D1417535

LOST

Also by Joy Fielding

Whispers and Lies
Grand Avenue
The First Time
Missing Pieces
Don't Cry Now
Tell Me No Secrets
See Jane Run
Good Intentions
The Deep End
Life Penalty
The Other Woman
Kiss Mommy Goodbye

LOST

A NOVEL

JOY FIELDING

DOUBLEDAY CANADA

Copyright © 2003 by Joy Fielding, Inc.

All rights reserved. The use of any part of this publication, reproduced, transmitted in any form or by any means electronic, mechanical, photocopying, recording or otherwise, or stored in a retrieval system without the prior written consent of the publisher—or, in the case of photocopying or other reprographic copying, a license from the Canadian Copyright Licensing Agency—is an infringement of the copyright law.

Doubleday Canada and colophon are trademarks.

National Library of Canada Cataloguing in Publication has been applied for.

This book is a work of fiction. Names, characters, places and incidents are products of the author's imagination or are used fictitiously. Any resemblance to actual events or locales or persons, living or dead, is entirely coincidental.

Jacket images: city scene © William Morris/woman © Ian Sanderson/Taxi
Jacket design: Julienne G. Ha
Printed and bound in the USA

Published in Canada by
Doubleday Canada, a division of
Random House of Canada Limited

Visit Random House of Canada Limited's website: www.randomhouse.ca

10 9 8 7 6 5 4 3 2

To Annie,
my sweet potato

ACKNOWLEDGMENTS

Once again, my thanks and gratitude to Owen Laster, Larry Mirkin, and Beverley Slopen for their continuing friendship, insight, advice, and unfailing generosity of spirit. Please know that your support means the world to me.

To my gorgeous editor, Emily Bestler, and her assistant Sarah Branham, for their smarts, hard work, and dedication. And to Owen's assistant, Jonathan Pecarsky, for always managing to sound pleased to hear from me.

To Judith Curr, Louise Burke, Laura Mullen, Estelle Laurence, and the wonderful people at Atria and Pocket, for their continuing efforts on my behalf—and for those wonderful chocolates at Christmas.

A special thank you to Michael Steeves from MacInfo, who responded to my frantic cries for help when my computer seemingly swallowed my disk. His efforts on my behalf were truly heroic.

To Maya Mavjee, John Neale, John Pearce, Stephanie Gowan, and the staff at Doubleday Canada, a division of Random House, who have never flagged in their support. Our association has spanned many years and several publishing upheavals, and I am both proud and happy we're still together.

Lost is the first of my novels to be set in my hometown of Toronto, and I realized as I was writing this book how much this beautiful city means to me. I am particularly indebted to Dr. Jim Cairns, the Deputy Chief Coroner for the province of Ontario, and to Gord Walker in the dispatch regional office for the time both so graciously took to answer my questions and share their expertise. My thanks also to the Toronto International Film Festival—the greatest film festival on earth—for providing both the backdrop for this book, and also some of my greatest film memories.

To my readers, again I thank you for your emails, your comments, and your enthusiasm. And a special thanks to those of you who show up at book signings. You make book tours worthwhile.

And lastly, to my family and friends, especially Warren, my amazing husband of almost thirty years, and our beautiful and talented daughters, Shannon and Annie. Without you, truly I would be lost.

LOST

ONE

T_{HE} morning began, as did so many of their mornings, with an argument. Later, when it was important to recall the precise order of events, the way everything had spun so effortlessly out of control, Cindy would struggle to remember what exactly she and her older daughter had been fighting about. The dog, the shower, her niece's upcoming wedding—it would all seem so mundane, so trivial, so unworthy of raised voices and increased blood pressure. A blur of words that blew past their heads like a sudden storm, scattering debris but leaving the foundation intact. Nothing extraordinary to be sure. The start of an average day. Or so it had seemed at the time.

(Images: Cindy, in the ratty, green-and-navy terry-cloth bathrobe she'd bought just after Tom left, towel-drying her chin-length brown hair as she emerges from her bedroom; Julia at the opposite end of the wide upstairs hall, wrapped in a yellow-and-white-striped towel, pacing back and forth in front of the bathroom between her room and her sister's, impatience bubbling like lava from a volcano inside her reed-thin, six-foot frame; Elvis, the perpetually scruffy, apricot-colored Wheaten terrier Julia brought with her when she'd moved back home just under a year ago, barking and snapping at the air as he bounces along beside her.)

"Heather, what in God's name are you doing in there?" Julia banged on the bathroom door, then banged on it a second time when no answer was forthcoming.

"Sounds like she's taking a shower," Cindy offered, regretting her interference as soon as the words were out of her mouth.

Julia glared at her mother from underneath a mop of ash-blond hair, painstakingly straightened every morning to obliterate even a hint of its natural curl. "Obviously."

Cindy marveled that one word could contain so much venom, convey so much disdain. "I'm sure she'll be out in a minute."

"She's been in there for half an hour already. There'll be no hot water left for me."

"There'll be plenty of hot water."

Julia banged her fist a third time against the bathroom door.

"Stop that, Julia. You'll break it if you're not careful."

"Oh, yeah, right. Like I could break the door." As if to prove her point, she thumped it again.

"Julia. . . ."

"Mother. . . ."

Stalemate, Cindy thought. As usual. The way it had been between the two of them since Julia was two years old and had balked at wearing the frilly white dress Cindy had bought her for her birthday, the stubborn toddler refusing to attend her own party even after Cindy had conceded defeat, told her she could wear whatever she liked.

Nineteen years had passed. Julia was twenty-one. Nothing had changed.

"Did you walk the dog?" Cindy asked now.

"And just when would I have done that?"

Cindy pretended not to notice the sarcasm in her daughter's voice. "When you got up. Like you're supposed to."

Julia rolled large green eyes toward the ceiling.

"We had a deal," Cindy reminded her.

"I'll walk him later."

"He's been cooped up all night. He's probably desperate to go."

"He'll be fine."

"I don't want any more accidents."

"Then *you* take him out," Julia snapped. "I'm not exactly dressed for a walk."

"You're being obstinate."

"You're being anal."

"Julia. . . ."

"Mother. . . ."

Stalemate.

Julia slammed her open palm against the bathroom door. "Okay, time's up. Everybody out of the pool."

Cindy absorbed the reverberation from Julia's hand on the door like a slap on the face. She lifted her fingers to her cheek, felt the sting. "That's enough, Julia. She can't hear you."

"She's doing it on purpose. She knows I have a big audition today."

"You have an audition?"

"For Michael Kinsolving's new movie. He's in town for the film festival, and he's agreed to audition some local talent."

"That's great."

"Dad set it up."

Cindy forced a smile through tightly gritted teeth.

"You're doing it again." Julia mimicked her mother's strained expression. "If you're going to go catatonic every time I mention Dad. . . ."

"I'm not catatonic."

"The divorce was seven years ago, Mom. Get over it."

"I assure you, I'm well over your father."

Julia arched one thin eyebrow, plucked to within a hair of its life. "Anyway, they're looking for an unknown, which probably means every girl in North America will be up for the part. Heather, for God's sake," Julia shouted, as the shower shuddered to a halt. "You're not the only one who lives here, you know."

Cindy stared toward the thick cream-colored broadloom at her feet. It had been less than a year since Julia had decided to move back home with her mother and sister after seven years of living with her father, and only because her father's new wife had made it clear she considered their five-thousand-square-foot lakeside penthouse too cramped for the three of them. Julia had made it equally clear to her mother that her move home was temporary, one borne of financial necessity, and that she'd be moving into her own apartment as soon as her fledgling acting career took off. Cindy had been so eager to have her daughter back, to make up for the time missed, the years lost, that even the sight of Julia's unruly dog peeing on the living room carpet did little to dampen her initial enthusiasm. Cindy had welcomed Julia back with open arms and a grateful heart.

The door to Heather's bedroom opened, and a sleepy-eyed teenage girl in an oversized purple nightshirt spotted with tiny pink hearts squinted into the hall. Delicate long fingers pushed several tendrils of loose brown curls away from the slight oval of her Botticelli face, then rubbed at the freckles peppering the tip of her upturned nose. "What's all the racket?" she asked as Elvis jumped up to lick her chin.

"Oh, for God's sake," Julia muttered angrily when she saw her sister, then kicked at the bathroom door with her bare feet. "Duncan, get your bony ass out of there."

"Julia. . . ."

"Mother. . . ."

"Duncan's ass is not bony," Heather said.

"I can't believe I'm going to be late for my audition because my sister's moronic boyfriend is using my shower."

"It's not your shower; he's not a moron; and he's lived here longer than you have," Heather protested.

"A huge mistake," Julia said, looking accusingly at her mother.

"Says who?"

"Says Dad."

Cindy's lips formed the automatic smile that accompanied each mention of her ex-husband. "Let's not get into that right now."

"Fiona thinks so too," Julia persisted. "She says she can't understand whatever possessed you to let him move in here."

"Did you tell that pea-brained twit to mind her own goddamned business?" The angry words flew from Cindy's mouth. She couldn't have stopped them if she'd tried.

"Mom!" Heather's dark blue eyes widened in alarm.

"Mother, really," Julia said, green eyes rolling back toward the ceiling.

It was the "really" that did Cindy in. The word hit her like an arrow to the heart, and she had to lean against the nearest wall for support. As if eager to add his opinion, Elvis lifted his leg into the air and peed against the bathroom door.

"Oh no!" Cindy glared at her older daughter.

"Don't look at me. You're the one who swore and got him all upset."

"Just clean it up."

"I don't have time to clean it up. My audition's at eleven o'clock."

"It's eight-thirty!"

"You have an audition?" Heather asked her sister. "What for?"

"Michael Kinsolving's in town for the film festival, and he's decided to audition local talent for his new movie. Dad set it up."

"Cool," Heather said as Cindy's lips curled again into a frozen smile.

The bathroom door opened and a cloud of steam rushed into the hall, followed by tall, skinny Duncan Rossi, wet black hair falling across playful brown eyes, and wearing nothing but a small yellow-and-white bath towel and a large, lopsided grin. He quickly ducked into the bedroom he'd been sharing with Cindy's younger daughter for almost two years. Of course, the original deal had been that he occupy the spare room in the basement, an arrangement that lasted all of three months. Another three months were spent denying the obvious, that Duncan was creeping up to Heather's bedroom after Cindy was safely asleep, and then creeping back down before she got up, until everyone finally stopped pretending, although no one ever actually acknowledged the move out loud.

In truth Cindy had no problem with the fact Heather and Duncan were sleeping together. She genuinely liked Duncan, who was considerate and helpful around the house, and had somehow managed to maintain his equilibrium and good humor even after the maelstrom that was Julia moved in across the hall. Both Heather and Duncan were nice, responsible kids who'd started dating in their first year of high school, and had been talking about marriage ever since.

Which was the only thing that really worried Cindy.

Sometimes she'd look over at Duncan and her daughter as they were reading the morning paper at breakfast—Honey Nut Cheerios for him, Cinnamon Toast Crunch for her—and think they were almost too comfortable with each other, too settled. She marveled at Heather's eager embrace of such a safe, middle-aged lifestyle, and wondered if being the child of divorce had played any part in it. "Why is she in such a hurry to tie herself down? She's only nineteen. She's in college. She should be out sleeping around," Cindy had shocked her friends recently by confiding. "Well, when else is she going to do it?" she'd continued, painfully aware of her own reluctant celibacy.

Cindy could count on one hand the number of affairs she'd had since her divorce, two of those in the immediate aftermath of

Tom's abrupt decision to leave her for another woman, a woman he'd left for yet another other woman as soon as his divorce from Cindy became final. Seven years of other women, Cindy thought now, each woman younger and tartier than the last. A dozen at least. A baker's dozen, she thought, feeling her jaw lock. And then along came little Fiona, the freshest tart of all. Hell, she was only eight years older than Julia. Not even a tart, for God's sake. A cookie!

"Mom?" Heather was asking.

"Hmm?"

"Is everything all right?"

"Mrs. Carver?" Duncan reappeared at Heather's side. The towel had been replaced by a pair of fashionably faded blue jeans. He slipped a navy T-shirt over his still-damp, utterly hairless chest. "Is something wrong? You have a very strange look on your face."

"She's thinking about my father," Julia announced wearily.

"What? I am not."

"Then why the rigor mortis smile?"

Cindy took a deep breath and tried to relax her mouth, feeling it wobble precariously from side to side. "I thought you were in such a hurry to get in the shower."

"It's only eight-thirty," Julia said as Elvis began barking.

"Would someone like to go for a walk?" Duncan asked the dog, whose response was to run around in increasingly frantic circles and bark even louder. "Let's go then, boy." Duncan bounded down the stairs, Elvis racing ahead of him, as the phone in Cindy's bedroom began to ring.

"If it's Sean, I'm not here," Julia told her mother.

"Why would Sean be calling on my line?"

"Because I won't speak to him on mine."

"Why won't you speak to him?"

"Because I broke up with him, and he won't take no for an answer. I'm not here," Julia insisted as the phone continued to ring.

Joy Fielding

"What about you?" Cindy asked her younger daughter play-fully. "Are you here?"

"Why would I want to speak to Sean?"

"Be back in twenty minutes," Duncan called from the front door.

My best kid, Cindy thought, entering her room and reaching for the phone on the night table beside her bed.

"I'm not here," Julia repeated from the doorway.

"Hello."

"It's me," the voice announced as Cindy plopped down on the edge of her unmade bed, a headache slowly gnawing at the base of her neck.

"Is it Sean?" Julia whispered.

"It's Leigh," Cindy whispered back as Julia rolled disappointed eyes toward the window overlooking the backyard. Outside, the late-August sun created the illusion of peace and tranquility.

"Why are you whispering?" Cindy's sister asked. "You're not sick, are you?"

"I'm fine. How about you? You're calling awfully early."

"Early for you maybe. I've been up since six."

It was Cindy's turn to roll her eyes. Leigh had elevated sibling rivalry to a fine art. If Cindy had been up since seven o'clock, Leigh had been up since five; if Cindy had a sore throat, Leigh had a sore throat *and* a fever; if Cindy had a million things to do that day, Leigh had a million and *one*.

"This wedding is going to be the death of me," Leigh said. "You have no idea what planning a wedding this size is like. No idea."

"I thought everything was pretty much taken care of." Cindy knew that Leigh had been planning her daughter's wedding ever since Bianca was five years old. "Is there a problem?"

"Our mother is driving me absolutely nuts."

Cindy felt her headache spreading rapidly from the top of her spine to the bridge of her nose. She tried picturing her sister, who was three years younger, two inches shorter, and fifteen pounds heavier than she was, but she couldn't remember the color of her hair. Last week it had been a deep chestnut brown, the week before that an alarming carrot red.

"What's she done now?" Cindy asked reluctantly.

"She doesn't like her dress."

"So change it."

"It's too late to change it. The damn dress is already made. We have fittings this afternoon. I need you to be there."

"Me?"

"You have to convince her the dress looks fabulous. She'll believe *you*. Besides, don't you want to see Heather and Julia in their dresses?"

Cindy's head snapped toward Julia, still watching from the doorway. "Heather and Julia have fittings this afternoon?"

"No way!" Julia exclaimed. "I'm not going. I hate that stupid dress."

"Four o'clock. And they can't be late," Leigh continued, oblivious to Julia's rant.

"I'm not wearing that god-awful purple dress." Julia began pacing back and forth in the doorway. "I look like a giant grape."

"The girls will be there," Cindy said pointedly, watching her daughter throw her arms up into the air. "But I'm getting a really bad headache."

"A headache? Please, I've had a migraine for two days now. Look, I have a zillion things to do. I'll see you at four o'clock."

"I'm not going," Julia said as Cindy hung up the phone.

"You have to go. You're a bridesmaid."

"I'm busy."

"She's my sister."

"Then you wear the damn dress."

"Julia. . . ."

"Mother. . . ."

Julia spun around on her heels and disappeared into the bathroom at the end of the hall, slamming the door behind her.

(Flashback: Julia, a chubby toddler, her Shirley Temple curls framing dimpled, chipmunk cheeks, burrowing in against her mother's pregnant belly as Cindy reads her a bedtime story; Julia, age nine, proudly displaying the fiberglass casts she wore after breaking both arms in a fall off her bicycle; Julia at thirteen, already almost a head taller than her mother, defiantly refusing to apologize for swearing at her sister; Julia the following year, packing her clothes into the new Louis Vuitton suitcase her father had bought her, then carrying it outside to his waiting BMW, leaving her childhood—and her mother— behind.)

Later Cindy would wonder whether these images had been a premonition of disaster looming, of calamity about to strike, whether she'd somehow suspected that the glimpse she'd caught of Julia disappearing behind the slammed bathroom door was the last she would see of her difficult daughter.

Probably not. How could she, after all? *Why* would she? It was far too early in the day to be mindful of the fact that great calamity, like great evil, often springs from the womb of the hopelessly mundane, that defining moments rarely have meaning in the present and can be seen clearly only in retrospect. And so the morning of the day Julia went missing was rightly perceived by her mother as nothing more than one in a long string of such mornings, their argument only the latest installment of their ongoing debate. Cindy thought little of it beyond that which was obvious— her daughter was giving her a hard time, what else was new?

Julia. . . .

Mother. . . .

Checkmate.

TWO

I met this great guy."

Cindy stared across the picnic table at her friend. Trish Sinclair was all careless sophistication and ageless grace. She shouldn't have been beautiful, but she was, her face full of sharp, competing angles, her Modigliani-like features further exaggerated by the unnatural blackness of her hair, hair that hung in dramatic swirls past bony shoulders, toward the ample cleavage that peeked out over the top buttons of her bright yellow blouse. "You're married," Cindy reminded her.

"Not for me, silly. For you."

Cindy lowered the back of her head to the top of her spine, lifting her face to the sun and inhaling the faintest whiff of fall. A month from now it would probably be too cool to be sitting on a picnic bench in a friend's backyard in the middle of the day, choosing what movies to see at this year's festival, while eating open-faced tuna sandwiches and sipping glasses of chardonnay. "Not interested."

"Let me tell you about him before you make any hasty decisions."

"I thought we were here to discuss movies." Cindy looked to her friend, Meg, for help. Meg Taylor, looking closer to fifteen than forty, was as fair and flat-chested as Trish was dark and voluptuous. She sat on the other end of the long picnic bench, wearing cutoff jeans and a red-and-white-striped tank top, seemingly engrossed in the dauntingly thick catalog for this year's festival.

"The new Patricia Rozema film sounds good," she offered, her voice small and crinkly, like tin foil unraveling.

"What page?" Cindy asked gratefully, eager to move on. The last time Trish had fixed her up, just before Julia's move home, had been an unmitigated disaster. At the end of the relentlessly confrontational evening with the thrice-divorced divorce attorney, the man had leaned in for what Cindy assumed was a conciliatory peck on the cheek, then rammed his tongue so far down Cindy's throat, she'd had visions of having to call a plumber to get him out.

"*Special Presentation,*" Meg told her. "Page 97."

Cindy quickly flipped through the pages of her festival catalog.

" 'Elegantly shot and finely performed,' " Meg read from the notes, " 'what is finally so impressive about Rozema's new work. . . .' "

"Isn't she the one who makes films about lesbians?" Trish interrupted.

"Is she?" Meg asked.

Cindy's eyes traveled back and forth between her two closest friends. Cindy and Meg had been inseparable since the eleventh grade; Cindy and Trish had bonded after colliding at the Clinique counter at Holt's ten years ago. "*Mansfield Park* wasn't about lesbians," Cindy said, thinking that neither woman had changed substantially over the years.

"It had lesbian overtones," Trish said.

"*Mansfield Park* is by Jane Austen," Meg reminded her.

"It had definite overtones."

"Your point being . . . ?"

"I don't want any lesbians this year."

"You don't want any lesbians?"

"I'm tired of lesbians. We saw enough films about lesbians last year."

Cindy laughed. "You have a quota on lesbians?"

"Does that include gays?" Meg grabbed a green apple from a nearby basket and took a loud bite.

"Yes." Trish pushed a thick layer of dark bangs away from her forehead, adjusted the heart-shaped diamond pendant at her throat. "I'm tired of them too."

"Well, there go half the movies." Cindy took a sip of wine, held it inside her mouth, feeling the late-August sun warm against her cheeks. Every year for the last six years, the three women had gathered in Meg's backyard to eat, drink, and select from the hundreds of movies being previewed at the annual Toronto International Film Festival. Another year had come and gone. Another festival was upon them. Not much had changed in the interim, except Julia had come home.

Which meant everything had changed.

"You'd really like him," Trish said, suddenly shifting gears, although it was obvious by the way she leaned into the table that she'd only been biding her time, waiting for her next opportunity to reintroduce the subject. "He's bright, funny, good-looking."

Cindy watched a parade of clouds float past her line of vision, several wisps breaking free to drape themselves across the sky, like cobwebs. "Not interested," she said again.

"His name is Neil Macfarlane, and he's Bill's new accountant. We had dinner with him last night, and he's to die for. I swear. You'll love him."

"What's he look like?" Meg asked.

"Tall, slim, really cute."

"How about *The Winds of Change*?" Cindy proposed, ignoring her two friends. "Page 257."

Trish groaned as the women flipped to the appropriate page.

"Yikes!" Meg said, almost choking on the apple she was chewing. "Are you kidding? An Iranian film? Have you forgotten *Caravan to Heaven*?"

"Was that the one where the camel got stuck in the sand and it took three hours to get him out?" Trish winced at the memory.

"That's the one."

"So much for Iran."

"What about France?" Cindy asked.

"All they do in French movies is talk and eat," Meg said.

"Sometimes they have sex," Trish told her.

"They talk during sex," Meg said.

"So France is out?" Cindy looked from Meg to Trish, then back again. "How about this one? *Night Crawlers*. Page 316. It's Swedish. Do we have a problem with Sweden?"

Meg lifted the thick, heavy catalog into her hands and read out loud, as if she'd been called on in class. " 'The film has a gritty feel for the seedy side of suburban life. Uncompromising and . . .' "

"Hold it," Trish interrupted. "What did we decide 'uncompromising' means?"

"Well," Cindy said, "let's see if we can remember the code. Lyrical means . . ."

"Slow," Meg answered.

"Visually stunning means . . ."

"Boring as hell," Trish said.

"Uncompromising means . . ."

Trish and Meg exchanged knowing glances. "Handheld camera," they agreed.

"Good. Okay," Cindy said. "So, we don't want lyrical, visually stunning, or uncompromising."

"And we've eliminated gays, lesbians, and Iran."

"Don't forget France."

"Let's not be too hasty about France," Cindy pleaded.

"What about Germany?"

"No sense of humor."

"Hong Kong?"

"Too violent," Meg said.

"Canada?"

The women stared at each other blankly.

"How about the new movie by Michael Kinsolving?" Cindy asked. "Page 186."

"Isn't he a bit passé?"

"He could use a hit, that's for sure." Again Meg lifted the heavy tome into the air and read aloud. " 'Fresh, stylish, contemporary, edgy.' " She lowered the catalog back to the picnic table, took another bite of her apple. " 'Edgy' is a bit troublesome. It could be a code word for 'low-life.' "

"Julia had an audition with Michael Kinsolving this morning," Cindy said.

"Really? How'd it go?"

"I don't know." Cindy pulled her cell phone out of her leopard-print purse, pressed in Julia's home number, then listened as it rang once, twice, three times. She was about to hang up when she heard Julia's breathy whisper in her ear.

"This is Julia," the recorded message began with seductive grace. *"I'm so sorry I can't answer your call at the moment, but I wouldn't want to miss a thing you have to say, so please leave a message after the beep, and I'll get back to you as soon as I can. Or you can reach me on my cell at 416-555-4332. Thanks so much, and have a great day."*

Cindy hung up, quickly called Julia's cell phone. "It's your mother, sweetie," she said when confronted by the same message. "Just phoning to see how your audition went. Call me if you get the chance. Otherwise, I'll see you at four o'clock," she added, unable to stop herself.

"What's at four o'clock?" Meg asked as Cindy tucked her phone back inside her purse.

"Fittings for bridesmaids' dresses."

"Ugh," Trish said. "I remember being a bridesmaid at my sister's wedding. She had the ugliest dresses you've ever seen. Pink taffeta, of all things. Can you picture me in pink?"

"I love pink," Meg said.

"I was so embarrassed. I just wanted to crawl in a hole and die. And of course, the marriage didn't last, which, to this day, I blame on the dresses. Did you have bridesmaids when you married Gordon?" she asked Meg.

"Eight," Meg said flatly. "In pink taffeta."

Cindy laughed at both the memory and the look on Trish's face. "I was one of them."

"She looks fabulous in pink taffeta," Meg said, laughing now as well.

Strains of Beethoven's Ninth suddenly filled the air. "My phone," Cindy announced, reaching back into her purse. "Probably Julia." She lifted the phone to her ear.

"I gave him your number," Trish said quickly.

"What?"

"I gave Neil Macfarlane your number."

"Hello?" A large male voice pushed its way out of the small phone in Cindy's hand. "Hello? Is anybody there?"

"I can't believe you gave someone my number without asking me first," Cindy hissed, holding the phone tight against her chest.

"He's really cute," Trish said, by way of explanation.

"Hello?" the voice asked again.

"I'm sorry. Hello," Cindy said, fighting the urge to throw the phone at her friend's head.

"Cindy?"

"Neil?" Cindy asked in return.

He laughed. "Trish obviously told you I'd be calling."

Cindy glared at Trish, who was pouring herself another glass of wine. "What can I do for you, Neil? I'm afraid I already have an accountant."

"Be nice," Trish whispered.

"In that case," Neil said easily, "maybe you'd let me take you out to dinner one night."

"Dinner?"

"Just because you're mad at me, don't take it out on him," Trish said.

"When exactly did you have in mind?" Cindy heard herself ask.

"How about tonight?"

"Tonight?"

"He's really cute," Trish said, her voice a plea.

"Tonight is fine," Cindy said, giving in, as Trish squealed with delight and Meg jumped up and down with girlish excitement. "When and where?"

"The Pasta Bar? Seven o'clock?"

"I'll meet you there." Cindy flung the phone back into her purse, then confronted her friend, whose always broad smile now stretched from one side of her face to the other. "I can't believe you did that to me."

"Oh, relax. You'll have a wonderful time."

"I haven't had a date in over a year."

"Then it's about time, wouldn't you say?"

"I won't know what to talk about."

"Don't worry. You'll think of something."

"I haven't a clue what to wear."

"Something stylish," Trish said.

"Something sexy," Meg said.

"Oh sure, something stylish and sexy. I haven't had sex in, what . . . ?"

"Three years," Trish and Meg said in unison.

Cindy laughed. "You probably told him that, didn't you?"

"Are you kidding? I tell everyone." Trish poured Cindy a full glass of wine, raised her own glass in a toast. "To great movies, great wine, and great sex."

Meg took another bite of her apple. "This is so French, don't you think?"

"I CAN'T BELIEVE she did that to me," Cindy muttered as she waited for the light at the corner of Balmoral and Avenue Road to change. "I can't believe she gave him my number." She shook her head, growing impatient and running across the busy thorough-fare at the first break in the traffic. "I can't believe I said I'd go. What's the matter with me?"

She could hear Elvis barking as soon as her toe hit the side-walk, even though her house was at the far end of the street. That meant no one was home, and the dog had probably peed on the hall rug, a favorite new protest spot for being left alone for more than thirty minutes. She'd tried locking him in the kitchen, but he always found a way out. He'd even figured out how to unlock the large wire crate Cindy had purchased, and that now sat empty in the garage. Cindy chuckled. He was Julia's dog all right.

A slight breeze whispered through the lush green leaves crowding the branches of the large maple trees lining the beautiful wide street in the heart of the city. Cindy and Tom had purchased the old, brown-brick home near the corner of Balmoral and Poplar Plains only months before Tom moved out, and she'd kept it as part of their divorce settlement. In return, Tom got to keep the oceanfront condo in Florida and the lakeside cottage in Muskoka, which was fine with Cindy, who'd always considered herself a city girl at heart.

It was one of the reasons she loved Toronto, and had loved it from the moment her father had relocated the family here from the suburbs of Detroit just after her thirteenth birthday. At first she'd been apprehensive about moving to a new city, a new coun-try—*It's always snowing up there; the people only speak French; stand absolutely still if you see a bear!*—but within days all such fears had been dispelled by the pleasant reality that was Toronto. More than the interesting architecture, the diverse neighborhoods, the plethora of art galleries, trendy boutiques, and theaters, what Cindy loved most about the city was the fact that people actually lived there, that they didn't just work there during the day only to disappear into distant suburbs at night. The entire downtown core was residential. Stately old mansions with backyard swimming pools shared the same streets as towering new office buildings, and everything was only minutes away from a subway line—the subways clean, the streets safe, the people polite, if admittedly more reserved than their neighbors to the south. A city of over three million people—five million if you counted the surrounding areas—and there were rarely more than fifty murders a year. Amazing, Cindy thought now, stretching her arms into the air, hugging the city to her breast, forgiving even the summer humidity that sent spasms through her already curly hair.

After her father died, Cindy's mother had briefly considered moving back to Detroit, where her brother and sister still lived, but her daughters, by then both married and with families of their own, had talked her out of it. In truth, Norma Appleton hadn't needed much persuading. Within months, she'd sold the old family home on Wembley Avenue, and moved into a brand-new condominium on Prince Arthur, only a block north of the shopping mecca that was Bloor Street, and less than a five-minute drive from either of her children.

("We should have let her move back to Detroit," Leigh had lamented on more than one occasion. "She's driving me nuts."

"You take her too seriously. Don't let her get to you."

"Easy for you to say. You're the one who can do no wrong."

"I do plenty wrong."

"You don't have to tell me.")

A laugh escaped Cindy's mouth and skipped down the empty

street. It always surprised Cindy that her mother and sister were so often at odds when, in fact, they were so much alike—a little of each went a long way.

Cindy checked her watch. It was almost three o'clock. She'd have just enough time to walk the dog and change out of her shorts before heading over to Marcel's for the fittings. Then she'd have to race back home and shower and change for her stupid date with Neil Macfarlane. And she still had no idea what she was going to wear. She didn't have any clothes that were both stylish and sexy. Whatever had possessed her to say yes? Did she need this kind of stress in her life? She crossed her fingers, said a silent prayer that Julia would be at the fitting promptly at four o'clock.

It was amazing, she thought, how much time and energy she expended fretting over her older daughter. When Julia was living with her father, Cindy had worried about her every minute of every day. Was she eating properly, getting to bed on time, doing her homework? Was she safe? Was she happy? Did the child cry herself to sleep every night, as Cindy often did, regretful of the choice she'd made? Did she wish she was home with her mother and sister where she knew in her heart she belonged? Was it misguided pride that kept her with her father year after stubborn year?

It seemed that even in her absence, Julia had taken up a disproportionate amount of space in the house on Balmoral Avenue. Missing Julia had become a steady part of Cindy's life, a persistent ache in the pit of her stomach, an ulcer that refused to heal even after Julia decided to move back home.

A slight movement caught Cindy's eye and she turned her head toward her next-door neighbor's house. Faith Sellick, a new mother at age thirty-one, was rocking back and forth on the top of her front steps, her long brown hair uncombed and all but covering her face.

"Faith?" Cindy cautiously approached her neighbor's front

path, watched as the normally friendly and outgoing young woman slowly raised her head from her knees, tears streaking a face that was round and pretty and totally void of expression. "Faith, what's going on? Are you all right?"

Faith glanced over her shoulder toward the house, then back again at Cindy. Cindy saw that the front of the young woman's white blouse was stained with the milk leaking from her swollen breasts, creating quarter-sized circles in the thin fabric.

"What's the matter, Faith? Where's the baby?"

Faith stared at Cindy with sad, dull eyes.

Cindy looked past the young woman, straining to detect sounds of life from the interior of the house, but the only thing she heard was Elvis barking next door. A thousand thoughts rushed through Cindy's mind: that Faith and her husband had had a terrible fight; that he'd walked out on her and the baby; that something horrible had happened to Kyle, the couple's two-month-old son; that Faith had come outside to get a breath of fresh air and inadvertently locked herself out. Except none of that explained the blankness in Faith's eyes, and why she was staring at Cindy as if she'd never seen her before in her life. "Faith, what's the matter? Talk to me."

Faith said nothing.

"Faith, where's Kyle? Has something happened to Kyle?"

Faith stared at the house, fresh tears falling the length of her cheeks.

In the next instant, Cindy vaulted past the young woman and into her house. She took the stairs two at a time, racing toward the nursery and pushing open the door, her breath stabbing at her chest like a hunting knife. Tears stung her eyes as she threw herself toward the crib, terrified of what she might see.

The baby was lying on his back in the middle of crisp, blue-and-white gingham sheets. He was wearing a yellow sleeper and a matching yellow cap, his beautiful face as smooth and round as his mother's, his perfect lips settled into a perfect pout, red little fists curled into tight little balls, tiny knuckles white. Was he breathing?

Cindy edged closer to the crib, and leaned her body over the side bar, pressing her cheek to the baby's mouth and breathing in his wondrous infant scent. Gently she touched her cool lips to his warm chest, holding her breath until she felt his body shudder with the effort of a single deep breath. And then another. And another. "Thank God," Cindy whispered, feeling the infant's forehead with her lips to make sure he wasn't feverish, then straightening up and backing slowly out of the room, her legs wobbling as she closed the door behind her, having to remind herself to breathe. "Thank God, you're okay."

Faith was still sitting on the top of the outside landing, swaying rhythmically from side to side, as if mimicking the branches of the maple tree in the middle of her front lawn, when Cindy stepped back outside, sat down beside her. "Faith?"

Faith said nothing, continued rocking from side to side.

"Faith, what's wrong?"

"I'm sorry," Faith said, so quietly Cindy wasn't sure she'd heard her at all.

"Why are you sorry? Did something happen?"

Faith looked quizzical. "No."

"Then what's the matter? What are you doing out here?"

"Is the baby crying?"

"No. He's sound asleep."

Faith ran unsteady hands across her breasts. "He's probably hungry."

"He's asleep," Cindy repeated.

"I'm a terrible mother."

"No, you're not. You're a wonderful mother," Cindy assured her truthfully, recalling Faith's excitement when she'd knocked on Cindy's door to announce her pregnancy, how sweetly she'd asked for any advice Cindy could give her, how wonderfully gentle and patient she was with the baby. "I think we should go inside."

Faith offered no resistance as Cindy helped her to her feet, the top of her head in line with Cindy's chin. Cindy guided her through the large front foyer into the rectangular-shaped living room at the back of the house. A powder blue sweater lay on the hardwood floor next to the baby grand piano and Faith reached down to scoop it up, pushing her hands roughly through the sleeves, and quickly securing its three white buttons. Then she sank down into the green velvet sofa, and leaned her head against the pillows.

"What's Ryan's number at work?"

"Ryan's at work," Faith said.

"Yes, I know. I need his phone number."

Faith stared blankly at the pale green wall ahead.

"It's okay. I'll find it. You stay here. Lie down."

Faith smiled and obediently lifted her feet off the floor, bringing her knees to her chest.

Cindy quickly located Ryan's work number from the bulletin board by the kitchen phone and punched in the correct numbers. It was answered on the first ring.

"Ryan Sellick," the man said instead of hello.

"Ryan," Cindy enunciated clearly, "this is Cindy Carver. I think you need to come home."

THREE

"Y o u ' r e late."

"I'm sorry. I got here as fast as I could."

"I said four o'clock," Leigh reminded her sister, square red nails tapping on the gold band of her watch for emphasis, then pushing newly streaked hair away from a face that was pinched with incipient hysteria. The impatience in her hazel eyes was underlined in heavy black pencil, and mascara sat like tiny lumps of coal on her lashes. Anxiety draped across her shoulders like a well-worn shawl. "It's almost four-thirty," she said. "Marcel has to leave at five."

"I'm really sorry." Cindy looked from her sister to the short, curly-haired man in tight brown leather pants who was conferring with his assistant in a far corner of the long, cluttered room. "There was a problem with my next-door neighbor. She's acting very strangely. I'm afraid things just kind of got away from me."

"They always do," Leigh said.

"What's that supposed to mean?"

"Look, you're here *now*. Let's not make a big deal out of it."

Cindy took a deep breath, silently counting to ten. If you

hadn't picked a dressmaker whose shop is halfway out of the city, I might have been able to get here on time, she wanted to say. If you hadn't scheduled the damn fittings for the height of rush hour traffic, I might not have been so late. Besides, you're the one making the big deal out of it, not me. Instead she said, "So, how's it going so far?"

"As expected." Leigh lowered her voice to a whisper. "Mother is driving me nuts."

"What are you whispering about?" a woman's gravelly voice called from one of the dressing rooms at the back of the shop.

Cindy spun around, absorbing the details of the small dress-making salon in a single glance: the wide front window, the bare white walls lined with racks of silk and satin gowns in varying stages of completion, bolts of bright fabric carpeting the floor and occupying the only two chairs in the room, a full-length mirror in one corner, three appropriately angled mirrors in another, another room at the back crowded with assorted tables, sewing machines, and ironing boards. Cindy sidled up to a rack of more casual suits and dresses that was pushed off to one side, wondering whether she might find something on it that was sufficiently stylish and sexy for her date with Neil Macfarlane.

"Cindy's here," Leigh called to her mother.

"Hi, dear," her mother's disembodied voice sang out.

"Hi, Mom. How's the dress?"

"You tell me." Cindy watched her normally vivacious, seventy-two-year-old mother push open the heavy white curtain that served as her dressing room door and frown uncertainly, her fingers pulling at the sides of the magenta satin gown.

"Tell her she looks beautiful," Leigh whispered behind cupped fingers, pretending to be scratching her nose.

"What did your sister say?"

"She said you look beautiful," Cindy told her.

"What do *you* think?"

"Naturally," Leigh said under her breath. "What *I* think doesn't count."

"What's your sister muttering about now?"

"I'm right here, Mother. You don't have to ask Cindy."

"I think you look beautiful," Cindy said, genuinely agreeing with her sister's assessment and reaching out to pat her mother's fashionable blond bob.

Norma Appleton made a dismissive gesture with her mouth. "Well, of course, you girls would stick together."

"What's the problem you're having with the dress, Mom?" Cindy asked, spotting a short red cocktail dress on the rack of more casual offerings, wondering if it was her size.

"I don't like the neckline." Her mother tugged at the offending area. "It's too plain."

The neckline might be too low-cut, Cindy thought, noting the daring bodice of the short red dress. She didn't want to give Neil Macfarlane the wrong idea. Did she?

He's really cute, Trish whispered in her ear.

"I've already explained to Mother a million times. . . ."

"I'm right here, you know," Norma Appleton said. "You can talk to *me.*"

"I've already told *you* a zillion times that Marcel will be adding beading along the top."

Cindy mentally discarded the short red dress, her eyes moving down the rack to a long, shapeless, beige linen sack. Definitely not, she decided, picturing herself lost inside its voluminous folds. She didn't want Neil Macfarlane to think he was dating a nun. Did she?

You haven't had sex in three years.

"I hate beading," her mother was saying.

"Since when do you hate beading?"

"I've always hated beading."

"What about a jacket?" Cindy suggested, trying to still the voices in her head. "Maybe Marcel could make up something in lace. . . ." She glanced imploringly at Marcel, who promptly left his assistant's side to join them in the center of the room.

"A lace jacket is a lovely idea," her mother agreed.

"I thought you didn't like lace," Leigh said.

"I've always liked lace."

The last time she'd had sex, Cindy recalled, she'd been wearing a lace peignoir. The man's name was Alan and they'd met when he came into Meg's shop to buy a pair of crystal-and-turquoise earrings for his sister's birthday. Cindy found out that he didn't have a sister when his wife came by the following week to exchange the earrings for something subtler. By then, of course, it was too late. The peignoir had been purchased; the deed had been done.

"What do you think, Marcel?" Cindy asked now, her voice unnaturally loud. The poor man took a step back, glancing anxiously at Cindy's mother, trying not to fixate on the deep creases her fingers were inflicting on the delicate satin of his design.

Without hesitation, Marcel reached for the tape measure that circled his neck like a scarf. "Whatever you desire."

Whatever you desire, Cindy repeated silently, savoring the sound. How long had it been since anyone had offered her whatever she desired? Would Neil Macfarlane?

He's to die for. I swear. You'll love him.

"Did I hear you say something about problems with a neighbor?" her mother asked, lifting her arms to allow Marcel to measure their length.

"Yes," Cindy said, grateful for the chance to get her mind on something else. "You remember the Sellicks from next door? They had a baby a few months ago?" she asked, as if she weren't sure. "I think she might have postpartum depression."

"I had that," Leigh said.

"You had hemorrhoids," her mother said.

Marcel winced, wrapped the tape measure across Norma Appleton's expansive bosom.

"I had postpartum depression with both Jeffrey and Bianca."

"I don't remember that."

"Of course not. Now if I were Cindy. . . ."

"Cindy never had postpartum depression."

"And speaking of Bianca," Cindy interjected, "just where *is* the beautiful bride-to-be?" She looked around the salon, realizing for the first time that neither her niece nor her daughters were anywhere in sight.

"They got tired of waiting and went to Starbucks."

"Heather looks so beautiful in her dress," Norma Appleton said.

"And the bride, Mother?" Leigh asked pointedly. "How does Bianca look in her gown? Or doesn't she rate a mention?"

"What are you talking about? I said she looked beautiful."

"No, you didn't."

"I most certainly did."

"What about Julia?" Cindy interrupted.

"Julia?" Leigh scoffed. "Julia has yet to honor us with her presence."

"She isn't here yet?"

"I'm sure 'things just got away from her,'" Leigh said, forcing a smile.

"I said I was sorry." Cindy reached into her purse for her cell phone. "She had an audition. Maybe she had to wait. . . ."

"What kind of audition?" Her mother turned around so that Marcel could measure her back.

"For Michael Kinsolving, the director. He's in town for the film festival." Cindy pressed in her daughter's number, listened to the telephone ring.

"You and that stupid festival," Leigh said dismissively.

"Isn't Michael Kinsolving dating Cameron Diaz?" their mother asked. "Or maybe it's Drew Barrymore. Ever since *Charlie's Angels,* I can't keep the two of them straight. Anyway, I hear he has quite a reputation with the ladies."

"Oh, for heaven's sake, Mother," Leigh exclaimed impatiently. "How would you know anything about this Michael whoever-the hell-he-is?"

Her mother pulled her shoulders back with just enough righteous indignation to cause Marcel to lose his balance and drop his tape measure. "I read about him in *People* magazine."

"Michael Kinsolving is a very important director," Cindy said, as Julia's breathy voice caressed her ear.

"I'm so sorry I can't answer your call at the moment," the recording whispered seductively. Cindy immediately hung up, dialed Julia's cell phone, listened to the same breathy message.

"He hasn't had a hit in a long time," their mother said knowingly. "Apparently he's some sort of sex addict."

"I believe that's Michael Douglas," Marcel piped up enthusiastically, regaining his footing and retrieving the tape measure from the floor.

"Really?"

"Before he married Catherine Zeta-Jones."

"Are we actually having this conversation?" Leigh threw her hands into the air in frustration.

"What's your problem, dear?" her mother asked.

"My problem," Leigh began, as little beads of perspiration began breaking out across her forehead, causing her newly streaked bangs to curl in several awkward directions, "is that my daughter's wedding is less than two months away, and nobody seems to give a good goddamn that time is running out and there's still tons of stuff to do."

"It'll all work out, dear." Her mother tugged at the long taffeta skirt. "Doesn't there seem to be an awful lot of material here? It makes me look very hippy."

"She's not answering." Cindy returned the phone to her purse and stared at the front door, as if willing Julia to walk through.

"She's forty minutes late."

"Maybe she got lost."

"Lost?" Leigh asked incredulously. "She gets on the subway at St. Clair; she gets off at Finch. How could she possibly get lost?"

"Maybe she missed her stop. You know Julia. Sometimes she gets distracted."

"Julia's never had a distracted moment in her life. She knows exactly what she's doing at all times."

"What's that supposed to mean?"

"Leigh, why don't you show us your dress?" their mother suggested.

"Yes," Cindy agreed wearily. "Mom says it's wonderful."

"Mom hasn't seen it."

"Good try," her mother whispered to Cindy as Leigh retreated to the dressing rooms at the back of the shop, shaking her head and muttering to herself. "You've got to say something to your sister, darling. She's driving me nuts."

Cindy caught her reflection in one panel of the three-sectioned full-length mirror, and advanced steadily toward it, horrified by what she saw but unable to turn away, as if she'd stumbled across the scene of an accident. When did I get so ugly? she wondered, hypnotized by the creases clustered around her large eyes and small mouth, staring at them until her still-delicate features blurred, then disappeared altogether, leaving only the telltale lines of middle age. She squinted, trying to find the young woman she'd once been, remembering that at one time, she'd been considered beautiful.

Like Julia.

When was the last time a man had told her she was beautiful? Cindy wondered now, backing away from the mirror, and pushing a bolt of fabric off one of the chairs. She sat down, her head heavy with conflicting emotions: impatience with her sister, anger at her older daughter, curiosity about Neil Macfarlane. Was he really as smart, funny, and good-looking as Trish claimed? And if so, why would he be interested in a forty-two-year-old woman with less-than-perky breasts and a collapsing rear end? Undoubtedly such a prize catch could have his pick of any number of perfect young females eager to make his acquaintance. Certainly Tom had considered the choice a no-brainer.

Cindy checked her watch. Almost four forty-five already. By the time she finished up here and got home, assuming she wasn't a raving lunatic and was still capable of handling an automobile, she'd be lucky if there'd be enough time to shower and change, let alone make sure there was something in the house for the kids to eat. She sighed, thinking that Heather and Duncan could order in a pizza, and remembering that Julia had mentioned she might be having dinner with her father. Was that where she was?

"Ta dum!" Leigh announced, pulling back the dressing room curtain and appearing before her mother and startled sister in yards of pink taffeta.

This is not happening, Cindy thought. She opened her mouth to speak, but no words emerged.

"Of course, I'm planning to lose ten pounds before the wedding, so it'll be tighter here." Leigh pulled at the tucks at her waistline. "And here." She flattened the taffeta across her hips. It made a swishing sound. "So, what do you think?" She lifted her hands into the air above her head, did a slow turn around.

"I wouldn't do that, dear." Norma Appleton pointed to the underside of her daughter's arms.

"Do what?"

"Your 'Hi, Helens,' " her mother said, grimacing.

"My what?"

"Your 'Hi, Helens,' " her mother repeated with a point of her chin.

"What are you talking about? What is she talking about?" Leigh demanded of Cindy.

"Remember Auntie Molly?" Cindy asked reluctantly.

"Of course I remember Auntie Molly."

"Remember she had this friend Helen, who lived across the street?"

"I don't remember any Helen."

"Anyway," Cindy continued, bracing herself for the explosion she knew would follow, "whenever Auntie Molly saw Helen, she used to wave to her and say, 'Hi, Helen. Hi, Helen.' And the skin under her arms would jiggle, and so Mom started referring to that part of the arm as the 'Hi, Helens.' "

"What!"

"Hi, Helen," her mother said, waving to an invisible woman on the other side of the room. "Hi, Helen."

"You're saying my arms jiggle?!"

"Everybody's arms jiggle," Cindy offered.

"Yours don't," her mother said.

"No, Cindy's arms are perfect," Leigh agreed angrily, pacing back and forth in front of her mother and sister. "That's because Cindy has time to go to the gym five times a week."

"I don't go to the gym five times a week."

"Because Cindy only has to go to work when she feels like it . . ."

"That's not true. I work three afternoons a week."

". . . so she has lots of time to do things like go to the gym and the film festival and . . ."

"What's this problem you have with the film festival?"

"I don't have any problem with it. In fact, I'd dearly love to spend ten days doing nothing but running from one movie to the next. I love movies as much as you do, you know."

"Then why don't you go?"

"Because I have responsibilities. Because I have four kids and a husband to look after."

"Your daughter's getting married, your sons are in college, and your husband can take care of himself."

"As if you'd know anything about taking care of husbands," Leigh said, then blanched visibly. "I didn't mean that."

Cindy nodded, unable to find her voice.

"This is all your fault," Leigh accused her mother. "You and your damn 'Hi, Helens.' "

"You take things much too seriously," her mother said. "You always did. Besides, that's no excuse for being mean to your sister."

Leigh acknowledged her guilt with a bow of her head. "I'm really very sorry, Cindy. Please forgive me."

"You're under a lot of stress," Cindy acknowledged, trying to be generous.

"Trust me, you have no idea." Leigh hugged her arms to her sides, kept them absolutely still. "It's been one disaster after another. The hotel double-booked the ballroom, which took days to get straightened out; the florist says lilacs are out of the question for October...."

"Who has lilacs in October?" their mother asked.

"My future in-laws haven't offered to pay for a thing, and now Jason has decided he wants a reggae band instead of the trio we hired."

"He's the groom," Cindy reminded her sister.

"He's an idiot," Leigh shot back as the front door opened.

"Who's an idiot?" Leigh's daughter, Bianca, marched into the store, followed by Cindy's daughter, Heather, two steps behind.

Cindy smiled at the two denim-clad young women standing before her. Like Leigh, twenty-two-year-old Bianca was slightly overweight, the extra weight concentrated mostly in her hips, which made her appear shorter than she actually was. Also like her mother, Bianca's eyes were hazel, her mouth full, her smile wide.

(Snapshots: Six-year-old Cindy, dressed in a Wonder Woman costume on Halloween, smiling shyly at the camera, while three-year-old Leigh, naked except for an awkward black mask, mugs outrageously in the background; thirteen-year-old Cindy and ten-year-old Leigh standing on either side of their mother in front of their new house on Wembley Avenue, Leigh's right hand stretched behind her mother, her fingers raised above Cindy's head like donkey ears; mother and teenage daughters sitting on a large rock at the edge of Lake Joseph, Cindy squinting into the sun, Leigh's face hidden in the shadows.)

"Hi, Aunt Cindy."

"Hi, sweetheart."

"Who's an idiot?" Bianca asked again.

Leigh shrugged off her daughter's question, pretended to be busy with the folds of her gown.

"Hi, Mom." Heather greeted Cindy with a kiss on the cheek.

"Hi, darling. I hear you're a knockout in your dress. Sorry I missed it."

"I'm sure there'll be other opportunities," Heather said with a wink. "Julia here yet?"

"Of course she isn't here," Leigh answered before Cindy had the chance.

"You look nice," Heather told her aunt.

Leigh raised one hand to her head, fiddled girlishly with her hair, before dropping her arm self-consciously back to her side, massaging the flesh above her elbow.

"Is your arm hurt?" Heather asked.

"Let me try Julia one more time." Again Cindy retrieved her phone from her purse, quickly punching in Julia's cell phone number. Again she heard the breathy voice, the fake regret. *I'm so sorry I can't answer your call at the moment.* Where are you, Julia? she wondered, feeling her sister's angry eyes burning holes in the back of her blue blouse. "Julia, it's almost five o'clock," Cindy said evenly. "Where the hell are you?"

FOUR

THE first time Julia disappeared, she was four years old. Cindy had taken the girls to a nearby park and was busy pushing Heather on a swing when she realized that Julia was no longer among the children playing in the sandbox. She'd spent the next twenty minutes running around in increasingly frantic circles, accosting strangers, and shouting at hapless passersby: "I've lost my little girl. Please, has anyone seen my daughter?"

Cindy had run home to call the police, Heather slung across her shoulder like an old purse, only to find Julia sitting on the front steps. "What took you so long?" the child demanded. "I've been waiting for you."

Was Julia somewhere waiting for her now? Cindy wondered, entering her bedroom and walking past her younger daughter, who lay sprawled across Cindy's king-size bed, watching television, Elvis beside her. "What on earth are you watching?" Cindy asked, mesmerized by the sight of a staggeringly well-endowed young woman with big hair and a tiny white bikini rubbing great gobs of green fingerpaint over the expansive chest of a muscular young man. The young man was grinning so hard, his face looked as if it might explode. Cindy inched back, picturing white teeth spraying toward the pale blue walls of her bedroom, like confetti.

"It's called *Blind Date.*"

How appropriate, Cindy thought, sitting down on the end of her bed, trying not to think of the night ahead. "What are they doing?"

"Getting to know each other," Heather deadpanned.

"I guess some people will do anything to get on TV." Cindy found herself thinking of Julia despite her best efforts not to. She was still angry that her older daughter hadn't shown up for her fitting, that she hadn't so much as called to offer an excuse. "Get down, Elvis," Cindy said sharply, transferring her anger at her daughter to her daughter's dog. Elvis looked at her with sleepy brown eyes, sighed deeply, and rolled over on his side.

The second time Julia had disappeared was less than a year after the first. This time Cindy had put Heather in bed for her afternoon nap and come downstairs to find the front door open and Julia gone. Cindy had torn the house apart looking for her, then raced up and down the block, screaming out her daughter's name. When she'd returned to the house, her phone was ringing. It was Tom. "Julia's here," he'd said simply, a smile lurking behind his words. Apparently, Julia had grown impatient with her mother, and walked the twelve blocks to her father's office. "You took too long with Heather," Julia scolded her mother when Tom brought her home.

Had Julia grown impatient with her mother yet again? Cindy wondered, pushing herself to her feet and walking toward her closet.

"You see, the premise of this show," Heather was explaining, "is that they fix two people up and then send them off to the beach, or rock climbing, or something like that, for the afternoon, and then later, they go out for an intimate dinner . . ."

Where *was* Julia? Why hadn't she phoned?

". . . and at the end of the date," Heather continued, "they each tell the camera whether or not they'd go out with that person a second time."

"Based on a deep spiritual connection, no doubt," Cindy said, snapping back into the present, her eyes scanning the line of wooden hangers in her closet for something that could conceivably pass for stylish and sexy. "There isn't a damn thing." Julia would be able to put together something, she thought.

"What?"

"I said I have nothing to wear."

"Me neither. Can we go shopping tomorrow?"

Cindy rifled through her pantsuits, dismissing one as too heavy, one as too lightweight, another as too formal for a first date, although it looked like something an accountant might like. She finally settled on a pair of gray linen slacks and a loose-fitting white blouse. At least they were clean.

"Oh, wow. You won't believe what they're doing now," Heather cried, her voice a mixture of shock and delight. "Mom, you've got to get out here and see this."

Cindy bolted from the closet in time to see the toothy muscleman aim a flowing waterhose down the bottom half of his companion's minuscule bikini, while the big-haired, big-breasted bimbo squealed with delight. "How can you watch this garbage?"

"Are you kidding? It's great." Then, noticing the clothes in her mother's hands, "What are you doing? Are you going out?" The latter question carried just a trace of indignation.

"I won't be late."

"Where are you going?"

"Just out for dinner. I won't be late."

"So you said. Who are you going to dinner with?"

"No one special."

"What does that mean?" Heather sat up on the bed, crossed her legs, balanced her chin in the palms of her hands, her radar on full alert.

"It doesn't mean anything."

"You're being very evasive."

"You're being very nosy."

You're being obstinate, she'd told Julia this morning.

You're being anal.

"I'm just curious," Heather was saying. "You always ask me where I'm going."

"That's because I'm your mother."

"Do you have a date?" Heather pressed. "You do, don't you? With who?"

"With *whom,*" Cindy corrected. "I thought you were majoring in English."

"With *whom* are you going out, Mother?" Heather asked in Julia's voice, the word "mother" snapping at Cindy like an elastic band.

Cindy shook her head in defeat. "His name is Neil Macfarlane. He's Trish's accountant."

"Is he cute?"

Cindy shrugged. "Trish says he is."

"You've never seen him?"

Cindy blushed.

"So this is like a . . . Blind Date?" Heather asked with exaggerated flourish, vocally capitalizing the last two words, and pointing toward the TV screen with both hands.

"You ever been part of a threesome?" the grinning Romeo was asking his giggling Juliet while hand-feeding her lobster, then licking at the butter that dripped from her chin.

"Oh my," Cindy said.

"Is that what you're going to wear?" Heather indicated the clothes in her mother's hands.

Cindy held the blouse up under her chin. "What do you think?"

"You might want to go with something a little more low-cut. You know, make more of an impression."

"I think this is exactly the impression I want to make. Where's Duncan?" Cindy asked, suddenly realizing she hadn't seen Duncan since they got home.

Heather feigned indifference, shrugged, leaned back on her elbows. "Don't know."

"You don't? That's unusual."

Heather shot her mother a look. "No, it's not. We're not joined at the hip, you know."

"You two have a fight?"

"It's no big deal."

Cindy could tell from her daughter's tone that it was a subject best not pursued. Besides, if Heather and Duncan were fighting, she really didn't want to know the details. In truth, she already knew way too much about their relationship. That was the problem with sleeping down the hall from your daughter and her live-in boyfriend. You heard every whisper, every playful sigh, every enthusiastic squeak of the bed. "Could you do me a favor?" Cindy said with a smile, waiting for her daughter to ask what, then continuing when she didn't. "Could you call your father for me?"

"Why?"

"Find out if Julia's having dinner over there."

"Why don't you call?"

"I don't want to," Cindy admitted.

"Why not?"

"Because I'm asking you to call."

Heather groaned. "What kind of answer is that?"

"Heather, please. . . ."

"I'll call when the show is over."

"When is that?"

"Another fifteen minutes."

"We connected on an intellectual level," the bimbo was telling the camera.

"Then you'll call your dad?"

"Julia's fine, you know. She told you she wasn't coming to the fitting. I don't know what you're so worried about."

"I'm not worried." Then, "You don't think she could have gotten lost, do you?"

"Lost?" Heather demanded in her aunt's voice.

The last time Julia disappeared, Cindy remembered, she was thirteen years old. Cindy was still reeling from her father's sudden death from a heart attack two months earlier, Tom was away on a "business trip" with his latest paramour, and Heather was singing a solo with her school choir that night. Julia was supposed to be home in time to accompany her mother to the concert, but by seven o'clock, she still wasn't back. Cindy spent the next hour calling all Julia's friends, checking with neighbors, driving up and down the rain-soaked streets. She'd tried reaching Tom in Montreal, but he wasn't at his hotel. Finally, at nine o'clock, distraught and unsure what to do next, she'd driven to the school to pick up Heather, only to find a defiant Julia comforting her sister. "I told you I'd meet you in the auditorium," Julia chastised her mother. "Don't you listen?"

Had Julia told her of her plans this morning? Cindy wondered now, throwing her clothes on the bed and walking into the bathroom. Was this mix-up all her fault? Had she not been listening?

"Look at me," she moaned. "I look awful."

"You don't look awful," Heather called from the bedroom.

"I'm short."

"Five six isn't short."

"My hair's a mess." Cindy pulled at her loose brown curls.

"Your hair is not a mess." Heather appeared in the bathroom doorway. "Mom, what's wrong?"

"Wrong?"

"Aren't I the one who's supposed to be whining about her appearance and you the one reassuring me with quaint, motherly platitudes?"

Cindy smiled. Heather was right. When had their roles suddenly reversed?

"You're probably just nervous about your date."

"It's not a date," Cindy corrected. "And I'm not nervous." She turned on the tap, began rigorously scrubbing her face.

"Shouldn't use soap," her daughter advised, stilling her mother's hand and reaching into the medicine cabinet for a jar of moisturizing cleanser. "I mean, you buy all this stuff. Why don't you use it?"

"It's too much work. I can't be bothered."

"Try this," Heather instructed. "Then this." She pulled an assortment of bottles off the shelf of the crowded cabinet and spread them across the cherrywood counter. "Then I'll do your makeup. And speaking of makeup, what's with Auntie Leigh and the Tammy Faye Baker eyes?"

"I'm hoping it's a phase."

"Let's hope it's over by the wedding."

The phone rang.

"It's about time." Cindy marched back into her bedroom, grabbed for the phone. "Hello," she said eagerly, waiting for Julia's voice.

"Cindy, it's Leigh," her sister announced, as if she knew they'd been speaking about her. "I just want to apologize again for what I said earlier—about you spending all your time at the movies, and not knowing how to take care of a husband."

"Oh," Cindy said flatly. "That."

"I was out of line."

"Yeah," Cindy agreed. "You were."

"Anyway, I'm sorry."

"Apology accepted."

"It's just this wedding. And Mom, of course."

"Of course."

"The pressure is nonstop. Sometimes I get a little over-whelmed."

Cindy nodded into the receiver.

Her sister sighed. "I wish I had your life," she said.

Cindy laughed as she hung up the phone.

"What's funny?" Heather asked.

"My sister's idea of an apology." Cindy stared at the TV. A second young woman, whose dark bikini matched her ebony skin, was climbing into a hot tub with a bald-headed, tattoo-covered man who looked like a black Mr. Clean.

"What's she sorry for?" Heather asked.

"That's just the point. She isn't." Cindy shook her head, trying to remember the last time she'd felt close to her younger sister.

(Memory: Eight-year-old Leigh shadowing Cindy's every move, following her from room to room, as if glued to her side. "Why does she have to do everything the same as me?" Cindy protests, pushing Leigh aside.

"The same as *I*," her mother corrects. "Besides, imitation is the sincerest form of flattery."

"I hate her."

"I hate her too," Leigh echoes.

"You'll love each other when you grow up," their mother promises.)

Did they? Cindy wondered now, watching as Mr. Clean explained his various tattoos to his curious companion. She and Leigh were so different. They had different interests, different styles, different tastes. In clothes, in politics, in men. Try as they might, and occasionally they really did try, they never quite seemed to connect. Their empathy was forced, their sympathy strained. They tolerated each other. Sometimes just barely.

Strangely enough, their relationship had been at its best just after Cindy got married and again just after she got divorced. When Cindy eloped with Tom to Niagara Falls without a word to anyone, it had been Leigh who'd convinced their parents to get over their anger and accept the young man Cindy had chosen. Leigh had been a regular guest at their tiny apartment, a co-conspirator after the fact.

After Tom walked out, taking Julia with him, Leigh had been equally supportive, dropping over dinners, going grocery shopping for her distraught sister, offering to baby-sit Heather. For months, she'd called first thing every morning and again before she went to bed. She'd made sure Cindy had the best divorce lawyer in the city. She'd literally clapped her hands when Cindy's settlement guaranteed her security for life.

Leigh's own marriage, to a high school principal, had always seemed happy enough. Warren was a kind man, patient to a fault, and he seemed to genuinely love his wife. "Warren would never cheat on me," Leigh had said on more than one occasion, and Cindy had nodded her agreement, confident in the rightness of her sister's assessment, pretending not to hear the silent addendum, "the way Tom cheated on you."

"Mom?" Heather was asking now. "What's the matter? Why are you smiling like that?"

Cindy unclenched her teeth. "Just this stupid TV show." She flicked off the remote control, watching Mr. Clean and his companion disappear into darkness.

"Hey . . ."

"Call your father for me. Please," Cindy added when her daughter failed to respond.

Heather slumped toward the phone. "I don't understand why you can't call him."

"I don't want to speak to the Cookie," Cindy muttered.

"What?"

"Just call him."

Heather punched in the numbers, shifting her weight from one foot to the other as she waited for someone to answer the phone. "Hey, Fiona," she said while Cindy scrunched up her nose, as if she'd just smelled something unpleasant. "It's Heather. I'm fine. How are you?"

Cindy walked back into the bathroom, stuck out her tongue at her reflection. "I'm just fine," she said in the Cookie's chirpy little voice. "Right as rain. Happy as a lark. Peachy perfect."

"Is my sister there?"

Cindy grabbed a brush, dragged it through her hair, listened for the answer.

"Is she expected there for dinner?"

So, Julia wasn't there. At least not yet. "Ask her if she's heard from her," Cindy instructed her daughter, returning to the bedroom, the brush dangling from her hair.

"Have you heard from her?" Heather asked dutifully, then shook her head in her mother's direction. "Okay, well, if you do," Heather continued over her mother's continued prompting, "have her call home. Okay? Yeah, everything's fine. I just want to speak to her. Okay, yeah. Bye." She hung up the phone.

"Julia's not there?"

Heather shrugged her indifference. "She's fine, Mom."

"It would be nice if she phoned, that's all."

"How come you call Fiona a cookie?"

Cindy shrugged, pulling roughly at the brush in her hair, feeling the handle break off in her hand. "Oh, that's just great."

"I'll do it." Slowly, gently, Heather extricated the head of the brush from her mother's hair. Then she slid it back into the handle and began tenderly manipulating Cindy's soft curls. "You'll see. I'm going to make you absolutely gorgeous for your date tonight."

"It's not a date."

"I know it's not."

"I probably shouldn't even be going."

"Don't be silly. I'll be fine here by myself."

"It's Julia I'm worried about."

Heather stopped her gentle ministrations.

"That's it? You're done?"

Heather nodded, returning the brush to her mother's hands. "You don't need me," she said.

FIVE

So, how do you know Trish?"

Cindy tucked her hair behind her right ear, less from necessity and more because it gave her something to do with her hands. She straightened the cutlery on the white tablecloth, although it was already perfectly straight, and refolded the burgundy-colored napkin in her lap. Then she tucked the hair behind her right ear a second time and stared out the long window behind Neil Macfarlane's head, watching the blue slowly leak from the sky, bathing the expansive panorama in muted gray. Soon it would be dark, she thought, mindful that the days were getting shorter. Hold that thought, she told herself. Save it for when the conversation runs dry, for when the small talk gets so tiny it threatens to disappear altogether. Isn't that why she stopped dating in the first place, why she vowed never to subject herself to the single scene's unpleasant vagaries again? Or was it because the men had simply stopped calling? "We met about ten years ago. At one of the makeup counters in Holt's. We actually walked right into one another, reaching for the same bottle of moisturizing cream," Cindy continued, unable to stop the unexpected torrent of words. "We were both in a hurry. It was during the film festival, and we didn't have much time between films."

The man across the table nodded. "I understand Trish is quite the movie fan."

"Yes. We both are." Of course, the most logical follow-up would be for her to ask, "And you? Do you like movies too?" But she didn't because such a question would imply she was interested in whether Neil Macfarlane liked movies or not. And she was determined not to be interested in anything about Neil Macfarlane at all. So instead, Cindy scratched at the back of her neck and reached for the bread basket, although she merely shifted it a little to the left before returning her hands to her lap. She didn't want to fill up on bread. She didn't want to get bread crumbs all over her white blouse and gray linen pants. She didn't want the waiter approaching with one of those frightening little gadgets they employed to clean the tables of assorted debris, each roll offering a silent rebuke for being such a sloppy eater. All she wanted was to finish her dinner, assuming the waiter ever came by to take their order, drink her wine, assuming the wine steward could locate the expensive Bordeaux Neil had ordered, and get the hell out of the restaurant and home to Julia, assuming her older daughter had finally decided to put in an appearance. Where was she anyway? At the very least, why hadn't she called? Cindy rifled through her purse and checked that her cell phone was on.

"Everything all right?" Neil asked.

"Fine." Cindy smiled, careful to avoid the intense scrutiny of his eyes, eyes she'd noticed immediately that were an amazing shade of blue. Somewhere between teal and turquoise. With a sparkle, no less, as if it had been dabbed on with silver paint. Trish hadn't been exaggerating. Neil Macfarlane was cute all right. More than cute. He was drop-dead gorgeous. Cindy had decided immediately that the less she looked at him the better off she'd be.

(First impressions: A man, tall and slender, wavy brown hair atop a boyish face, waits for her at the bottom of the elegant, open, red mahogany staircase, the city stretched out tantalizingly behind him in the long expanse of glass; he smiles, deep dimples creasing his cheeks as she warily approaches and the city blurs behind him; he is wearing a blue shirt that underlines the fierce blue of his eyes; his hands are warm as they reach for hers; his voice is soft as he speaks her name. "Cindy," he says with the quiet confidence of someone who is used to being right. "Neil?" she asks in return, feeling instantly foolish. Who else would he be? Already she feels inadequate.)

"So what kinds of movies do you like?" Neil was asking as the wine steward approached the table, proudly displaying the requested bottle for Neil's perusal. "Looks fine," Neil told him, although his eyes never strayed from Cindy.

Cindy, in turn, focused all her attention on the wine steward, watching as he slowly and expertly began the process of removing the cork from the bottle. "I like all movies," she said vaguely, disappointed when the cork put up no real resistance, sliding out of the bottle with ease.

The steward offered the cork to Neil, who dutifully sniffed at it and nodded his approval, then tasted the sampling the steward poured into his glass. "Fine," he said. "Excellent. It just needs a few minutes to breathe," Neil advised her.

I know how it feels, Cindy thought, but didn't say, watching as the steward filled her glass just short of halfway.

"So, you have no preferences at all?" Neil was asking.

What was the matter with him? Cindy wondered impatiently. Why did he insist on making conversation? He didn't really give a damn what kinds of movies she liked, or how she and Trish had met, or anything about her, for that matter. And if he did, it was only because he wanted to sleep with her, and he knew his chances would be greatly improved if he at least feigned an interest in her. Although why he would want to sleep with her was a total mystery. Look at him, for heaven's sake, Cindy thought, deliberately looking at the floor. On any given night, he undoubtedly had his choice of any number of much more attractive, much fitter, much *younger* women. Why would he want to sleep with her? That was easy, she decided. He wanted to sleep with her because she was here. It was as simple as that. It didn't mean anything.

It doesn't mean anything.

How many times had Tom told her exactly that?

Cindy raised her head, stared directly into Neil Macfarlane's brilliant blue eyes. "I like sex and violence," she stated honestly, the first time she'd admitted that to anyone.

"What?"

"You asked what kind of movies I like. I like sex and violence," she repeated, reaching for her wineglass, taking a long sip, feeling the wine slightly abrasive as it scratched against her throat. He was right. It needed a few more minutes to breathe. Cindy tossed her hair back, took another sip. "You look shocked."

Neil smiled, the dimples framing his mouth like quotation marks. "I understand liking sex. But blood and guts?"

"Not blood and guts so much," Cindy countered, feeling the wine curl into her stomach, like a contented cat in a wicker basket. "I don't like watching people get blown up ad nauseum. I guess what I like is more the threat of violence, the possibility that something terrible is about to happen."

"Women-in-jeopardy," Neil said matter-of-factly, nodding as if he understood, as if he already understood everything there was to know about her, as if there was nothing more to discover.

"I hate that term," Cindy said, stronger than she'd intended. "*Women-in-jeopardy*," she repeated, taking another sip of wine, emboldened. "It's condescending. You never hear people say *men-in-jeopardy*. And, I mean, isn't that what drama is all about? *People* in jeopardy? Why is it somehow less valid when it concerns women? I'm really sick of that attitude." Whoa, she thought. Where had that come from?

Neil leaned back, lifted his hands in the air in a gesture of surrender. Cindy braced herself for his comeback, some smart remark that would put her in her place, reduce her to the role of angry, man-hating feminist. Instead he said, "You're right."

I'm right? she thought, relief washing over her, like an unexpected shower. She tapped her heart with her open palm. "I don't think anybody's ever said that to me before."

He laughed. "I guess I've just never really thought about it, but now that I do, I see your point—all drama is about people in peril, at a time in their lives when they're at risk, when they have to take a chance, make key decisions, get out of sticky situations, save themselves. The term 'women-in-jeopardy' *is* condescending. You're absolutely right."

Cindy smiled. He must really want to sleep with me, she thought. "Did Trish tell you I haven't had sex in three years?" The words were out of her mouth before she could stop them.

Neil's hand froze as he reached for his glass. "I don't think she mentioned that, no." Slowly, carefully, he brought the glass to his lips, then took a long sip of wine, holding it in his mouth, almost as if he were afraid to swallow.

"You think it's breathed long enough?" Cindy asked, enjoying his discomfort.

He gulped it down, exhaled deeply. "Definitely breathed long enough." The waiter approached, and asked if they'd reached a decision about their order. Neil grabbed for his menu. "Forgot what I wanted," he said sheepishly, blue eyes quickly scanning the night's offerings. "I guess I'll just have the special."

"The calves' liver sounds wonderful," Cindy said, thinking how nice it felt to be in control for a change. When was the last time she'd felt in control? Of anything? "And I'd like the endive and pear salad to start." Suddenly she felt ravenous.

"I'll start with the calamari," Neil said.

"Good choice," the waiter told him before departing with the menus.

What was the matter with my choice? Cindy wondered, feeling oddly slighted, her power already deflating. What was the matter with her? What on earth had possessed her to tell a virtual stranger she hadn't had sex in three years? Trish's accountant, for God's sake. What he must think of her! "Have you noticed the days are getting shorter?" she asked, a bit desperately.

Neil looked toward the windows that embraced the east and south walls of the tony restaurant. "I guess they are." He looked back at Cindy, the look in his eyes a mixture of bemused curiosity and wary anticipation, as if he were slightly afraid of what she might say next, but was looking forward to it just the same.

"So tell me all about the joys of accounting. Are there any?"

"I like to think so," Neil answered, his voice a smile. "There's something very satisfying about numbers."

"How so?"

"Numbers are what they are. They're very straightforward. Unlike people."

Cindy nodded her agreement. "I can't imagine you have much trouble with people."

Neil shrugged, lifted his glass in a toast. "To people."

Cindy clicked her glass against his, avoided his eyes. "So, I guess you were always really good at math, right?"

"Right."

"I was horrible in math. It was my worst subject."

"English was my worst."

"My best," Cindy said.

There was a moment's silence. "Can we go back to talking about sex now?" Neil asked, and Cindy laughed in spite of her desire not to.

"Can we just forget I said anything about that?"

"That might be difficult."

"Can we try?"

"Absolutely."

Another moment of silence. "Look, I'm obviously not very good at this."

"At what?"

"This whole scene. Dating. You know."

"What makes you say that?"

"Well, I'm not exactly a sparkling conversationalist."

"On the contrary. You sure got my attention."

Again Cindy laughed. "Yeah, well, sex is a cheap way to get someone's attention."

"Not always so cheap."

Cindy quickly finished off the wine in her glass. "So, what *did* Trish tell you about me?"

Neil sat back in his chair, gave the question several seconds thought. "She said that you were bright, beautiful, and extremely picky when it came to men."

"Which is a nice way of saying I haven't had sex in three years," Cindy heard herself say before throwing her hand over her mouth. "God, what's the matter with me?"

"You haven't had sex in three years," Neil answered with a sly smile.

A wave of heat spread across Cindy's face and neck, like a sunburn. She felt all eyes staring at her. "Maybe I should just make a general announcement. Hell, I think there are some people in the far corner over there who might not know."

"Why haven't you had sex in three years? Are you really that picky when it comes to men?"

"*Prickly* is probably a better word," Cindy admitted. "Men don't like angry women."

"And you're an angry woman?"

"Apparently."

I've always had trouble dealing with your anger, her ex-husband had told her.

"You okay?" Neil asked.

"Yes. Why?"

"I don't know. You just got this funny little look on your face."

"I'm fine," Cindy said. "I mean, other than the fact that I feel like a total idiot, I'm fine."

"I think you're charming. I'm having a great time."

"You are?"

"Aren't you?"

Cindy laughed. "Actually, yes. I am."

"Good. Have some more wine." He filled both their glasses, then clicked his glass against hers. "To angry women."

Cindy smiled. "To brave men."

(Memory: Tom's voice on the answering machine: *Hi, it's me. Look, there's no easy way to say this, so I'll just come right out with it. I'm leaving. Actually I've already left. Call me a coward, and a few other choice words I'm sure you'll think of, but I just thought it was better if we didn't speak in person. You know I've always had trouble dealing with your anger. Anyway, I'm at the Four Seasons Hotel. Call me when you stop swearing.*)

"So, Trish tells me you work in Hazelton Lanes," Neil was saying.

"Yes. A friend of mine owns this neat little jewelry store. I help her out three afternoons a week."

"How long have you been doing that?"

"About seven years."

"Since your divorce?"

"Trish told you about that?"

"She said you've been divorced seven years."

This was the part of dating Cindy liked least. The emotional résumé, where you were expected to trot out your dirty laundry and bare your soul, vent your frustrations, recount your pain, and hope for a sympathetic ear. But Cindy had no interest in trotting, baring, venting, and recounting. And she'd long since given up on hope. She took a deep breath. "Okay, I'm going to get this over with as quickly as possible, so listen carefully: My husband walked out on me seven years ago for another woman, which was no huge surprise since he'd been cheating on me for years. What was surprising was that my older daughter chose to go with him, although I probably shouldn't have been so surprised because she was always her father's little princess. Anyway," Cindy continued, glancing toward the phone in her purse, "my settlement ensured I didn't have to worry about finding a job, which was good because I only had a high school education, having eloped when I was eighteen. Still with me?"

"Hanging onto every word."

"After I got married, I worked at Eaton's for a couple of years, selling towels and bedding and exciting stuff like that, helping put my ex through law school, pretty standard stuff, and then I got pregnant and I quit work to stay home with Julia, and then two years later, Heather came along, something for which Julia never quite forgave me." Cindy strained to keep her voice light. "Witness her decision to go live with her father."

"But you saw her, didn't you? Weekends? Holidays?"

"She was a teenager. I saw her whenever she could fit me into her busy schedule. Which wasn't too often." Cindy felt her stomach cramp at the memory.

"That must have been very difficult for you."

"It was awful. I felt as if someone had ripped my guts out. I cried every day. Couldn't sleep, wondering what I'd done wrong. Sometimes I could barely get out of bed. I honestly thought I'd lose my mind. That's when Meg, my friend, offered me a job working at her little boutique. At first I said no, but eventually I decided I had to do something. And it's been great. I work three afternoons a week; I take off whenever I feel like it. And to top it off, my daughter's come back." Again Cindy glanced toward her purse.

"Do you keep her in there?" Neil asked.

Cindy smiled. "Sorry. It's just that she was supposed to call. Anyway, sorry about unloading on you like that. Can we do us both a favor and never mention my ex-husband or my divorce again?"

"I'll drink to that." They clicked glasses.

"Your turn." Cindy leaned back in her chair, sipped on her wine. "Family history in fifty words or less."

He laughed. "Well, I was married."

"For how long?"

"Fifteen years."

"And you've been divorced for how long?"

"I'm not divorced."

"Oh?"

"My wife died four years ago."

"Oh, I'm so sorry."

"She woke up one morning, said she wasn't feeling quite right, and six weeks later, she was dead. Ovarian cancer."

"How awful. Trish didn't tell me. . . ."

"I doubt she has any idea. I've only known her a short time, and all she asked me was whether I was married, and if I'd be interested in going out with her friend."

Cindy shook her head. "And you, poor man, said yes."

"I said yes."

"Do you have children?"

"A son. Max. He's seventeen. Great kid."

Cindy tried picturing Julia at seventeen, but the years between fourteen and twenty-one had pretty much melted together in Cindy's mind, like chocolates left too long in the sun. All those years lost. Years she could never get back.

The waiter was suddenly standing beside them. "Endive and pear salad for the lady," he announced, as if she might have forgotten. "Calamari for the gentleman." He put the dishes on the table. "Enjoy."

"Thank you." Cindy lifted her fork, stabbing it into her salad as she stole another glance at the phone in her purse. *Hi, Mom. Sorry about not calling earlier, but I've had the most incredible day.* But Cindy's phone remained stubbornly silent, and Julia remained, as ever, tantalizingly out of reach.

SIX

THE phone rang at just after 2 A.M., cutting through Cindy's sleep like a dull blade. She flung her arm toward the sound, knocking the back of her hand against the night table beside her bed, and crying out in pain as she groped for the receiver. "Hello?" she said, barely recognizing the sound of her own voice.

"I understand you've lost your daughter," the caller said.

Instantly Cindy was wide awake, her body rigid, her feet on the floor, poised to run. "Who is this?"

"It doesn't matter who I am. What matters is, I found her."

Cindy's eyes shot through the darkness to the window, as if Julia might have been spirited through the slats of the California shutters and was now hidden among the leaves of the red maple trees in the backyard. Her heart pounded loudly against her ears, like a restless ocean surf. "Where is she? How is she?"

"You should take better care of your children," the caller scolded.

"Please, can you just tell me where she is?"

"You know what they say, don't you? Finders, keepers . . ."

"What?"

". . . losers, weepers."

"Who are you? What have you done with Julia?"

"I have to go now."

"Wait! Don't hang up. Please, don't hang up!" Cindy felt the line go dead in her hands, as if Julia herself had just died in her arms. "No! No!"

"Mom?" a frightened voice called from the doorway. "Mom, what's the matter?"

Cindy spun around, the blankets falling from her naked body as she jumped from the bed, her pupils dilating with disbelief as she absorbed the identity of the person walking toward her. "Julia! You're here. You're all right." She threw her arms around her daughter, wrapped her in a smothering embrace. "I was having the most awful nightmare. It was so real. But you're okay. You're okay." She kissed Julia's cheek and forehead, felt Julia's skin grow colder with each brush of her lips. "My poor baby. You're freezing. Come get into bed. What's the matter, darling? Are you sick?" Cindy maneuvered her daughter into her bed, Julia's body going limp as she lay back against the pillow, her blond hair floating around her face, like seaweed in a shallow lake. "Everything's okay now, sweetheart. Mommy's here. I'll take care of you."

Julia stared at her mother through cold, dead eyes. She spoke without moving her lips. "This is all your fault," she said.

Cindy screamed.

And then suddenly someone was at her side, touching her shoulder, stroking her arm. "Mom! Mom! What's the matter? Mom, wake up. Wake up." And then something wet on her cheek, a rhythmic thumping at the side of the bed.

Cindy opened her eyes, saw Heather trembling beside her, the moonlight through the bedroom shutters drawing a series of broad horizontal stripes across her face. Elvis was on his hind legs at the side of the bed, his eager tongue extending toward her face, his tail slapping enthusiastically at the sideboard. "What's happening?"

"You tell me. Are you all right?" Somewhere behind Heather, something stirred.

Cindy arched forward, strained through the darkness past her younger child. "Is someone there? Julia? Is that you?"

"It's me, Mrs. Carver," Duncan replied, joining Heather and Elvis at Cindy's side. He was wearing only the bottom half of a pair of blue-and-white-striped pajamas; Heather was wearing its matching top.

"Oh." Cindy quickly pulled the covers up around her chin. "My robe," she said, motioning vaguely toward the foot of the bed.

Heather reached for the green-and-navy terry-cloth robe, draped it across her mother's shoulders. "You must have been having a nightmare."

Cindy stared blankly toward the foot of the bed, the details of her dream already receding, bursting like bubbles against the night air, evaporating, taking Julia away. "A nightmare. Yes. It was awful."

"You want some warm milk or something?" Heather asked. "I can make you a cup."

Cindy shook her head. "Is Julia home?"

Even in the dark, Cindy could see the frown on her younger daughter's face.

"Her door's closed," Duncan volunteered.

"It's always closed," Heather reminded him. "You want me to check?"

"I'll do it." Cindy secured her robe around her and climbed out of bed. "You two go back to bed. Get some sleep. It's late." She followed them out of the room and into the wide hall, stopping with them in front of Julia's door, Elvis licking at her bare toes. Her fingers stretched toward the doorknob.

"She's gonna be real mad if you wake her up," Heather warned.

She's going to be really angry, Cindy corrected silently, too tired to say the words out loud. She felt the doorknob twist in her palm, heard the loud creak as she pushed open Julia's door. Cindy poked her head inside the room, her eyes straining through the darkness toward the bed.

It was empty.

Cindy knew it instantly, even before Elvis went charging past her and began wrestling with the stuffed animals propped against Julia's pillows. Heather ran after him, stubbing her toes on several of the CDs scattered across the blue carpet, and swearing loudly.

"Shit," she cried as Cindy flipped on the overhead light.

"Good thing Julia's not here," Duncan observed wryly as Elvis began barking.

"Where the hell is she?" Cindy surveyed the mess that was her daughter's room. Discarded clothes lay scattered across the floor, on the bookshelves lining one wall, on the walnut desk propped against another, and over the back of the black leather chair in front of it. A hot pink mini-dress was draped across the top of the white shutters; a pair of outrageously high-heeled sandals hung from their straps on a bedpost.

"She's probably at Dad's," Heather said, shooing Elvis off Julia's bed.

"Then why hasn't she called?"

"Because she's Julia," Heather reminded her mother. Then, "Maybe she's with Sean."

"I thought they broke up."

"So?" Heather asked.

Cindy nodded, wondering whether she could call Sean at this hour of the morning.

"Don't even think about it," Heather warned, as if reading her mother's mind. "She's fine, Mom. Stop worrying. You can bet she's not worrying about you."

"You're right," Cindy said, trying not to picture Julia lying bleeding and alone in some ditch at the side of a dark road. Or worse.

"You never said how your date went tonight." Heather stared at her mother expectedly.

"It wasn't a date."

"Yeah, okay, so, the question is, did you connect on a deep intellectual and spiritual level?"

Cindy pictured Neil's wondrous dimples when he laughed, felt the touch of his skin as his hand repeatedly brushed up against her arm as he walked her home, tasted his sweet breath as he leaned in to kiss her cheek good night. "We connected."

"So there'll be a second nondate?"

"We'll see." Cindy kissed Heather's forehead, patted Duncan's bare arm. "Get some sleep."

"You too," Heather said. "Come on, Elvis."

Elvis immediately spread himself across Cindy's feet, refused to move.

"Looks like he's sleeping with you tonight," Heather said, following Duncan into their bedroom and closing the door.

"Great." Elvis rolled over onto his back, offered his stomach to be rubbed. "Come on, you nut. Let's go to bed." Elvis flipped back onto his feet, took two steps, then stopped, sat down, and stared back at Julia's room, as if he, too, were confused by her absence. "She's fine," Cindy told him, as Elvis cocked his head to one side attentively. "Except that I'm going to kill her when she gets home." She shuffled toward her room, plopped down on her bed, then lay down on top of her covers. Elvis immediately jumped on the bed and burrowed in against the inside of her knees. Cindy turned on one side; Elvis snuggled closer. "I don't think this is going to work," Cindy told the dog after several minutes spent in a futile effort to get comfortable. "I guess I'm just not used to sharing my space anymore. Sorry about that." She sat up, flipped on the light beside her bed, reached for the phone.

Don't even think about it, she heard Heather say.

But it was too late. Already Cindy's fingers were punching in the numbers she hadn't realized she knew by heart.

The voice that answered the phone on its fourth ring was wary and weighted with sleep. "Hello?"

Cindy pictured the young woman sitting up in bed, pushing lush red ringlets away from her Kewpie-doll face, the strap of an expensive pink silk peignoir slipping down one milk-white shoulder, full bosom heaving fetchingly in the soft moonlight. A book cover, Cindy thought, picturing it in her mind: *Romance for Cookies.*

"Fiona," Cindy said, imagining Tom sitting up beside his young wife, playful fingers sliding the errant strap back over her shoulder. "It's Cindy."

"It's two o'clock in the morning, Cindy."

"I know what time it is."

"Is something wrong?"

"Is Julia there?"

"Julia? No."

"What's going on?" Cindy heard Tom grumble.

"She's your ex-wife. You ask her," the Cookie said, as Cindy pictured her flopping back on her pillow and covering her eyes with a disinterested hand.

"Cindy, what the hell's going on? It's after two o'clock."

Cindy felt her throat constrict, as it always did when she was forced to actually speak to her former husband. "Fiona has already told me the time. And I'm sorry to bother you at this hour, I really am, but Julia's not home, and I haven't heard from her all day, and I just wondered if you'd spoken to her."

There was a long pause. "Not since around ten-thirty this morning."

"She didn't call you after her audition?"

"No."

"And you're not worried?" Cindy heard the growing panic in her voice.

"Why would I be worried?" Cindy recognized the once-familiar tone. His lawyer's voice. I don't have time for your petty insecurities, it said. "I don't demand that my daughter check in with me every minute of the day and night."

"Neither do I."

"You have to let go, Cindy . . ." Tom said.

Tears stung Cindy's eyes. How can I let go of something I never had? she thought.

". . . or you'll drive her away again."

I didn't drive her away, Cindy thought bitterly. *You* drove her away. In your goddamn BMW.

"She's probably with Sean."

Cindy nodded.

"Don't even think of calling him now," Tom said.

Cindy hung up without saying good night. "Bastard," she whispered, as if afraid he could still hear her. She remained motionless in her bed for several seconds, Elvis pressing against her side. "What about you?" she asked the dog. "You think I'm overly protective? You think I've driven her away again?"

In response, Elvis jumped off the bed and ran to the bedroom door, then stopped and looked back, as if expecting her to follow.

"I don't think you understand."

The dog began pacing restlessly back and forth in the doorway.

"What? You have to go out?"

Elvis barked.

"Ssh! Okay, okay. I'll take you out." Cindy tightened the sash of her terry-coth bathrobe and slid her feet into a pair of well-worn white slippers, stomping down the stairs to the front door. "I can't believe I'm doing this. You better have to pee, that's all I can say." She opened the door to the cool night air and stepped onto the front landing. Elvis immediately took off down the front steps and disappeared. "Elvis, wait! Where are you going?" A sudden blur raced across her front lawn, cutting through the bushes that separated her property from her next-door neighbor's. "Elvis! Get back here. I can't believe this." Her slippers flopping noisily around her feet like rubber flippers, Cindy inched her way down the front steps. "Elvis, get back here. You're a very bad dog." Oh, sure, she thought, that'll get him back here in a hurry. "You're a really good dog, Elvis," she said, trying again. "Come to Mommy." Except she wasn't his mommy. Julia was his mommy. Which made her Elvis's grandmother. "Dear God," she wailed.

"It's okay, Cindy. He's over here," a voice announced from somewhere beside her.

Cindy gasped, her head snapping toward the sound.

"Sorry. I didn't mean to scare you." The voice was coming from beyond the bushes. "It's me. Ryan."

Cindy kicked off her slippers and pushed herself through the bushes, several branches slapping against her face as she stepped onto Ryan Sellick's front lawn, the damp grass creeping between her bare toes. Ryan was sitting on his top step, in much the same position his wife, Faith, had occupied earlier in the day. Light from two brass lanterns hanging to either side of the front door illuminated his fine features: the long, straight nose; the thin lips; the sculpted cheekbones; the slight cleft in his chin. Dark hair fell across his forehead and over the back collar of his shirt, a shirt that was either black or brown, as were his eyes. Julia had always considered him terribly handsome, Cindy remembered as she approached, seeing Elvis with his head resting comfortably in Ryan's lap, contently licking at the crisp denim of Ryan's jeans. She noticed Ryan's feet were as bare as her own, and that there was a long, fresh scratch beneath his right eye that hadn't been there earlier in the day. "I'm sorry to bother you." Cindy remained at the foot of the outside steps, not wanting to intrude any further into his privacy. "Elvis, get down here."

"He's fine." Ryan stroked behind the dog's ears. "Actually, I'm grateful for the company."

"Are you okay?"

"Couldn't sleep."

Cindy nodded. "How's Faith?"

He shrugged, as if he weren't sure how to answer the question.

"My sister had postpartum depression," Cindy offered. "With two of her children."

"Really? And what happened?"

Cindy struggled to remember, but like her mother, she actually had no recollection of Leigh having suffered from any such affliction. "I guess it just went away with time."

"That's pretty much what her doctor says will happen. Apparently it's not all that uncommon."

"So I've heard."

"You never had it?"

"No. I was lucky, I guess." Cindy had sailed through both her pregnancies and their aftermath, relishing the time when her daughters were infants, despite the fact that Julia had been collicky and demanding from the moment of her birth. Heather, on the other hand, had slept through the night at ten weeks, settled into a three-feedings-a-day schedule the week after that, and potty-trained herself at thirteen months. Cindy sat down on the bottom step and stared down the quiet street, half expecting to see her older daughter emerge from the shadows of the streetlamps. "Has the doctor recommended any medication?"

"He prescribed Valium, but it doesn't seem to be doing much good. Maybe she needs something stronger."

"Maybe she needs to talk to a psychiatrist."

"Maybe." Ryan Sellick massaged the bridge of his nose, as if trying to keep a budding headache at bay.

"What about Faith's mother? Any chance she could help out for a few weeks?"

"Her mother's been back and forth from Vancouver several times already. I can't expect her to keep flying over every time there's a problem. And my parents are both dead, so . . ."

"What about hiring a nanny?"

"Faith won't hear of it. 'What kind of mother can't take care of her own child?' she says whenever I so much as mention the idea." Ryan shook his head, gingerly patting the deep scratch beneath his eye. "I don't know what to do. I can't keep taking time off work, that's for sure. I didn't get to the office today till almost noon, and then I had to leave again when you called."

"Maybe I could drop by a few times a week," Cindy suggested.

"No. I couldn't put you to that much trouble."

"It's no trouble," Cindy assured him. "And I'll talk to Heather and Julia, see if they'd be willing to baby-sit occasionally."

Ryan laughed, an unexpectedly hearty sound.

"What's funny?"

He shook his head. "Julia just doesn't strike me as the baby-sitting type."

Cindy had to agree. "I didn't realize you knew my daughter so well."

"It's all in the way she walks. Nobody struts a street quite like Julia."

Cindy watched Julia's image step out of the shadows and walk toward them, head high, shoulders rotating in time with her hips, arms swinging at her sides. She moves as if a camera is following her, Cindy thought, recording her every move.

"Everything all right at home?" Ryan asked.

What was he talking about? "What do you mean?"

"Well, Julia and Heather's boyfriend, I've forgotten his name. . . ."

"Duncan."

"Yeah, Duncan. They were going at it pretty good this morning."

"They were fighting?"

"In the driveway. I heard the yelling from inside my house." He motioned toward the dining room to the left of the front door.

It must have been when I was out shopping for chardonnay,

Cindy thought, recalling today's lunch with genuine nostalgia. Already it seemed so long ago. Why would Julia have been fighting with Duncan? And why hadn't he mentioned their argument to her earlier? Why hadn't Heather?

"What time was that?"

"A little before eleven, I think."

So Julia had been fighting with Duncan just before she'd had to leave for her appointment. Maybe the argument had upset her, caused her to blow the most important audition of her career. Maybe that's why she hadn't come home—because she was too angry and embarrassed and upset. Damn that Duncan anyway, Cindy thought, pushing herself to her feet. She should never have allowed him to move into her house. "I should get home. Let you get some sleep," she said. "Come on, Elvis. Party's over." Surprisingly, the dog immediately jumped to his feet and followed after her.

"Thanks for being such a good neighbor," Ryan called as Cindy reached the sidewalk in front of the house.

Cindy waited while Elvis relieved himself against the side of a tall maple tree. "Everything's going to work out fine. You'll see." Confidence radiated from her voice, and it was only later, when she was lying in her bed, wide awake at nearly 4 A.M., Julia still not home, that Cindy wondered who it was she'd been trying so hard to convince.

SEVEN

At precisely seven-thirty the next morning Cindy phoned Sean Banack. "Sean, this is Julia's mother," she said instead of hello. "Is Julia there?"

"What?" The sleepy voice was raspy with cigarettes and alcohol. "I'm sorry, what?" he said again.

"It's Cindy Carver. Julia's mother," Cindy repeated, picturing Sean Banack slowly propping himself up on one elbow in the middle of rumpled white sheets, his free hand pushing long blond hair away from his forehead, then rubbing at tired brown eyes. She wondered if Julia was stretched out beside him. *I'm not here,* she could almost hear her daughter whisper before flipping onto her other side and covering her head with a pillow.

"Mrs. Carver?" Sean asked, as if he still wasn't sure who she was.

"I'm sorry to be calling so early, but I need to speak to Julia."

"Julia's not here."

"Please, Sean. This is really important."

"She's not here," he repeated stubbornly.

"Do you know where she is?"

Sean made a sound halfway between a laugh and a cry. "I'm very sorry, Mrs. Carver, but Julia is no longer my problem."

"What does that mean?"

"It means we broke up. It means I don't have a clue where she is. It means it's seven-thirty in the morning and I didn't get to bed till after three. Which means I'm still a little drunk and I've got to get some sleep."

"Sean," Cindy cried before he could disconnect. "Please. Julia didn't come home last night and I'm very worried. If you have any idea at all where she might be. . . ."

"Sorry, Mrs. Carver," Sean said before hanging up the phone. "I'm not the one you should be speaking to."

"What do you mean? Who should I . . . ?" Cindy stared at the dead phone in her hands for several long seconds before dropping it back into its carriage. "Great. Just great." Elvis stirred beside her, then jumped from the bed, stared at her expectantly. "What does that mean, 'I'm not the one you should be speaking to?' " she asked the dog, who cocked his head from side to side, as if carefully considering his response. Then he ran to the bedroom door and barked. "That's all you have to say?" Elvis barked again, and began digging at the carpet. "I know. I know. You have to go out. Give me a minute, okay?" Elvis promptly sat down, patiently waiting as Cindy showered and slipped into a pair of jeans and an old orange T-shirt. "Did Julia come home while I was in the shower?" she asked the dog as he dutifully followed her into Julia's empty room.

Cindy glanced toward the closed door of the bedroom Heather shared with Duncan. It bothered her that neither of them had said anything about Duncan's fight with Julia, a fight so acrimonious it had spilled from the house to the street, so loud it had attracted the attention of their next-door neighbor. She thought of storming into their room and demanding an explanation, but decided such confrontations were better left till she got back from walking the dog. Perhaps by that time, Julia would be home.

"Come on, boy." Cindy attached Elvis's leash to his collar and grabbed a plastic bag from the kitchen. It was only after she'd stepped outside and closed the front door behind her that she realized she'd forgotten her key. At least now she had an excuse for having to wake everyone up early.

"Where are you, Julia?" Cindy asked the sun-dappled street, listening to the whir of cars already clogging Avenue Road. Avenue Road, she repeated silently, turning in the opposite direction and waiting as Elvis relieved himself on a neighbor's front lawn. What a strange thing to call a street. Almost as if the city council had run out of names. "Where are you, Julia?" she repeated, stopping again while Elvis left his mark on a newly planted strip of grass.

She turned left on Poplar Plains and proceeded south, letting Elvis lead the way. It was going to be a beautiful day, she thought, feeling the sun warm on her arms, the slightest of breezes teasing the leaves on the trees. A week from now, the University of Toronto's fall semester would be getting under way, and Heather and Duncan would be back in class, Cindy would be sitting in a crowded movie theater with hundreds of other avid film devotees, and Julia . . . Julia would be where?

Where was she now?

"Where are you, Julia?" Cindy asked again, tugging on Elvis's leash when he stopped too long at the corner of Poplar Plains and Clarendon, picking up the pace as they turned the corner onto Edmund. "Hurry up and do your stuff," Cindy instructed, amazed when the dog immediately squatted, leaving a large, steaming deposit in the middle of the sidewalk. Cindy held her breath as she scooped the dog poop into the clear plastic bag. "Good boy," she said. All my children should listen so well, she thought.

What had Sean meant when he said Julia was no longer his problem? Clearly he was upset about their breakup, but he'd sounded so bitter. *I'm not the one you should be speaking to.* What did that mean exactly? *Whom* should she be speaking to?

"Damn it, Julia. Where are you?" Cindy nodded hello to a heavyset man who was skipping rope in front of a mustard-yellow apartment building on the other side of the street. Even from this distance she could see he was sweating profusely, and she wondered if such intense exercise was good for him. She checked her watch. It was a little past eight o'clock. Maybe that's where Julia was—at an early-morning exercise class. Yes, that was it. She'd probably met up with a group of friends after her audition and they'd spent the afternoon together, gone out for a dinner of sushi and wine, then partied until it was too late to call home. When she woke up, she'd gone directly to her yoga class. There was nothing to worry about; nothing awful had happened. Julia hadn't been hurt, molested, kidnapped, murdered, dismembered, her body parts hurled into the middle of Lake Ontario. She was perfectly fine, and she'd be back within the hour to shower and blow-dry her hair razor-straight for the undoubtedly busy day ahead. She hadn't called because she simply wasn't used to reporting her whereabouts to her mother. Her father had never demanded that she—how was it he so sensitively put it?—check in with him every minute of the day and night.

"I hope you're picking up after your dog," a woman called from a nearby apartment window.

Cindy waved the plastic bag full of poop above her head. "What do you think this is?" she snapped. "A purse?"

The woman quickly retreated, lowering her window with a loud bang.

So many angry people, Cindy thought, proceeding up Avenue Road, dropping the plastic bag into a garbage bin already overflowing with them. She turned west on Balmoral, heading for home. *I've always had trouble dealing with your anger,* she heard Tom say, as she ran up the steps and banged on her front door.

* * *

"I DON'T UNDERSTAND how you could leave the house without your keys," Heather scolded her mother, yawning as she poured herself a large bowl of Cinnamon Toast Crunch and plopped down at the kitchen table, burying her face in the morning paper.

"You didn't tell me Duncan and Julia had a fight yesterday," Cindy said in return.

"It was no big deal."

"Big enough to concern several of the neighbors," Cindy embellished.

"Really? Who?"

"That's not the issue."

"There is no issue."

"What was the fight about?"

"Nothing." Heather shrugged, tossed the front section of the *Globe and Mail* onto the round pine table. "You know Julia."

"And you know what Julia and Duncan were fighting about. Tell me."

Heather lowered the paper and released a deep breath of air, looking imploringly toward the doorway, as if hoping Duncan would miraculously appear. But the shower was still running and it was unlikely Duncan would be down for a while. "It was nothing. Really. Her Highness was running late, as usual, and she wanted a ride to her audition. When Duncan said he was going in the opposite direction and didn't have time to chauffeur her around, she got angry and started yelling. She even followed him to his car."

Cindy silently berated herself for not having been home to drive her daughter to her audition. "Would it have killed him to give her a lift?"

"Would it kill her to get her driver's license? How can anyone fail that stupid test three times?"

Cindy had occasionally wondered the same thing. But not

even the sight of Julia's mesmerizingly long legs had been enough
to influence the instructor's decision. "That's not the point."

"The point is that not everyone's life revolves around Julia.
Stop worrying, Mom. She's fine."

"Then where is she? Why hasn't she called?" Cindy braced herself for her daughter's careless shrug, but surprisingly, none came.

"Did you check with Dad?"

Cindy nodded.

"And Sean?"

"He says Julia is no longer his problem. He hinted she might be
seeing someone else."

"Really?"

"You have no idea who that might be?"

"No, but then I'm not exactly Julia's main confidante. You
could ask Lindsey."

"Lindsey?"

"Lindsey—Julia's latest, greatest, best friend ever. She met her
last month. The one with the enormous implants."

A huge bosom balancing precariously atop a skinny torso
flashed before Cindy's eyes. The implants wafted into the air like
two helium-filled balloons, blocking the young woman's face. "Do
you know her number?"

"It's probably in Julia's address book."

Several minutes later, Cindy was in Julia's bedroom, guiltily
rummaging through her things. But if Julia had an address book,
she'd taken it with her. Cindy looked under every piece of clothing, searched through every drawer. Amid a sea of debris, she
found a crumpled five-dollar bill, a sweater she'd been looking for
all winter, and several packets of condoms, but no address book.
Did it matter? She couldn't remember Lindsey's last name. Cindy
slapped angrily at her thighs. What kind of mother doesn't know
the names of her daughter's friends?

"I'm absolutely positive she's okay," Heather said when Cindy returned to the kitchen. "But maybe you should call the hospitals," she added quietly. "Just in case."

CINDY SPENT THE next hour calling every hospital in the city. She started with the downtown hospitals—Mount Sinai, the Toronto Hospital, Women's College, the Western, St. Mike's, even the Hospital for Sick Children, and then she branched out, calling Sunnybrook, North York General, Humber Memorial, and even Scarborough. They all told her the same thing. No one named Julia Carver was registered as a patient; no one fitting her description had been brought into the emergency department in the last twenty-four hours.

She called the police, asked whether there'd been any accidents or incidents that might have involved her daughter, but the answer was no, and she hung up, feeling relieved, grateful, and alarmed all at the same time.

She noted the time on the microwave oven. It was ten o'clock. A full day had elapsed since she'd seen Julia.

Cindy looked around the now-empty kitchen. Heather and Duncan were upstairs, engaged in a quiet but unmistakable argument. They'd tried to pretend nothing was amiss, but Cindy could feel the tension between them. Was Julia in any way responsible for that tension? She found herself remembering how often she and Tom had put on similar fronts, smiling pleasantly for the children before retreating to their bedroom to unleash angry words between tightly gritted teeth, their hostility all the more intense for being so zealously suppressed. Cindy reached for the phone, punched in Tom's office number, smiling tightly as she waited for his secretary to answer.

"Thomas Carver's office," the secretary chirped in her little-girl voice, although the woman was almost Cindy's age.

"Mr. Carver, please."

"Cindy?" the secretary asked. "Is that you?"

"Irena," Cindy acknowledged, amazed her voice was still recognizable after all this time. "How are you?"

"Great. Run off my feet, as usual. Haven't heard from you in forever. How are you doing?"

"I'm doing very well, thank you," Cindy lied. "Is he in?" she asked, not sure exactly what to call her ex-husband. Couldn't very well ask to speak to "the shithead."

"He's not. He's in meetings most of the day, and I don't think he's planning on coming back to the office. Being Friday and the long weekend and everything. You know."

Cindy nodded, although she didn't know. When she and Tom had been married, one day was pretty much the same as the next. There'd been no such thing as a weekend, let alone a long one. He was always at the office. As was Irena. "Will he be checking in this morning?"

"I'm sure he will."

"Could you please tell him to call me as soon as possible? It's very important."

"Is it anything I can help you with?" Irena asked.

"I don't think so." Cindy pictured the attractive, middle-aged woman leaning forward in her chair, crossing one dimpled knee over the other, and tucking her short blond hair behind her right ear. She'd known about Irena's long-standing affair with her husband almost from its inception. It wove in and around his other affairs like threads in a large tapestry. Cindy wondered if it was still going on, or whether it had ended with the Cookie's arrival. That's the way the cookie crumbles, she found herself thinking as she hung up the phone.

It rang immediately.

"Julia?" Cindy felt her heart pounding against her chest, the blood rushing to her ears.

"No, it's Trish. Just calling to see how last night went."

"Last night?"

"Your date with Neil Macfarlane?"

"My date with Neil," Cindy repeated, trying to calm herself down.

"It didn't go well?"

"No, it went great."

"Details," Trish pressed with a girlish giggle. "I need details. Tell me everything."

"Trish, can I call you later?" Cindy implored. "I'm expecting an important call."

"Everything all right?"

"Everything's fine."

There was a brief pause. "Okay. Call me later."

Cindy replaced the receiver, glared at the phone. Why hadn't she told Trish about Julia? "Damn it, Julia. Call me." As if on cue, the phone rang. "Julia?"

"No. Me," her sister said.

Cindy felt her shoulders slump toward the floor. "Leigh, can I call you back later?"

"Are you kidding? Your line's been busy all morning. I'm not waiting around for you to fit me into your busy schedule."

"It's just that I'm expecting Julia to call. . . ."

"Yeah, and when she does, would you tell her that I rescheduled her fitting for next Wednesday at two o'clock, and that if she doesn't show up then, there's no way Marcel can have her dress ready on time, which would mean she won't be in the wedding party."

"I'll tell her." What was the point in saying anything else?

"Tell her Bianca's counting on her," Leigh said instead of goodbye.

As soon as Cindy hung up, the phone rang yet again. "Hello? Julia?"

"It's Meg. How'd your date go last night?"

Cindy felt her knees go weak. She grabbed onto the side of a chair for support. "It was fine."

"Just fine?"

"Great. It was great."

"Was he as cute as Trish claimed?"

"He's very cute," Cindy said.

"Are you okay? You don't sound like yourself."

"Actually, I'm not feeling so hot."

"Oh no. You can't get sick now. The festival starts next week."

"I'm sure I'll be fine."

"Well, we're not taking any chances. Don't come in this afternoon. I can manage the store by myself."

"Would you mind terribly?"

"Of course not. Just feel better."

Cindy hung up the phone, wondering why she hadn't told her two closest friends that Julia hadn't come home last night, that she hadn't seen or heard from her since yesterday morning? She'd been desperate to tell them, but something had held her back. What? Embarrassment? Shame? Fear? Fear of what exactly? That if she spoke the words out loud, they might come true, and Julia might be lost forever?

She thought of Lindsey, Julia's *latest, greatest, best friend ever.* Who was she anyway? Unlike both Cindy and Heather, Julia was always forming attachments that were as short-lived as they were intense. Men and women flitted around the circumference of Julia's life, drifting in and out, occasionally penetrating the inner circle, but more likely succumbing to the force of gravity and falling, unheralded, off the ever-rolling curve. Some emerged unscathed, grateful for the ride, however brief. Some left resentful and angry, nursing ugly wounds that refused to heal.

Why hadn't she kept a closer vigil? What kind of mother was she?

Cindy crossed to the counter on the other side of the room, holding her hands beneath her arms to keep them from shaking. Luckily, there was still some coffee in the coffeemaker, and she poured herself a cup. It tasted bitter, but she drank it anyway, repeatedly glancing back at the phone, silently begging Julia to call, assure her she was alive and well. "This is silly. You're making yourself nuts," Cindy said out loud. "Just calm down. Breathe deeply. Repeat after me: there is nothing to worry about, there is nothing to worry about."

The phone rang.

Cindy lunged at it as if she'd been shot from a canon. "Hello? Julia?"

"Neil Macfarlane," the voice announced. "Cindy, is that you?"

Cindy swallowed the threat of tears. "Yes. Neil. Hello."

"Is this a bad time?"

"My daughter didn't come home last night," she heard herself whimper. "I'm so scared."

"I'll be right over," he said.

EIGHT

H AS she ever done anything like this before?"

"You mean, stayed out all night?"

Neil nodded. He was sitting beside Cindy on one of two tan leather sofas in her living room. Behind them a wall of windows overlooked the spacious backyard. Facing them were three paintings of pears in varying degrees of ripeness. Cindy couldn't remember the name of the artist who'd painted these pictures. Tom had bought them without asking either her opinion or approval, *I make the money; I make the decisions,* being pretty much the theme of their marriage. Along with the never-ending parade of other women, Cindy thought, smiling sadly at the good-looking man perched on the opposite end of the couch and wondering if he'd ever cheated on his wife. She ran her hand across the sofa's buttery surface. Fine Italian leather. Guaranteed to last a lifetime. Unlike her marriage, she thought. The sofas had also been Tom's decision, as was the checkered print of the two wing chairs sitting in front of the black marble fireplace. Why had she never bothered to change anything after he left? Had she been subconsciously waiting for him to return? She shook her head, trying to excise her former husband from her brain.

"Cindy?" Neil was asking, leaning forward, extending his hands toward hers. "Are you all right? You have this very strange look on your face."

"Yes, she's stayed out all night before," Cindy said, answering his question, wondering how long ago he'd asked it. "But she always calls. She's never not called." Except once just after she moved back home, Cindy recalled, when she was making a point about being an adult and no longer answerable to her mother. Her *father,* she'd argued pointedly, had never placed any such restrictions on her. Her *mother,* Cindy had countered, needed to be assured of her safety. It was a matter of consideration, not constraint. In reply, Julia had rolled her eyes and flounced out of the room, but she'd never stayed out all night again without first phoning home.

Except one other time when she forgot, Cindy remembered, but then she'd called first thing the next morning and apologized profusely.

"Shouldn't you be at work?" she asked Neil, trying to prevent another example from springing to mind.

"I take Fridays off in the summer."

Cindy vaguely recalled him having told her that last night. "Look, you don't have to stay. I mean, it was very thoughtful of you to come over and everything. I really appreciate it, but I'm sure you have plans for the long weekend. . . ."

"I have no plans."

". . . and Julia should be home any minute now," Cindy continued, ignoring the implications of his remark, "at which point I'm going to strangle her, and everything will be back to normal." She tried to laugh, cried out instead. "Oh God, what if something terrible has happened to her?"

"Nothing terrible has happened to her."

Cindy stared at Neil imploringly. "You promise?"

"I promise," he said simply.

Amazingly, Cindy felt better. "Thank you."

Neil reached over, took her hands in his.

There was a sudden avalanche of footsteps on the stairs, and Heather bounded into view. "I heard the door. Is Julia home?"

Cindy quickly extricated her hands from Neil's, returned them primly to her lap.

"Who are you?"

"Heather, this is Neil Macfarlane."

"The accountant." Heather advanced warily, quick eyes absorbing Neil's black jeans and denim shirt.

"Neil, this is my younger daughter, Heather."

Neil stood up, shook Heather's hand. "Nice to meet you, Heather."

Heather nodded. "I thought maybe Julia was back."

"No," Cindy said.

Heather swayed from one foot to the other. "Duncan and I were just going to head down to Queen Street. Unless you need me for anything."

"No, honey. I'm fine."

"You're sure? 'Cause I can stay if you want."

"No, sweetheart. You go. I'll be fine."

"You'll call me as soon as Julia gets home?"

Cindy nodded, looked anxiously toward the front door.

"You know my cell number?"

"Of course." Cindy pictured a series of numbers, realized they were Julia's. "Maybe you'd better write it down."

Heather walked into the kitchen. "I'm leaving it by the phone," she called back as Duncan came barreling down the stairs.

"Julia home?" he asked.

"Not yet."

He stared blankly at Neil, crossed one arm protectively over the other. "Are you a cop?"

Cindy blanched. Why would he ask that?

"He's an accountant," Heather said, reentering the room. "We should go." She guided Duncan toward the front door. "Remember to call me when Julia gets home."

Cindy nodded, watching them leave. "Do you think I should call the police?"

"If you're worried, yes," Neil said.

"It's only been twenty-four hours."

"That's long enough."

She thought of Tom. Probably she should wait for him to return her call, discuss the matter with him before she did anything rash. "I should probably wait a little longer."

"Have you checked with the place where Julia had her audition, to make sure she showed up?"

"I don't know who to contact," Cindy admitted. "I mean, I know the audition was for Michael Kinsolving, but he's probably just renting some space, and I don't know the address or the phone number." I don't know anything, she wailed silently. What kind of mother am I, who doesn't know anything? "Tom will know," she said. "My ex-husband. Julia's father. He arranged the audition. He'll know." All the more reason to wait until she spoke to him before calling the police, she acknowledged to herself.

Neil walked to the fireplace, lifted a Plexiglas frame from the mantel. "Is this Julia?"

Cindy stared at the picture of Julia that had been taken several days after her eighteenth birthday. She was smiling, showing a mouthful of perfect, professionally straightened and whitened teeth, elegant shoulders thrust proudly back in her new cream-colored Gucci leather jacket, a present from her father. Diamond studs sparkled from each ear, another present from Daddy. The night this picture was taken, Cindy had presented her daughter with a delicate necklace with her name spelled out in gold. Less than a month later, Julia had broken it while trying to pull a turtleneck sweater over her head. *I forgot I had it on,* she'd announced nonchalantly, returning the necklace to her mother to be fixed. Cindy dutifully had the necklace repaired, only to have Julia lose it a few weeks later. "That's an old picture," Cindy said now, taking the photograph from Neil's hands and returning it to the mantel, one finger lingering, caressing her daughter's cheek through the small square of glass.

"She's a very beautiful girl."

"Yes, she is."

"Like her mother."

The phone rang. Cindy raced to the kitchen, tripping on the large sisal rug in the front hall, banging her hip against the side of the kitchen door. "Damn it," she swore, lifting the phone to her ear. "Hello?"

"Well, damn it yourself," her mother replied. "What's the matter, darling? Forgot to put on your makeup?"

Cindy raised a hand to her bare cheek, realized she had indeed forgotten to put on any makeup. Still Neil had said she was beautiful, she thought gratefully, shaking her head as he approached, signaling the caller wasn't Julia. "I'm fine, Mom. Just a little busy at the moment. Can I call you back?"

"You don't have to bother. I'm just checking in. Everything all right? Your sister said you sounded pissy, and I'm afraid I have to agree with her."

Cindy closed her eyes, ran her free hand through her hair. "Everything's fine, Mom. I'll call you later. Okay?"

"Fine, darling. Take care."

"My mother," Cindy said, hanging up the phone and immediately checking her voice-mail to make sure no one else had called. "My sister told her I sounded pissy when she called earlier."

"I'm sure she meant pithy," Neil offered.

Cindy laughed. "Thanks for coming over. I really appreciate it."

"I just wish there was something more I could do."

Something clicked in Cindy's mind. "You can take me to see Sean Banack," she announced suddenly.

"Who?"

"I'll explain on the way." Cindy grabbed a piece of paper and scribbled a note for Julia, leaving it in the middle of the kitchen table, in case her daughter should return while she was gone. On the way out the door, she called Julia's cell phone again and left another message. There'd been something in Sean's voice when she'd talked to him earlier, Cindy thought, replaying their conversation in her mind, word for word. Something more than cigarettes and alcohol. Something more than fatigue and impatience and hurt feelings.

Anger, she realized.

He'd sounded pissy.

"Is Sean here?"

"He isn't," the young man said, standing in the doorway, blocking Cindy's entrance to the small, second-floor apartment that was situated over an old variety store on the south side of Dupont Street near Christie. The man was tall and black, with an athletic build and a shiny, bald head. A silver loop dangled from his left ear. A set of earphones wrapped around his neck, like a noose. He was wearing a sleeveless white T-shirt and black sweatpants, and his left hand clutched a large, plastic bottle of Evian.

"You must be Paul," Cindy said, pulling the name of Sean's roommate from the recesses of her subconscious. She extended her hand, gently pushing her way inside the stuffy, nonairconditioned apartment, Neil following right behind.

The young man smiled warily. "And you are?"

"This is Neil Macfarlane, and I'm Cindy Carver. Julia's mother."

The expression on the young man's face altered ever so slightly. "Nice to meet you, Mrs. Carver, Mr. Macfarlane. Excuse the mess." He looked sheepishly toward the cluttered L of the living-dining room behind him.

Cindy's eyes followed his. Books and papers covered the light hardwood floor and brown corduroy sofa in the middle of the room. A deeply scratched wooden door balancing on four short stacks of red bricks served as a coffee table. Several old copies of the *Toronto Star* lay stretched across the small dining room table, like a linen tablecloth. HUSBAND PHONED WIFE AFTER BEHEADING HER screamed an inside headline. MAN STALKED VICTIM FOR THREE DAYS BEFORE FATAL ATTACK announced another.

"Sean's doing research on aberrant behavior," Paul explained, following her eyes. "For a script he's writing."

Cindy nodded, remembering Julia had once boasted that Sean was writing a script especially for her. As far as Cindy knew, Sean had yet to find a producer for any of his efforts. He supported himself by bartending at Fluid, a popular downtown club. "Has Julia been around lately?" she asked, straining to sound casual.

"Haven't seen her since . . ." There was an uncomfortable pause. "You should probably talk to Sean."

"Do you have any idea when he's coming back?"

"No. I wasn't here when he went out."

"Do you mind if we wait?" Cindy immediately plopped herself down on the sofa, moving a well-thumbed copy of a paperback book to the cushion beside her. The book was called *Mortal Prey*.

Paul hesitated. "The thing is . . . I have to be somewhere by noon, and I was just gonna hop in the shower. . . ."

"Oh, you go right ahead," Cindy instructed. "We'll be fine."

"Sean could be a while."

"If he's not back by the time you're ready to leave, we'll go."

"All right. I guess it's all right," the young man muttered under his breath, perhaps sensing Cindy's determination, and not wanting to make a scene. "I won't be long."

"Take your time."

As soon as Cindy heard the shower running, she was on her feet.

"What are you doing?" Neil asked. "Where are you going?"

The second question was by far the easier of the two to answer. "To Sean's room," she said, trying to decide which of the two rooms at the back of the apartment was his, opening the first door she came to, grateful when she saw a row of high school football trophies bearing Sean's name lined up in front of the open window.

Posters from popular movies covered the walls: *Spider-Man; Invasion of the Body Snatchers; From Hell; The Texas Chainsaw Massacre.* Cindy winced at the image of a horrifying, leather-faced figure brandishing a chainsaw in front of him like a giant phallus, a helpless young woman secured to the wall behind him. She remembered that movie, hated herself now for enjoying it. What was the matter with her that she liked such things?

"I don't think this is such a good idea," Neil said, his voice a strained whisper as he followed her inside the tiny bedroom.

"Probably not," Cindy admitted, looking from the unmade bed to the water-stained desk on the opposite wall. An empty picture frame sat to one side of a bright blue iMac in the middle of the desk; a neat stack of blank paper was piled on the other.

"What is it you're looking for?"

"I don't know." Cindy took a step back, her ankle brushing up against the wastepaper basket on the floor. Her attention was immediately captured by the torn and crumpled remains of an eight-by-ten glossy. She bent down and scooped the battered picture of her daughter into her shaking hands. "It's Julia's most recent head shot. She just had it taken a few weeks ago." Cindy tried vainly to

iron out the creases of the black-and-white photograph, piece together the smile on her daughter's face. Obviously Sean had torn
it from its frame in a fit of fury. Was it possible he'd attacked her
daughter in a similar rage?

"Maybe you should just leave it," Neil advised, removing the
picture from her trembling hands.

"What else is in here?" Cindy asked, ignoring Neil's warning,
turning the wastepaper basket upside down, and watching as scrap
pieces of paper, used tissues, pencil shavings, and a browning apple
core tumbled toward the floor. "Garbage, garbage, garbage," she
muttered, her fingers loosening their grip on the white plastic
container, allowing it to slip from her hand. She began pulling
open the desk drawers, poking around inside them. There was
nothing of consequence in the first drawer, and she was just about
to close the second when her fingers located something at the very
back. An envelope, she realized, pulling it out, and opening it, a
small gasp escaping her lips.

"What is it?"

Cindy's mouth opened, but no words emerged, as her fingers
flipped through a succession of small color photographs, all of
Julia, all in various stages of undress: Julia in a see-through laven-
der bra and thong set; Julia wearing only the bottom half of a black
string bikini, her hands playfully covering obviously bare breasts;
Julia in profile, the curve of one naked breast visible beneath the
crook of her elbow, the top of her bare bottom rounding out of
the frame; Julia wrapped provocatively in a bedsheet; Julia wearing
high heels and a man's unbuttoned shirt and crooked tie.

"Why would she do this?" Cindy wondered out loud, showing
the pictures to Neil before tucking them into the pocket of her
khaki cotton pants. What was the matter with Julia? Had she no
common sense whatsoever?

Cindy rifled through a few more items, and was about to close
the drawer when her eyes fell across a sheet of densely typed paper.

The Dead Girl, she read.

By Sean Banack.

Cindy pulled the piece of paper from the drawer and carried it over to the bed, where she sank down, her lips moving silently across the page as she read.

THE DEAD GIRL
by Sean Banack

CHAPTER ONE

She stares up at him defiantly, despite the fact her hands and feet are bound behind her naked body and she knows beyond any shadow of a doubt that he is going to kill her. He should have taped her eyes shut as well as her mouth, he thinks; then he wouldn't have to see the look of contempt he knows so well. But he wants her to see him. He wants her to know what's coming, to see the knives and other medieval instruments of torture spread out across the floor, and understand what hell he has prepared for her. He lifts the smallest, yet sharpest of the knives into his hands, cradles it delicately between his fingers, fingers she claims are hopelessly inept. Fairy fingers, she calls them to his face. A faggot's hands.

He draws a fine line down the taut flesh of her inner arm. Her eyes widen as she watches a thin red streak wind its way across the whiteness of her skin. Slowly he lifts a second knife into the air in a graceful arc, then plunges it into her side, careful to keep the blade a safe distance from her vital organs, making sure the thrust isn't hard enough to kill her, because what would be the fun in that? Over so soon, so quick, before he's had a chance to really enjoy himself, before she's had a chance to fully suffer for her sins. And she must suffer. As he has suffered for so long.

What are you doing? Let go of me, she'd yelled when he pulled up beside her, then bundled her into the trunk of his car. She, this spoiled child of privilege, who claimed nosebleeds anywhere north of Highway 401, is about to bleed to death in an abandoned shed just south of the King Sideroad, in the middle of bloody nowhere. Serves you right, bitch, he says, slicing at her legs before throwing her on her back, pushing the largest of the knives between her thighs.

Green eyes widen in alarm as the knife slides higher, cuts deeper. Not laughing now, are you, bitch? Where's all that defiance now? With his free hand he grabs another knife, slashes at her breasts. Her blood is everywhere: on her, on him, on the floor, on his clothes, in his eyes, beneath his fingernails. His faggot fingernails, he thinks, rejoicing as he plunges the knife deep inside her, then savagely rips the duct tape away from her mouth so that he can hear her final screams.

"Oh, dear God," Cindy cried, rocking back and forth.

Neil extricated the paper from Cindy's hands. "What is it?"

"No, please no."

It was then she heard the noise from somewhere beside them. "What's going on in here?" Paul asked from the doorway. "Mrs. Carver? What are you doing in here?"

Cindy scrambled to her feet, lunged at the startled young man, naked except for the white towel wrapped around his waist. "Where's my daughter? What have you done with her?"

Paul took a step back, clutching the towel at his hips. "I don't know. Honestly, I have no idea where she is."

"You're lying."

"I really think you should leave."

"I'm not going anywhere until I speak to Sean."

"I already told you I don't know when he'll be back."

"Is he with Julia?"

"No way. Julia ripped his guts out, man. Look, I'm gonna have to call the police if you don't clear out of here right now."

Neil looked up from the pages he was reading and yanked the phone from the small table beside Sean's bed, thrust it toward Paul. "Call them," he said.

NINE

A dark green Jaguar was parked in Cindy's driveway when she got home.

"Oh no," Cindy said, panicking as Neil pulled his black Nissan alongside it. "It's my ex-husband. Why is he here?"

"Maybe he brought Julia home," Neil offered hopefully.

Cindy bolted from the car and was halfway up the steps when her front door opened. Tom stood in the doorway to her house, one well-toned arm crossed over the other, a look of bemused impatience creasing his tanned face. He was dressed head to toe in beige linen, a color that complemented the recent blond streaks in his still shockingly full head of hair. His feet were bare inside brown tassled loafers. As smugly handsome at forty-five as he'd been at twenty-five, Cindy thought, disappointed that middle-age hadn't damaged him in any obvious way, that he hadn't grown fat or bald, that his wrinkles actually added to his appeal. Elvis was sitting at his feet, as if he were used to having Tom there, Cindy groused silently, when behind him, something moved. A young woman, Cindy realized, relief pulsing through her veins. "Julia!" she cried out.

A shape emerged from the inside shadows, took its place in the doorway, snaked a proprietary hand through Tom Carver's arm. "Hello, Cindy," the Cookie said, pushing the dog away with her feet. She was wearing a tight cream-colored jersey over tight cream-colored pants, which at first glance, made her seem nude. A most disconcerting thought, Cindy decided, thinking of the pictures of Julia in her pocket, and watching the Cookie lean her head on Tom's shoulder, as if to say, "He's mine now."

I get the point, Cindy said to herself. You don't have to work so hard. Aloud she said, "Is Julia inside?"

Tom shook his head.

"We don't know where Julia is," the Cookie informed her. Then, noticing Neil standing in the driveway, "Who's this?"

Cindy spun around as Neil came up behind her. "This is Neil Macfarlane. My accountant," she added, stumbling over the lie. "Neil, this is my ex-husband, Tom Carver, and the . . . Fiona, his current wife." She stressed the word current, as if the condition were temporary.

"I didn't realize accountants made house calls," Tom said slyly, extending his hand.

"Special circumstances," Neil said genially. Then quietly, to Cindy, "Would you like me to leave?"

"No. Please stay. The police might want to ask you some more questions."

"The police? What's going on here?" Tom stood back to let them enter.

As if the house is still his, Cindy thought, feeling herself bristle as she sidestepped around her ex-husband's young wife, Elvis licking at her legs. "Julia didn't come home last night," she reminded him, looking around for Heather. "Heather?"

"Heather's not here," the Cookie said.

"What do you mean, she's not here? Who let you in?"

Tom smiled sheepishly. "I have a key," he said, having the grace to look at least moderately embarrassed. "Look, let's not make this into a big deal, okay?"

"What do you mean, you have a key?"

"I said, let's not make this . . ."

"And I said, what do you mean, you have a key? I changed the locks seven years ago. What do you mean, you have a key?"

"Julia thought I should have one."

"Julia gave you a key to the house?"

"The key *and* the alarm code," the Cookie said, possible payback for Cindy's earlier use of the word *current*. "She thought her father and me should have a key in case she ever needed something or . . ."

"Her father and *I,*" Cindy corrected impatiently. "And with all due respect, this really isn't any of your business."

"It certainly *is* my business."

"Okay, okay," Tom said, arms outstretched, as if trying to placate both women. He glanced over at Neil. Women, his eyes said, clearly enjoying the fuss, knowing it was about him.

"I can't believe you came into my house when I wasn't here."

"Here's your key." Tom dropped the key into Cindy's outstretched hand.

"I don't understand what you're so worked up about," the Cookie said. "We're the ones who should be upset. We were halfway to the cottage when Irena called, and we had to come racing back."

"I thought you were in a meeting," Cindy said to her exhusband, pointedly ignoring his young wife. "Secretary's still lying for you, I see."

Tom shrugged.

(Scenes from a marriage: Cindy cleans up the kitchen after getting both children ready for bed. She wraps Tom's dinner in plastic wrap and puts it in the fridge for him to eat when he gets home, then recorks the bottle of wine. "When's Daddy coming home?" Julia calls out from the top of the stairs.

"Soon," Cindy assures her.

"He promised to read me a story," Julia says an hour later, sitting up in her bed, stubbornly refusing to fall asleep.

"I'll read to you," Cindy offers, but Julia turns from her, covering her face with her pillow, as if she senses her father's absence is somehow her mother's fault.

Cindy retreats to her own room, thumbs through the latest issue of *Vanity Fair,* and watches TV until her eyes are so heavy with fatigue she can no longer focus. It's ten o'clock. She reaches for the phone, her arm stopping in midair, falling to her side. Irena has already told her Tom is stuck in meetings and can't be disturbed. At eleven o'clock, Cindy turns off the lights and gives in to sleep. At twenty minutes after midnight, she awakens to the sound of a key turning in the front door, and hears her husband's guilty footsteps on the stairs.

"Daddy!" she hears Julia cry with sleepy delight as he visits her room to kiss her good night.

Cindy feigns sleep as he creeps into their room and takes off his clothes, crawling in beside her without washing up. Even though he has undoubtedly showered before coming home, she can smell another woman on his skin. She moves to the far side of the bed, hugs her knees to her chest till morning.)

"Earth to Cindy." A voice snapped at the silence.

Cindy turned toward the grating sound.

"My husband asked you a question," the Cookie said.

"You called the police?" Tom asked a second time.

"Yes, I did. They should be here any minute."

"Julia's going to be so pissed," the Cookie said.

"I don't understand why you felt it necessary to involve the police."

"What exactly is it you don't understand?" Cindy asked her ex-husband, checking her watch. "It's almost one o'clock. Nobody has seen or heard from Julia since yesterday morning."

"She's going to be so pissed."

"Do you know where she is?"

"No," Tom admitted. "But . . ."

"But what?"

"You don't think it's a little early to be sending in the cavalry?"

"Did you know she broke up with her boyfriend?"

"Yes, I knew that. So what? Kid's a loser."

"A very angry loser," Cindy said. "So angry he wrote a really scary story about a man who kidnaps his former girlfriend and tortures her to death."

Tom waved a dismissive hand in front of his face, as if swatting away a fly. "I think you're overreacting."

"Really? Well, the police don't think so. They've asked me for a recent photograph of Julia." She patted the pocket of her khaki pants, tried not to see the pictures inside it.

"I still don't understand when exactly you spoke to the police."

"I'll explain," Neil said, motioning Tom and Fiona toward the living room. "You go find the photograph," he directed Cindy.

"And what exactly is your part in all this?" Tom was asking Neil as Cindy left the room, running up the stairs, Elvis at her heels.

Cindy stood motionless outside Julia's bedroom for several seconds, as if waiting to be invited in, Elvis's tail slapping happily against the door. Her daughter wouldn't like her snooping around in her room any more than Cindy had appreciated seeing Tom on the wrong side of her front door. How dare he come inside the house, make himself at home, bring that silly twit he married into her space, rub her nose in his new life—what was the matter with him? Did he think that just because he'd once lived here that gave him some kind of residual rights?

I make the money. I make the decisions.

Cindy took a deep breath, trying to calm herself down. What exactly was she so angry about? The fact that Tom seemed so unconcerned about their daugher's whereabouts, or the fact that he still looked so damned good, that despite the years and everything that had happened, he still had the power to make her go weak in the knees? "It's not fair," she muttered, turning around in helpless circles, trying to think where Julia might have stored her most recent head shots. Probably in the same place she keeps her address book, she thought, shaking her head, aware this was the second time this morning she'd invaded her daughter's privacy.

"She's going to be so pissed," she told the dog in the Cookie's voice, as once more, she rifled through the drawers of Julia's desk. Getting pretty good at this, Cindy thought, counting three boxes of unused stationary, at least thirty black pens, several scraps of paper with nameless phone numbers scribbled across them, four unused key chains, two empty picture frames, a leopard-print chiffon scarf, a dozen matchbooks, and three unopened packages of Juicy Fruit gum.

No head shots.

She opened the closet, slapped at the size-two clothing dangling precariously from the wooden hangers, again rummaging through the stacks of sweaters piled carelessly on the built-in shelves, and straightening the shoes lined up across the closet floor.

No head shots.

She ransacked each drawer of her daughter's dresser, suppressing a shudder when she came across Julia's collection of sexy push-up bras and thong panties. Doesn't she have any normal underwear? Cindy wondered, recalling the days of her own youth, how she hadn't even owned a bra when she married Tom. Her sister, Leigh, who was several cup sizes larger than Cindy, used to tease her about her lack of endowment. "My breasts might be small," Cindy had countered, "but they're perfect."

Now they're just small, she thought dryly, closing the last of Julia's dresser drawers, and looking out the front window in time to see a police cruiser pull up in front of the house.

The police had arrived at Sean's apartment within twenty minutes of his roommate's call. They'd listened with interest as Paul apprised them of the situation, told them that he'd asked Cindy and Neil to leave repeatedly, and that they'd refused. Cindy, in turn, patiently explained that her daughter had recently broken up with her boyfriend, Paul's roommate, and that she was now missing. She and Neil had come by to talk to Sean, only to find Julia's torn picture in his wastepaper basket and this alarmingly odious little story, she said, her voice cracking, her patience evaporating, as she thrust the offending piece of paper at the two police officers, and suggested they start combing the area immediately south of the King Sideroad for any abandoned shacks. "Hey, hey, hold on a moment," they'd said, trying to slow her down.

"Slow down," Cindy repeated now, falling to her knees and peeking under her daughter's bed, the dog's nose wet against her cheek. She saw an old electric keyboard and a new acoustic guitar, both covered in dust, which wasn't surprising since Cindy couldn't remember the last time she'd heard Julia play either. She was about to give up in defeat, go downstairs and tell the police that Julia must have taken the head shots with her when she went to her audition, when she saw the large manila envelope peeking out from under the shaft of the guitar. "Perfectly logical place to keep them," Cindy said, stretching to retrieve the envelope and opening it as the front doorbell rang. Elvis barked loudly in her ear, then ran from the room. "I'll be right down," she called over the dog's repeated yapping.

"Hello, Officers. Please come in," she heard Tom say, as if this were still his house.

Cindy pulled a handful of photographs out of the envelope, smiled sadly at her daughter's beautiful face. She looks so radiant,

Cindy thought, admiring the determination in her daughter's eyes. As if nothing can stop her, as if nothing can get in her way. "Julia gives good attitude," Tom had once remarked, and as much as Cindy hated to admit her ex-husband was right about anything, he was right about that. Julia stared back at her mother from the black-and-white glossy, her head tilted provocatively to one side, straight blond hair cascading toward her right shoulder, her skin flawless, with just the hint of a smile on her enviously full lips.

And yet Cindy knew that beneath all the bravado lay a bundle of insecurities, wriggling like snakes inside a canvas bag. Unlike Heather, who had the confidence but not the attitude, Julia had the attitude without the confidence. It was an interesting contradiction, Cindy thought, removing several of the head shots from the top of the pile to give to the police. She thought of the pictures in her pocket. Can't very well show these to the police, she thought, removing them from her pocket and glancing through them.

"Cindy?" Tom appeared in the doorway, as if he'd been lurking there all along, just waiting for the right moment to pop into view. Clearly a man who understood the value of good timing, who knew how to make an entrance. "What's taking you so long? The police are waiting."

Cindy jumped to her feet, only to stand frozen to the spot, unable to move.

"What's going on?" Tom said. "What are you doing?" He walked to her side and removed the pictures from Cindy's hand.

"I found them in Sean's apartment."

"She looks pretty good," Tom remarked casually.

Cindy shook her head in dismay. "You're unbelievable."

"Come on, Cindy. Lighten up. You can't see anything."

"You can see she's naked."

"You can also see she's enjoying herself thoroughly."

"Which makes it all right?"

"Which makes it none of our business."

"She's your daughter!"

"She's a consenting adult."

"Do you think I should show these pictures to the police?"

"Only if you want to cloud the issue," he warned her.

"What do you mean?"

"I mean the police are easily distracted. One look at these and they aren't going to take your concerns too seriously. I thought the objective here was to find our daughter."

"So suddenly I'm not overreacting?"

"Of course you're overreacting. It's part of your charm."

"Don't patronize me."

"Don't punish me for something that happened seven years ago."

Cindy's eyes widened in disbelief. "You think this is about you? About our divorce?"

"Isn't it?"

"It's about our daughter."

"Our daughter who's missing," he reminded her, as if she didn't know.

The air rushed from Cindy's lungs. "You don't think something's happened to her, do you?"

"No, I don't," Tom said evenly. "I think she just decided to get away for a few days."

"Without telling anyone?"

Tom shrugged. "It wouldn't be the first time."

"She's done this before?"

"Once," he admitted. "She was upset about my getting married, so she took off, came back a couple of days later, apologized, said she'd just needed some time to get her head clear."

"And you didn't tell me?"

"I didn't want to worry you unnecessarily." He reached over, touched her arm. "I know our daughter. She likes to stir things up a little. Like her mother," he added with a smile.

Cindy looked toward the window. "You're so full of shit," she said.

"Maybe," he conceded. "But I still think we should wait until Tuesday before dispatching the troops, or we're going to be awfully embarrassed when Julia comes waltzing home."

"I don't give a rat's ass about being embarrassed."

"Really, Cindy, your language. . . ."

"Fuck you," Cindy told her ex-husband, watched him wince.

"Well, I guess there's a certain comfort in knowing that some things never change." He shook his head. "Look. Your *accountant* suggested I call Michael Kinsolving to see if Julia showed up for her audition. Who knows? Maybe she mentioned something to him about her plans for the weekend."

"Do you think that's possible?"

"Anything's possible. Come on, the police are waiting." They were halfway down the stairs before Cindy realized that Tom hadn't returned the photographs of Julia. She was about to ask for them back when one of the police officers appeared at the bottom of the stairs, staring toward them expectantly.

Cindy watched her former husband smile as he slipped the provocative photographs of Julia into the pocket of his linen pants.

TEN

"M AYBE she eloped," the Cookie was suggesting to the second police officer as Cindy and her ex-husband reentered the living room beside Detective Andy Bartolli. Detective Bartolli was the elder of the two men, and the stockier; his partner, Detective Tyrone Gill, was younger by a decade and taller by several inches. Both had necks the size of tree stumps.

"What did you say?" Cindy felt the sudden constraint of Tom's hand on her arm, as if he feared she was about to throw herself at his wife's head.

The Cookie tossed long red hair from one shoulder to the other. "Maybe she eloped," she repeated, as if she really thought Cindy might not have heard her the first time.

Cindy stole a glance at the two detectives, sensing their interest already starting to wane.

There's no urgency here, the looks they exchanged suggested.

"What makes you think she might have eloped?" Detective Bartolli asked.

"Julia would never elope," Cindy interjected.

"Oh, please," the Cookie said. "How many times have I had to

listen to that stupid story about you and Tom running off to Niagara Falls without telling anyone? She thought it was so romantic."

She did? Cindy fought back tears. Julia had never said anything
of the sort to her.

The police waited as Tom called Michael Kinsolving, whose assistant said the famous director had left town until Tuesday and
couldn't be reached, although the assistant confirmed that Julia
had indeed shown up for her fifteen-minute audition promptly at
eleven o'clock.

After asking several pointed questions about Julia's recent state
of mind—*Has she been depressed lately? How upset was she about the breakup
with her boyfriend?*—the policemen left with several copies of her
head shots, promising to phone as soon as they spoke to Sean Banack. With Tom's approval, and over Cindy's objections, they decided to wait until after the long weekend before launching a
more formal investigation.

"What now?" Cindy asked when they were gone.

"Try to relax," her ex-husband advised. "Call me in Muskoka if
you hear anything."

"You're going to the cottage?" Cindy asked incredulously.

"I can't do anything here."

"Julia's fine," the Cookie said with a yawn. "She's a big girl. She
probably just needed some time away from her mother."

"Would somebody please get this moron out of my house?"
Cindy pleaded, looking from Tom to Neil.

The Cookie turned a sickly shade of beige that perfectly
matched her outfit. The dog started barking. "I think it's time we
left," Tom said.

"Yes. You're very good at that," Cindy agreed, only half under
her breath.

The phone rang. Both Tom and Cindy strode purposefully
into the kitchen, colliding in the doorway as they reached for the

phone. "Hello," Cindy said, pressing the phone to her ear, her eyes warning Tom to back off.

"What's wrong?" her mother asked.

Cindy's shoulders slumped with disappointment. "What makes you think something's wrong, Mom?"

Tom rolled his eyes toward the ceiling. So that's where Julia gets it, Cindy thought.

"A mother always knows when something's wrong," her mother said, and Cindy felt her heart sink, thinking of Julia.

"We'll go," Tom whispered.

"Who's that?" her mother asked. "Was that Tom?"

"You're amazing, Mother." Cindy watched Tom usher the Cookie out the front door.

"What's he doing there? Now I know something's wrong."

"It's nothing."

"I'll be right there."

"No. Mom! Mother! Damn it!" She dropped the phone into its carriage. "Shit!"

"What's up?" Neil asked good-naturedly, coming into the kitchen.

"My mother's coming over. Sorry for the language," she said, still smarting from Tom's earlier admonition.

"What language?"

Cindy fought the urge to kiss him full on the mouth. "You should probably go."

"I'm happy to stay."

And I would dearly love you to stay, Cindy thought. "I think you've met enough of my family for one day," she said instead, walking him to the door, thinking how his body contrasted with Tom's. While both men were approximately the same height and weight, Tom had a way of overwhelming everything in his path, rather like Julia. Neil was more like Heather, an easier, more accommodating fit. "Thank you," Cindy told him, both eager and reluctant to say good-bye. Talk about bad timing. "I don't think I could have managed without you."

He smiled. "I bet you say that to all your accountants."

Cindy reached out, touched his cheek. Beside her, Elvis growled. "Got a little more than you bargained for, didn't you?"

"I'll call you later," he said, patting Elvis on the head.

She watched him back his car out of the driveway. "I won't hold my breath," she said wistfully, as his car disappeared down the street.

It was only then that Cindy became aware that she herself was being watched. She swiveled toward her neighbor's house. "Faith," she said, returning the other woman's wan smile. "I didn't see you there. How are you feeling?"

"Fine." Faith Sellick was wearing a sloppy red-and-black-checkered shirt over a pair of black capris. A red ribbon dangled from her hair. "Lots of activity at your house today."

"Yes."

"I saw the police car."

"It was nothing."

Faith nodded, stared at the street.

"Where's the baby?"

"Ryan took him to the office this morning."

"That was nice of him. It gives you a chance to relax."

"I guess."

"It's such a beautiful day," Cindy remarked when she could think of nothing else to say. "Would you like a cup of tea?" she heard herself ask, realizing she was reluctant to go back inside the house, that she was afraid to be alone. Time alone meant time to think. Time to think meant time to worry. Time to worry meant time to imagine the worst.

"That would be nice," Faith said, carefully measuring out each word. "Tea would be very nice."

"Good. Come on over."

She walks as if she's asleep, Cindy observed, her eyes following Faith Sellick as the young woman floated down her front steps and along the sidewalk. Elvis ran forward to nip at her heels.

"Hello, boy," Faith said absently.

"Come inside." Cindy stood back to let Faith enter.

"This is really very sweet of you."

"My pleasure." Cindy led Faith into the kitchen, motioned toward the four pine chairs at the rectangular pine table. Faith sank into the closest one, stared at Cindy expectantly. "Regular or herbal?" Cindy asked as Elvis spread himself across the top of Faith's feet.

Faith said nothing, and for a moment, Cindy wondered if she'd understood the question. She was about to ask it again when Faith finally answered. "Herbal," she said, her sudden smile at odds with the sadness in her eyes.

"Ginger peach or spearmint?"

"Spearmint." Faith laughed, a delicate tinkle that danced in the air like wind chimes.

Cindy filled the kettle with water, turned on the burner, turned back to Faith, thinking that the young woman looked much older than her years, closer to forty than thirty, Cindy thought, noting the dark circles rimming Faith's eyes, the sallowness of her complexion. "Did you get any sleep at all last night?"

Faith nodded. "A bit."

"It's not easy being a new mother." Cindy pictured Julia as a baby. "It's not easy being a mother, period," she added, picturing her now.

"Seems easy enough for most people."

"Don't kid yourself."

"Your girls are so beautiful. They've turned out so well."

"Thank you." Cindy crossed her fingers, said a silent prayer.

"Did you worry about them a lot when they were babies?"

"Of course."

"I worry about Kyle all the time."

"That's perfectly normal."

"I worry about everything," Faith continued as if Cindy hadn't spoken. "His safety, his health, whether he'll be happy when he grows up."

"I don't think you ever really stop worrying about those things." Again Cindy thought of Julia.

"I mean, look at what's going on in the world today. Terrorists, suicide bombers, AIDS, poverty, child abuse . . ."

"Faith," Cindy advised gently, interrupting the seamless flow of catastrophes, "you'll make yourself nuts if you worry about all those things."

"How can you not worry? All you have to do is pick up the morning paper."

"Don't pick it up."

"You have to know what's happening. You can't just bury your head in the sand."

"Why can't you?"

"Because things won't get any better that way."

"And you think worrying yourself sick is going to make things better?"

"No, but you should be aware."

"You can be aware again when Kyle starts sleeping through the night."

"It just doesn't seem right to bring a child into a world where so many bad things are happening, where there are so many evil people."

"There are good people too," Cindy said, trying to reassure them both.

"I try to be a good person."

"You *are* a good person."

Faith grimaced, as if she'd had a sudden spasm. "I'm not a very good mother."

"Why would you think that?"

"Kyle cries all the time."

"He has colic. It has nothing to do with you."

"I try to comfort him. I feed him. I hold him. I even sing to him. But he still cries."

"Julia was the same when she was a baby. The only one who could get her to stop crying was Tom."

"Tom's your ex-husband?"

"Yes."

"Was that him before? With the redhead?"

"That was him."

"Is she his new girlfriend?"

"Wife."

"I think Ryan has a girlfiriend," Faith said matter-of-factly as the kettle began whistling.

"No," Cindy started, then stopped. How would she know whether or not Ryan had a girlfriend? "What makes you say that?" she asked, busying herself with making the tea.

"I can see it in his eyes."

"What do you see?"

"It's more what I don't see."

Cindy understood without asking exactly what Faith meant. She'd seen the same lack of substance in Tom's eyes before he walked out, as if he were already gone. Still she said, "He's probably just tired."

"No. It's more than that. Less," she corrected. "I don't think he loves me anymore."

"I'm sure Ryan loves you, Faith." Cindy pictured Ryan's troubled face as he sat on his front steps, Elvis's head in his lap. The subtle scent of spearmint filled the air as Cindy deposited the steaming mug of herbal tea on the table in front of Faith. "He's just worried about you, that's all."

"Worry isn't love." Faith lifted the mug to her lips, quickly laid it back down. "It's hot."

"Better give it a few minutes to cool off."

"My grandmother used to say that." Faith smiled at the memory. " 'Give it a few minutes to cool off,' " she repeated in a voice not her own. "She died last year. Cancer."

"I'm sorry."

"She'd had this really hard life. Her oldest son commited suicide, you know."

"How awful."

"Yeah. My uncle Barry. He was schizophrenic. I don't really remember him. He died when I was still a kid. He hanged himself in the bathroom. My grandmother found him." Faith raised the mug to her lips a second time, breathed in the aromatic steam still rising from its surface. "Suicide kind of runs in my family."

"What?" Cindy recalled Detective Bartolli's questions about her daughter's recent state of mind. *Has she been depressed lately? How upset was she about the breakup with her boyfriend?*

"I had a great-aunt who threw herself off a tall building," Faith was saying, "and two cousins who slashed their wrists. And my mom took too many pills once, but then she called all the neighbors and told them what she'd done, so they rushed her to the hospital and she had to have her stomach pumped."

"That's terrible." Cindy gingerly sipped at her tea, not quite sure what to say next. "You would never . . ."

Julia would never . . .

"What? Oh. Oh no! No, of course not. I would never do anything like that."

"Because things are never as black as they seem," Cindy said earnestly, the cliché filling her mouth like a wad of cottonballs. "Things always get better." Unless they get worse, she added silently.

"I don't have the courage to kill myself," Faith was saying.

"You think it's a question of courage?"

Has she been depressed lately?

"I know some people consider suicide the coward's way out,

but I never thought of it that way. I mean, to do something as drastic as taking your own life, I think that requires tremendous guts. More guts than I have, that's for sure."

"Good." Cindy suppressed a shudder as she settled into the chair across from Faith, vaguely recalling an article she'd read about the ripple effect of suicide, how the suicide of one family member often served to validate another's, that such action came to be seen as an acceptable alternative, a viable option for solving one's problems. She shook her head. The women in her family might be emotional, headstrong, and impulsive, but they were definitely not suicidal. And they were far too interested in having the last word to take themselves out of the argument early. "Because you have everything to live for," Cindy heard herself continue. "I mean, it's hard now. You're going through a very difficult time. You're exhausted. Your hormones are raging. But it'll get better. Trust me. A year from now, you'll feel so much better about everything."

"Do you think Ryan will leave me?"

"Ryan's not going anywhere, Faith."

"He says he wants three more children."

"What do you want?"

"I don't know."

"What about your job?"

"I'm on maternity leave till the new year. But I don't think I should go back."

"Why not? I thought you loved teaching."

"How can I possibly handle twenty-five kids when I can't take care of one?"

Cindy watched ominous clouds gather in Faith's eyes as she sipped steadily at her tea. "Well, you don't have to make any major decisions right now."

"I guess that's right."

"You have plenty of time."

Faith's eyes filled with tears. "Ryan's so busy these days. I hardly see him anymore." She lifted her shoulders to her ears in a prolonged shrug. "When he first started working at Granger, McAllister, it was just this tiny firm. Now there are seven architects, secretaries, assistants, so many people, and they're busy all the time. He's always having to rush off somewhere. This tea is really good," she said, finishing what remained in her mug.

"Would you like some more?"

"Oh no, thank you. I should be getting home. I promised Ryan I'd try to straighten things up a bit. He says the house is a pigsty."

"Why don't you take a nap first?" Cindy suggested, hearing a car pull into the driveway. Julia! she thought, running to the door, opening it in time to see a cab backing into the street and her mother walking up the front steps as Elvis ran down to greet her.

"What's the matter?" her mother said, ignoring the dog. "And don't tell me nothing. I can see it in your face. Who's this?" Cindy followed her mother's eyes to the woman standing behind her.

"Mom, this is Faith Sellick, my neighbor. Faith, this is my mother."

"Pleased to meet you." Faith stepped outside, shielding her eyes from the sun. "Thanks again for the tea."

"You don't have to leave on my account," Cindy's mother said.

"No, I have to go. I have so much to do."

"First, you have to take a nap."

"Right." Faith ambled down the steps.

"There's something not quite right about that one," her mother remarked as soon as Faith was out of earshot.

"She's the one I was talking about yesterday. With the postpartum depression."

Her mother nodded. "So, are you going to invite me in, tell me what Tom was doing here?"

Cindy led her mother into the kitchen, motioned toward the recently vacated chair. "I think you better sit down."

ELEVEN

At exactly 2:29 A.M. Cindy bolted upright in her bed and cried, "Oh no, I forgot!" She jumped out of bed and rushed into the bathroom, Elvis jumping excitedly into the air beside her, as if this were some great new game they were playing. Almost tripping over him as she lunged toward the medicine cabinet, Cindy tried to focus on the assorted bottles of headache remedies, half-empty boxes of Band-Aids, partially squeezed tubes of ointments, abandoned spools of dental floss, and discarded brands of hair gel that met her half-closed eyes. The detritus of everyday life, she thought, reaching into the cabinet, hoping she wasn't too late. The doctor had warned her that if she didn't take her pills at the same time every day, she would die. How long ago was that? Weeks, months, years? How long had it been since she'd last remembered to take her pills? Oh no. Oh no.

"What the hell am I doing?" Cindy suddenly asked herself, coming wide awake and staring at her reflection, regarding the woman in the glass as if she were some alien being. "What is the matter with you? What pills?"

Slowly, Cindy took stock of the situation, her panic gradually subsiding, her heartbeat returning to normal. She was standing naked in her bathroom in the middle of the night searching for pills that didn't exist on the advice of a doctor who also didn't exist. Obviously she'd been having another nightmare, although she couldn't remember a single detail. "It's that damn herbal tea," she told the woman in the glass. "That stuff'll kill you."

Her reflection nodded.

Cindy watched the woman run a tired hand through her lifeless hair, her eyes filling with tears. "Would somebody please just shoot me now. Put me out of my misery."

In response, her reflection dropped her chin toward her chest, the silence buzzing around their respective heads like determined mosquitoes.

"You've got to get some sleep," Cindy muttered on her way back to bed, but even as she was climbing back under the covers, she knew sleep was lost to her, that the hours between now and seven o'clock would be spent in restless tossing and turning, that if she slept at all, it would be in fits and starts, and that she would wake up feeling even less refreshed and more tired than before. She closed her eyes, trying not to picture her daughter hog-tied and bleeding on the dirt floor of some abandoned shack in the middle of nowhere. "Please, no," she whispered into the pillow, feeling it wet against her skin. "Please let Julia be all right. Please let this whole thing be nothing but a bad dream." A terribly long, bad dream, Cindy thought, flipping onto her other side, hearing Elvis groan beside her, knowing that this nightmare was horribly real, and that if her daughter didn't come home soon, she would most assuredly die, as the imaginary doctor of her dreams had warned.

"Oh God." Cindy sat up only to flop back down. She rolled onto her other side, sat up, turned on the light, reached for the paperback novel on the nightstand beside her bed, and glared at the phone. Undoubtedly Tom and the Cookie were having no such trouble sleeping. She pictured the cottage on Lake Joseph, the large, rustic bedroom she'd once shared with Tom, the long, side window open to allow the cool Muskoka breezes entry. The image of her former husband in bed with his young wife pasted itself across the pages of her book. Cindy brushed it aside with a disdainful swipe of her hand, accidentally ripping off the top corner of the page. She read, then reread the first few paragraphs of the chapter before tossing the novel to the foot of the bed in defeat. How could she read when she couldn't concentrate? "Where are you, Julia?"

Had she really considered her parents' elopement so romantic? Was it possible she might have pulled the same stunt herself? With whom?

Just come home, Cindy prayed. Please. Come home.

When she comes home, Cindy vowed silently, I'm going to buy her those brown suede boots she was admiring in David's, the ones I told her were way too expensive.

When she comes home, I'm going to take her to her favorite sushi restaurant for dinner. And lunch. And even breakfast, if that's what she wants.

When she comes home, I won't yell or complain or get on her case about inconsequentials. I'll be more understanding of her problems, less judgmental, more patient, less critical. I'll be the perfect mother, the perfect friend. Our lives will be perfect when she comes home.

When she comes home, Cindy repeated hopefully in her head, as she'd been repeating for so much of Julia's life.

She'd already lost her daughter once. She wasn't about to lose her again.

Cindy pushed herself out of bed, slipped a pink cotton night-shirt over her head, and tiptoed down the hall to Julia's room, Elvis at her heels. She stood in the doorway, and peered toward Julia's bed.

"Is someone there?" a voice asked, cutting through the darkness like a laser.

Cindy gasped as a figure sat up in the bed, reaching for the lamp on the night table just as Cindy flipped on the overhead light. "Julia!" she cried, arms extending into the room, then dropping heavily to her sides, her feet coming to an abrupt halt, as if she'd just waded into cement.

"Sweetheart," her mother said softly, getting out of Julia's bed and walking slowly toward her. "Are you all right?"

Cindy shook her head, dislodging a steady flow of tears. "I'm sorry. I forgot you were here." Her mother had insisted on spending the night after Cindy confided that Julia was missing. "Did I wake you up?"

Her mother led her to the side of Julia's bed, sat down next to her. "Not really. I heard some kind of noise a few minutes ago. I thought it might be Julia coming home."

"That was probably me. I woke up in a sweat because I'd forgotten to take my pills."

"What pills?"

"There are no pills." Cindy raised her hands helplessly in the air. "I must be losing my mind."

Her mother laughed.

"Something funny about that?"

Norma Appleton took Cindy's hands in hers. "Only that I remember going through a very similar experience years ago, constantly waking up in the middle of the night, convinced I'd forgotten something terribly important. I think it has to do with menopause."

"Menopause? I'm not in menopause."

"Close."

"No way. I'm only forty-two."

"All right, dear."

"That's all I need to worry about right now."

"You're missing the point here, darling."

"The point being?"

"The point being that I think this is pretty common in women of a certain age."

"Mother. . . ."

"I used to call it the OFIFs."

"The what?"

"The OFIFs—'Oh, fuck—I forgot!' "

"Excuse me?"

"What—you think you're the only one who knows words like that? Close your mouth, dear. A bug will fly in."

Cindy stared at her mother in disbelief. So that's where I get it, she thought.

Here comes the mouth, Tom used to say at the start of any argument. *You and that mouth,* he used to say.

Sorry for the language, she'd apologized to Neil earlier.

What language? he'd asked.

"What are you thinking?" her mother asked now.

"What?"

"You're smiling."

"I am?" God, her mother didn't miss a thing. "Must be gas."

"She'll come home," her mother said, her eyes on the distant past, her voice heavy with experience. "You'll see. Tomorrow morning she'll come waltzing through the front door as if nothing's happened, amazed at all the fuss, angry you were worried, furious you called the police."

A flush of shame bowed Cindy's head. "I put you through hell when I ran off with Tom," she acknowledged.

"You were young and in love," her mother said generously.

"I was willful and self-absorbed."

"That too."

Cindy shook her head. "What was I thinking?"

"I don't think you were."

"I was actually angry at you for having worried?"

"You were livid. How dare I call your friends! How dare I embarrass you like that! How could I involve the police? You were gone less than forty-eight hours! You're a grown woman! A married woman, no less! What was the matter with me? Oh, you went on and on."

"Is it too late for me to apologize?"

Her mother draped a protective arm around Cindy's shoulder, hugged her to her side. "It's never too late," she whispered, kissing her daughter's wet cheek.

"You think this is payback time? God's idea of poetic justice?"

"I like to think that God has better things to do with His time."

"Do you think Julia could have eloped with some guy?"

"Do you?"

Cindy shook her head. When Julia spoke about getting married, she talked about Vera Wang dresses and a photo spread in *People* magazine. "It's not her style. Besides, she broke up with her boyfriend." She thought of Sean Banack. "You don't think she was overly upset about that, do you? I mean, upset enough to do something stupid."

"Julia hurt herself over a man?"

Her mother's question was answer enough. "Then what's happened to her? Where is she?"

"I don't know, sweetheart. I *do* know you need to get some sleep or you're not going to be in any shape to yell at her when she comes home. Come on," her mother urged, pulling down the covers on the other side of Julia's queen-size bed. "Why don't you sleep with me tonight? I could use the company."

Wordlessly, Cindy climbed into Julia's bed, burrowing in against her mother's side, her mother's arm falling across her hip, as Elvis flopped down between their feet. The lingering aroma of Julia's Angel perfume on her pillow filled Cindy's nostrils. She closed her eyes, sucked at the scent as if she were a baby at her mother's breast. When Julia comes home, Cindy recited silently, I'll buy her the biggest bottle of Angel perfume they sell. When she comes home, I'll get her a Gold Pass to the film festival, so she can attend all the galas. When she comes home, I'll hold my tongue, hold my temper, hold my baby in my arms again.

When she comes home, Cindy repeated over and over again in her mind, until she fell asleep.

When she comes home. When she comes home.

"MOM? GRANDMA?" Heather asked from somewhere above their heads. "What's going on?"

Cindy opened her eyes, saw Heather looming above her, the pull of gravity distorting her sweet features. Cindy pushed herself up against the headboard, rubbing her eyes as Elvis bounded over to lick her face.

"My heavens, what's that?" Cindy's mother asked, as the dog poked his nose under the covers. "Get out of here," she groused as Elvis's long tongue flicked toward her lips. "He stuck his tongue in my mouth! Get away from me, you silly dog."

Heather shooed Elvis off the bed. "I didn't know you were here, Grandma."

"I was in bed before you came home."

"I thought Julia was back."

Cindy felt her heart cramp. "No. I take it you haven't heard anything. . . ."

Heather shook her head. "Why are you sleeping in here?"

Cindy and her mother shrugged in unison. "What time is it?" Cindy asked.

"Almost nine o'clock."

"Nine o'clock?" When was the last time she'd slept till nine o'clock, even on a weekend?

"What's the matter?" Heather asked. "Do you have to be somewhere?"

"No," both women answered.

"But I have a lot to do," Cindy added quickly.

"Like what?"

Cindy brushed the question aside with an impatient wave of her hand. "Is Duncan still asleep? I need to talk to him."

"He's not here."

"Where is he?"

Heather shrugged. "Not here."

"Heather. . . ."

"Look, Mom, I'm real sorry, but I don't know where Duncan is every minute of the day."

"*Really* sorry," Cindy and her mother corrected together.

"What?"

"It's an adverb," Heather's grandmother explained.

Heather nodded, backing slowly out of the room. "I think I'll take Elvis out for his walk now, if that's all right with the grammar police."

Cindy smiled. "Thank you, darling."

"I made coffee," Heather said.

"Thank you," Cindy said again, marveling at her daughter's easy grace. Even dressed in tight, low-fitting jeans and a navel-baring, candy-apple-red tank top, she somehow managed to look elegant.

"She's a very sweet thing," her mother said after Heather had left the room.

"Yes, she is."

"Like her mother." She kissed Cindy's forehead.

Cindy felt her eyes fill with tears. "Thanks for being here, Mom," she said.

BY TEN O'CLOCK, Cindy had showered and dressed and was on her fourth cup of coffee.

"You should eat something," her mother advised.

"I'm not hungry."

"You should eat something anyway. You have to keep up your strength."

Cindy nodded, irritation beginning to mingle with gratitude. While it was nice to have her mother here, to feel her love and support in this difficult time, Norma Appleton had an annoying tendency of taking up more than her fair share of oxygen. Prolonged exposure to her company rendered breathing increasingly difficult. Grown women had been known to run screaming from the room, overcome by intense feelings of suffocation. Was that how Cindy made Julia feel? As if there weren't enough air in the room? "Don't feel you have to stay here with me, Mom," she said delicately. "I'm sure you have a million other things to do."

"What things?"

"I don't know."

"What's more important than this?"

Cindy shook her head in defeat, finished the coffee in her cup, poured herself another.

"You should eat something," her mother said.

Cindy pulled several crumpled pieces of paper out of the pocket of her gray sweatpants, glanced at the phone.

"What's that?" her mother asked.

"Just some phone numbers I found in Julia's room."

"Whose are they?"

Cindy studied the numbers on the scraps of paper, tried willing them into familiarity. "I don't know."

Her mother reached across the kitchen table, turned the pieces of paper in Cindy's hand toward her so that she could read them, then repeated the numbers out loud. "Are you going to call them?"

"Should I?"

"Might as well."

"What'll I say?" Cindy crossed the room in three quick strides, then lifted the phone to her ear, her fingers already pressing in the first of the numbers.

"Start with hello."

"Thanks, Mom," Cindy said as the phone was answered on its first ring.

"Esthetics by Noelise," a woman's voice announced.

"I'm sorry. What?"

"Esthetics by Noelise?" the woman repeated, as if she were no longer sure.

"Oh. Oh, I'm sorry. I must have the wrong number."

"No problem."

"Esthetics by Noelise," Cindy told her mother, hanging up the phone.

"What's that?"

"Where Julia gets her legs waxed."

"Try the next one."

The second number belonged to Sushi Supreme, the third to a local talent agency Julia was hoping to sign with. "Last one," Cindy said, punching in the final set of numbers, listening as the phone rang four times before being picked up by voice-mail.

"You have reached the offices of Granger, McAllister," the taped message began. "Our normal hours of operation are from nine to five, Monday through Friday. If you know the extension of the person you wish to speak to, you may enter it now. If you would like to access our company directory . . ."

Cindy hung up the phone.

"What's the matter?" her mother asked, already at her side.

"Granger, McAllister," Cindy repeated. "Why do I know that name?"

"A law firm?"

"No, I don't think so." Cindy pictured the name written in broad strokes across the beige tile floor.

When he first started working at Granger, McAllister, it was just this tiny firm.

"They're architects," Cindy said flatly, hearing Faith's voice.

"What would Julia want with an architect?"

"I have no idea." *I think Ryan has a girlfriend.* Was it possible Julia and Ryan were involved? "But I'm damn sure going to find out."

The phone rang just as she was reaching for it.

"It's Julia's line," Cindy said, her finger hesitating over the key for line two.

"Answer it," her mother urged.

Cindy took a deep breath, pressed the appropriate key, picked up the phone. "Hello."

"Julia, it's Lindsey. I'm at the Yoga Studio. What's taking you so long?"

"I'll be right there," Cindy replied in Julia's breathy whisper, then hung up the phone, her heart racing. "I've got to go."

"What do you mean, you've got to go? Where are you going all of a sudden? What are you doing?"

Cindy didn't answer. The truth was she had no idea what she was doing, or what she would do when she got to the Yoga Studio. She grabbed her purse from the front closet and was already at the door when the phone rang again. Her line. She turned toward the sound, Julia's name freezing on her lips, as her mother picked up the phone.

"It's Leigh," her mother said. "She's calling to see if you know where I am."

Cindy opened the front door, swallowed a deep gulp of air. "Don't tell her anything."

Her mother nodded understanding. "I'm sorry you were worried," Cindy heard her say as she was closing the front door. "But something's happened here. Julia's missing."

TWELVE

THE Yoga Studio was located in an old six-story building on the north side of Bloor Street just west of Spadina, across the street from a large grocery store and the central branch of the JCC. For some reason, in the last several years, this nondescript studio in an unfashionable part of town had become a favorite spot for visiting celebrities to unwind and work out, which was the main reason Cindy knew her daughter frequented the place. Occasionally Julia had regaled her mother with tales of stretching out beside the likes of Gwyneth Paltrow and Elisabeth Shue. One day, she'd vowed, other girls would be telling their mothers they'd worked out beside Julia Carver.

There was nowhere out front to park, so Cindy spent almost fifteen minutes navigating the area's frustrating arrangement of one-way streets before ending up back on the main road. Spotting someone pulling out of a space on the south side of Bloor, Cindy promptly executed an illegal U-turn, causing the driver in the car behind her to jam on her brakes, and eliciting a raised middle finger from the driver in the oncoming lane, a middle-aged man who pulled up beside Cindy's tan-colored Camry as she was backing into the freshly vacated spot and sat on his horn until she turned off her engine. Cindy sat staring out her front window, refusing to look at the man in the car beside her, knowing he hadn't left her enough room to open her door, and that if she wanted to leave her car, she'd have to climb across the front seat and use the passenger door. She checked her watch, feeling the man's eyes burning acid-powered holes through the car window.

"What's the hurry, lady?" she heard him shout through two layers of glass. "You have a bladder problem?"

Oh dear, she thought, not sure what to do. So many angry people in this world. So many crazy people. She shuddered. What if Julia had encountered such a man? Suppose she'd inadvertently said or done the wrong thing, offended someone in some inno-cent, unforeseen way?

"You almost got us both killed back there," the man raged.

Cindy saw his arms waving with much agitation around his head, as if he'd stumbled into a nest of bees. She pictured a knife in those hands, heard Julia's distant screams. Her eyes filled with tears. Behind the man's car, horns began beeping, urging him for-ward. Still he didn't move. Was he planning to sit there all day?

Cindy pushed the tears from her cheeks and rechecked the time. It was getting late. The yoga class would be half over by now. Lindsey might have already given up on her tardy friend and gone home. She couldn't just sit here all morning waiting for this lu-natic to leave. "I'm sorry," she said sincerely, turning in the man's direction, noting that fury had reddened his complexion and dis-torted his features, like a clumsy finger through clay. "I didn't mean to cut you off."

"Lady, you should be shot," came the man's instant retort. Then he pulled away, extending his middle finger high out the window in a final blistering farewell.

Cindy pushed open her door, hearing the blast of another horn, and feeling a hot gust of exhaust on her legs as a red Porsche barely missed running over her toes. Another middle finger waved back in her direction. She fought back the renewed threat of tears as she waited for a break in the traffic. A man begging for change in front of a nearby convenience store shook his head in dismay as she scurried across the street, then turned away as she approached, as if repelled by her carelessness. "Fine, then," she muttered, returning a fistful of coins to her pocket. "Don't take my money."

Cindy pulled open the outside door to The Yoga Studio and approached the ancient elevators, pressing, then re-pressing the call button at least four times before she heard the old wires groan somewhere above her head, signaling the elevator's excrutiatingly slow and shaky descent. She pushed her way through the elevator's heavy metal doors before they were fully open, then realized she didn't know what floor the studio was on. "What's the matter with you? How could you be so stupid?" she asked out loud, exiting the elevator just as a sloppily dressed young woman chewing an enormous wad of gum shuffled in. "Excuse me, do you know what floor The Yoga Studio is on?" she asked the girl, who stared at her blankly and continued chewing her gum. "Could you hold the elevator a minute, please?"

Cindy raced to the directory on the wall to the left of the building's entrance. She quickly scanned the list, noted the correct floor, and ran back just as the elevator doors were drawing to a close. "Could you hold the door . . . ?" she began, but the girl chewed her gum and stared right through her, as if Cindy didn't exist.

"I don't believe this! Would it have killed you to wait two goddamn seconds?" Cindy's voice followed the elevator's ascent as her fist slammed repeatedly against the call button. "Oh God, I'm losing it." She looked around for the stairs, taking them two at a time. So many angry people in this world, she was thinking again. So many crazy people. "And I'm definitely one of them," she acknowledged, reaching the fourth-floor landing, her thighs quivering, her knees about to give way, the tips of her fingers brushing against the concrete floor as she collapsed from the waist, gasping for breath.

What was the matter with her? Where was she going in such a hurry? And what was she going to do when she got there?

Cindy pushed damp hair away from her face, straightened her shoulders, and waited until her breathing had returned to normal before stepping into the hall, and winding her way past the offices of several small companies, until she found the door to the Yoga Studio. She pressed her forehead against it, listening to the silence.

Suddenly the door opened and Cindy fell into the room.

"I'm so sorry. Are you all right?" A middle-aged woman in an un-flattering black leotard reached out to block Cindy's fall. "I had no idea anyone was there." Wild gray hair shot out at right angles from the woman's worried face, as if she'd been struck by lightning.

I did that to her, Cindy thought. "Forgive me," she said. "It was my fault."

"Can I help you?" a voice asked from somewhere behind the shock of gray hair.

Cindy's eyes swept from one end of the long, rectangular room to the other. An old brown sofa and a couple of shabby beige chairs were hunched around a low coffee table in one corner, a high glass cabinet containing yoga-related books and merchandise stood in another, and a cluttered reception desk sat in the middle. Several styles of white, gray, and black T-shirts imprinted with The Yoga Studio logo were pinned to one wall, like artwork, and the scent of oranges, courtesy of several plates of freshly cut orange quarters, filled the air, like cologne. Two women were sipping bottled water and eating oranges on the sofa; another woman was straightening a bunch of yoga mats that were stacked beside the doors to the inner rooms.

"Can I help you?" the receptionist asked again. She was a pale young woman approximately Julia's age, with fine reddish-blond hair and a smattering of oversized freckles that was smeared across her nose like peanut butter.

"I'm looking for Lindsey."

"Lindsey . . . ?"

"Lindsey," Cindy repeated, as if the simple repetition of the name was enough. "I was supposed to meet her here at ten o'clock. She may already be in class. I'm very late," Cindy added unnecessarily.

The receptionist nodded. "We have several classes going on at the moment. Do you know who her class was with?"

"No. But how many Lindseys can there be?"

"Actually, we have several Lindseys, and I believe two of them are here this morning." The girl checked the register. "Yes. Lindsey Josephson and Lindsey Krauss."

Lindsey Josephson and Lindsey Krauss, Cindy repeated silently. Neither name was the least bit familiar. "She was waiting for my daughter, Julia. Julia Carver."

A smile danced across the receptionist's face. "Julia's your daughter?"

Cindy nodded, feeling a surge of motherly pride so strong it brought tears back to her eyes.

"She's so gorgeous."

"Yes, she is."

"Julia's going to be famous. Then I'll get to say 'I knew her when.' "

Again Cindy nodded. Please, God, she was thinking, just let Julia be all right.

"It's Lindsey Krauss."

"What?"

"Her friend. It's Lindsey Krauss. She's in Peter's class." She pointed toward one of the closed doors beyond the cabinet at the far end of the room.

"Can I go in?"

"Well, it's eighteen dollars and the class is almost over. Why don't you just wait until it finishes." She indicated the sofa and chairs with her chin.

Cindy dropped a twenty-dollar bill onto the desk, and headed toward the studio.

"Wait. Your change . . ." the receptionist called after her. Then, when Cindy failed to respond, "You'll need a mat."

Cindy grabbed a bright blue mat from the shelf as she opened the door and peeked inside the room. Ten people, eight women and two men, all with their eyes closed, stood beside their mats, balancing on the hardwood floor on one foot, like human flamingos. Their other legs were crossed over the knees of their standing legs, their hands brought together in front of them, as if in prayer, their elbows extended at their sides. Several of the women wobbled precariously on the balls of their feet, fighting to stay upright, and the face of one man was pinched in such concentration he looked in danger of imploding. There were no movie stars that Cindy could identify, but she did recognize Lindsey Krauss, a tall, willowly brunette whose surgically enhanced bosom overwhelmed her otherwise boyish frame. Cindy made her way over slowly to where Lindsey was standing in the center of the room, setting her mat down behind her and wondering how best to approach her. She isn't wobbling at all, Cindy thought, marveling at the young woman's effortless mastery of the exercise. She's perfect, Cindy thought.

Like Julia.

The teacher, a supple young man with light brown hair and clear blue eyes, nodded almost imperceptively at Cindy as she tried to assume the proper position. What the hell am I doing? she wondered, struggling to balance on one foot. Why hadn't she just relaxed in the comfortable waiting area, sipping bottled water and eating fresh orange quarters until the class was over? What did she possibly hope to accomplish in here?

"Focus on your breath," the instructor advised gently, his voice a whisper. "If your mind starts to wander, just bring it back to the breath. It will help you stay balanced."

Not when you're as seriously *un*balanced as I am, Cindy thought, sliding her left foot up along her right thigh, her right foot cramping in protest.

"Now, slowly lower your leg," Peter instructed, as Cindy's foot hit the floor with a resounding thud. A slight grimace creased Peter's unlined brow. "Very good. Now, let's take a final Vinyasa before we move into relaxation."

A final what? Cindy wondered, as the instructor lifted his hands into the air above his head. The class immediately followed suit, lifting their own arms into the air, then bending from the waist and rapidly extending one leg forward, the other one back.

Lindsey's right leg shot back, kicked at Cindy's shin. She swiveled around guiltily. "I'm sorry," she whispered.

"Lindsey," Cindy said, seizing the opportunity.

Lindsey glanced over her shoulder as she brought her other leg back to meet the first. "Mrs. Carver?"

"And now slide gently into the Cobra," Peter directed.

"I need to talk to you."

Lindsey, along with the rest of the class, slid forward on her belly, then raised herself up on her arms, before pushing herself into something the instructor referred to as the Downward Dog. She stared at Cindy upside down from between legs spread shoulder-distance apart. "I don't understand. What are you doing here? Where's Julia?"

"That's what I need to talk to you about."

"Allow your shoulders to relax," the instructor intoned, a slight edge creeping into his voice.

"I don't understand," Lindsey said again, pushing herself into an upright position.

"Ladies, please. Can we save the conversation until after class?"

"Sorry," Lindsey said.

"Can we talk later?" Cindy whispered. "It won't take long."

"All right."

"Thank you."

"Ladies, please."

"Sorry," Cindy said.

"Very good. Now slowly, lie down on your back and concentrate all your energy on your breathing."

Cindy lay down, feeling the muscles in her back melt into the rubber of the mat. She took a deep breath, the air filling her nostrils and traveling to her lungs, her abdomen gradually expanding. Like when I was pregnant with Julia, she thought, remembering the pride she'd felt as her stomach filled with life.

"Very good," Peter was saying. "Now release that breath, ridding all toxins and stress from your pores. Blow the worries of the world gently from your lips. Feel them leave your body."

Cindy had loved being pregnant despite the morning sickness and overwhelming fatigue of the first few months. She'd loved that her breasts were so voluptuous, her skin so glowing. She'd even loved the ugly, loose-fitting clothes. And she'd loved that Tom was so solicitous, so caring, so eager to be a father. Looking back, their marriage was probably its happiest during her first pregnancy.

"Now take another deep breath and open your heart, feel it fill with positive energy."

Her second pregnancy had been a completely different story. This time the morning sickness lasted all day and water retention caused her to swell from head to toe. The constant nausea meant Cindy was unable to devote much time or energy to Julia, who'd grown used to both, and it was during those nine months that Julia's allegiance had subtly shifted from her mother to her father. It was also during this time that Cindy first discovered Tom was cheating on her.

"If your mind starts to wander," Peter was saying somewhere above her head, "bring it back to the breath."

Cindy had blamed herself for Tom's affair. The fact that she was always sick, always tired. Sick and tired of feeling sick and tired. As special as she'd felt during her pregnancy with Julia was how superfluous she felt during her pregnancy with Heather, almost like an afterthought in her own home. Tom had taken over Cindy's role with relish, playing Barbie with Julia for hours on end, reading her story after story, taking her to the park on weekend afternoons. After he'd tucked Julia into bed at night, he'd lock himself in the den, or go back to the office to catch up on his work. Or he'd go for a drive. To relax, he said.

"Relax," the voice continued now, floating across the room. "Relax. Let go."

The pattern had continued after Heather's birth. The fact that Heather had proved as easy an infant as Julia had been difficult strangely only made things worse. Julia blamed Cindy for bringing this unwanted intruder into their lives, turned increasingly to her father, shut her mother out almost completely. "She's never forgiven me for Heather," Cindy told her mother, who said that Cindy had once felt the same way about Leigh.

"Let go," Peter was saying, soft hands on Cindy's, trying to manipulate her fingers. "Let go. Let go."

"I'm sorry," Cindy whispered, realizing how tightly her fists were clenched at her sides.

"Feel your breath seep into your fingertips. Allow your hands to relax."

Cindy felt her fists gradually open under Peter's expert and gentle touch. Tom used to touch her with that same kind of tender strength, she thought. The best lover she'd ever had, his caress as addictive as the most powerful narcotic. They'd made love through all his infidelities, made love that awful night he'd told her he was leaving, and for several months after he'd moved out, when she thought there was still a chance he might come home, and for several months after that, while they were hammering out a settlement, and even after their divorce was final, when she knew there was no hope at all. The lovemaking had finally stopped the afternoon Julia packed her new suitcase and left her mother's house to go live with her father.

"That's it," Peter said, his voice filled with quiet pride as he patted Cindy's fingers. "You're smiling."

"WHAT'S GOING ON?" Lindsey asked as Cindy followed her into the main reception area. "Is Julia sick?" She grabbed an orange quarter from the bowl on the desk.

"Here's your change," the receptionist offered Cindy, holding out a two-dollar coin.

Cindy ignored the money, watching Lindsey suck the juice from the sliver of orange. "When was the last time you spoke to Julia?"

"This morning."

"This morning?" Cindy's heart began to race.

"Yeah, I called and asked her what she was doing. We were supposed to meet for coffee at nine-thirty."

Cindy felt her heart sink. "That was me."

"What?"

"That was me you spoke to."

"I don't understand. Why would you . . . ?"

"Julia's missing."

"What?"

"Since Thursday." Cindy saw the movement in Lindsey's brown eyes as the girl retraced the last two days in her mind. "Have you heard from her since then?"

"No. No, I haven't. I left her a message yesterday, but she didn't get back to me."

"Is that unusual?"

"Not really. Julia's not great about returning calls."

"Do you have any idea where she might be?"

Lindsey shook her head, discarded the orange peel.

"Please, Lindsey," Cindy urged, sensing that Lindsey knew something she wasn't telling. "If you know anything at all. . . ."

"Excuse me." A woman from Lindsey's class reached between them to grab a piece of orange.

"I know she had an audition with that big-shot Hollywood director, Michael something . . ."

"Kinsolving. Yes, we know that."

"We?"

"The police have been notified," Cindy said, hoping to shock Lindsey into revealing whatever it was she knew. Around her, several women lingered, pretending not to listen.

"The police? You really think something's happened to Julia?"

"I don't know what to think."

"I'm sure she's all right, Mrs. Carver."

"How are you sure?"

Lindsey grabbed another orange slice, stuffed it inside her mouth. "I just can't imagine. . . . Look, I really have to go. My boyfriend's waiting downstairs."

"Let him wait, damn it."

"Excuse me," the receptionist asked meekly. "Is there a problem here?"

"My daughter is missing," Cindy announced to a chorus of Oh, my's. "And I think this girl might know something about it."

"I don't," Lindsey protested to the gathering crowd. "Honestly, I don't."

"But?" Cindy demanded. "I know there's a 'but' there. What aren't you telling me?"

Lindsey lowered her head, spoke out of the side of her mouth, her voice no more than a whisper. "There was this guy. Maybe she's with him."

"What guy?"

"I don't know his name. Really, I don't," Lindsey insisted as Cindy was about to interrupt. "She was very secretive about him. She wouldn't tell me anything except . . ."

"Except what?"

"Except that she was crazy about him."

"She told you she was crazy about him but she wouldn't tell you his name?"

"She said she couldn't."

"What do you mean, she couldn't?"

"She said it was a very complicated situation."

"Complicated in what way? Is he married?" Ryan Sellick winked at her from the dark corners of her imagination. "What exactly did she tell you about him?"

"Nothing. Honestly. I've told you everything I know. I really have to go now. I'm sure there's nothing to worry about."

Lindsey fled the room as a woman from her class approached. "Can I get you a glass of water?" the woman asked Cindy.

Tears filled Cindy's eyes, causing the woman's face to blur, her features to overlap, like a cubist painting.

"Do you need a ride home?" another woman offered.

"Thank you. I have my car," Cindy said, her voice a monotone.

"Is there anything we can do?"

Cindy nodded. "You can find my daughter."

THIRTEEN

As soon as she left the Yoga Studio, Cindy drove north on Spadina to Dupont, fully intending to go home. But instead of turning right toward Poplar Plains, she turned left, continuing west to Christie, where she pulled to a stop across the street from an old convenience store on the corner, then turned the engine off and sat staring up at Sean Banack's apartment. What am I doing here? she thought now, pressing her forehead against the leather of the steering wheel. Hadn't the police told her to let them handle things?

Except that the police were waiting until Tuesday.

And Tuesday might be too late.

Cindy lifted her head, looked across the street. Sean Banack was standing in front of the convenience store, staring at her.

In the next instant Cindy was out of the car and running across the road. "Sean, Sean, wait," she shouted at him over the tops of the passing cars. "I need to talk to you."

Sean Banack took several steps back as Cindy drew near, muscular arms raised, as if warning her to keep her distance. He was of medium height and build, handsome in a careless sort of way, his normally long blond hair cut very short, his blue jeans worn very tight, light brown eyes challenging hers. "I don't think we have anything to talk about, Mrs. Carver."

"I do."

"So . . . what I want doesn't count?" Sean lifted his palms into the air, as if already conceding defeat. "Now I see where Julia gets it."

"Gets what?"

"Her—how can I put this politely?—her single-minded determination."

Cindy smiled at the thought that her daughter might resemble her in any way at all. "Where's Julia?"

"Not here."

"Where then?"

"I have absolutely no idea."

"I don't believe you."

Sean Banack took another step back, until he was literally up against the redbrick wall of the convenience store. "Mrs. Carver, what's going on here?"

"My daughter is missing, Sean. She hasn't been home in two days."

"And that gives you the right to show up at my apartment and hassle my roommate? To go through my things? To tell the police I had something to do with Julia's disappearance?"

"You're saying you didn't?"

"Of course I didn't."

"I read your story."

Sean looked at the sidewalk, swayed from one foot to the other, scratched the side of his head. "It was just a story. I'm a writer. It's what I do."

"It was a vile, horrible story."

"I didn't say I was a good writer." He looked sheepishly at his feet, as if ashamed of his meager stab at humor. "Look, Mrs. Carver, I can see that you're really upset, and I understand why reading that story would freak you out in light of what's happened. . . ."

"What's happened?" Cindy repeated. "What did you do to her?"

"I didn't do anything."

"Please, just tell me where she is."

"I don't *know* where she is."

"You wrote that you had her tied up in an abandoned shack. . . ."

"What I wrote was a goddamn story! A story that has nothing whatsoever to do with Julia. For God's sake, Mrs. Carver, I loved your daughter. I could never hurt her."

Two young boys suddenly bounded from the convenience store, laughing and punching one another in the arm.

"What happened between the two of you?" Cindy persisted, stepping aside to let an elderly couple pass by. "Why did you break up?"

"That's really none of your business."

"Please, Sean. Just tell me."

Sean laughed, but the laugh was hollow, joyless. "You want to know why your daughter and I broke up, Mrs. Carver? All right, I'll tell you. Julia and I broke up because she was cheating on me. I found out she'd been seeing someone behind my back for months."

"Who was it?"

"I don't know."

Cindy felt her knees wobble, then give way. She crumpled to the sidewalk like a balled piece of paper tossed from someone's fist.

Sean Banack was instantly on his knees beside her. "Mrs. Carver? Mrs. Carver, are you all right?"

"My little girl is missing," Cindy cried helplessly.

"I'll get you some water," Sean offered. "Stay where you are. I'll be right back." He disappeared into the convenience store.

But when he returned, Cindy was already gone.

* ★ ★

"WHERE HAVE YOU BEEN?" her sister asked as Cindy walked through the front door, Elvis immediately at her feet. "Your phone's been ringing all morning."

"Julia . . . ?" Cindy asked, staring at her sister, afraid to say more.

"No," Leigh said, following Cindy into the kitchen. "Nobody's heard from her. I can't believe she's been missing for two days and you didn't tell me. I had to hear it from Mom."

Norma Appleton shrugged from her seat at the kitchen table as Leigh crossed the room. "I made some fresh coffee," Leigh said. "You want some?"

"Thank you." Cindy sank into the chair beside her mother, feeling displaced, like an unwelcome guest in her own home, admiring the effortless way her sister had assumed control. Elvis stretched himself heavily across her feet. "When did you get here?"

"Couple of hours ago." Leigh deposited the cup of black coffee on the table in front of Cindy. "Where have you been? It's almost one."

"I talked to a friend of Julia's."

"And?"

"Nothing."

"I'll have another cup of coffee," her mother said.

"You've had enough coffee today."

"Leigh. . . ."

"Mom, don't argue with me, okay? It's lunchtime. I'll make you some soup."

"I don't want soup. What kind of soup?"

Leigh crossed to the cupboards, her eyes scanning the shelves. "Cream of mushroom, cream of asparagus, split pea."

"Split pea."

"Where's the can opener?"

Cindy pointed to a corner of the crowded counter, next to a spice rack that had fallen off the wall, and behind a stack of un-opened mail and old fashion magazines Julia had been saving.

"You've been gone all morning. Where else did you go?" Leigh opened the soup tin and poured its contents into a waiting pot.

Cindy retraced in her mind all the streets she'd traveled since leaving Sean. North on Poplar Plains, east along St. Clair, north on Yonge, east on Eglinton, south on Mount Pleasant, east on Elm, circling blindly through the expensive, old-money labyrinth that was Rosedale, escaping to the blossoming seediness of Sherbourne, heading south to the downtown core, then west, then north again, up and down, back and forth, eyes scanning each pedestrian on both sides of the streets, peering into parked cars, squinting into the sun, hoping the shadow on the opposite corner might be Julia's. "Who phoned?" she asked, not bothering to answer Leigh's question, and thinking how much softer her sister looked without her normal layers of makeup, how much prettier she looked with her hair brushed away from her face.

"Meg. Wondered how you were feeling. Said she'd call you later. And Trish. Said to tell you she picked up the tickets for the film festival. I take it they don't know about Julia."

Cindy nodded, feeling both guilty and relieved. Guilty she hadn't yet confided in her two best friends, relieved her sister knew that.

"And your neighbor. Faith? Is that her name? It was hard to make out what she was saying with that baby screaming in the background."

Again Cindy pictured Ryan, saw his phone number scribbled across the scrap of paper she'd found in Julia's room. What would Julia be doing with Ryan's phone number at work? Was it possible he was the mystery man her daughter was involved with? Or was it someone else at Granger, McAllister? "What did she want?"

"Just to tell you she's feeling a hundred percent better, she and her husband are off to Lake Simcoe for the day, she'll call you to-morrow, she didn't want you to worry."

So Ryan would have to wait till tomorrow.

"Oh, and Heather called to see if Julia was back yet."

Cindy looked toward the hall. "What about Duncan? Is he here?"

"Haven't seen him. You want some soup?"

"No."

"You should eat," Leigh said. "It's important to keep up your strength. Mom says you didn't get much sleep last night."

"She had a bad dream," their mother explained. "Thought she forgot to take her pills."

"What pills?"

"It was just a dream," Cindy said.

"Wish bad dreams were all I had." Leigh carefully measured out two bowls of soup. "Me, I have something called benign positional vertigo."

"What's that?" her mother asked.

"Apparently the calcium stones in my inner ear have come loose, and they send a signal to my brain that I'm moving when I'm not. So the minute I lie down on my back or turn over on my side—only my right side, mind you, good thing I sleep on my left—the next thing I know, the room is spinning around like I'm on one of those crazy rides at the Exhibition. The doctor says it's benign positional vertigo." She put the bowls of soup on the table. "Don't let it get cold."

"Aren't you having any?" Cindy asked.

"Nah. I hate canned soups. If I have time tomorrow, I'll make you some real soup."

Tomorrow, Cindy thought, desperately hoping that by this time tomorrow, Julia would be standing where her sister was now.

Tomorrow, she thought, silently repeating the word as if it were a prayer.

Tomorrow.

* * *

WHEN CINDY WOKE up the next morning, Leigh was already in the kitchen preparing breakfast.

"Bacon and eggs." Heather marveled, smiling at her mother from her seat at the kitchen table. She was wearing an old pair of pink pajamas Cindy hadn't seen in years. Elvis was sitting beside her expectantly, clearly hoping a few errant scraps might come his way.

"You're up early." Cindy kissed her daughter's cheek, patted the top of Elvis's head.

"I smelled the bacon."

"You didn't have to do this." Cindy said as her sister handed her a plate of crispy bacon slices and two depressingly perfect sunny-side up eggs.

Leigh popped two pieces of raisin bread into the toaster. "How'd you sleep?"

"Okay," Cindy lied, sitting down and cutting into the eggs. "You?"

"Not great. That mattress downstairs is a killer. But what can you expect from a sofabed? Mom still asleep?"

Cindy nodded. "What about Duncan?" she asked Heather.

The familiar shrug. "Don't know."

"You don't know?"

"He slept at Mac's last night."

"Mac?" Leigh repeated, turning the name over on her tongue. "Why does that name . . . ? Oh, my God." She turned to Cindy. "You had a call yesterday from a Neil Mac-something. I'm so sorry. I didn't recognize the name and I couldn't find a piece of paper to write on, so I forgot all about him. You really should keep a pad and pencil by the phone. Then this sort of thing wouldn't happen."

"It's okay, Leigh," Cindy said, Neil's face appearing before her eyes, only to smudge, fade, be blinked to the periphery of her line of sight. Bad timing, she thought again, banishing the image altogether. She had enough on her plate at the moment. When Julia came home, maybe. . . . "Why is Duncan sleeping over at Mac's?"

"Why shouldn't he sleep at Mac's?" came Heather's too-quick reply.

"Well, it's the long weekend. I assumed you'd have plans."

"Trouble in Paradise?" asked Leigh, grabbing the pieces of raisin bread as they popped from the toaster.

"Everything's fine," Heather said. "No toast for me, thanks." She swallowed the last of her bacon, and carried her plate to the sink. "I have to get dressed."

"It's not even eight o'clock," Leigh said. "Where are you going?"

"Thanks for the breakfast," Heather said sweetly. "It was a real treat."

"Is she always so forthcoming?" Leigh asked after Heather left the room.

"She's not used to getting the third degree."

"You're not curious where she's off to? Coffee?" Leigh asked in the same breath.

"Yes, and no," Cindy said. "Yes to the coffee."

"You were always way too lenient with them."

"I beg your pardon?"

"I'm just saying that it doesn't hurt to ask a few simple questions." Leigh poured her sister a cup of coffee, and put it on the table along with the raisin toast. "Honestly, Cindy, I just don't understand you. I mean, it's one thing to respect your kids' privacy, but you always go too far."

"I go too far?" Cindy repeated numbly.

"You're almost pathologically fair."

"*Pathologically* fair? What does that mean?"

"It means you can't be both their mother *and* their friend."

"What are you talking about?"

"Please don't take that tone with me."

"Then stop talking to me like I'm one of your kids."

"I'm just trying to help."

"Well, news flash—this isn't helping."

"Look, I know you're upset, but don't try to make me feel badly because I made some polite inquiries."

"*Bad,*" Cindy snapped.

"What?"

"Don't try to make me feel *bad,*" Cindy continued, feeling the anger rise in her throat. "You don't say, 'I feel sadly,' do you? No. You say, 'I feel sad.' In the same way, you shouldn't say, 'I feel badly.' You should say, 'I feel bad.' You feel *what,* not *how.* It's an emotion, not an adverb."

Leigh's mouth fell open. "You're correcting my grammar?"

Cindy lowered her head. Not even eight o'clock in the morning and already she was exhausted. Maybe she'd spend the day in bed. Maybe she'd go to church and pray. Maybe she'd badger the police, even though she knew they were waiting until the end of the long weekend, confident Julia would turn up on her own.

Would she?

There had to be something she could do. Something to keep her from going out of her mind. She just couldn't sit idly by and wait until Tuesday, especially with Supermom hovering, telegraphing her disapproval with every look and utterance. "Look. I can manage here," she told her sister. "You don't have to stay."

"Don't be silly. Of course I'll stay."

"You have your own family to look after."

"You're my family."

Tears filled Cindy's eyes. "Where is she, Leigh?" she asked, burying her face in her hands.

"Have you checked her voice-mail for messages?"

Cindy was immediately on her feet and at the telephone. Why hadn't she thought to check her daughter's voice-mail? What was the matter with her? "I don't know her code," she whispered, suspecting that Leigh knew all her children's voice-mail codes by heart.

Cindy heard Heather's footsteps on the stairs. "Everything okay?" Heather asked, freshly changed into jeans and a light blue jersey.

"Heather," Leigh said, "do you know your sister's voice-mail code?"

Heather quickly rattled off the four digits. "I've got to go." She kissed her mother's cheek. "I'll call you later. Try not to worry."

Even before the front door closed, Cindy was entering the code to Julia's voice-mail, feeling guilty for snooping into her daughter's personal life. When Julia got home, she'd apologize, Cindy decided, hearing her sister's earlier pronouncement ringing in her ear. Almost pathologically fair, she'd said.

"You have seven new messages," a recorded voice chirped in Cindy's ear.

"Seven new messages," Cindy repeated, looking around in vain for a pencil and a piece of paper.

Her sister lifted her hands in the air. *Told you so,* said the expression on her face.

In the end there was no need for paper and pencil. Five of the messages were from Cindy, forwarded from Julia's cell phone, one was from Lindsey, the last one was a hang-up. Cindy replaced the receiver, desperation gnawing at her insides, like a dull hunger.

"Are you all right?" Cindy heard Leigh asking through the ringing in her ears. "You don't look so hot."

Cindy watched the room sway precariously from side to side, as if she were riding on a high swing, the earth pulling away from her feet. Benign positional vertigo, she thought, watching the ceiling swoop toward her, like a giant bird. It plucked her into the air, shaking her this way and that, leaving her limp and helpless, before abuptly letting go. Cindy felt herself plummeting to the ground. Just before she landed, she heard Elvis yelp, saw her sister's eyes widen in alarm. "What are you doing?" Leigh demanded, hands on her hips.

Cindy's last thought before the darkness overtook her was that she hoped Leigh could move fast enough to catch her before her head hit the floor.

FOURTEEN

WHEN Cindy opened her eyes, she saw Neil Macfarlane's handsome face. I'm in heaven, she thought, watching her mother and sister insert themselves into the frame. I'm in hell, she thought, quickly amending her earlier assessment.

The tan leather of the living room sofa groaned as Cindy pushed herself into a sitting position. "What's going on?"

"Apparently you fainted," Neil said from the seat beside her. He was casually dressed in jeans and a yellow golf shirt. His amazingly blue eyes were flecked with worry.

"Scared the hell out of me," Leigh said, backing away from the sofa and rubbing her right hand with her left. "I think I may have done something to my wrist when I blocked your fall."

Cindy tried shaking the heavy fog from inside her head, but it hung on, like a dead weight. "I don't understand. How long was I out?"

"Not more than a couple of minutes," her mother answered. "I was in the bathroom when I heard your sister screaming."

"Well, she scared the hell out of me," Leigh repeated.

"And then the doorbell was ringing."

"That was me," Neil said with a smile.

"He brought bagels," Cindy's mother said.

"He helped me lift you onto the sofa," Leigh told her.

"And so concludes our up-to-the-minute report," Neil said.

Cindy shook her head. "I don't think I've ever fainted before."

"It's because you don't eat enough," her sister pronounced.

"Which is why I brought bagels," Neil said.

"Maybe later." Cindy smiled, so grateful for his presence she almost cried. "You've obviously met my mother and sister."

"The necessary introductions have all been made."

"Can I get you a cup of coffee, Mr. Macfarlane?" Leigh asked, hovering like a waiting helicopter.

"No, thank you."

Cindy pushed herself to her feet. "I could use some fresh air."

"How about a walk?" Neil asked.

Elvis barked his enthusiastic approval, headed for the door.

Cindy laughed. "You said the magic word. Actually, a walk sounds great." Elvis began circling the hall, barking even louder. "Okay, okay, you can come." She walked slowly into the kitchen, retrieved Elvis's leash, and attached it to his collar.

"You're sure you're all right to go out?" her mother asked.

"I'm fine, Mom."

"Don't go too far," she advised as Cindy and Neil headed down the outside stairs, Neil's hand guiding Cindy's elbow. "Don't let her do too much," her mother called after them.

"For heaven's sake, Mom," Cindy heard Leigh hiss from the doorway. "She's not a child. Stop fussing over her. Ouch, my arm. . . ."

"You're sure you're okay?" Neil asked Cindy as they continued down the street.

Cindy felt her legs grow stronger, her footing more secure, with each step away from her house. "I'll be fine as soon as we get around the corner." The dog yanked on Cindy's arm, demanding that she pick up the pace.

Neil took the leash from Cindy's hand. "Let me do this."

"Thank you." Cindy marveled at the way the dog immediately slowed down, fell into step beside Neil. "How did you do that?"

"It's all in the pressure."

"I'm not very good with pressure," Cindy said.

"Well, there's only so much anyone can take." They turned south on Poplar Plains. "I assume no one's heard from Julia."

Cindy nodded, pointed to her right. "Let's go to the park." They walked in silence for several seconds along Clarendon. "What made you drop by?"

"I wanted to see how everything was. I called yesterday. . . ."

"I didn't get your message until today."

"Yes, your sister mentioned something about there being no pad and pencil by the phone."

"She doesn't waste any time."

"That's the impression I got."

Cindy smiled. "She's really a very nice person."

"I'm sure she is."

"I shouldn't sound so ungrateful."

"You don't." They stopped for Elvis to pee against a line of scraggly red and yellow rosebushes. "Anyway, when I didn't hear back from you, I thought I'd take a chance and drop by, see for myself how you were doing."

"And you found me sprawled across the kitchen floor."

He nodded. "What happened to make you faint?"

Cindy shook her head. "Damned if I know. One minute I was looking at my sister; next minute, I was looking at you."

"Maybe you should call your doctor."

"I'm sure my mother is doing exactly that as we speak."

They crossed Russell Hill Road and headed up the side entrance to Winston Churchill Park, where Cindy bent down and unhooked the leash from Elvis's collar, letting the dog run free. He bounded up the slight incline to the foot of a steep hill. DANGER, a sign proclaimed in big, bold letters at its base. SLOPE & FENCE HAZARD, SLEIGHING, TOBOGGANING PROHIBITED. A collapsing orange wire fence looped casually along the ground; a flight of wooden steps ran diagonally up the right side of the hill. Elvis was already halfway to the top by the time Cindy and Neil began their climb.

"You sure you're up for this?" Neil asked.

"Lead on."

The top of the hill plateaued into a small field of dry, yellow grass. Cindy and Neil arrived at the top step in time to see Elvis bound between a father and his young son, who were struggling with a large, blue-and-gold kite, then pounce on a young couple sunbathing near the row of tennis courts at the far end of the park. "Elvis, stop that. Come back here," Cindy called as the dog chased after a jogger in a pair of lime green shorts who was puffing along the well-worn perimeter of the park. An elderly Chinese woman, who was exercising with meticulous deliberation near a set of concrete stairs that led to a nearby ravine, stopped to give Elvis a pat on the head. "I'm sorry if he bothered you," Cindy said just as she was hit in the leg by a well-chewed, misaimed rubber ball. Immediately, a large white poodle was at her feet, grabbing the ball in his teeth, then taking off for the middle of the park, Elvis in quick pursuit, to where a group of pet owners were clustered together.

"Quite the scene," Neil remarked as Elvis raced circles around the other dogs.

"Elvis!" a woman shouted warmly in greeting. "How are you, boy?"

"Sorry about that ball," a middle-aged man apologized as Cindy approached the group. "Didn't realize I could throw that far. How you doin', Elvis?"

"You know my dog?"

"Oh, sure," another woman answered easily. "We all know Elvis. You want a treat, boy?" The woman, her short pixie hair peeking out from under a Blue Jays baseball cap, reached into the side pocket of her baggy olive green pants and pulled out a biscuit. "Sit," she instructed.

Elvis promptly did as he was told.

"Amazing," Cindy said.

Immediately, six other dogs rushed the woman, begging for treats. Along with the white poodle, there was a smaller red one, a big German shepherd, a bigger Golden Lab, and two medium-sized black dogs whose breeds Cindy couldn't identify.

"Where's Julia?" a young girl asked as Elvis chewed on his treat. The girl was about twelve years old, with thin yellow hair and a mouthful of braces. She stood beside a younger girl with the exact same face, minus the hardware.

Cindy hadn't expected to hear her daughter's name. It stabbed at her heart like a sharp stick. Instinctively, her hand reached for Neil's. She felt his fingers fold over her own. "You know Julia?"

"She's so pretty," the younger of the two sisters answered with a laugh.

"Haven't seen her around in a while," the woman with the treats said, pushing gray-streaked black hair away from her narrow face. "Did she take off for Hollywood?"

Did she? Cindy wondered. "When was the last time you saw her?" she asked, trying to make the question sound as casual as possible.

"I'm not sure. About two weeks ago, I guess."

"Was she with anyone?"

The woman looked puzzled by the question.

"She was with her new boyfriend," the younger of the two sisters offered with a giggle.

"Her new boyfriend?" Cindy felt her throat constricting, as if a stranger's hands were around her neck, strangling further attempts at conversation. "Do you know his name?" she whispered hoarsely, kneeling down on the grass in front of the younger, yellow-haired girl.

The child shook her head, looked anxiously toward her sister.

"Can you tell me what Julia's boyfriend looked like? Please, it's very important."

The little girl shrugged, backed against her older sister's side.

"Is there a problem?" someone asked from above her head.

"Julia's been missing since Thursday," Cindy said, eyes focused on the two girls.

"Oh, dear."

"I saw her yesterday," a man said.

Instantly, Cindy was on her feet, advancing toward him. "You saw her yesterday?"

The man, who was fortyish, heavyset, and balding, took a step back. "She was sitting right over there." He pointed toward a lone bench at the far end of the park. "She was crying."

"Crying?"

"That wasn't Julia," the man's wife corrected. "It was the other one. Heather. Is that her name? Such a nice girl."

"Heather was here yesterday?"

"About four o'clock. Sitting right over there," the man repeated. "Crying her heart out. You're sure that wasn't Julia?" he asked his wife.

Was she?

"It was the other one," his wife insisted.

What would Heather be doing in the park, crying?

"I wanted to ask her if there was anything we could do to help, but . . ." The woman shook her head in her husband's direction, as if her failure to take action was his fault.

"We decided it was none of our business," her husband replied defensively.

"Have you called the police?" someone asked, the voices beginning to blend together in Cindy's ears, becoming indistinguishable one from the other.

"The police have been contacted," Neil answered for her. "But if any of you can think of anything that might be of help. . . ."

"Can't think of a thing," someone said.

"I'm sure she'll turn up."

"I'm so sorry," said someone else.

"Good luck."

Their voices receded as their footsteps pulled away. Cindy stared at the trampled grass until it grew quiet. When she looked up again, she and Neil were alone in the center of the park.

"Are you all right?" Neil asked.

Cindy shrugged, realized she was still holding tightly onto Neil's hand. "Sorry," she said, releasing his fingers from her vise-like grip.

"Any time."

Cindy's eyes swept across the dry field. The father and his young son were still struggling with their uncooperative kite; the sunbathers were still stretched out on their blanket by the tennis courts; the jogger in the lime green shorts was still running in hapless circles around the track; the elderly Chinese woman was still doing her exercises. "Where's Elvis?" Cindy asked, spinning around. "Elvis!" She ran to the edge of the hill, looked down, saw a bunch of other dogs playing at the bottom. No Elvis. "Oh no." She raced to the other side of the park. "Elvis! Where is he? Elvis! Where are you?"

Neil was right beside her. "Take it easy, Cindy. We'll find him."

"I can't believe it. I can't believe I lost Julia's dog."

"We'll find him," Neil repeated.

She was crying now. "Julia will never forgive me. She'll never forgive me."

Neil took her arm, deliberately slowed her pace, led her toward the tennis courts. "Elvis!" he called out, his voice racing ahead of them as they walked around the side of the double row of courts to the front part of the park. They passed a group of young men playing soccer, dodged between two teenage boys tossing a bright orange Frisbee back and forth.

"He's not here," Cindy said, eyes scanning the crowded children's playground by the front row of tennis courts. She approached a group of young mothers pushing their children on the swings. "Excuse me, have you seen a Wheaten terrier, about this big?" She held her hand about two feet off the ground. "He's apricot-colored," she continued, even as the women were shaking their heads no. Cindy ran toward the tiny brick building that was the headquarters of the Winston Churchill Tennis Association. "I can't believe it. First I lose Julia; now I lose her dog."

"You haven't lost anyone." Neil poked his head inside the men's washroom to the left of the small structure. "We'll find him," he said. "Elvis! Elvis!"

"Elvis!" Cindy echoed.

"Is this your dog?" someone called from inside the main room.

Cindy poked her head into the open door of the tennis association's headquarters. The single room was long and casually furnished, with a large desk to one side, a soft drink machine at the back, and several rows of blue chairs positioned around a small TV that was tuned to the U.S. Open. Two young men in tennis whites were lounging across a dark blue couch propped against one wall, a large pizza box open between them. Elvis was sitting on the floor in front of them, his eyes glued to what remained of the pizza.

"Elvis!" Cindy cried, falling to her knees and hugging the dog to her chest, feeling his wet tongue on the underside of her chin. "You scared me half to death."

"Your dog sure loves pizza," one of the boys said as Elvis barked his desire for more.

"I'm very sorry he bothered you." Cindy quickly attached

Elvis's leash to his collar and pulled at the stubborn dog. "Come on, you."

"Elvis has left the building," she heard one of the young men say as they stepped outside.

The sun smacked Cindy full in the face, so she didn't see the two young sisters in her path until she was almost on top of them. "I'm so sorry," she apologized. How many times had she said that in the last several days?

"Does Julia have a baby?" the younger of the two girls asked.

"What?"

"Come on," the older girl urged, pulling on her sister's arm.

"Wait," Cindy said. "Please. What makes you think Julia has a baby?"

" 'Cause I saw her with one."

"Come on, Anne-Marie. We have to go home."

"You saw Julia with a baby?" Cindy pressed.

"She was pushing it in a carriage. I asked her if it was her baby, and she laughed."

Cindy took a long, deep breath, tried to digest this latest piece of information. What did it mean? Did it mean anything at all? "Damn it," she muttered, as once again Ryan's face imposed itself on her consciousness. "That miserable son of a bitch."

Anne-Marie gasped. "You said a bad word."

"I'm sorry. I didn't mean . . ." Cindy began, but the two girls were already fleeing the park.

"What is it?" Neil asked.

Cindy stared blankly at the horizon. Somewhere above her head, the old children's rhyme kept circling: *First comes love, then comes marriage. Then comes Julia with a baby carriage.*

"CINDY, HI," Faith Sellick said, pulling open her front door, seemingly oblivious to the streak of green bile staining the front of her white shirt.

"Can I speak to Ryan for a minute?"

"He's not home."

"Where is he?"

"Golfing. Somewhere up north."

"Could you have him call me as soon as he gets back?"

"Sure. Is something wrong?"

"I just need to talk to him."

"He might be pretty late."

"That doesn't matter."

From upstairs, a baby's cry pierced the air. Faith's eyes closed as her shoulders slumped. "We had such a nice day yesterday," she said wistfully.

"Do you need some help?" Cindy asked, glancing down the front steps to where Neil stood waiting.

"No. You go. I'll be fine."

But when Cindy reached her own front door, she saw that Faith was still standing in her doorway, not moving, eyes tightly closed.

"Maybe it's better to wait until Tuesday, let the police talk to Ryan," Neil advised later that night.

They were sitting at Cindy's kitchen table, finishing off the last of a bottle of red Zinfandel. It was almost midnight. Heather and Duncan were out; her mother was upstairs asleep; her sister had gone home.

Ryan still hadn't phoned.

"Bastard," Cindy said. "Where is he?" She checked her watch. "Do you think I'm overreacting?" Tom would have said she was overreacting.

"No."

"I mean, the kid could be mistaken. It might not have been Julia she saw with the baby. And the baby doesn't have to be Ryan's. Even if it was, that doesn't necessarily mean that Ryan is

Julia's mystery boyfriend. Do you think I'm jumping to conclusions?" Tom would have said she was jumping to conclusions.

"I think you have good instincts. You should trust them."

Cindy smiled across the table at a tired-looking Neil Macfarlane. I think I could love this man, she thought. Out loud she said, "It's late. You should probably go."

AT EIGHT O'CLOCK the next morning, Cindy was knocking on Ryan Sellick's front door.

"Hold your horses," Ryan called groggily from inside.

Cindy heard him shuffling toward the door, braced herself for the encounter to follow. "Easy does it. You catch more flies with honey than with vinegar," she could almost hear her mother advise.

She'd been up most of the night preparing what she was going to say, rehearsing exactly how she was going to say it. She'd even spent twenty minutes doing deep-breathing exercises to help her relax, and she was determined to stay calm. But the minute she saw Ryan standing in the doorway, black shirt unbuttoned, light khaki pants hanging low on his hips, a line of short, black hairs twisting down from his belly button and disappearing under his waistband, feet bare, long hair falling into sleepy eyes, the scratch beneath his right eye still prominent, it took all her resolve to keep from hurling herself at his throat. *You lying, motherfucking, son of a bitch,* she wanted to shout. "I need to talk to you," she said instead.

Ryan wiped some sleep from the corner of his right eye. "Is something wrong?"

"I'm not sure."

"Is this about Faith?" He glanced warily over his shoulder toward the stairs.

"No."

He looked confused.

"It's about Julia."

"Julia?"

"She's been missing since Thursday."

"Missing?"

"Have you seen her?"

"Not since I saw her arguing with Duncan in the driveway. Was that Thursday?"

"You haven't seen her since then?"

Ryan shook his head. He was wide awake now.

"She didn't say anything to you about maybe going away for the long weekend?"

The same stubborn shake of his head. "Nothing."

"Has she confided in you lately about being depressed or upset?"

"Why would she confide in me?"

"I don't know," Cindy answered simply. "Maybe because the two of you were sleeping together?" The words tumbled from her mouth before she could stop them. *Trust your instincts,* she heard Neil say, remembering he had also suggested waiting until Tuesday, letting the police question Ryan. Why hadn't she listened? she thought now, watching the summer tan drain from Ryan's complexion. Why was she always barreling off half-cocked?

Ryan raised the fingers of his left hand to his lips, his eyes shooting toward his upstairs bedroom. "Look, maybe we should take this outside. I don't want to wake Faith. She was up half the night with the baby." They stepped onto the front landing. "What the hell are you talking about?"

"Where were you yesterday?"

"Where was I?" he repeated, as if trying to make sense of the question.

"Where were you?" Cindy repeated.

"I was golfing up at Rocky Crest. Why? What . . . ?"

"Was Julia with you?"

"Of course not."

"Where did you get that scratch under your eye?"

"What?"

"Did Julia do that to you?"

"No. Of course not. I walked into a branch in the backyard." Ryan pressed down on the scratch, as if trying to make it disappear. "Look, I think you better tell me what's going on." He lowered his voice to a whisper. "Why would you think I'm involved with Julia?"

"Julia recently broke up with her boyfriend. He says she was seeing someone else."

"What would make you think that someone is me?"

"You were seen together. In the park. With the baby."

Ryan's face was a road map of confusing wrinkles. "I don't know . . . wait . . . okay. Yes, I did run into Julia in the park. A few weeks ago, I think it was. I was there with Kyle. Julia was walking the dog. We talked for a few minutes. Is that what this is about?"

Cindy quickly digested this new information. Could she be mistaken? Had Ryan and Julia simply bumped into each other in the park? Was that all there was to it? "I found the phone number for Granger, McAllister among Julia's things," she said with renewed determination.

"So?"

"So . . . what would Julia be doing with the number for Granger, McAllister?"

"I have no idea."

Hadn't Tom once told her that innocent people rarely embellish, that only the guilty feel compelled to provide answers or excuses? Was she wrong about Ryan being the new mystery man in Julia's life? Was he as innocent as he appeared to be?

The door swung open, as if by itself, and a ghostly apparition suddenly materialized in the front hall. "That's probably my fault," Faith said, her voice seeming to emanate from somewhere outside her body. "I'm so sorry, Cindy. I forgot to tell Ryan you wanted him to call."

Ryan rushed toward his wife, who was looking pale and glassy-eyed in her long white cotton nightgown. He snaked his arm protectively around her waist. "What do you mean? What's your fault?"

"About a month ago," Faith recited without emotion, "I locked myself out of the house. I didn't know what to do—the baby was inside—and then I saw Julia coming down the street, so I asked her to please call Ryan at work. But then I remembered we keep a spare set of keys under the mat, so there was no need to call him after all. I'm so sorry."

Cindy shook her head, feeling both foolish and dejected. "There's nothing for you to be sorry about. If anything, I'm the one who should be apologizing to both of you."

"Is something wrong?" Faith asked.

"Julia's missing," her husband told her.

"Missing?"

"Since Thursday morning," Cindy said. "I was hoping Ryan might know something. Anything."

"I wish I could help you," Ryan said.

"We haven't seen her," Faith added.

"Okay, well, if you think of anything, anything at all. . . ."

"We'll call you," the Sellicks said together.

Cindy walked down the outside steps, hearing their front door close behind her.

FIFTEEN

T H E police arrived at just after ten o'clock Tuesday morning.

Cindy had been up since three, when she'd jumped out of bed in a sweat, certain she'd forgotten to take the pills that were keeping her alive. She'd let out a long chain of expletives and climbed back under the covers. But, of course, sleep was now impossible. Too many thoughts, too much fear. Too many possibilities, too much anger.

How could she have confronted Ryan that way? What was the matter with her?

At five, she'd given up on sleep and turned on the TV, hoping for something suitably mind-numbing to lull her back into unconsciousness. Something like *Blind Date,* she'd hoped, thoughts drifting to Neil.

She doubted she'd hear from him again. Despite his promises to call later, she recognized there was only so much unsolicited drama a man could take. There was a point when intrigue degenerated into irritant. Cindy suspected she'd already passed that point.

At seven she was walking Elvis around the block. At seven-thirty, Tom called to say he'd just driven back from Muskoka, had she heard from their daughter?

She told him Julia was still missing and he should get his ass over to her house as soon as possible. He told her he didn't appreciate the profanity. She told him to fuck off.

An hour and a half later, resplendent in a dark blue suit, a lighter blue shirt, and a blue-and-gold-striped tie, Tom arrived with the Cookie, who was wearing black pants and a pink silk shirt. She took one look at Cindy in her baggy jeans and old mauve T-shirt and shook her head, as if she couldn't quite believe her husband had once actually shared a bed with this woman, let alone produced a child as beautiful and fashion-savvy as Julia.

At nine-thirty, Cindy called the police. A few minutes after ten o'clock, Detectives Bartolli and Gill were at her door.

Cindy ushered them into the living room, introducing the policemen to her mother and her younger daughter, as Elvis ran around in excited circles, convinced they were all there to see him. Cindy remained in the entranceway, as everyone arranged themselves around the room, the two policemen pulling out their notepads and perching on the ends of their chairs.

"What was your daughter wearing when you saw her last?" Detective Gill asked, his voice carrying traces of a soft Jamaican lilt.

A towel, Cindy realized, looking to Heather for help.

Heather was sitting on the sofa between her father and her grandmother. Norma Appleton had insisted she wasn't going anywhere until Julia was found. ("What? I'm going to leave with you fainting all over the place?" she'd asked.) Thank God Leigh had gone home, although she was threatening to come back later.

"She was wearing her red leather pants and that white top she has with the V-neck and short sleeves," Heather said.

Detective Bartolli jotted that down, then held up the photograph Cindy had given him Friday. "And this is the most recent picture you have of her?"

Cindy looked from her husband to the Cookie, who was standing in front of the fireplace, as if afraid she might crease her pants were she to sit down. "Yes." Cindy tried not to picture the other photographs of her daughter in varying stages of undress.

"Can you describe Julia's mood on Thursday morning?" Detective Bartolli asked, as he had asked last Friday.

She was screaming at everyone, banging on doors, being totally unreasonable, Cindy thought. What she said was, "She was excited, a little nervous. She had a big audition coming up." She was being Julia, Cindy thought, listening as Tom explained the nature of Julia's audition.

"I'll need an address for this Michael Kinsolver," Detective Gill said.

"Kinsolving," Tom corrected, spelling the name slowly. "Three-two-zero Yorkville. Suite two-zero-four. I can get you his phone number. . . ."

"That won't be necessary, thank you."

"So, you last saw Julia at what time, Mrs. Carver?"

"I haven't seen her since last Tuesday," the Cookie replied.

"He was talking to me," Cindy said icily.

The Cookie raised her eyebrows, arranged her lips in a stubborn pout.

"It was a little after ten," Cindy said. "I was going out, so I went to her room to say good-bye and wish her good luck on her audition." And she yelled at me not to come in because she was naked, said I was slowing her down. "I just peeked my head in the door. Wished her good luck," she repeated.

"And then you went out?" the Cookie asked accusingly.

"Yes, I'm allowed out every now and then."

"I was here," Heather volunteered.

"You were here when Julia left?"

"Yes. It was around eleven o'clock."

"Apparently Julia had a fight with Heather's boyfriend just before she went out," Cindy interjected.

"It was nothing." Heather glared at her mother. "She was yelling at me too."

Detective Gill looked up from his notepad, exchanged looks with his partner. "Your boyfriend's name is . . . ?"

"Duncan. Duncan Rossi."

"Address?"

"He lives here."

Again the partners exchanged glances, while Cindy's mother shifted uncomfortably in her seat and the Cookie rolled her eyes.

Tom gave a look that said, It wasn't my idea.

"Where is Duncan now?"

"Out," Heather said. "I don't know where," she added when the look on everyone's faces made it clear more information was expected.

"We'll have to talk to him," Detective Bartolli said.

Heather nodded, turned away.

"We'll need a list of all Julia's friends," Detective Gill said.

Cindy felt a wave of guilt so strong it nearly knocked her off her feet. What kind of mother was she that she didn't know her daughter's friends?

"I can probably be of help to you in that regard," Tom said, as if reading Cindy's mind. "Until quite recently, Julia lived with me."

The officers nodded, as if this was something they heard every day. But Cindy knew what they were thinking. They were questioning what kind of mother she was that her daughter had chosen to live with her father. She couldn't blame them. How many times had she asked herself that same question?

"But she was living with you now?"

"Yes," Cindy said. "For amost a year."

"Do you mind my asking why she was no longer living with you, Mr. Carver?" Detective Bartolli asked.

Tom smiled, although Cindy could tell from the tight set of his jaw that he most certainly did mind. He was uncomfortable with being questioned, unused to being put on the spot. That was *his* job, after all.

"Tom and I moved into a new condo after we got married," the Cookie answered for him. "There's only so much room."

"Five thousand square feet," Cindy said, just loud enough to be heard.

"How did Julia feel about your remarriage?" Detective Gill asked Tom. "Was she upset about it?"

"The marriage was almost two years ago, and no, Julia wasn't the least bit upset. She loves Fiona."

The Cookie smiled and tossed her hair proudly from one shoulder to the other.

"And where were you on Thursday, Mr. Carver?"

"I beg your pardon!"

"We have to ask," Detective Gill apologized.

"Are you insinuating I had anything to do with my daughter's disappearance?"

"My husband is a very important attorney," the Cookie said.

Cindy rolled her eyes, amazed that people actually said things like, "My husband is a very important attorney," except on television.

"I was at my office," Tom replied testily. "You can check with my colleagues, if you honestly think that's necessary."

Detective Bartolli nodded, jotted this information in his notepad, and turned toward Cindy, who'd been discreetly enjoying her ex-husband's discomfort. How often, after all, did she get to see Tom squirm? "Was your daughter on any kind of medication?" he asked.

"Medication?"

"Painkillers, antidepressants . . ."

"Julia wasn't depressed," Cindy told the two officers, as she had told them at least half a dozen times already. "Why do you keep insisting she was depressed?"

"Mrs. Carver," Detective Bartolli explained patiently, "you have to understand that we get missing persons reports like this every day, and half the time, the person in question turns out to be someone who was feeling a little down and just decided to take off for a few days."

"And the other half?"

Detective Bartolli looked toward his partner. Detective Gill closed his notepad, leaned forward sympathetically. "To be frank, with people your daughter's age, suicide is our biggest worry."

"Suicide," Cindy repeated numbly.

"Julia would never commit suicide," Heather protested.

"Suicide is not an option," Cindy said, recalling her conversation with Faith Sellick. "What else do you worry about?"

"Well, of course, there exists the possibility of foul play. . . ."

Cindy put her hand across her mouth, stifled the cry pushing against her lips.

"But we're getting way ahead of ourselves here, Mrs. Carver. There's nothing to suggest any harm has come to your daughter."

"Except that nobody's heard from her for five days," Cindy reminded him.

"And that's unusual?"

"Of course it's unusual."

"Cindy," Tom said, in the voice he used whenever he sensed she was about to lose control. She'd heard that voice often during their marriage. There was something perversely comforting in hearing it now.

"Does she have any friends who live out-of-town?"

"She has several acquaintances in New York," Tom said.

Cindy stared blankly out the back window. This whole conversation was ridiculous. "Don't you think she would have told me if she were planning a trip to New York?"

"Maybe she told you and you forgot," the Cookie said.

"Is it possible she told you and you forgot?" Tom repeated, as if the Cookie had never spoken.

(Flashback: Julia, at thirteen, gets up from the kitchen table after dinnner and walks out of the room. Her mother calls her back, reminds her to put her dishes in the dishwasher. Her father immediately echoes that request. "Julia, put your dishes in the dishwasher," he repeats. Julia reluctantly saunters back to the table, does as her father says.

"Why do you always do that?" Cindy demands after Julia has retreated to her room.

"Do what?"

"I tell her to do something, then you repeat it, as if my word doesn't carry enough weight."

"I'm supporting you, damn it."

"No. You're undermining me.")

Nice to see some things never change, even if wives do, Cindy thought now, smiling in spite of herself. "She didn't tell me," she told her ex-husband. "I didn't forget."

"You're sure?"

"She didn't," Cindy repeated, biting off each word. "I didn't."

"Fine. No need to get upset."

"No need to get upset?" Cindy countered. "Nobody has seen or heard from Julia since Thursday morning. I'd say there's plenty of reason to get upset."

Tom glanced at the detectives, as if to say, You see what I have to deal with? You understand now why I left?

"So you were of the understanding that Julia was coming home directly after her audition?" Detective Bartolli asked.

"I wasn't sure what her plans were, but she was supposed to be at a dress fitting at four o'clock."

"My granddaughter, Bianca, is getting married," Norma Appleton interjected. "Julia and Heather are bridesmaids."

"So, she didn't show up for her fitting." Detective Gill scribbled this fact in his notepad. "Was it common for Julia not to show up for appointments?"

"No," Cindy said.

"Yes," Tom corrected. "Julia can be very willful."

"In what way?"

"In the way of most twenty-one-year-old women." Tom smiled knowingly at the two detectives.

"But you can't think of any reason your daughter might take off for a few days without telling anyone?"

"No," Cindy said.

"Yes," the Cookie disagreed.

"Excuse me?"

"Why is that, Mrs. Carver?"

"Because she's a moron," Cindy answered.

"I believe Detective Gill was talking to *me,*" the Cookie said pointedly.

"You think Julia might have taken off without telling anyone?"

"I think it's possible."

"Why is that?"

"Because she was always complaining that she didn't have any privacy, that her mother was always on her case. . . ."

"You are so full of shit," Cindy said.

"Cindy, please," Tom warned.

"What exactly is this birdbrain trying to do here, Tom?"

"What did you call me?"

"Is she trying to sabotage this investigation? Is she trying to make it seem less urgent than it is?"

"Excuse me, but I'm right here," the Cookie said, waving her hand in the air, the huge diamond sparkler on her ring finger flashing like a strobe light in Cindy's eyes.

"Maybe it *is* less urgent than it *seems*," Tom said.

"Very clever," Cindy admitted, despising his easy glibness. "Our daughter has been missing for five days."

"I know that."

"Then what's the matter with you? Why aren't you more concerned? Why aren't you tearing your hair out?"

"Because you won't let me." Tom jumped to his feet, began pacing back and forth, Elvis barking beside him. "Because you're frantic enough for everybody. Somebody has to stay calm. Somebody has to behave like a rational human being. Shut up, Elvis."

"Oh God."

"Are you going to faint again?" Cindy's mother demanded, rushing to her daughter's side.

"You fainted?" Heather asked. "When?"

"The other day," her grandmother said. "Good thing her sister was here to catch her."

"I'm fine," Cindy assured everyone. "I'm not going to faint."

"I'll make some coffee," Norma Appleton offered, heading for the kitchen. "You sit down."

"I don't want to sit down."

"Don't be so stubborn," Tom said.

"Don't tell me what to do."

Again Tom looked at the detectives, as if to say, You see what I have put up with? You see why I had to leave?

"Mrs. Carver," Detective Bartolli said.

"Yes?" said Cindy.

"Yes?" said the Cookie.

Cindy gritted her teeth, took a deep breath, grabbed one hand with the other to keep from wrapping them around the Cookie's neck.

"Can we go over the events of last Thursday morning one more time?" Detective Bartolli asked.

"There's nothing to go over," Cindy insisted. "Julia was getting ready for her audition. She was excited, nervous. I went out about ten-fifteen to buy some wine. Apparently she was running late, so she asked Duncan to give her a lift. They had a fight," Cindy said. A fight so intense it spilled out into the street, so loud it attracted the attention of the neighbors.

"What was the fight about?"

"Julia got angry when Duncan said he didn't have time to take her to her audition," Heather explained patiently, "and she threw her usual tantrum. She was fighting with everyone that morning." She looked guiltily toward her mother.

"You had a fight with your daughter, Mrs. Carver?" Detective Gill asked.

"It was hardly a fight."

"What were you fighting about?" Tom asked.

"It was nothing." Cindy motioned toward the dog. "I wanted her to take Elvis for a walk. She said she had to take a shower. She was banging on the bathroom door, trying to get Duncan to hurry up. I told her to stop. Stuff like that. Nothing important."

"Nothing else?"

"She didn't want to go to the fitting," Heather said.

"She would have gone," Cindy insisted. "She wouldn't just not show up. She wouldn't not come home for five days. She wouldn't not call."

"Take it easy," Tom cautioned.

"I don't want to take it easy. I want these policemen to stop asking questions and go out and find my daughter. Have you talked to Sean Banack?"

"What's Sean got to do with this?" Norma Appleton asked, coming back into the living room. "Coffee'll be ready in just a minute."

"We talked to him briefly on Friday. And we'll be talking to him again this morning."

"What about?" Cindy's mother asked.

"Mom, please. I'll tell you later."

"I understand this is a very difficult time for you, Mrs. Carver," Detective Gill said, staring directly at Cindy, leaving no doubt whom he was talking to, "but the more we know about Julia, the better our chances are of finding her. Can you tell me anything else about her? Her hobbies, what she likes to do, places she frequents. . . ."

"She likes the Rivoli," the Cookie answered before Cindy had a chance to formulate a response.

"The Rivoli?"

"Comedy club on Queen Street," Heather said.

I didn't know that, Cindy thought. Why didn't I know that?

"What about the dance clubs?"

Tom smiled. "She gave that scene up years ago."

"Does your daughter drink?"

"No," Cindy said.

"Occasionally," Tom corrected.

"What about drugs?"

"What about them?" Cindy asked.

"She went through the usual phase all young people do," Tom said.

She did? Cindy wondered. Why wasn't I told? Why didn't I know?

"But I sat her down," Tom continued, "had a long talk with her, told her that if she wanted to be a successful actress, she had to get serious, that I'd help her as much as I could, but only if she stopped goofing around and started focusing. Luckily, she listened."

You sat her down, Cindy thought. *You* talked to her. *You* told her she had to get serious, that *you'd* help her as much as *you* could. *You* pompous ass. Cindy rubbed her forehead. "What happens now?" she asked.

"We go back to the station, file a missing person's report."

"The reporters'll be all over this one." Detective Gill held up Julia's picture. "A pretty girl like this. Actress. Daughter of a prominent attorney. It'll be front page news."

"Is that good or bad?" Cindy asked.

"A bit of both. The public can be very helpful, but don't be surprised if once this news gets out, you start getting a lot of crank calls. If necessary, we'll put a tap on your phone, try weeding out the crazies."

"Try not to worry, Mrs. Carver," Detective Bartolli said. "She'll turn up."

Cindy stared at the detectives through eyes rapidly filling with tears. "Thank you," she said.

"In the meantime, if you think of anything else . . ."

"There is something," Cindy said, seeing Ryan's face in the blur of her tears, wondering again if he was really as innocent as he claimed.

"What's that?"

"My neighbor, Ryan Sellick. You might want to have a talk with him."

SIXTEEN

OKAY, Cindy, what's going on? Why haven't you returned any of our messages?" Meg was asking. "Cindy? Cindy, are you there?"

Cindy brushed her lips against the receiver, pictured Meg and Trish huddled together on the other end of the line. "Julia's missing," she whispered.

"What? I didn't hear you."

"Julia's missing," Cindy repeated, louder this time.

"What do you mean, she's missing?"

Cindy said nothing. What more was there to say?

"We'll be right over."

Cindy replaced the receiver, shifted her gaze to the floor. She didn't look up. If she did, she knew she'd see her mother and daughter watching her from their seats at the kitchen table, and she'd have to contend with the worry in their eyes, and she didn't want to have to deal with their worry, she didn't want to have to deal with their fears, she didn't want to have to deal with anybody else's problems, damn it, she just wanted Julia to come home.

Wasn't that all she'd ever wanted?

"Who was that?" her mother asked.

"Meg. She and Trish are coming over." Cindy's voice wobbled, like a tire running out of air.

"I better make some more coffee."

Cindy continued staring at the floor.

"Mom?" Heather asked. "Are you okay?"

I can't move, Cindy thought. I can't think. I can't breathe. "I'm okay," she said.

"You're not going to faint again, are you?" her mother asked.

"I'm not going to faint."

"Is there anything you want me to do?" Heather asked.

"You can take the dog for a walk."

"Sure. Come on, Elvis. Let's go to the park."

Elvis was immediately up and at the front door, his tail wagging in blissful abandon.

I saw her yesterday, Cindy heard a man say. *She was sitting right over there.* He pointed at the park bench. *She was crying her heart out.*

"Heather, wait."

"What?"

Cindy watched her daughter's feet cut across her line of vision. She needs new sneakers, Cindy thought idly. And some new clothes for school. Didn't classes start this week? Cindy shook her head. She couldn't remember. "Why were you crying in the park?"

"What?"

"A man saw you there last week. Crying your eyes out, he said."

Heather shrugged, shook her head. "Wasn't me."

"Heather. . . ."

"Be back soon." She headed for the front door.

"Why don't you sit down," Cindy's mother advised after Heather was gone.

"I don't want to sit down."

"You'll make yourself sick."

"By standing?"

Her mother approached, put gentle arms around Cindy's shoulders, led her to the nearest chair, sat her down. "You've done everything you can, sweetheart. Now you have to let the police handle things."

"What if they can't? What if they never find her?"

"They'll find her."

"Young women disappear all the time. Sometimes they never come home."

"She'll come home," her mother insisted as Cindy sucked the words into her lungs, as if she were running out of air.

Suddenly she was back on her feet. "I can't just sit here and do nothing."

"You have to stay calm. You have to stay hopeful. The police will call as soon as they have any information."

"I can't wait. I have to do something." Cindy ran to the front door and opened it.

"Wait! Cindy! What are you doing? Where are you going?"

"I have to get out of here." Cindy ran down the steps to her driveway, climbed inside her car.

"Darling, please. Your friends will be here any minute. Where are you . . . ?"

Cindy backed her car onto the street, shot toward Avenue Road.

Less than five minutes later, she was running along Yorkville, almost colliding with several camera-toting tourists on the popular, boutique-lined street. "I'm sorry," she shouted as she ran, her eyes scanning the numbers of the tony, two-story buildings until she found Number 320. She pulled open the front door, took a deep breath, then waited until she was confident she'd regained her composure before slowly walking up the stairs to Suite 204. Seconds later, she was standing in a small waiting area, in front of a pencil-thin young man with pointy black hair. "I'm here to see

Michael Kinsolving," she told him with a confidence that surprised her.

The young man raised his fingers to his face, the back of his left hand resting against the tip of his long nose, then leaned across his desk to check his datebook. "And you are?"

"Cindy Appleton," she replied, her maiden name feeling clumsy on her tongue, like a once-stylish suit that no longer fit. "I'm with the film festival."

"Do you have an appointment?"

"Of course." Cindy checked her watch. "Eleven-thirty. Right on time."

The young man rifled through the pages of his appointment calendar. "I'm sorry. There's obviously been some mistake. I don't seem to have you down. . . ."

"It's very important. I'm afraid there's a scheduling problem with regard to Mr. Kinsolving's new film . . ."

"A scheduling problem? Oh dear. Well, hold on. I'll see if Mr. Kinsolving can spare a few minutes. Your name again?"

"Cindy Appleton," Cindy repeated, the name a more comfortable fit the second time. Why had she never thought to reclaim it?

The skinny young man disappeared into the inner office, popped his head out seconds later. "Mr. Kinsolving will see you now."

"Thank you." Cindy slowly crossed the sparsely furnished waiting room, its walls lined with posters from past Toronto film festivals, thinking, What now?

AT FIRST SHE saw no one, just the back of a tall black leather chair, a large desk, and the grainy image of a beautiful young woman filling a large-screen TV on the opposite wall of the small room. "Well, well, look who's here," the young woman said, as if speaking directly to Cindy. Cindy froze, her eyes glued to the young woman's face, a face that was similar to Julia's in certain respects, but fuller, slightly coarser. "What happened? Forget your cigarettes?"

A click of a button and the image suddenly halted, reversed, stopped, started up again. "Well, well, look who's here," the woman repeated. "What happened? Forget your cigarettes?"

Another click. This time the image froze, vibrating slightly in its enforced stillness.

"Well, what do you think?" a deep voice asked from behind the high-backed leather chair. "Would you like to fuck her?"

"What?" Cindy took a step back, felt the crunch of the assistant's toes beneath her feet as he tried in vain to get out of her way.

The chair swiveled around abruptly, revealing a gnome-like man with a handsomely craggy face. Cindy recognized the famous director immediately from his rumpled hair and trademark black T-shirt. "I'm sorry," he said, not bothering to get to his feet, a slow smile spreading across his cherubic face. Magazine profiles always mentioned his roguish green eyes and acne-scarred skin. Both were more pronounced in person than in photographs. "I thought you were a man. I should have realized 'Sydney' could be a woman's name as well."

"Cindy," she corrected.

"Cindy," Michael Kinsolving repeated slyly, and Cindy understood in that moment that no mistake had been made, that this was a man who knew what he was doing at all times, that he'd said what he did to throw her off-guard, a subtly sadistic way of controlling the situation and putting her in her place. Clearly this was a man who was used to directing his reality. He motioned toward the TV screen. "Fucking her aside, what do you think of her?"

Cindy struggled to maintain her composure. "I'm not sure what you want me to say."

"Do you think she's beautiful?"

"Yes."

"Sexy?"

"I suppose."

"Her eyes aren't too small?"

"I don't think. . . ."

"Her lips aren't too thin?"

Cindy straightened her shoulders, took a deep breath. "Mr. Kinsolving. . . ."

"I'm going for a very specific look here. I want women to look at this girl and think 'lost soul.' I want men to look at her and think 'blow-job.' That's why I think her lips might be too thin," he said, as if they were discussing the weather.

Cindy tried not to give him the satisfaction of looking shocked. Was this how all directors talked about the young women who auditioned for them? Young women who bared their souls, and often a good deal more, for a chance to make their dreams come true? Women examined and dissected and ultimately reduced to a series of body parts that never quite measured up? Eyes that were too small; lips that were too thin. Souls that were lost. "What about talent?"

"Talent?" Michael Kinsolving looked amused.

"Is she a good actress?"

Michael Kinsolving laughed out loud. "Who cares? They're all good. That's the least of it."

"The least of it?"

"You have to want to fuck them," the gnomish director declared, leaning back in his chair. "That's what makes a star. They're bankable if they're fuckable."

"Mr. Kinsolving . . ."

"Who are you?" he asked, studying his manicured fingernails. "I know you're not who you say you are. You're certainly not from the film festival."

Cindy released a deep breath of air, eyes flitting across the bare white walls. "My name is Cindy Carver."

"Carver," Michael repeated, still not looking at her. "Why is that name familiar?"

"My husband, my *ex*-husband, is Tom Carver." A smile forced its way onto her lips.

Still no sign the Hollywood director had any idea who she was.

"My daughter is Julia Carver. She had an audition with you last Thursday morning at eleven o'clock."

Michael Kinsolving glanced questioningly at the skinny, spiky-haired young man hovering in the doorway.

"Yes," the young man replied, drawing out the word into several syllables. "I believe someone from Mr. Carver's office called to ask whether she'd kept that appointment."

"And had she?" Michael Kinsolving's voice was strong and clear, the voice of a man used to giving orders.

"Yes."

"So, what's the problem?" the director asked.

"She's missing," Cindy told him, watching his brow crease, his green eyes narrow. The same color eyes as Julia, she thought.

"Missing?"

"Nobody has seen or heard from her since she left this office."

"What are you saying? That she walked out of here and vanished into thin air?"

"We don't know what's happened to her," Cindy admitted, her voice filling with tears. "I guess I was hoping you might be able to shed some light on the situation. If you know anything at all that might help us find her. . . ."

Michael Kinsolving stood up slowly and walked to Cindy's side, the top of his head in line with the tip of her nose. "And what would I know exactly?"

"I guess I was hoping that she might have said something to you about her plans."

"Why would she do that?"

"I don't know." Already Cindy regretted her decision to come here. Had she really thought Michael Kinsolving might be able to help her?

"She probably took off with some guy she knew you wouldn't approve of," he offered with a smirk. "Trust me, I know whereof I speak. I have three daughters myself."

Cindy vaguely recalled having read that Michael Kinsolving had five children from four different marriages.

"Of course they live with their mothers."

Of course, Cindy acknowledged with a nod. Didn't all daughters choose to live with their mothers after their parents divorced? All except Julia.

"I'm sorry, but I don't see how I can help you." The director pulled a tissue from his jean pocket and offered it to Cindy.

Cindy noted how muscular his arms were despite his diminutive size. "Did she give a good audition?" *Talent is the least of it.* "Did you say anything to her that might have upset her?" *Your eyes are too small; your lips are too thin.* "Did she seem depressed to you when she left?" *Did women look at her and think 'lost soul'? Did men look at her and think . . .* Dear God.

"I wish there was something I could tell you to put your mind at ease," Michael Kinsolving was saying. "But to be perfectly frank, I don't even remember the girl."

"Oh, you'd remember Julia. She's twenty-one, very beautiful, slim, blond . . ." Cindy stopped, looked at the television screen, understanding that for the past week, Michael Kinsolving's office had been inundated with slim, blond, beautiful women.

The director looked to his assistant for help. "Do we have a tape on her?"

The assistant nodded. "I'll get it." He backed out of the room.

Michael Kinsolving guided Cindy around his desk to his chair. "Would you like some bottled water or maybe an espresso?"

"Water would be great."

"With gas or without?"

Cindy shook her head, unable to choose.

"Philip," Michael Kinsolving called toward the next room, "some Perrier for Mrs. Carver. Can I call you Cindy?"

"Of course."

"Cindy." The director smiled, extended his hand. "Michael."

She took his hand, felt the strength in his fingers, suddenly understood why women found him so attractive. "My hands are cold," she apologized.

"Cold hands, warm heart," he said with a smile.

Was he flirting with her? Cindy wondered, quickly returning her hand to her lap, disconcerted by the thought. Was it possible he'd come on to Julia?

Philip reentered the room carrying a glass of sparkling water and a tape cassette. He handed the glass to Cindy, then crossed to the television against the far wall. "I believe she's on this tape. Shall I put it on?"

"Please," Michael directed as his assistant removed the existing tape and replaced it with another.

Cindy took a small sip of water, felt the bubbles bursting against her nose, like smelling salts. She watched the tape flicker on, held her breath as a young woman's face filled the screen. Like the woman before her, this woman was blond and beautiful. Cindy found herself focusing on her lips. Were they too thin? she wondered.

"I believe she's number eight." Philip fast-forwarded the tape.

A parade of lovely young women flew across the large-screen TV, their arms jerking up and down like marionettes, their heads turning this way and that, as if controlled by invisible strings, their blond hair shaking from one shoulder to the other, as the tape raced to find her daughter.

"So many women, so little time," Michael mused out loud. "Sorry. Didn't mean to sound glib."

Cindy shook her head. In truth, she'd barely heard him, and it was only his apology that gave the words weight, allowed them to sink in. She winced as the tape came to an abrupt halt, Julia's face filling the screen. Philip pressed another button and the image froze. Julia sat across the room, staring at her mother from inside a large, rectangular box, her bright smile frozen on her face.

"Oh yes," Michael said. "I remember her now. Her father's a lawyer. He does some work for our company."

"That's the one," Philip confirmed, once more receding into the background.

"Yes, she gave a very nice reading," Michael continued absently, leaning back against the front of his desk. "Are you sure you want to see this?"

"Please."

He signaled to his assistant, who pressed the appropriate button, unfreezing the frame and bringing Julia to life.

(Julia's Audition: A beautiful young woman sits on a small wooden chair, crosses one spectacular leg over the other. She is wearing red leather pants and a white blouse, which glares slightly under the harsh light. The camera slowly moves in on her face as she states her name. "Julia Carver," she pronounces clearly, then gives the name of her agent. She lowers her head, her hair falling across her face. Several seconds pass before she raises her head again, and when she does, it is almost as if Julia has disappeared and another girl has taken her place. This girl is tougher, angrier, sexier. And there is something else, something her defiant posture tries to hide. Behind the anger, the toughness, the undeniable sexuality, there is a sadness, a hunger, a raw need. Julia leans back, throws one elbow over the back of her chair, her eyes moving up and down an invisible visitor. The eyes of a lost soul. "Well, well, look who's here," she says. "What happened? Forget your cigarettes?"

"I came back to see you," an off-camera voice replies.

Julia's eyebrows arch in a gesture that is achingly familiar. "Is that supposed to make me go all weak in the knees?" she asks. "Is it? Because if it is, it's not working. See? My knees aren't weak at all." She recrosses her legs with provocative slowness, then leans forward, speaks directly into the camera lens. "What's the matter, baby? Disappointed? Surprised? Thought you could just waltz back into my life and everything would be the same as it was before you ran off with my best friend? How is Amy, by the way? No, don't tell me. The fact you're back is all the answer I need."

"Caroline . . ." the off-camera voice interrupts.

"I could have told you she was a lousy lay." The words roll off Julia's tongue like a stray caress. "I could have spared you the time and trouble. I was her roommate for . . . how many years? I saw the men come and go. I heard the phony groans, the fake orgasms she thought were fooling them. But none of them were the fool you turned out to be." Julia throws her head back, laughs unpleasantly. "What's the matter, baby? You come back for a real woman? Someone who doesn't have to fake it when you touch her? Someone who loves the feel of you pounding away inside her? Night and day. Day and night." Julia begins fidgeting in her seat, moving her hips in time to some distant, obscene rhythm. "Any time. All the time. Is that what you miss, baby? Is that why you've come home?"

"Caroline," the voice says flatly. "Amy and I got married last night."

The hard mask covering Julia's face melts away as tears overwhelm her eyes. "You got married?"

"Last night."

Julia says nothing. She simply stares into the camera, her tears spilling down her cheeks, washing away all traces of pride, her face an open wound.)

The push of a button. The scene ended. Julia's anguished face stared at her mother from inside her fifty-two-inch prison.

"I had no idea . . ." Cindy began.

"How good she is?" Michael asked quietly.

"Yes."

"Yes, she's very good," Michael agreed. "Would you like to see it again?"

Cindy shook her head. Another viewing of the tape and they'd have to scrape her off the floor.

"I could have a copy made, if you'd like."

"Thank you."

There was the sound of footsteps on the stairs. Philip stepped into the waiting room, returned seconds later, his pale face ashen. "It's the police."

"You called the police?" Michael asked, clearly more amused than annoyed.

Cindy shook her head as the two detectives strode purposefully into the room.

"Michael Kinsolving?" Detective Bartolli asked, his partner right behind. Both men stopped abruptly when they saw Julia's face on the large TV screen. Slowly, they pivoted in Cindy's direction. "Mrs. Carver?"

"What are you doing here?" Detective Gill asked accusingly.

Michael Kinsolving shook the officers' hands. "Mrs. Carver was hoping I might be able to be of some help in finding her daughter."

"And were you?"

"I'm afraid I have no idea where her daughter might be."

"We were just showing Mrs. Carver a tape of Julia's audition," Philip volunteered from the doorway. "Can I get anyone some bottled water or an espresso, perhaps?"

Detective Bartolli shook his head. "Detective Gill will drive you home, Mrs. Carver," he said, his voice bristling with annoyance at her unexpected presence.

"That's all right. I have my car."

"I'll walk you to it," Detective Gill said, leaving no room for discussion.

"I'll get a copy of the audition tape over to you as soon as possible," Michael said.

"Thank you." Cindy rose slowly from the chair, depositing her barely touched glass of Perrier on the director's desk, then shuffling toward the door, her feet numb, unable to feel the floor. She paused in the doorway. "Good luck at the festival."

"Thank you. Good luck finding your daughter."

Julia nodded, aware of Detective Gill's firm grasp on her elbow.

"I'd like to have a look at that tape," she heard Detective Bartolli say as the door to the inner office closed and Detective Gill led her toward the stairs.

SEVENTEEN

Dark clouds were gathering overhead as Cindy pulled into her driveway. She recognized Meg's red Mercedes on the street as she ran up the front stairs to her house, fumbling in her purse for her key.

The front door opened just as she was reaching for it. "Where have you been?" Trish asked, pulling her inside, Elvis leaping toward her thighs. "Your mother's been frantic."

"Just like old times," Meg said, joining Trish in the hallway and taking Cindy into her arms. "Are you all right?"

Cindy nodded against her friend's shoulder. "I'm okay."

"Where have you been?" Trish asked again.

"Where did you go?" Norma Appleton demanded, joining the women in the front hall.

"I went to see Michael Kinsolving."

"Michael Kinsolving, the director?" Trish asked.

"Why'd you go see him?" Meg asked.

"Does he know where Julia is?" Cindy's mother asked at the same time.

Cindy shook her head. "He says he doesn't."

"You don't believe him?"

"I don't know." *Would you like to fuck her?* she heard the director ask, wondering if he'd posed the same question to others regarding Julia. "He claimed he didn't even remember her, that he's seen so many girls . . ." Her voice faded, disappeared. But then he acknowledged how very good she was. And how could anyone forget Julia?

"Have some lunch," Norma Appleton urged, ushering the women into the kitchen.

"I'm not hungry."

"Your mother's been filling us in," Meg said. "I can't imagine what you're going through."

"What do the police think?" Trish asked.

Cindy shrugged. "That it's too early to panic."

"They're right."

"I know."

"Doesn't help, does it?"

"No."

Trish hugged her, sat down beside her, as Meg pulled up another chair, wrapped her arms around Cindy.

"Where's Heather?" Cindy asked.

"Out. Said she'd be back later." Norma Appleton swayed from one foot to the other, as if weighing her options. "I think I'll go upstairs and watch TV," she announced finally. "Come on, Elvis, you can keep me company. Meg," she called from the top of the stairs, "make sure she eats something."

"Will do," Meg called back. Then, "Is she driving you nuts?"

"Only a little."

"I remember when my mother came to help out after Jeremy was born," Trish began. "What a time that was!"

"Trish," Meg said, "that was twenty years ago."

"Trust me, I'm still reeling."

Cindy laughed, a tentative trickle that wobbled through the still air.

"She flew in from Florida, arrived in the middle of a giant snowstorm, the plane was like three hours late arriving, and she was angry because no one could get to the airport to pick her up, and God forbid, she had to take a limo, and she marched into the apartment complaining about all things Canadian, especially her oldest daughter, who was inconsiderate enough to have given birth in February, of all months. I can still hear her say that—*February, of all months!* Anyway, she proceeded to wreak havoc for the next several weeks. I couldn't do anything right. Why had I allowed myself to gain so much weight during my pregnancy? Why was I nursing when I probably didn't have enough milk? I was going to have one awfully spoiled baby on my hands if I insisted on feeding him each time he cried. I could literally hear her gasp with horror every time I picked him up. *His head! Watch his head!* Like I was this total moron. Of course, I couldn't yell at her, so I took it out on Bill. Almost ended the marriage right then and there. No wonder Jeremy's an only child."

"Families." Meg shook her head. "You gotta love 'em."

"Do you?" Trish asked.

"In the end, what else is there?"

"Friends," Cindy said, reaching for their hands, entwining her fingers with theirs, trying to ignore the echo of Tom's distant voice in her ear. *Friends,* he'd said dismissively. *Friends come and go.* Which probably accounted for Julia's revolving door approach to friendship.

"So, tell your friends exactly what's going on," Trish said.

Cindy immediately recounted the details of last Thursday morning, the chaos surrounding her final moments with Julia.

"So, you'd been arguing," Trish said in summation.

"We weren't arguing."

"All right. You weren't arguing. You were upset. . . ."

"I wasn't upset. . . ."

"Okay. You weren't upset."

"Maybe her audition didn't go well," Meg offered, as others had offered before. "Maybe she just needed some space."

"Could there be a new guy?" Trish asked.

"It's been five days," Cindy interrupted her friends, verbally italicizing each word.

"Yes, but . . ."

"But what?"

"This is Julia we're talking about," Trish reminded her.

"You know how she can be," Meg said.

"Do you honestly think she's that inconsiderate, that she'd disappear for this long without a word to anyone?" Had Trish always been this obtuse? Cindy found herself wondering.

"Tom hasn't heard from her either?" Meg asked.

"Tom hasn't heard from her either," Cindy repeated, sliding her hands into her lap as a tight smile froze on her lips. She imagined her body melting into liquid and spilling off her chair, forming an unwieldy puddle on the floor, much like the Wicked Witch of the West, who dissolved when Dorothy threw water at her head.

Meg's question was like that water, Cindy thought. Seemingly innocent on the surface, but capable of great damage, like acid. It seeped painfully between Cindy's ears, burning the words into delicate tissue.

Tom hasn't heard from her either?

Cindy felt strangely insubstantial, a feeling she'd often experienced during her marriage, and then again immediately after her divorce, as if she were somehow less solid without Tom at her side, as if his presence was necessary to give hers relevance, as if her opinions, her worries, her observations, weren't enough without his acknowledgment and approval.

Tom hasn't heard from her either?

Cindy knew that Meg would be both alarmed and horrified to think her words had been interpreted in such a manner, so Cindy tried hard to give the question context, assign it its proper perspective. Still, the words lingered, small thorns tearing at her already bruised flesh. She smiled at her oldest and closest friend, understanding that despite Meg's obvious sympathy for her plight, she had absolutely no idea of the turmoil raging inside her brain.

How little we know of what really goes on in people's minds, Cindy was thinking, her eyes traveling back and forth between the two women, the smile slowly sliding from her lips. How little we know one another at all.

"Are you all right?" Meg asked, her hand reaching over to smooth some fine hairs from Cindy's forehead.

Cindy shrugged, stared toward the backyard.

"So, tell us about Michael Kinsolving," Trish said. "Is he as sexy as people say?"

Cindy recognized Trish's question for the diversionary tactic it was. Still, it felt strange to be talking about Michael Kinsolving's sexuality under the circumstances. *Bankable is fuckable,* she heard him say. "His face is all pockmarked," she answered, deciding to go with the flow. "And he's short."

"How short?"

"Tom Cruise–short."

"Why are all the men in Hollywood so little?" Trish asked.

"And he didn't remember Julia?" Meg asked incredulously.

Cindy's heartbeat quickened at the mention of her daughter's name. "Not at first. But after we watched the tape . . ."

"What tape?"

"Julia's audition. You should see it. She's amazing."

"I'm not surprised," Meg said.

"She's so talented," Trish concurred, although neither woman had ever seen Julia act.

Cindy recalled the director's face at the conclusion of the viewing. "I think he was impressed. I think he'd forgotten how good she was." *Talent? Talent is the least of it. Do you want to fuck her?*

"Well, that's great then," Meg enthused. "It means he'll remember her. When she comes home," she added, her voice trailing away, disappearing into the air, like smoke from a cigarette.

When she comes home, Cindy repeated, clinging to the words, as if they were life buoys in a choppy sea. When she comes home, I'll buy her those Miss Sixty jeans she's been coveting. I'll take her to New York for a holiday weekend. Just the two of us.

"She's okay, Cindy," Trish was saying. "She'll turn up. Safe and sound. You'll see."

"How can that be?" Cindy demanded, hearing her voice rise. "How can someone disappear for almost a week and then just show up, safe and sound? How is that possible? Julia's not a child. She didn't wander off and get lost. And she didn't run away from home because she had a fight with her mother."

Had she?

"She's not a silly romantic like I was. She didn't elope with some guy to Niagara Falls."

Had she?

"She's not flighty or naïve. She's had disappointing auditions before. She knows the odds of getting cast in a major Hollywood movie."

Did she?

"I know you both think she's selfish and self-absorbed. . . ."

"No. We don't think that."

"It's okay, sweetie," Meg said soothingly. "It's okay."

"It's not okay," Cindy shot back angrily. "Julia wouldn't just take off without telling me. She certainly wouldn't take off without telling her father."

"I didn't mean . . ." Trish began.

"I was just trying . . ." Meg continued.

"She knows her actions have consequences. She knows I'd be worried sick. She wouldn't put me through this."

"Of course she wouldn't," the two friends agreed.

"So, where is she?" Cindy wailed, the sound of her voice bringing Elvis galloping back down the stairs, his barking mixing with her cries, underlining and surrounding her anguish. "Where is she?"

C INDY WAS LY I NG in her bed, watching a peppy young woman named Ricki Lake interviewing a bunch of alternately sullen and giggly teenage girls. "Why do you think your friend dresses like a slut?" Ricki asked sprightly, pushing the phallic-shaped microphone into a girl's face.

Her lips aren't too thin?

Cindy flipped the channel before the girl could reply, watched as a handsome man named Montel Williams cast overly earnest eyes toward a trembling young woman in the seat beside him. "How old were you when your father first molested you?" he asked.

I want women to look at this girl and think, "lost soul." I want men to look at her and think, "blow-job."

Another press of the button and Montel was replaced by Oprah, then Jenny, then Maury, then someone named Judge Judy, a thoroughly unpleasant woman who seemed to think that justice could best be served by insulting all those who stood before her. "Did she ask for your advice?" Judge Judy demanded angrily of the hapless middle-aged woman in front of her. "Just because she's your daughter doesn't mean you can tell her how to run her life."

My daughter is Julia Carver.

Cindy flipped to Comedy Central, hoping for a laugh. "My mother's from another planet," a young female comic was espousing. She paused. "Actually, she's from Hell."

Cindy turned off the TV, tossing the remote to the end of the bed, just missing Elvis, who glanced at her with accusing eyes before jumping to the floor and skulking from the room. Downstairs, she could hear her mother in the kitchen, preparing dinner. Probably she should get out of bed, go down and help out, but she was too tired to move, too drained to offer even token assistance.

The phone rang.

"Hello?" Cindy prayed for the sound of her daughter's voice, braced herself for the inevitable disappointment.

"Are you okay?" Meg asked on the other end of the line.

"I'm fine."

"I felt terrible after we left," Meg continued. "Like we failed you somehow."

"You didn't."

"I just wish there was something we could say or do. . . ."

"There isn't."

"I could come over later. . . ."

"No, that's all right. I'm pretty tired."

"You need your rest."

"I need Julia."

Awkward silence.

"Try to think positive."

Sure. Why not? Why didn't I think of that? "I'm trying."

"I love you," Meg said.

"I know," Cindy told her. "I love you too."

Cindy replaced the receiver, buried her face in her hands. "Think positive*ly,*" she corrected, feeling her breath warm inside her cupped palms. She lifted her head, glared at the phone. "Did I ask for your advice?" she demanded in Judge Judy's strident voice.

She knew she was being unfair, that Meg was only saying what she herself would probably say if their situations were reversed. She knew her friend's concern was genuine, her love and support unwavering. She understood that both Meg and Trish wanted to be there for her, to comfort and protect her, but she also recognized that despite their best intentions, they could never really understand what she was going through. Just as they'd never wholly comprehended the sorrow she'd lived with all those years Julia spent living with her dad. Trish, with her husband and perfect son,

Meg with two wonderful boys of her own. "Mothers of just sons," her own mother had once told her. "They're a different breed. They have no idea."

It wasn't that her friends were insensitive, Cindy thought. In fact, they were kind and considerate and thoughtful and everything true friends should be. They just didn't get it. How could they? They had no idea.

This is Julia we're talking about.

You know how she can be.

(Defining Moment: Tom across from her at the breakfast table, fingers digging into the morning paper he holds high in front of his face. "Nothing's ever enough for you," he says between tightly gritted teeth.

They've been fighting since last night. Cindy can barely remember what the argument is about. "That's not true," she counters weakly, lifting her glass of orange juice to her lips, wishing he would put the paper down so that she could see his face.

"Of course it's true. Face it, Cindy. I just don't measure up to your lofty standards."

"What are you talking about? I never said that."

"You said I stabbed Leo Marshall in the back."

"I said I was surprised you bad-mouthed the man in front of his client."

"His client is worth four hundred milion dollars. He wasn't getting his money's worth with Leo. He will with me."

"I thought Leo Marshall was your friend."

"Friends." Tom sniffs. "Friends come and go."

Cindy feels the glass of orange juice tremble in her hands. "So the end justifies the means?"

"In most cases, yes. Can you get off your high horse now?"

"Can you put the paper down?"

"I don't know what more you want from me."

"I want you to put the paper down. Please."

He lowers the paper, glowers at her from across the table. "There. You happy? Paper's down. You got your way."

"This isn't about getting my way."

"Paper's down, isn't it?"

"That's not the issue."

Tom glances impatiently at his watch. "Look, it's eight-thirty. Much as I'd love to sit here arguing issues with you all morning, some of us have to go to work." He pushes back his chair. "I have a meeting tonight. Don't count on me for dinner."

"Who is she this time?" Cindy asks.

Tom gets to his feet, says nothing.

"Tom?" she says, her grip on her glass tightening.

He looks at her, shakes his head. "What now?" he says.

Probably it is the *now,* and not the fact of another woman that gets her. "This," she says simply, then hurls the contents of the glass at his face.)

That moment was the end of her marriage.

Although she and Tom remained together for several more years, the minute that orange juice left her glass, divorce was inevitable. It became strictly a matter of time, a gathering of energy.

It was the same with Meg and Trish, Cindy realized now, an ineffable sadness seeping through her pores, settling into her bones.

This is Julia we're talking about.

You know how she can be.

Maybe it hadn't been as dramatic as a tossed glass of juice, but another defining moment had quietly, yet inexorably, slipped by. Yes, Meg and Trish were her dearest friends. Yes, she loved them and they loved her. But unforeseen circumstance had intervened, and their friendship had been subtly and forever altered. Try as the three friends might to pretend otherwise, Cindy understood that their relationship would never quite be the same again.

Another woman had come between them.

Her name was Julia.

EIGHTEEN

CINDY opened her eyes to find Julia staring at her from across the room.

She pushed herself away from her pillow, holding her breath, watching as the familiar photo of her daughter enlarged to fill the entire TV screen. Cindy lunged toward it, straining to hear the announcer's voice, but the words failed to register. She reached for the remote control to raise the volume, but it wasn't beside her. "Where are you, damn it?" she said, frantic hands pawing at the folds of the blue-and-white-flowered comforter. She vaguely remembered having tossed it toward the end of the bed earlier in the day. How long ago? she wondered, glancing at the clock, noting that it was just minutes after 6 P.M., that despite the bleakness of the sky, darkness was still several hours away.

She must have fallen asleep, she realized, as the back of her hand slapped against the remote, knocking it from the bed. It shot into the air and plummeted to the floor, landing with a dull thud on the carpet, before bouncing out of sight.

Instantly, Cindy was off the bed and on her hands and knees, the carpet's stale scent pushing into her nostrils as she pressed her cheek against its soft pile. She lifted the white dust ruffle and poked her head under the bed, her hands fumbling around in the dark until they connected with the stubborn object. "Damn it," she said, bumping her head as she struggled to her feet, aiming the remote at the television screen, as if it were a gun, increasing the volume until the announcer's voice was all but shouting in her ear. Except that he was no longer talking about Julia. Her daughter's picture had been replaced by an aerial view of Canada's Wonderland, where the announcer intoned solemnly, a little boy of eight had been sexually molested only hours before.

Cindy changed the channel. A farmer's field popped into view. It took Cindy several seconds to realize she was looking at an old, dilapidated barn in a sea of swaying cornstalks. "Oh no." Cindy clasped her hand across her mouth to still the screams building in her throat. They'd found Julia's body in an abandoned barn off the King Sideroad. Sean's story had led them to her torn and battered remains. "No. No. No."

"Cindy!" her mother was yelling as Elvis began barking from somewhere beside her. "Cindy, what's wrong?"

Her mother was suddenly beside her, sliding the remote control unit from her daughter's hands, returning the TV's volume to a normal level. It was only then that Cindy was able to digest the announcer's words, to understand that the cornfield in question wasn't anywhere near the King Sideroad, but rather somewhere outside Midland, that the story concerned bumper crops of corn and had absolutely nothing to do with Julia.

"I thought. . . ."

"What, darling?"

"Julia. . . ."

"Was there something about Julia?" Her mother began flipping through the channels.

"I saw her picture. They were talking about her." Were they? Or had she just dreamed it?

And then there she was again: the tilted head, the dazzling eyes, the straight blond hair falling toward her shoulder, the knowing smile.

"Turn it up, turn it up."

"Police are searching for clues in the disappearance of twenty-one-year-old Julia Carver, daughter of prominent entertainment lawyer, Tom Carver. The aspiring actress was last seen Thursday morning, August twenty-ninth, after leaving an audition with noted Hollywood director Michael Kinsolving."

Julia's photo was instantly replaced by one of Michael Kinsolving, his arms around two voluptuous blond starlets.

"Police have questioned the famed director, in town to preview his latest film at the Toronto International Film Festival, and to scout locations for his next movie, but insist he is not a suspect in the young woman's disappearance."

The newscaster's bland face replaced Michael Kinsolving's, while Julia's picture reappeared in a small square at the right top of the screen. *"Anyone with any information regarding Julia Carver's whereabouts is urged to contact local police."*

"I guess that makes it official," Norma Appleton said, collapsing on the end of the bed, her face ashen, her eyes wide and blank.

Immediately Cindy was at her mother's side. "Oh, Mom," she said. "I'm so sorry. I've been so consumed with my own worry. I haven't even thought about how this might be affecting you."

"The last thing I want is for you to start worrying about me."

"You're her grandmother."

Her mother lowered her head. "My first grandchild," she whispered.

"Oh, Mom. What if she doesn't come home? What if we never find out what happened to her?"

"She'll come home," her mother said, her voice strong, as if the sheer force of her will could keep her granddaughter safe, bring her back home.

Cindy nodded, afraid to question her further. The two women

sat at the foot of the bed, holding tightly onto one another, waiting for more news of Julia.

I T   W A S   A L M O S T   ten o'clock when Cindy heard the front door open and close. She leaned forward in her bed, pressed the mute button on the TV, and waited as footsteps filled the upstairs hall. "Heather?" she called. Heather had phoned to say she wouldn't be home for dinner, that she was meeting up with friends but wouldn't be late.

Elvis jumped from the bed, ran out of the room. "Heather?" Cindy called again.

"It's me," Duncan answered, his face appearing in the doorway, Elvis leaping against his legs with such enthusiasm he almost knocked him over.

"Duncan," Cindy acknowledged. "Is Heather with you?"

Duncan shook his head. Dark hair fell across his forehead. He looked tired, as if he hadn't slept in days. His normally smooth skin was splotchy and pale. The stale odor of too many cigarettes wafted from his clothes. "I'm sure she'll be back soon," he said, swaying. He leaned his shoulder against the wall, as if to steady himself.

"Are you okay?" Then, "Are you drunk?"

Duncan's eyebrows drew together at the bridge of his nose, as if he were giving the question serious consideration. "No. Well, maybe. Just a bit."

"Why?"

"Why?" he repeated.

"Why were you drinking?"

He laughed, an annoyingly girlish giggle Cindy hadn't heard before. "Does there have to be a reason?"

"I don't think I've ever seen you drunk before."

"Yeah, well . . ."

"When did you start smoking?" Cindy pressed.

"What?"

"Smoking and drinking—it's just not you."

"I don't do it very often," Duncan said defensively. "Just every now and then. You know."

"I don't know."

"Mrs. Carver, you're making me a little nervous here."

"What are you nervous about?"

"Are you upset with me about something?"

"Why would I be upset with you?"

"I don't know. You just seem . . ."

"Upset?"

"Yeah."

"You don't think I have good reason to be upset?"

Duncan glanced down the hall toward the bedroom he shared with Heather. "I didn't say that." He paused, pushed himself away from the wall, wobbled on his heels. He took two steps, then stopped, stared hard at Cindy. "Has there been any news?" he asked, carefully. "About Julia?"

"No. Duncan . . ." Cindy called as he was about to turn away.

"Yes?"

"What's going on with you and Heather?"

Duncan swallowed, rubbed the side of his nose. "I don't know what you mean."

"Something's obviously not right between the two of you. . . ."

"We're just going through a bit of a rough patch, Mrs. Carver. That's all. I really don't feel comfortable talking about it."

"You'd tell me, wouldn't you, if there was anything I should know?"

"I don't understand."

"You know something, don't you?"

"I know I'm drunker than I thought I was." He tried to laugh, coughed instead.

"You know something about Julia," Cindy said over the sound of his hacking.

Blood drained from the young man's already pale face. He seemed to sober up on the spot. "About Julia? No. Of course not."

"You were fighting with her . . ."

"Yeah, but . . ."

"And then she disappeared."

"Mrs. Carver, you can't think I had anything to do with Julia's disappearance."

"Did you?"

"No!"

Cindy fell back against her pillow. Did she really think the boy she'd welcomed into her home, this young man who was her younger daughter's lover, was in any way responsible for her older daughter's disappearance? Could she really think that? She shook her head. She didn't know what to think anymore.

Duncan stood silently in the doorway, his arms hanging limply at his sides. "Maybe I should spend the night at Mac's," he said finally. "You'd probably feel more comfortable if I weren't around."

Cindy said nothing.

"I'll just get a few of my things."

Cindy listened as he shuffled down the hall. She thought of running after him, wrestling him to the ground, beating a confession out of him. Then she thought of her mother asleep in Julia's bed. What was the point in waking her up by creating a scene? Duncan wasn't about to confess to anything. Did she really think he had anything to confess?

Cindy heard him rummaging around in the closet. A few seconds later, she caught sight of his shadow as it hurried by her room. He left without saying good-bye.

"How have you been holding out, Mrs. Carver?" the doctor was asking, his face drifting in and out of focus. He was a big man with a full beard, bushy eyebrows, and thinning gray hair.

"I've been better," Cindy said, adjusting the white sheet tucked around her breasts.

"Remembering to take your pills?"

Cindy rubbed her eyes, watching the doctor's features flatten and slide across his face. "What pills?"

"It's very important that you take your pills, Mrs. Carver," he was saying. "If you don't take your pills, you'll die."

"Oh no!" Cindy shot up in bed. "I forgot. I forgot." She was halfway to the bathroom, her heart pounding against her chest when she stopped. "What pills?" she asked out loud, glancing toward the television set, realizing it was still on, that she'd fallen asleep sometime before midnight during a rerun of *Law & Order,* and that she was standing naked in the middle of her room in the middle of the night in the middle of the recurring nightmare that was her life. "What pills?" she asked again, collapsing on the floor, and staring at a handsome man in an orange jumpsuit walking glumly across her TV screen. The camera lowered to reveal the man's hands in shackles as his head of curly brown hair was pushed roughly inside a waiting police car.

It took Cindy a minute to realize that the man she was watching was Ted Bundy, notorious killer of dozens, possibly even hundreds, of young women. She shuddered, unable to turn away, transfixed by the announcer's deep voice and the killer's bottomless stare. *"Stay tuned as Ted Bundy makes a daring escape,"* the announcer intoned solemnly. "American Justice *continues after these messages."*

Was that what happened to Julia? Cindy couldn't stop herself from wondering. Had she run into a man whose boyishly handsome exterior belied the heart and soul of a deranged killer? Had he tricked her into getting into his car, charmed her into going back to his place? Had she tried to fight him off? Had he used drugs or chains to subdue her? Was he keeping her prisoner in some dank underground cave?

So many madmen out there, Cindy was thinking. So many *mad men*. Had one of them taken out his rage on her little girl?

She pushed herself to her feet just as Ted Bundy's smiling face once again filled the screen, his crazed eyes quickly settling on her own, daring her to confront him.

"The boy next door," the announcer proclaimed as Cindy groped for the remote control. For a station that was ostensibly about art and entertainment, it seemed to spend an awful lot of time detailing grisly murders. She clicked it off, watching the room go instantly dark, as if the TV itself had swallowed the light. Eating its young, she thought, walking to the window, pushing aside the curtains to stare at the backyard. There was only a sliver of moon, and it was pretty much hidden by the tall maple tree that sat in the center of the Sellicks' unruly and overgrown lawn. She should really do something about the cedar fence that divided their property, she thought absently. It was starting to cave in at the far end, buckling under the extended pressure of a nearby sumac tree. All it would take was one good snowfall and that fence would collapse altogether.

And "Good fences make good neighbors," she thought, recalling the lines by Robert Frost, projecting ahead to the coming winter, trying to imagine herself in three months time. Would she still be standing by her bedroom window, staring into the darkness, waiting for her daughter to come home?

It was then she saw her.

She was sitting on the bottom step leading from the patio off the kitchen to the backyard, and while Cindy couldn't see her face, she knew immediately it was Julia. "Julia. My God—Julia!" She pulled on her terry-cloth robe and raced down the stairs, Elvis at her heels. She ran into the kitchen, unlocked and opened the sliding glass door in one fluid gesture, and vaulted outside, the cool night air whipping against her face like a wet towel. "Julia!" she cried, as the girl on the bottom step jumped to her feet and backed into the night.

"Mom, no. It's me."

"Heather?!!"

"You scared me. What are you doing?"

"What am *I* doing? What are *you* doing?" Cindy demanded. "It's after three in the morning."

"I couldn't sleep."

"I saw you from my bedroom window. I thought you were Julia."

"Sorry," Heather said. "It's only me." There was a strange, gargled quality to Heather's voice.

"Are you crying?" Cindy inched her way down the steps, as if her daughter were a stray kitten who might run away if she moved too fast.

Heather shook her head, the sliver of moonlight catching her cheek, revealing a path of still-wet tears.

"What is it, sweetheart? And please don't tell me, nothing," she added just as the word was leaving Heather's lips. "Does it have something to do with Duncan?"

Heather turned away. "We split up," she acknowledged, after a long pause.

"You split up? When?"

"Tonight."

"Why?" Cindy asked, her voice low.

"I don't know." Heather released a deep breath of air, lifted her palms into the air. "We've been fighting a lot lately."

"About Julia?"

Heather looked confused. "About Julia? No. What's Julia got to do with this?"

"What were you fighting about, sweetheart?" Cindy asked, ignoring the question.

Heather shook her head. "I don't know. Everything. Nothing. It's just so stupid."

"What is?"

"We were at this party a few weeks ago," Heather began slowly, "and I was talking to this guy. I was just talking to him. It was perfectly innocent, but Duncan said I was flirting, and we had this whole big argument. I thought we'd patched it up, but then it started up again last week. I'd gone to this club with Sheri and Jessica, and Duncan was really upset about it. He said I shouldn't be going places like that without him, and I said, Why shouldn't I? I'm not doing anything wrong. Why can't I just hang out with my girlfriends and have a good time? And he said, if that's what I wanted, I could hang out with my girlfriends every night. Then tonight we had another big fight, and Duncan got pretty drunk, and I got mad and left with Jessica, and when I got home, I saw his stuff wasn't here, so I called him at Mac's, and he said he wasn't coming back, that it was over between us."

"Oh, sweetie, he doesn't mean that."

"Yes, he does. He said he doesn't want anything more to do with any of us, that we're all crazy. Why would he say that?"

"I don't know," Cindy lied, thinking of their earlier confrontation.

"Did you see him when he came home?"

"Yes," Cindy admitted.

"And?"

"He was pretty drunk."

"What did you say to him?"

"Nothing. I just asked him a few questions."

"What sort of questions?"

"I just asked him . . . if there was anything he thought I should know."

"About what?"

"About Julia."

"About Julia? Why would you ask him about her?"

"I don't know."

"Why does everything always have to be about Julia?" Heather demanded suddenly. "I am so sick and tired of everything always being about Julia. This isn't about her. It's about me. Heather. Your other daughter. Remember me?"

"Heather, please. Your sister is missing. . . ."

"Julia's not missing."

"What?"

Heather looked toward the ground.

"What are you talking about? Are you saying you know where she is?"

"No."

"What *are* you saying?"

Heather reluctantly met her mother's gaze. "I didn't think she was serious. I didn't think she'd actually do it."

"What are you saying?" Cindy repeated, her voice a low growl. "Tell me."

"The whole thing is just so stupid," Heather began. "Julia was mad at Duncan because he wouldn't give her a lift. She was calling him names, accusing him of being selfish and ungrateful. She said if he was going to live here free of charge, the least he could do was make himself useful. He told her he wasn't her chauffeur; she told him to get the hell out of the house. I told *her* to get the hell out, that everyone was sick and tired of her stupid tantrums, and she said she couldn't wait to get out, that she hated me, that I was 'the bane of her existence.' And then she said that maybe she wouldn't wait until she'd saved up enough money to get her own place, maybe she'd move out right away. Today, she said. Maybe she wouldn't even bother coming home after her audition."

The words pounded against Cindy's consciousness like a boxer's fists. "What?"

"I didn't think she really meant it."

"Why didn't you tell me this before?"

"When? When the police were here? You got so angry when Fiona suggested Julia might want some time to herself. You said she was trying to sabotage the investigation. I didn't want . . . I mean, just in case . . . I didn't know . . ."

Cindy fought to make sense of her daughter's words. Was it possible Julia had simply taken off in a fit of pique? That she could be so vengeful, so thoughtless, so cruel? That she could disappear as a way of making a point?

No. It wasn't possible. No matter how angry Julia was at her sister, no matter how selfish and self-absorbed she might be, she would never put her family through this kind of prolonged torture. She might have stayed away a few hours to teach her sister a lesson, possibly even overnight. But not this long. Not this long. "No," Cindy said out loud. "Julia would never pull a stunt like this. She knows how worried we'd all be."

"Mom, wake up," Heather said forcefully. "The only person Julia has ever worried about is Julia. She . . ."

Whatever else Heather was about to say was lost as the palm of Cindy's hand came crashing down against the side of her daughter's face. Heather gasped, fell back, staggered to the ground.

"Oh, my baby, I'm so sorry," Cindy cried immediately, reaching for her daughter in the darkness, the sliver of moon spotlighting the trickle of blood slowly spreading across Heather's mouth like lipstick carelessly applied.

Heather recoiled from her mother's touch. "No, you're not." She pushed herself to her feet and ran up the back steps to the patio. "Face it, Mom," she said, clinging to the sliding glass door, "the only thing you're sorry about is that I'm standing here and Julia isn't." The simple sentence tumbled down the steps, then ricocheted off the damp grass to hit Cindy right between the eyes.

Cindy stood at the bottom of the outside steps, too weak to

move, too numb to fall. This must be what it feels like to be shot, she thought, as Heather disappeared inside the house. The moment right before you collapse.

Cindy looked up at the moon's thin arc, searching for stars in the cloud-carpeted sky. But if there were stars, they were hiding, she thought, her eyes drifting toward the house next door.

Faith was at her bedroom window, staring down at her. It was too dark to read the expression on her face.

NINETEEN

THE phone rang at seven o'clock the next morning, abruptly pulling Cindy out of a boxing ring in the middle of a close match with a faceless opponent. Blood seeped from her bandaged fingers as she stretched her hand toward the phone, the dream receding as she opened her eyes, disappearing altogether at the sound of her voice. "Hello," she said, trying to sound as if she'd been up for hours, and not, as was the case, as if she'd just fallen asleep.

"Cindy Carver?"

Cindy pushed herself into a sitting position as Elvis adjusted his position at her feet. "Who is this?"

"It's Elizabeth Kapiza from the *National Post.* First, let me say how very sorry I am about your daughter."

"What's happened?" Cindy grabbed for the remote control and turned on the television, rapidly flipping through the channels, her heart pounding wildly against her chest, as if trying to escape before the dreadful news descended.

"Nothing," Elizabeth Kapiza assured her quickly. "There's nothing new."

Cindy fell back against her pillows, fighting the urge to throw up, her forehead clammy and bathed in sweat.

"I don't know if you're familiar with my work," Elizabeth Kapiza was saying.

Cindy pictured the thirty-five-year-old woman with the pixie haircut and gold loop earrings that were her trademark smiling at her from the side of newspaper boxes across the city. "I know who you are." Everyone knew Elizabeth Kapiza, Cindy thought, even if they didn't read her columns. Her increasingly high profile was the result of a canny mixture of talent and self-promotion, achieved by carefully injecting herself into the middle of every tragedy she covered, be it a local case of child abuse or a case of international terrorism. In theory, she wrote human interest stories. In actual fact, she wrote about herself.

"I was wondering if I could come by and talk to you."

"It's seven o'clock in the morning," Cindy reminded her, glancing at the clock.

"Whenever it's convenient for you."

"What is it you want to talk about?"

"About Julia, of course," Elizabeth answered, the name sliding easily off her tongue, as if she'd known Julia all her life. "And you."

"Me?"

"What you're going through."

"You have no idea what I'm going through." Cindy brushed an unwanted tear away from her cheek, felt another one rush to take its place.

"That's what I need you to tell me," the woman urged gently.

Cindy shook her head, as if Elizabeth Kapiza could see her. "I don't think so."

"Please," the reporter said softly. "I can help you."

"By exploiting my daughter?"

"Cindy," Elizabeth Kapiza said, the name wrapping itself around Cindy's shoulder like a lover's arm, "the more publicity there is in cases like this, the more chance there is of a happy ending."

A happy ending, Cindy repeated silently. How long had it been since she'd believed in happy endings? "I'm sorry. I don't think there's anything I can tell you that would help."

"You're her mother," Elizabeth said simply.

"Yes," Cindy agreed, unable to find the strength to say more.

"Would you at least think about it, and call me if you change your mind?" Elizabeth Kapiza relayed her office telephone number, her home number, and the number of her cell phone, then repeated them all again as Cindy obligingly scribbled them across the bottom of a Kleenex box, although she had no intention of calling the woman back.

She barely had one foot out of bed when the phone rang again. This time it was a reporter from the *Globe and Mail,* calling for a quote. Cindy mumbled something about just wanting her daughter back home safe and sound, then mumbled roughly the same sentiments to the reporters from the *Star* and the *Sun,* both of whom phoned just after she'd emerged from the shower. *How long has your daughter been acting?* they asked. *What are some of her credits?*

Cindy combed her wet hair away from her face, then pulled on a pair of blue jeans and a white T-shirt, and went downstairs, Elvis running along ahead of her, impatiently pacing back and forth in front of the door as she opened it.

Julia's face stared up at her from the front pages of both the *Globe* and the *Star*. ACTRESS, 21, MISSING 6 DAYS, read the copy beneath the familiar black-and-white photograph. From the kitchen, the phone started ringing. Cindy ignored it as she walked into the room, and spread the papers across the table.

Police are investigating the disappearance of beautiful aspiring actress, Julia Carver, 21, missing since last Thursday. Ms. Carver, daughter of prominent enter-

tainment lawyer Tom Carver, vanished without a trace after a meeting with renowned Hollywood director Michael Kinsolving.

Cindy read the paragraph once, then read it again out loud as the phone continued its stubborn ringing.

" 'Police are investigating the disappearance of beautiful aspiring actress, Julia Carver, 21, missing since last Thursday. Ms. Carver, daughter of prominent entertainment lawyer Tom Carver. . . .' "

Cindy smiled, pushing the *Globe* out of the way, and reaching for the *Star*. The phone stopped ringing, started up again almost immediately.

ACTRESS GOES MISSING AFTER AUDITION WITH HOLLYWOOD DIRECTOR, read the caption underneath Julia's picture. *Julia Carver, 21, the beautiful actress-daughter of entertainment lawyer Tom Carver, has been missing from her Toronto home since Thursday, August 29.*

"No," Cindy said, reading it again, and then again.

Beautiful actress-daughter of entertainment lawyer Tom Carver.

Daughter of prominent entertainment lawyer Tom Carver.

As if Julia has only one parent, Cindy thought, a feeling of outrage growing inside her stomach, like a malignant tumor. When had she become nonexistent? When had she ceased to matter? It was almost as if, like her daughter, Cindy Carver had suddenly and without notice vanished from the face of the earth. The newspapers, with a couple of careless phrases, had erased her from the landscape, swept her from her daughter's life.

Once again, Tom had stolen Julia from her. This time, without even trying.

The press had made it official: Julia was Tom Carver's daughter.

Her mother was nowhere in sight.

The phone stopped ringing.

"I don't exist," Cindy told Elvis, whose response was to lift his leg and pee against the side of her chair. Cindy stared at her daughter's scruffy terrier, torn between crying and laughing out loud. "It's okay," she said, grabbing some paper towels from the counter and soaking up the mess, quietly accepting the blame for the dog's errant behavior. It was her fault, after all. She should have taken him out. *Everything* was her fault. She was as lousy a mother to Elvis as she'd been to Julia. "Julia Carver," she whispered, staring at her daughter's picture on the front pages of the papers, "daughter of Cindy. Daughter of *Cindy*, damn it." And I will not be brushed aside again, she added silently. I will not just disappear.

I don't think there's anything I can tell you that would help, she'd told Elizabeth Kapiza.

You're her mother.

"Yes, I am," Cindy said, pushing herself to her feet and walking to the phone, quickly punching in the last of the numbers she'd scribbled on the bottom of the Kleenex box earlier, and had no trouble recalling now. "Elizabeth Kapiza?" she asked the woman who answered on the first ring, as if she'd been waiting for Cindy to call. "This is Cindy Carver."

"When can I see you?" the reporter asked.

"How's nine o'clock?"

BY EIGHT-THIRTY, Cindy had changed her clothes three times and was on her fourth cup of coffee.

"You look nice," her mother told her, coming into the kitchen, neatly dressed in varying shades of blue. "Is that a new blouse?"

Cindy smoothed the front of a pink silk shirt she'd bought on impulse at Andrew's the previous summer, but had never worn because it wasn't really *her*. Was it her now that she was no longer a person of substance? she wondered, securing the button at the top. "You want some breakfast?"

"Coffee's fine for now," her mother said, helping herself. "Who's been phoning so early in the morning?"

"Who hasn't?"

Her mother shrugged. "I take it nothing's new."

Cindy pushed the morning papers toward her. "See for yourself."

Norma Appleton scanned the front pages of both papers. "Oh, my," she said, sinking into one of the kitchen chairs.

"Elizabeth Kapiza's coming to the house in half an hour to interview me."

"You think that's wise?"

"I phoned the police," Cindy told her mother. "They said they don't have a problem with it as long as I don't talk about the investigation. They said it might even help."

Her mother sipped her coffee slowly, ran shaking fingers along her granddaughter's grainy cheek. "Where's Heather off to so early?"

Cindy regarded her mother quizzically. What was she talking about?

"Where's Heather going?" Norma Appleton asked again.

"I don't understand."

It was her mother's turn to look confused. "When I got up, she was packing."

"Packing? What are you talking about?" Cindy ran into the front hall just as Heather appeared at the top of the stairs, an overnight bag in her hands. "What are you doing?"

"I thought I'd stay over at Daddy's for a few days," Heather said, proceeding slowly down the steps, dropping the black leather overnight bag to the floor as she reached the bottom. "Hi, Grandma." She waved to the woman watching from the kitchen doorway.

"Hi, sweetheart."

"Why are you doing this?" Cindy asked.

"What's going on?" Norma Appleton's eyes darted back and forth between her daughter and her grandchild.

"Things are pretty intense around here. I thought Mom could

use a little space," Heather explained. "And it's been a while since I spent any serious time at Dad's. It's just for a few days," she said again.

"Heather, please, if this is about last night. . . ."

"What happened last night?" her mother asked.

"I've already called Dad," Heather said. "He's picking me up in a few minutes."

"You know how sorry I am. You know I didn't mean to slap you."

"You slapped her?" her mother said.

"It's not that," Heather said.

"Then why are you going?"

Heather hesitated, her eyes filling with tears. "I just think it'll be better for everyone if we take a small break."

Cindy shook her head. "Not for me."

Heather hesitated, her body swaying toward her mother. "I've already called Dad."

"Call him back."

The doorbell rang.

"Please, darling," Cindy continued, following Heather to the front door. "Tell him you changed your mind. He'll understand."

Heather took a deep breath, opened the door.

"I take it you've seen the morning papers," Leigh said, her hair a war zone of conflicting curls. She dropped a small suitcase to the floor at Heather's feet.

"What's this?" Cindy eyed the beat-up, brown leather suitcase suspiciously.

"I've been calling you for over an hour. Either the phone is busy or nobody answers. I finally got fed up and told Warren that's it. I can't stand not knowing what's going on. He'll have to manage without me for a while. I'm moving in with you guys until we know what's what."

"No," Cindy said quickly. Then, "That's really not necessary."

"Heather and Duncan can sleep downstairs. I'm sure they won't mind. My back's too fragile for sofa beds."

"Actually, I'll be staying at my father's for a few days."

"Well, then, that worked out perfectly, didn't it?" Leigh said.

"No," Cindy protested again, as outside a car horn honked twice.

"That'll be Dad." Heather glanced out the open door as Tom's dark green Jaguar pulled into view.

"Please, Heather," Cindy tried one last time.

"Don't worry, Mom. It'll be okay. I'll call you later." Heather's lips brushed against her mother's cheek. Then she ran down the front steps, throwing her overnight bag into the backseat of her father's car, and climbing into the front seat beside him.

(Flashback: Julia carries her new Louis Vuitton luggage to Tom's waiting BMW, waits while he puts it inside the trunk, then slides into the front seat next to him.)

Cindy watched as Tom's car pulled away from the curb.

She was still standing at the front door staring down the empty street when Elizabeth Kapiza showed up at precisely nine o'clock, tape recorder in hand, photographer in tow.

THE NATIONAL POST   *Thursday, September 5, 2002*

A Mother's Anguish

BY ELIZABETH KAPIZA

TORONTO, SEPTEMBER 5 — She sits in the living room of her spacious, art-filled home in midtown Toronto, a woman whose pale face is ravaged by uncertainty and fear. Tears are never far from her expressive blue eyes; they stain the front of her stylish, pink silk blouse. "I'm sorry," she apologizes repeatedly, twisting an already shredded tissue in her lap. She offers me coffee and a bagel, inquires after my health, asks if I'm comfortable. A typical mother, I find myself thinking. Except sadly, Cindy Carver is anything but typical.

Because Cindy Carver is the mother of Julia Carver, the stunning twenty-one-year-old actress who went missing a week ago, and whose father is well-known entertainment lawyer Tom Carver, from whom Cindy has been divorced for seven years. Cindy smiles at the mention of her ex-husband's name, and it is obvious that whatever their past differences, their daughter's disappearance has brought them closer together.

It is also obvious that beauty runs in the family, for Cindy Carver, despite the anguish of her situation, is still, at forty-two, a very beautiful woman. As she perches on the end of one of two exquisitely appointed tan leather sofas, one can see traces of Julia in her face, in the tilt of her head, in the soft fullness of her lips, in the determination of her gaze. "My daughter *will* be coming home," she says, and I ache to believe her.

The odds, of course, aren't good. Young women who go missing rarely come home. Once lost, they are rarely found. And if they are, it is usually in shallow graves, after weeks, months, even years of soul-destroying searching. One has only to think of the grisly discoveries on that infamous pig farm in British Columbia, or the recent rash of kidnappings south of the border. One has only to mention the names Amber and Chandra. One has to pray that the name Julia will not be added to the list.

"What do you think has happened to your daughter?" I ask gently, thinking of my own daughter, age five, safe at home.

Cindy shakes her head, dislodging several fresh tears, unable to formulate a response, to say out loud what must surely be going through her mind, that her beloved firstborn child has fallen victim to the kind of senseless violence that is so much a part of big-city life, that her daughter's sweet smile might have been misinterpreted by a mind unhinged by alcohol and drugs, that her natural exuberance might have acted as a red flag waving in the face of insanity.

"Julia is so full of life," her mother says lovingly. "She's got all this energy, all this drive. You take one look at Julia and you know she's going to be a success at whatever she decides to do."

What she's decided to do, of course, is act. Julia, according to the woman who is her biggest fan, is an extremely gifted actress whose talent and beauty are matched only by her determination to succeed. Indeed, according to famed Hollywood director Michael Kinsolving, no stranger to beautiful, talented women, and the man for whom Julia not only auditioned on the morning of her disappearance, but who may have been the last person to have seen her, Julia had stardom written all over her. "An extraordinary talent," he confides later over cocktails. "Gorgeous, of course. But more than that. She has that extra something that defines a star."

What does Julia's mother think of the rumors swirling around the well-known ladies' man, rumors that hint at a possible romantic involvement between the aging Lothario and the young starlet? "Ridiculous," Cindy Carver scoffs succinctly. "They just met that morning." Does she give any credence to the speculation that Michael Kinsolving might somehow be involved in her daughter's disappearance? "I can't imagine . . ." she begins, her voice breaking.

Immediately, her mother and sister, both of whom are staying with Cindy until Julia comes home, rush to her side, smoothing several wayward hairs away from her face, wrapping her in their protective embrace. Families, I marvel, as I show myself to the door, anxious to get home to my daughter and her three-year-old brother. Already I picture their wondrous smiles as I walk through the door, their eager arms extended to welcome me home. How lucky I am, I think, aching to hold my babies in my arms. Tonight, when I tuck them into their beds, I will ask them to say a little prayer for Julia.

And one for her mother as well.

TWENTY

ON Saturday morning, another girl was reported missing.

Like Julia, she was described as tall, blond, and beautiful, although the photograph that ran on the front page of all four major Toronto papers revealed a slight cast in her left eye that made her appear slightly cross-eyed. Her name was Sally Hanson, and she was three years older than Julia, and maybe ten pounds heavier. Since her graduation from Queen's University two years earlier, she'd been working in the editorial department of *Toronto Life* magazine, and according to the hastily assembled remarks from a number of her coworkers, she was outgoing and popular.

Like Julia, Sally Hanson had recently broken up with her boyfriend, whom police were reportedly most anxious to contact. Apparently he'd taken off on his motorcycle around the same time Sally's worried parents were letting themselves into their daughter's empty apartment.

Like Julia, Sally had disappeared on a Thursday, and like Julia, Sally was a movie buff, having planned her vacation to coincide with the film festival. She'd bought thirty coupons and, according to her mother, she'd been looking forward to seeing three films a day, every day, for the ten days of the festival's duration. Among those films for which she had tickets was Michael Kinsolving's highly anticipated new movie, *Lost*.

And yet, police were downplaying the speculation that there was any connection between the two disappearances. *"We have no reason at all to suspect these two cases are related,"* someone named Lieutenant Petersen was quoted as saying. The *Globe* and the *Post* largely echoed that sentiment, while the *Star* printed a lengthy article comparing and contrasting the lives of the two young women and the events leading up to their disappearances. Only the *Sun* asked the obvious question: SERIAL KILLER STALKING TORONTO FILM FESTIVAL? it queried in headline type.

"Don't read that garbage," Leigh said, wresting the tabloid from Cindy's hands.

"Hey, give that back." Cindy jumped up from her seat at the kitchen table and reclaimed the paper before her sister could stuff it into the trash container under the sink.

"Really, Cindy. What's the point?" Leigh assumed their mother's once-familiar stance, legs spread shoulder-length apart, hands on her hips, chin lowered, eyes raised, as if she were peering up over the top of a pair of reading glasses. She was wearing an unflattering, sky blue track suit that flattened her bosom and widened her hips, and a matching blue headband that pulled her eyebrows into her forehead and made her look vaguely deranged.

"The point is I want to read it," Cindy said.

"What for? It'll only upset you."

Cindy shrugged. What else is new? the shrug said.

"It's all just speculation anyway," Leigh told her.

"I know that."

"I'm sure that if the police thought there was any connection between the two cases, they'd say so."

Cindy stared at her sister, trying to digest Leigh's latest pronouncement. When had Julia lost her humanity, become merely a "case"?

The phone rang.

"I'll get it." Leigh was instantly at the phone. "Hello?" Immediately her face darkened. "Who is this?"

"Who is it?" Cindy echoed.

"You sick fuck!" Leigh slammed the phone into its carriage.

"Who was that?" Cindy asked, more amused than alarmed by her sister's outburst. "Who was that?" she asked again, although she already knew the answer.

"What difference does it make? They're all the same."

"What'd this one say?"

"The usual crap."

"Such as?"

"*I have your daughter. I'm going to cut her up into little pieces.* Yada, yada."

Cindy shook her head, amazed, though no longer surprised, by the cruelty of others. The police had warned her about all the twisted minds out there, the perverts who feasted on other people's suffering, who wallowed in their misery. *Hang up,* they'd told her. *Better still, don't answer your phone.* Sometimes Cindy heeded their advice. Other times, she didn't.

Ten minutes later, the phone rang again.

"I'll get it," Cindy said, this time beating her sister to the phone.

"Honestly, Cindy, you almost knocked me down."

"Hello," Cindy said.

"Hi, yourself," the voice answered.

The voice was both husky and light, soothing and creepy, alien and familiar. An obvious attempt at disguise. Why? Was it someone she knew?

"Who is this?"

"Have you seen the morning papers?"

"Who is this?" Cindy repeated.

"They think Julia might be the victim of a serial killer."

"Who is it?" Leigh asked impatiently. "What's he saying?"

"It would serve her right," the voice continued. "Your daughter's a slut, Cindy. She's nothing but a cheap whore."

A sharp cry suddenly stabbed at the air, tore through the phone wires, pierced Cindy's ear.

"My God," Cindy said, feeling her face drain of blood as she identified the sound.

"For heaven's sake, Cindy," Leigh said, "hang up the damn phone."

Cindy held her breath, listened for the sound again. It didn't come, but it didn't matter. Cindy knew exactly what it was.

The sound of a baby crying.

"Faith?" Cindy whispered.

The phone went dead.

In the next second, Cindy was out of the kitchen and at her front door, Leigh following right behind.

"Where are you going? What are you doing?" her sister shouted after her, as Cindy ran down the steps and cut through the bushes into her neighbor's front yard.

Cindy felt Leigh's hand on her arm, tried shaking it away, but Leigh's fingers were like stubborn vines, refusing to be severed with a simple shrug. "Let go," Cindy hissed between tightly gritted teeth as she yanked her arm away.

"Cindy!" she heard Leigh shout as she raced up the front steps of the Sellick home, not looking back.

The door opened just as Cindy reached the top step. "Cindy!" Faith exclaimed, clearly surprised to see her. She closed the door behind her and adjusted the green corduroy Snuggly at her breasts. Inside it, Kyle was sleeping soundly, his eyes tightly closed, his lips sucking contentedly at his pacifier. "What's happened? Has there been any news?"

"Did you just call me?" Cindy asked.

"What?"

"Did you just call me?"

"Call you? No. Why?"

"You didn't just phone me?"

"What's going on?" Faith glanced past Cindy to Leigh, who was now standing at the bottom of the stairs.

Leigh lifted her hands into the air, as if to say, You tell me.

"Somebody just phoned my house. I heard a baby crying in the background."

"Well, no wonder you thought it was me." Faith smiled, tenderly stroking the top of her baby's head. "It wasn't Kyle. Believe it or not, he's been sleeping like an angel all morning. I really think we've turned a corner. Are you okay? You don't look so hot."

"Come on, Cindy," Leigh was saying. "We'll let the police handle it."

"The police?" Faith asked.

"They're tapping the phone."

"The police are tapping your phone? Why?"

"We've been getting a lot of crank calls," Leigh explained. "Which wouldn't happen so often," she continued, reaching for Cindy's hand, "if my sister would get Caller ID." She guided Cindy down the stairs toward the sidewalk. "We'll take the long way home, if you don't mind."

"I'm sorry I yanked your arm like that," Cindy said.

"Don't give it another thought."

"SHE ALMOST BROKE my arm, she yanked it so hard," Leigh told her mother as soon as she returned from walking the dog.

"You yanked your sister's arm?" their mother asked Cindy incredulously, following the dog into the kitchen. "Hmm, what smells so good?"

"I'm making a lemon cake," Leigh said.

"You shouldn't fight with your sister," her mother said with a shake of her head. "Honestly, I can't leave you girls alone for a minute."

The phone rang.

"Don't answer it," Leigh instructed.

"Maybe it's Julia," Cindy said hopefully.

"This wouldn't happen if you had Caller ID," her mother said.

Cindy picked up the phone, braced herself for the worst.

It was Meg. "How're you doing?" Her voice sounded rushed, as if she were talking while running. Which, of course, was exactly what she was doing, Cindy realized, picturing Meg racing along Bloor Street, trying to get from one movie to the next as quickly as she could, desperate not to miss anything. The festival had been up and running for two days now, and although neither Meg nor Trish had so much as mentioned the festival, Cindy knew they were going without her.

Life goes on, she understood, wishing she could press a button, freeze time as easily as she could freeze an image on her television screen.

She knew she shouldn't judge Meg and Trish harshly. Her friends couldn't be expected to drop everything, abandon all their plans, put their lives on hold, because of something that didn't directly concern them. She shouldn't resent them for enjoying themselves, for laughing, for forgetting about her for hours at a stretch. She shouldn't, she thought. But she did.

"I read in the paper about that other missing girl," Meg said, as a car honked in the background. "What do the police really think?"

Cindy shook her head, said nothing.

"Look, you must be going stir-crazy over there. Why don't you come to a movie with us?"

"A movie?"

"I know it sounds frivolous, and I don't mean to sound insensitive. I just think it might be a good idea for you to get out of the house for a while, get some fresh air, get away from your mother, take your mind off everything."

"You think it's that easy?"

Meg sighed the sigh of the deliberately misunderstood. "Of course it's not that easy. I didn't mean to imply. . . ."

"I know. I'm sorry."

"Will you think about it?"

"Sure," Cindy said, although she had no intention of doing so.

"Call me on my cell. I'll keep it on all day."

Cindy smiled, recalling how enraged festival patrons got whenever anyone's cell phone rang during a screening.

"I love you," Meg said.

"I love you too."

Her mother and sister were staring at her from across the room, their bodies tensed to take action at the first sign of distress. Ever since Cindy had fainted, their eyes were on constant vigil, never allowing her far out of their reach. She wondered whether anyone would ever look at her the way they used to—without pity, without sadness, without fear.

Cindy shook her head, trying to rid her brain of such depressing thoughts. Meg was right—she was going stir-crazy. She needed air.

"I'm going upstairs to shower," her mother said. "Why don't you lie down for a while?"

"Because I'm not tired," Cindy said.

"You're sure?" Leigh asked as their mother left the room.

Cindy sank into one of the kitchen chairs, watched as her sister began preparing the icing for the cake. "You don't have to do this, you know."

"I know."

"Have you spoken to Warren today?"

"Of course."

"I'm sure he's wondering when you're coming home."

"He's fine. He'll be over later."

Cindy nodded. "Is everything all right?"

"What do you mean?"

"Between the two of you?"

"Of course it's all right," Leigh said. "Why wouldn't it be all right?"

"I don't know. I'm just asking."

"Everything's fine."

"Good."

"Warren's a good man. Not the most exciting man in the world, maybe. Not like Tom. . . ."

"Thank goodness."

"But he's sweet and he's decent, and he'd never cheat on me."

"I didn't mean to imply. . . ."

"I don't understand why you'd ask me something like that."

"I'm sorry. I honestly didn't mean. . . ."

"It's just this damn wedding. You know. People get tense."

"I'm sure."

"It's a huge expense, and we're not getting any help from the groom's parents. I've told you."

"Yes."

"So there's bound to be tension. Especially now, with Julia missing, and everything so up in the air."

"I'm sorry."

"There's nothing to be sorry for. We're fine."

"Good."

The doorbell rang.

"I'll get it," Cindy said, walking briskly to the front door, trying to sort out in her mind what had just happened.

"Check who it is before you open the door," Leigh called after her.

It was the police. Cindy held her breath as she tried reading the expressions on their faces.

"Can we come in?" Detective Bartolli asked.

"Oh God." Cindy fell back into the house, covered her mouth with her hand, as Leigh rushed to her side.

"What's happened?" Leigh asked, as Cindy struggled to stay upright.

"It's all right," Detective Gill assured the two women quickly. "We've just come to fill you in on what's been happening."

"Julia . . . ?"

"There's nothing new."

"Can we come in?" Detective Bartolli asked again as Elvis bounded down the stairs to jump against his thighs.

Cindy led the two men into the living room, motioned for them to sit down. Above her head, Cindy could hear the water from the shower running through the pipes.

"I assume you've heard about the Hanson girl," Detective Gill stated as he lowered himself onto one of the tan leather sofas.

"Do you think there's any connection?" Cindy asked.

"We have no reason at this time to assume the two incidents are related," came the automatic response from Detective Bartolli.

"But you think there's a chance?"

"It's a possibility," Detective Gill admitted. "We're looking into it."

"How exactly are you doing that?" Leigh asked.

The detectives exchanged glances, ignored the question. "We've had several conversations with Sean Banack," Detective Bartolli said.

"And?"

"We're still checking out his alibi for last Thursday. Unfortunately, because we don't know the exact time your daughter disappeared . . ."

"We know it was between eleven-fifteen and four-thirty," Cindy said.

"Yes, but that's a lot of time to account for. Sean can account for his whereabouts for part of the day, but not all."

"Then arrest him."

"We need evidence to arrest him, Mrs. Carver."

"That story he wrote. . . ."

"Not enough."

"We've had someone watching him," Detective Gill said.

"And?"

"So far, nothing."

"Have you talked to Lindsey Krauss?"

Detective Bartolli checked his notes. "Yes. And to the other names on the list your husband gave us."

"Ex-husband," Cindy said.

"Ex-husband, yes. Sorry about that." The detective smiled sheepishly, scratched at his ear. "The consensus among several of Julia's friends is that she was involved with a married man."

"That's ridiculous," Leigh said.

Cindy said nothing.

"Cindy?" her sister said.

"Have you talked to Ryan Sellick?" Cindy asked.

"He denies any romantic involvement with your daughter."

"Do you believe him?"

"Is there some reason we shouldn't?"

Cindy shrugged, filling the policemen in on everything that had taken place in the last week between herself and the Sellicks. She watched Detective Gill dutifully jot this information down, and wondered whether she really believed Ryan and Julia were having an affair, whether Faith had phoned her earlier, whether either one could have played a part in her daughter's disappearance. "What about Michael Kinsolving?" she asked.

"We have no evidence to suggest he was in any way involved."

"He left town right after he saw Julia," Cindy reminded them.

"He claims he was in the country, scouting locations."

"And? Was he?"

"We're still checking into that."

Cindy lowered her head. "So, basically what you're telling me is that we're no farther ahead than we were last week. Except now, another girl has disappeared."

"Mrs. Carver . . ."

"I know. There's no reason to assume the two cases are connected."

An hour later, Cindy was lying on her bed, looking through her festival catalog. In the section marked *Masters,* she found a photograph of what appeared to be an ambulance or a police car racing along a dark, metropolitan street, the deliberately blurred image bathed in an eerie orange-red light, a woman's darkened silhouette in the foreground. The notes underneath it read: **Lost,** *Michael Kinsolving's sensational new film deals with the underside of contemporary society, with disaffected youth and the appalling generation who created and raised them. We meet Catherine, age twenty-two and already a seasoned con artist, and her sister, Sarah, five years her junior, addicted to cocaine and men old enough to be her father.*

Cindy closed the book, rifled through the envelope of movie coupons Meg had left for her, then scanned the *Volkswagen Guide to the Festival Official Film Schedule* booklet, locating the listing for *Lost.* Tonight at seven-fifteen at the Uptown I, she read, reaching for the phone.

"Hello?" Meg answered, her voice a hoarse whisper. "Cindy?"

Cindy pictured Meg crouching down in her seat in the darkened theater, felt the angry glares of the people sitting around her.

"I'll meet you inside the theater at seven," Cindy said, then hung up before she had a chance to change her mind.

TWENTY-ONE

THE Uptown 1 was already filled to capacity by the time Cindy arrived at just after seven o'clock that evening. She searched through the dim light of the large, old-fashioned auditorium for her friends, praying she wouldn't run into anyone else she knew. She could only imagine what they might say. *Can you believe it? Her daughter's been missing for over a week, God only knows what's happened to her, and she's out galavanting around. She's going to the movies!*

And they'd be right, Cindy thought, wondering what the hell she was doing here. Did she seriously think she'd glean anything of significance from Michael Kinsolving's new film? That there'd be hidden clues pointing to her daughter's whereabouts? That she'd gain insight into the director's tortured psyche? Or had she merely been desperate to get out of the house? Away from her mother, her sister, the dog? *What is my objective?* she asked herself, twisting sharply around, fleeing the crowded auditorium for the equally crowded lobby, coming to an abrupt halt in front of a long table covered with sushi and exotic sandwiches.

"Can I help you?" A young woman stared at her expectantly from behind the food-laden table.

Cindy suddenly realized she was ravenously hungry, not having eaten anything since breakfast, despite Leigh's constant efforts to stuff food down her throat. She'd pleaded exhaustion when Warren invited them all out for dinner, insisting her mother and sister go without her, then vaulted from the house the minute they were gone. She'd left them a note—*Needed some air. Back by ten,* she'd scribbled—so they wouldn't worry. Although they'd worry anyway, she knew, guilt sitting heavy in her chest, like heartburn. She'd grab a sandwich and head straight for home, she decided now. Coming here had been a mistake. What had she been thinking? "What kind of sandwich is that?" she asked the pale-faced young woman whose name tag identified her as a festival volunteer.

"Tomato, Havarti cheese, and avocado on whole wheat."

Cindy nodded her approval, her mouth watering as she reached inside her purse for some money.

"I'll get that," a man said from somewhere behind her, and Cindy turned to see Neil Macfarlane.

"Where did you come from?" Cindy said, startled by his unexpected presence. What was he doing here?

Neil motioned toward the inside auditorium. "We're sitting near the back. Meg was just about to call you when you went running out."

"I didn't realize you'd be here."

"Trish had an extra ticket." Dimples creased the skin around Neil's mouth as his lips flirted with a smile. "She called me, told me you were coming. I hope you don't mind. If it makes you at all uncomfortable. . . ."

"It doesn't."

"Good." He took her elbow, led her toward a relatively quiet corner of the old lobby, whose walls were the color of dark blood. "I've called a few times. . . ."

"Yes, I know. I'm really sorry I haven't returned your messages." I wanted to call you, she thought. So many times. "It's been so crazy," she said.

"You don't have to explain."

"Thank you." Cindy smiled, fought the urge to caress his cheek. Had his eyes always been so blue? she wondered, before deliberately looking away.

"Are you ready to go back inside?"

Cindy straightened her shoulders, took a deep breath. "Ready or not."

It was completely dark in the auditorium as Neil led Cindy up the steep rows of stairs to where Meg and Trish were sitting near the back of the theater. The two friends greeted her with prolonged hugs and kisses.

"You okay?" Meg grabbed Cindy's hand and held it tightly in her lap. "I'm so glad you came."

"We were afraid you'd bolted," Trish said.

"I thought about it."

"You don't mind . . . about Neil?" she whispered.

"I don't mind."

"Ssh," said several nearby voices as a large spotlight jumped across the stage, ultimately coming to rest on a solitary figure standing to the left of the giant screen.

"Hello, I'm Richard Pearlman, and I'm one of the organizers of this year's festival," the casually dressed young man announced to a smattering of light applause. "First, I want to thank our sponsors," he said, gamely naming each one in turn. "Tonight, we are extremely privileged to be hosting the North American premiere of Michael Kinsolving's amazing new movie, *Lost,* a film of astonishing power and resonance. We are also honored to have Michael Kinsolving here with us this evening."

A pleased gasp trickled through the audience, like a breeze through a wheatfield.

"Ladies and gentlemen . . . Michael Kinsolving."

The applause was heartfelt and enthusiastic as the famed Hollywood director in his trademark black T-shirt and tight jeans, hopped onto the stage and waved. Then he cupped his right hand over his eyes, and stared out at the audience.

Can he see me? Cindy wondered, torn between leaning forward and sinking low in her seat.

"I hope you still feel like clapping after you see the film," Michael said to much laughter. "Anyway, what can I say? I love this festival. I love this city. As you may know, I'm planning to film my next movie here." Another burst of applause. "We tried to do something a little different with *Lost,* so I hope you don't mind. Anyway, I'll be available for a Q&A after the film." More applause. "Enjoy."

He jumped from the stage and the spotlight promptly evaporated. Enjoy, Cindy repeated silently as a haunting musical refrain began swirling about her head, and the screen filled with a group of ghostly, seminude dancers, whose arms and legs were painted in the black-and-white stripes of a movie clapboard, an arresting series of images that were part of this year's festival's logo. After several more promos, the movie began.

Cindy sank back in her chair as Meg squeezed her hand. What am I doing here? she wondered again, as the credits rolled across a deserted inner-city street. What do I hope to achieve? *What is my objective?*

(Documentary Footage: Cindy, in the bedroom of the house on Balmoral Avenue, the month before Tom packs his bags and moves out. It's a few minutes after 10 P.M. and he's just come home. Cindy has been waiting for him all night, intent on putting their marriage back on track, ready to accept at least part of the blame for its derailment. It's possible she's been too demanding, too critical, too angry all the time, as Tom is always saying. They've been married for seventeen years, nearly half her life.

They were children when they eloped. Her entire adult life has been interlocked with his. Could she survive without him? And what of their two beautiful daughters, daughters who would be devastated should she fail to make things right between them? While she finally recognizes that she can't change her husband's behavior, she can certainly change her own. She can show Tom the love and respect he needs, even if he is not always deserving of either. To that end, she is wearing a new, short, red satin night-gown and pointy-toed shoes with skinny stiletto heels, the kind he's always admired on other women.

He pleads exhaustion as she burrows into his arms and tugs at his tie. She can smell another woman's perfume on his skin. Stub-bornly, even recklessly, Cindy closes her eyes, covers her husband's lips with her own. She tastes another woman's lipstick, and fights the urge to gag, determined to ignore the bile rising in her throat, as Tom's body slowly, reluctantly, begins to respond to her minis-trations. Soon, they are on the bed and he is unzipping his pants, lifting up her nightgown, although he doesn't look at her, has barely looked at her since he walked into the room, as if she no longer exists for him, as if she no longer exists at all. Can you see me? Cindy wonders, feeling herself shrink beneath his weight, be-come less visible, less viable, with each mindless thrust of his hips. "Look at me," she demands suddenly, grabbing his chin in her hands, forcing his eyes to hers, the fierceness in her voice catching them both by surprise. Immediately she feels him grow soft. He pulls away from her in disgust.

She tries to apologize, to explain, but apologies and explana-tions lead only to recriminations, recriminations to accusations, accusations to more accusations. They end up fighting, the same fight they've been having for weeks, months, years. "What do you hope to achieve when you say things like that?" he asks. "I mean, really, Cindy. *What is your objective?"*)

I don't know, Cindy acknowledged now, watching as a young

woman's face overtook the screen, light bouncing off her long black hair, so that it sparkled like diamonds against the night sky. Her full lips were open and trembling. Huge, coffee-colored eyes scanned the desolate street.

I don't know anything anymore, Cindy thought, following the young woman on the screen into a run-down diner, noticing the hungry looks from the men and boys already inside.

"Has anyone here seen Julia?" the girl asked the decidedly motley crew.

Cindy gasped, clutched her stomach, the sandwich in her lap dropping to the floor.

"What's wrong?" Neil leaned forward as Meg's hand tightened its grip on Cindy's fingers.

"Jimmy doesn't come around much these days," someone answered.

Jimmy, Cindy realized, collapsing forward in her seat, the air rushing from her lungs as if she'd been sucker-punched. Jimmy. Not Julia.

"Are you okay?" Trish asked.

Cindy nodded, unable to find her voice.

"I'll get you another sandwich," Neil offered.

"No," Cindy whispered hoarsely, her appetite gone. "It's all right."

"Ssh," someone said from the row behind.

The rest of the movie passed in a merciful blur. Cindy saw a succession of faces, a panorama of flesh. Raised voices, loud sighs, long silences. Sex, drugs, and rock 'n' roll. Love and pain, and the whole damn thing. When it was over, the entire audience jumped to its feet, hooting and hollering its prolonged approval. "I think he finally has another hit," Meg exclaimed, sitting back down, clapping wildly.

Cindy realized that, although her eyes had never left the screen, she hadn't absorbed a single frame. Although she'd heard each word, she couldn't recall a single one. If there'd been anything of value to be gleaned by being here, she'd missed it. She'd missed everything. As usual.

The lights came up. Richard Pearlman vaulted back to the stage. "Ladies and gentlemen, once again I give you Michael Kinsolving."

The director acknowledged the deafening ovation with a modest bow. "Does that mean you approve?"

The audience roared. Loud whistles pierced the air.

"Thank you," Michael said, clearly reveling in the sound. "You're very kind."

The applause abated as Richard Pearlman leaned his lanky torso into the microphone. "Michael's generously agreed to answer some questions." He peered into the audience.

Can he see me? Cindy thought. Can anybody see me?

"Yes," Richard Pearlman said. "You, there, in the middle."

A heavyset woman in stretch leopard-print pants scrambled to her feet. "First, I want to congratulate you on a brilliant film. And I couldn't help but be struck by the parallels to Dante . . ."

"Show-off," Trish muttered.

"What parallels to Dante?" Meg asked.

"And I wondered whether you were consciously going after something more literary with this film?" the woman continued.

"More literary?" the director repeated, obviously tickled by the question. "First time I've ever been accused of that."

The audience laughed.

Richard Pearlman pointed to a man in the second row. "Yes?"

"How long did it take you to shoot the film?"

"A little over three months."

"Where did you find the lead actress?" a woman shouted, not bothering to wait her turn.

"Monica Mason, yes. She was great, wasn't she?"

More applause.

"I wish I could say that I discovered her sitting at the soda fountain at Schwab's, or tell you one of those apocryphal Holly-wood stories you always hear about, but the truth is that she was just one of dozens of very talented young actresses who auditioned for the part. Her agent sent her over one afternoon, she read for us, and that was that. Nothing very dramatic, I'm afraid."

Richard Pearlman pointed to a middle-aged woman in the upper right corner of the theater. "Yes?"

"Speaking of dramatic stories," the woman began, "do you know anything about what's happening with the police investigation into the two missing girls?"

"Oh, my God," Cindy whispered. Was this what she'd been waiting for? Was this the reason she was here?

"No," Michael answered curtly. "I don't know any more than you do."

"I understand one of the girls is an actress," the woman continued.

"Yes, I believe that's true."

"Didn't she audition for you the morning she disappeared?"

"I believe she did, yes." Michael scratched uncomfortably at the tip of his nose, looked to Richard Pearlman for help.

"Could we confine your questions to the wonderful movie we've just seen?" Richard asked. "Thank you." He pointed to another woman on his left.

"How does it feel to be the subject of a police investigation? Do you feel like you're in the middle of one of your own movies?"

Michael laughed, but the laugh was strained. "A bit, yes. Any more questions about *Lost*?"

"If they find her, you should give her the part," a man shouted out from the last row. "Then you'd have that apocryphal Holly-wood story to tell us next time."

"That's true," Michael conceded as the audience laughed.

An apocryphal Hollywood story, Cindy thought, feeling sick to her stomach. Her daughter's disappearance reduced to an amusing anecdote for the film cognoscenti. "I have to get out of here," she said, jumping to her feet, Neil right beside her.

"Are you all right?" Meg asked.

"I have to go."

"We'll come too," Trish offered.

"No."

"I'll take her home," Neil said.

"We'll come with you," Meg insisted, following after them down the stairs.

"No," Cindy said forcefully, spinning around. "Please."

Meg stopped, tears filling her eyes. "You're sure?"

Cindy nodded. "I'll call you tomorrow."

"The gentleman in the third row," Richard Pearlman was saying as Cindy and Neil clambered down the steps and into the lobby.

The man's voice trailed after her. "Has being questioned by the police changed your opinion about Toronto?"

An hour later, Cindy was quietly ushering Neil inside her front hall. "I think everyone's asleep," she whispered. "Can I get you anything? Something to drink?"

"I'm fine," he whispered back.

"Follow me." Cindy tiptoed down the stairs leading to the bottom floor, cringing at each creak of the floor beneath her feet, feeling like a teenager sneaking home after curfew. "Can you see okay?" she asked, relying on the half-moon peeking through the windows to guide them, reluctant to turn on any lights.

"I'm fine," he said again, settling in beside her on the family room sofa.

"Thanks for dinner." Cindy was glad it was too dark to make out the stains on the old brown corduroy couch, a couch that pulled out into a queen-size bed, Cindy thought, and felt her face flush. "I was hungrier than I realized."

And suddenly she was moving toward him, taking his face in her hands and drawing his lips toward hers, then kissing him full on the mouth, her tongue seeking his, her arms wrapping around him, crushing him tightly against her, her hands burying themselves in his hair, pulling him closer, as if there were still too much space between them, her legs curling around his hips, as if she could somehow manage to climb out of her own body and escape into his, as if she needed the air in his lungs to breathe.

"Oh God," she cried, abruptly pulling away and pushing herself toward the far end of the sofa. "What am I doing? What's the matter with me?"

"It's all right, Cindy. It's all right."

"It's not all right. I was all over you."

"Cindy," Neil said, trying to calm her, "you didn't do anything wrong."

"What you must think of me."

Neil stared at her through the semidarkness. "I think you're the most beautiful, most courageous woman I know," he said softly.

"Courageous?" Cindy swiped at the tears now falling the length of her cheeks. "Courage implies choice. I didn't choose any of this."

"Which makes you all the more courageous in my book."

Cindy stared wistfully at the man beside her. Where had he come from? Were there really men like this in the world? "Make love to me," she said. Then more forcefully, "I really need for you to make love to me."

Neil said nothing. He simply reached for her, strong arms surrounding her like a cape. He kissed her once, then again and again, tender kisses, like the gentle flutter of a butterfly's wings against her skin, then deeper, his touch sure, unhurried, deliberate, as he began to caress and undress her. She felt the warmth of his fingers, the cool wetness of his tongue, and cried out with joy when he entered her, urgency replacing delicacy as he rocked inside her.

Gradually, almost reluctantly, she felt her body building to a climax and tried hard to fight it, to prolong the moment as long as humanly possible, until it was no longer something she could control, and she cried out again, her nails digging into the flesh of his back, her fingers clinging to him as if he were a life preserver in a treacherous ocean. Seconds later, they collapsed against one another, their bodies bathed in a thin coating of sweat.

"Are you all right?" Neil asked after a silence of several seconds.

"Are you kidding?" Cindy asked in return, then laughed out loud.

Neil laughed with her, kissed her forehead, gathered her inside his arms.

"Thank you," Cindy said.

"Now who's kidding?"

He kissed her again, drawing her back against the well-stuffed pillows, their bodies folding comfortably together, their breathing steady and rhythmic.

And then there were footsteps shuffling above their heads, and upstairs' lights being turned on, and familiar voices sliding down the banister. "I told you there's no one here," Cindy's mother was saying as Elvis began barking beside her.

"And I'm telling you I heard something," Leigh argued. "Hello? Hello?"

"Hello?" Norma Appleton echoed. "Is someone there?"

The dog raced down the steps, bounded into the family room.

"Oh, for Pete's sake," Cindy said, fending off Elvis's eager paws as she scrambled into her clothes.

"Cindy? Cindy, is that you?"

"It's me, Mom," Cindy called out, pulling her T-shirt over her head as Elvis jumped against Neil's thighs. "It's all right. You don't have to come down."

"What are you doing downstairs?" Two sets of footsteps headed for the stairs.

"Please don't come down," Cindy urged, pulling her slacks over her hips, knowing such exhortations were futile, that it was only a matter of seconds before her mother and sister peeked their heads into the room. "I can't believe this," she whispered to Neil, who was hurriedly tucking his shirt inside his pants. "It's like when I was fifteen and she caught me making out with Martin Crawley."

"What do you mean, don't come down?" Leigh was asking, her voice edging closer. "What are you doing down here in the dark?" Her hand reached into the room, flipped on the switch for the overhead light, her eyes taking a second to adjust to the sudden brightness, another second to adjust to the fact that Cindy wasn't alone. "Oh."

"What's going on down here?" Norma Appleton asked.

"I think maybe we should go back upstairs," Leigh ventured, trying to back out of the room.

But her mother was already blocking her exit. "Don't be silly. What's . . . ? Oh." She stared at Neil Macfarlane. "I'm sorry, Cindy. I didn't realize you had company."

"You remember Neil," Cindy ventured meekly.

"Yes, of course," her mother said. "How are you, Neil?"

"I'm fine, thank you, Mrs. Appleton."

"Hi," Leigh offered weakly.

"Nice to see you again," Neil said.

Nobody moved.

"I guess I should probably go," Neil said finally.

"Please don't leave on our account," Norma Appleton said.

"It's late. I really should get going."

"I'll walk you to the door." Cindy followed him up the stairs. She, in turn, was trailed by her mother, her sister, and the dog.

Cindy closed the front door behind her as she walked Neil to his car. "I don't suppose I'll hear from you again," she said, smiling as he leaned over to kiss her good night.

"Was Martin Crawley so easily deterred?"

Cindy smiled, waited until his car disappeared down the street before turning back to the house. The front door opened just as she was reaching for it, her mother and sister waiting on the other side, Elvis between them.

"Sort of like old times," her mother said with a smile.

"I'll make us some tea," said Leigh.

TWENTY-TWO

HAVE you seen a copy of this morning's *Sun*?" Meg asked Cindy, at barely seven o'clock Monday morning.

It had been eleven days since Julia went missing.

Cindy lowered the phone in her hand and stared at Elvis, who was waiting for her by the front door. "No. I haven't been out yet. I was just about to take the dog for a walk when you called."

"Maybe you should let someone else take him," Meg suggested.

"Why? What are you getting at? What's in the *Sun* that you don't think I should see?"

"I just think you should be prepared."

"For what? Has another girl disappeared?" There'd been nothing in the other papers about any more disappearances.

"There's a picture of Julia on the front page," Meg said.

"Again?"

"It's a different picture. She's . . . well, it's pretty suggestive. And there are more pictures inside. I don't know where they got them. . . ."

Cindy dropped the receiver, ran for the door.

"Cindy?" she heard Meg's voice call after her. "Cindy, are you there?"

Elvis barked in angry protest as Cindy slammed the door behind her and ran down the street. What was Meg talking about? What picture? She'd only given the police that one head shot of Julia. Where could they have gotten more? "What pictures, damn it?" she asked out loud, hurling herself at the newspaper box on the corner, recoiling in horror at the full-page photograph of her daughter that stared back at her with almost deliberate provocation.

Julia was staring directly into the camera lens, her eyes challenging the viewer. She was wearing only the bottom half of a black string bikini, her hands cupped coyly over high, bare breasts. JULIA'S LOST JEWELS, the caption beside the picture read.

Cindy stumbled back on her heels as if she'd been struck. It was one of the photographs she'd found in Sean's apartment, photographs Tom had stuffed inside the pocket of his beige linen pants. How had the paper gotten its hands on it? And what of the other pictures inside? Were they part of the same collection?

She reached into her pocket for some change, realized she'd forgotten to bring any, and slammed her fist on the top of the red metal box in frustration. She cast a wary glance over each shoulder to make sure no one was watching, then kicked at the side of the box, and jiggled its handle, trying to force it open. The damn thing refused to budge. "Shit!" she yelled, spinning around in helpless circles.

A woman walking a small white dog rounded the corner at Lynwood. "Excuse me," Cindy called to her. "I don't suppose you have some spare change for the paper? I could pay you back later."

The woman's eyes narrowed, as if she'd just been approached by a foul-smelling panhandler, and she promptly picked up her dog and crossed to the other side of the street.

"Great," Cindy muttered, racing back down Balmoral toward

her house, hearing Elvis barking all the way down the street. "Okay, okay," she said, opening her door and trying to keep the dog from knocking her down as she rifled through her purse for some change. "Okay, you can come," she told the dog, grabbing his leash, heading back out the door.

"What's all the commotion?" her mother called from the top of the stairs.

"I'm just getting the paper," Cindy said. "Go back to sleep."

She hurried down the steps and along Balmoral to Avenue Road. But Elvis refused to be rushed, stopping repeatedly to sniff at the grass and lift his leg. "Come on. Come on. We haven't got all day."

Cindy stopped abruptly, the absurdity of what she'd just said hitting her square in the forehead, as if she'd just walked into a brick wall. *We haven't got all day?* All day was exactly what she had. And the day after that. And the day after that. How many days? she wondered, importuning the cloudless sky. How many more awful, blank days waiting to be filled? How many more endless days spent in aimless, if frantic, pursuit of her daughter? How many more useless meetings with police, well-meaning conversations with friends, sadistic phone calls from strangers? How many more such days could she tolerate? How many more could she survive?

As many as it takes, Cindy understood, continuing toward the corner. What choice did she have? "No choice, no control," she told the dog as he lifted his rump into the air and dropped several steaming turds into the middle of the sidewalk. "That's just great," she said, realizing she'd forgotten to bring a plastic bag. She looked helplessly up and down the street, wondering what to do. What *could* she do? She wasn't about to pick it up with her hands. "I'll come back later," she apologized to the empty street, stepping around the unsightly pile, pulling Elvis after her before he could do more damage.

She reached the newspaper box at the same time as an immaculately dressed, middle-aged man, who nodded hello as he dropped the appropriate coinage into the slot and pulled out a paper, his fingers unconsciously folding across her daughter's partially exposed breasts. Cindy felt a scream rising in her throat, and turned away. "Have a nice day," the man said in parting.

Cindy's eyes trailed after him. Did he know anything about her daughter's disappearance? He obviously lived in the area, had probably seen Julia around. He was neatly dressed to the point of fastidiousness, nattily bland, unnecessarily polite. Middle-aged. Repressed. Probably lived alone, or with his mother. Exactly the type you always read about, the quiet ones, the ones with smiles on their lips and mayhem in their hearts.

Men like him were everywhere, Cindy thought as she dropped her money in the slot and reached inside the box for the paper. She couldn't look at a man anymore without wondering whether he knew something about Julia, whether he'd seen her, or talked to her, or plotted her harm. Every stranger was a possible fiend; every friend a possible foe. How well do we really know anybody?

How well do we know ourselves?

Cindy's thoughts drifted to Neil, to the events of last Saturday night. Again she felt his arms around her, his lips on hers, his hands in her hair, on her breasts, between her legs. She felt him moving inside her, and even now, it felt wonderful. To lose herself so completely in the moment, to forget for a brief spasm of time what else she might have lost. Followed by the dog's paws on her bare thighs, the priceless looks on the faces of her mother and sister, the reassuring smile in Neil's eyes as he kissed her good night. The Lord giveth, she found herself thinking, as she stared at the picture of her daughter in the morning paper, trying to make sense of what she was seeing.

And the Lord taketh away.

More pictures, page 3.

Cindy flipped the page over, gasped when she saw two more familiar photos—one of Julia wearing a push-up bra and matching thong, the other of Julia in profile, her elbow pressing against the curve of her naked breast, the bare cheeks of her round bottom playing peekaboo with the camera.

How did the *Sun* get these pictures? Was it possible Sean had duplicates, that he'd sold the negatives to the tabloid? She stuffed more coins into the box, pulling out the last remaining copies of the paper, and running with them along the street, feeling one of her sandals suddenly connect with something squishy. "Oh, shit!" she yelled, sliding to a stop, knowing exactly what she'd stepped in. "Serves me right," she shouted. "Serves me goddamn right." She ripped off her sandal, the bottom of which was covered in dog poop, and hurled it into the middle of the road.

"Where's your sandal?" her mother asked as Cindy limped into the kitchen several minutes later on only one shoe.

Cindy waved the question aside as she spread the papers across the kitchen table, then walked to the phone, asked information for the number of the *Toronto Sun*.

"Oh, my," her mother whispered, staring at the pictures. Then again, "Oh, my."

"I need to speak to Frank Landau," Cindy said, checking the name under the article that accompanied the racy pictures of her daughter.

"This is Frank Landau," a man answered seconds later.

"Where did you get those pictures of my daughter?"

"Excuse me?"

"The pictures of Julia Carver. Where did you get them?"

"Mrs. Carver?"

"I will sue your goddamn paper. I will sue you personally. . . ."

"Mrs. Carver, wait. Wait. Calm down. Please."

"Don't tell me to calm down. Tell me how you got those pictures."

There was a long pause. By the time the reporter answered, Cindy knew what he was going to say. "I got them from your ex-husband," he told her evenly. "Tom Carver hand-delivered them to me in person yesterday afternoon."

"WHERE IS HE?" Cindy demanded as she pushed through the door to Tom's office at just after one o'clock that afternoon.

Irena Ruskin jumped to her feet behind her appropriately cluttered desk. "He's not here. Wait," she called, scrambling after Cindy into Tom's inner office. "Mrs. Carver! Cindy!"

Cindy spun around, absorbing the faithful secretary in a single glance. Her hair was still the same unsubtle shade of blond, although a few inches longer than Cindy last remembered it, possibly to hide the scars of her most recent plastic surgery, Cindy thought unkindly, wondering whether the woman chose her wardrobe to coordinate with the dark blue of the two chairs in front of the massive oak desk. "Where is he?"

"He's in a meeting."

"He's been in that meeting since nine o'clock this morning."

"I gave him all your messages."

"I need to speak to him, Irena. It's pretty urgent or I wouldn't be here."

"Cindy. . . ."

"Could you get him for me? Please?"

"Was that Cindy Carver I just saw walk by?" a man's voice asked from the doorway.

Cindy took a deep breath, forced herself to smile as she extended her hand to one of her ex-husband's law partners. "Hello, Alan. How are you?"

"I'm well. How are holding up?"

"Today isn't a great day." Cindy marveled at her use of understatement. She might even have laughed had Alan Reynolds not looked quite so earnest. "I'm sure you saw the pictures in the *Sun.*"

Alan Reynolds nodded. "You're waiting for Tom, I take it."

"Apparently he's stuck in one of those all-day meetings." Cindy glanced at Irena, who nodded uncomfortably.

"Really? Well, they must be taking a break. I just saw him talking to Mitchell Pritchard. Let me see if I can get him for you."

"I'd appreciate that."

"Can I get you anything in the meantime? A cup of coffee? Some water, perhaps?"

"Nothing, thank you."

"Has there been any news about Julia?" Irena asked when he was gone.

"You didn't see the spread in the *Sun*?"

"I saw it."

"Quite impressive, don't you think?"

Irena shuffled from one foot to the other, looked as if she were seriously considering jumping out the twenty-fifth-floor window. "If there's anything I can do for you during this difficult time. . . ."

You're the first person I'll call, Cindy thought. Aloud she said, "Thank you." She turned toward the floor-to-ceiling window with its magnificent view of the waterfront, saw her own pathetic image reflected back. She was wearing her standard uniform of blue jeans and faded T-shirt, and her hair was greasy from constantly tugging at it. *Take your hands away from your hair,* she could hear Tom scold. "How many partners are there in the firm now?" she asked Irena, in an effort to silence him.

"Sixteen partners. Forty-eight associates."

"Wow," Cindy said without enthusiasm.

"Half a dozen students," Irena continued.

Cindy wondered if Irena was still sleeping with Tom. She folded her arms across her chest, as if to keep her heart from falling out.

"Are you sure you wouldn't like a cup of coffee?"

"Quite sure, thank you."

"Well, I could certainly use one," Tom said, sweeping into the room, resplendent in a gray suit and red print tie. "If you wouldn't mind."

"No problem." Irena obediently slipped from the room, drawing the door closed behind her, then leaving it open a small crack.

"So, what brings you all the way down here?" Tom asked, examining his ex-wife as if she were an unpleasant document.

Cindy walked to the door, pushed it shut all the way, then turned back to her ex-husband. "You miserable son of a bitch," she began.

"Okay, ground rules," Tom stated, retreating behind his heavy oak desk. "No swearing. No name calling. No yelling."

"No shit," Cindy said.

Tom shook his head. "You look like crap."

Tears stung Cindy's eyes. Seven years after he'd left, and still, his words had the power to wound. "What the hell is wrong with you?"

"What's wrong with *me?*" he countered.

"How could you do it?"

"Do what?"

"Don't play games with me."

"I take it you're upset about the pictures in the *Sun.*"

"Pictures you hand-delivered yourself, you son of a bitch. Don't try to deny it."

"Why would I deny it?"

"Why would you *do* it?"

"Think about it a minute."

"Think about what? What's to think about?"

"Think about the best way to keep Julia front and center on everyone's minds," Tom said evenly, sitting down and leaning forward, elbows on his desk. "She's been missing for eleven days."

"I know exactly how long she's been missing."

"Then you also know her disappearance is old news. Another girl's already taken her place. Not to mention, the city is filled with visiting celebrities and movie stars, eager for a good photo-op. I had to do something to make sure Julia wouldn't be forgotten. Those pictures will more than accomplish that."

"So the end still justifies the means," Cindy said, aware there was a grain of truth to what Tom was saying, not wanting to acknowledge it.

"Cindy, be reasonable. How long do you think the police are going to keep Julia's case a priority?"

"How seriously do *you* think they're going to treat her disappearance after seeing these pictures? They'll dismiss her as flighty and foolish, maybe even flighty and foolish enough to take off without telling anyone. Or worse—they'll think she's a little tramp who got what she deserved."

"They'll think they better get off their asses and solve this case before it gets international exposure," Tom snapped. "I'm already fielding calls from Associated Press and *People* magazine."

"Oh God." Cindy felt her body crumpling like tissue paper, and collapsed into one of the two blue chairs in front of Tom's desk.

Tom stood up, warily approached his former wife. "Cindy, you have to calm down. You can't keep flying off half-cocked. It's not good for you."

"You mean it's not good for *you,*" she said, refusing to look at him.

"Look at you." He smoothed some hairs away from her face.

Cindy slapped his hand aside. "I know. I look like crap. You already told me."

"I'm just worried about you."

Cindy pushed herself out of the chair, and walked to the window, stared toward Lake Ontario. "If you're so damn worried about me, why didn't you tell me what you were planning to do with the pictures? Why didn't you warn me?"

"Because I knew you wouldn't approve. And I didn't feel like going through . . ."

"This?"

"Exactly."

"Coward."

Tom shook his head. "Okay, look. I think we've said all we have to say."

"I haven't."

"Of course," he said with an audible sigh. "Okay, I'm ready. Give it your best shot."

Cindy looked at her former husband, his feet spread shoulder-distance apart, his arms hanging limply at his sides, handsome face void of all expression. She'd once loved this man, she found herself thinking. Loved him from the time she was seventeen. Loved him so much she'd eloped with him at eighteen, had two children with him. *Two* children, she reminded herself, her lower lip quivering as once again, tears clouded her eyes. "How's Heather?" she asked, realizing she'd barely thought about Heather since she left.

"She's fine."

"Did she tell you what happened?"

"Just that the house was getting a little crowded." Tom paused. "You know I'm right about the pictures, don't you?"

Cindy pushed her hair impatiently behind her ears. "I hate it when you're right."

"You hate everything about me," he said softly, going to her side.

"Pretty much," Cindy acknowledged, allowing him to gather her into his arms and pull her toward him. She cried softly against his chest, his silk tie serving as a blotter for her tears. How had she ever allowed herself to fall in love with someone she'd never really liked?

"Cindy . . ."

"What?"

"Everything will be all right," he said, as the door to his office opened, and Irena stepped inside, a coffee mug shaking in her hands, the color drained from her face. "Something the matter?" Tom asked as Detectives Bartolli and Gill strode into the room. "What is it? Has something happened?"

Detective Bartolli stepped forward, his gaze shifting uneasily from Tom to Cindy. "We've found a body," he said slowly. "We'd like you to come with us."

TWENTY-THREE

THE regional office of the Chief Coroner for the Province of Ontario is located at 26 Grenville Street, at the corner of Yonge, next to the large Credit Union Bank, in the heart of downtown Toronto. It is a squat, two-story structure fashioned in brown stucco and glass that manages to be both bland and ominous. A giant, government-operated funeral parlor, Cindy found herself thinking as the police car pulled to a stop in the adjacent parking lot. Which is exactly what the damn thing is, she thought, suppressing the panic that was bubbling inside her body, like water boiling in a pot.

You have to stay calm, she admonished herself, scratching painfully at her arms, her skin on fire, as if she'd just slipped into a burning sweater. She wanted to jump from the car, strip off all her clothes, accost total strangers, laugh hysterically in their faces, scream at them until she was hoarse, but she couldn't do any of those things because Tom would tell her she was behaving inappropriately. And he'd be right, of course. He was always right. She did behave inappropriately. She yelled when whispers would suffice, laughed when others might cry, lashed out when what she wanted most was the comfort of someone's arms.

How was it that Tom managed to stay so focused, so in control? Cindy wondered, glancing over at her ex-husband, who was sitting beside her in the backseat of the police car, staring out the side window. How was it that his feathers never seemed to ruffle? That even faced with the loss of his daughter, he remained stoic and cool?

Was it possible such composure was all an act? That underneath the deceptively placid surface, a smoldering geyser was waiting to erupt? That behind the pat phrases, the condescending nods, the maddening reserve, he was every bit as panicky as she was?

"Do you remember how much Julia used to talk when she was a little girl?" Cindy asked Tom, who either didn't hear her question or chose to ignore it. "You couldn't shut her up," Cindy continued, undeterred. "She'd start talking the minute she opened her eyes in the morning, and she didn't stop until she closed them again at night. And sometimes she'd even talk in her sleep. It was so cute. Remember, Tom?"

Tom's shoulders stiffened. "Cindy. . . ."

"You'd keep waiting for her to take a breath, so you could get a word in, but it would never come. You'd think, surely she has to come up for air at some point, but she just breezed from one topic into the next. Isn't that right, Tom?"

Tom's head turned slowly toward her. "Cindy. . . ."

"And you didn't dare interrupt her," Cindy continued, chuckling at the memory. "If you did, she'd just start all over again from the beginning. And you'd have to listen to the whole thing again until she got to the part where you'd cut her off, and then she'd give you this little look. Remember that look, Tom? You used to say it could cut glass."

"Cindy. . . ."

"*What?*" Cindy snapped, understanding now how Julia must

have felt at being interrupted. Why had she always interrupted her? Why couldn't she just have let her speak?

"I think we should go inside now," Tom said quietly.

"Why? What's the rush? Is she going anywhere?" Cindy caught the look of horror on her ex-husband's face. "Oh, I'm sorry. Was that inappropriate?"

"Mrs. Carver, are you all right?" Detective Gill asked from the front seat.

"I'm fine," Cindy told him. "I mean, why wouldn't I be fine? We're just here to identify my daughter's body, right? Nothing to get upset about."

"Mrs. Carver . . ." Detective Bartolli said.

"She always wanted to be an actress, you know," Cindy told the two detectives, trying to prolong her time in the car, to postpone the inevitable. "She used to prance around the house in my high heels and nightgowns, like a fairy princess—you should have seen her—and she'd make up these cute little plays, and act out all the parts. She'd sing and dance. She was really very good. Wasn't she, Tom?"

"Cindy. . . ."

"I remember one afternoon when Julia was maybe four years old. I was busy with Heather, and Julia was playing with her Barbies— she had at least fifty of them—and I suddenly realized it was awfully quiet in Julia's room. So I put Heather in her crib and went to see what was going on. And there was Julia standing naked in the middle of her bedroom, in front of all her Barbies, whom she'd arranged in this kind of free-floating semicircle, and she was holding up this pencil, and she was saying, 'And now, audience, we're going to operate on my vagina.' " Cindy laughed out loud.

"Cindy, for God's sake," Tom said.

The smile slid from Cindy's face, as if rubbed off by a harsh abrasive. "What? Not appropriate?"

"Mrs. Carver," Detective Bartolli said gently. "Maybe Detective

Gill should take you home. Mr. Carver can make the identification."

"No!" Cindy said quickly. "I'm fine."

"You're not fine," Tom said.

"There is no way you're going to go into that room without
me."

"Cindy. . . ."

"She's my daughter too."

"Nobody disputes that."

"We recognize how difficult this is for you," Detective Gill said.

"Then you also recognize there's no way you're keeping me
from her."

"Mrs. Carver," Detective Bartolli continued, "it's very important that if you go inside, you stay calm."

"Why?" Cindy asked, genuinely curious. "Are you afraid I'll
upset the other corpses?"

"Okay, that's enough," Tom said. "Clearly my wife is hysterical."

"I'm not your wife," Cindy reminded him curtly.

"But you *are* hysterical."

"I'm fine," Cindy assured the two detectives. "I'll be okay. I
promise." I'll be a good girl, the child in her protested, pulling
back her shoulders, and taking a deep breath, determined to prove
she could be as rational, as grown-up, as they were. I'll be as cool as
a cucumber, she decided, puzzling over the origin of that expression. Why a cucumber? Why not "cool as a carrot" Or "cool as a
cabbage"? How about "cool as a corpse"?

Now *that's* appropriate, she thought, almost laughing as she
pushed open the car door and stepped onto the pavement, the
unseasonably hot September air descending on her head like a collapsing parachute. Better to keep such musings to herself, she decided. Any more outbursts and they wouldn't let her into the
building, let alone into the viewing room. They wouldn't let her

see her daughter. Or what was left of her. "Oh God," she said, trying not to picture Julia lying battered and lifeless on a cold, steel slab.

She felt her knees buckle, her legs give way, as if someone had kicked at them from behind, the reality she'd worked so hard to keep at bay pushing itself on top of her, holding her down, tearing through her body, like a rapist.

"Cindy," Tom said, catching her by the elbow before she could collapse.

"I'm all right," she told him, regaining her composure, putting one tenuous foot in front of the other.

"Mrs. Carver?"

"I'm fine."

They walked slowly around to the front of the building, Detective Gill rushing ahead to open the heavy glass door, then stepping back to allow them entry. Cindy crossed into the main lobby, a cold but efficient use of space that was typical of most government buildings. Detective Bartolli checked in with the dispatcher, a middle-aged man whose lush black beard was in stark contrast to his shiny bald head, then quickly ushered the small group toward a room to the right of the lobby.

"What's in here?" Cindy asked, pulling back as they reached the door.

"It's just a room," Detective Gill assured her as they stepped over the threshold.

"This is Mark Evert." Detective Bartolli introduced the surprisingly robust-looking morgue attendant, who was waiting for them inside.

"Mr. Evert," Tom said, shaking the man's hand.

"What is this, some sort of bereavement room?" Cindy asked.

"We call it the comfort room," Mark Evert replied.

"Really? What kind of comfort are you offering exactly?"

Mark Evert smiled sadly, as if he understood her pain. "If you'd

like to sit down. . . ." He pointed toward a grouping of recently re-
furbished sofa and chairs. "And there's a bathroom, if you'd
like. . . ."

"To freshen up?" Cindy asked.

"Cindy. . . ." Tom's voice warned from somewhere beside her.

She looked around the small room, its dim lights meant to be
soothing, the smell of new carpeting permeating the cool air. "I
think I *would* like to use the bathroom," she said, disappearing into
the tiny room, and locking the door after her. She turned on the
tap, splashed several handfuls of cold water at her face. "Stay
calm," she whispered at her reflection in the mirror over the sink.
The face in the glass stared back at her through hopelessly dazed
eyes. Cindy noted the greenish-yellow of the woman's cheeks, the
dark circles under her eyes, the circles spreading out in ripples, like
a still lake disturbed by a stone. You can do this, her reflection admonished silently. You can do this.

"No, I can't," Cindy said out loud. "I can't."

There was a gentle knock on the bathroom door. "Cindy?"
Tom called. "Are you all right in there?"

I'm fine in here, she wanted to answer. It's out there I have a
problem. Instead she said, "I'll just be half a minute." She took a
deep breath, then reached for the door, stopped, walked back to
the toilet and flushed it, watching as the water swirled aimlessly
around the bowl before being sucked down the drain. Gone. Just
like that. "Okay," she said, coming back into the so-called comfort
room, noting how quiet it was. This is what they mean by the term
"deathly quiet," she thought, knowing it would be *inappropriate* to
voice such an observation out loud. "What happens now?"

"We go inside." Mark Evert indicated the door directly behind
him. "We'll show you the body of a young woman. She's been
strangled."

Cindy drew in a sharp intake of air, automatically reached for
Tom's hand, felt his fingers close around hers.

"I thought you had closed-circuit TVs for this," Tom said, his body stiffening along with his voice.

The morgue attendant nodded. "We do, and generally speaking, we prefer to make identifications that way, especially in cases where's there's been significant trauma to the face. . . ."

"There's been trauma to her face?" Cindy repeated, struggling to understand the man's words.

"There are a few bruises, along with some swelling and discoloration."

"Oh no."

"You can't just show us a photograph?" Tom pressed.

"Unfortunately, in cases of homicide, this isn't an option. We require a direct identification."

"But on TV, people usually stand behind a window or something."

"Procedures vary in every jurisdiction," Mark Evert explained patiently. "If you need a few more minutes, Mr. Carver. . . ."

"Are you all right?" Cindy asked her ex-husband, surprised to find their roles suddenly reversed.

"Just tell us what to expect," Tom said tersely.

"The young woman you're going to see was strangled some time in the last forty-eight hours. We haven't done an autopsy yet to determine the exact time of death, but decomposition has started. . . ."

"Decomposition?" The terrible word assaulted Cindy's ears like an icepick to the brain.

"We'll try to spare you as much as we can. I'm afraid we aren't allowed to clean up the body in any way."

"Is there a lot of blood?" Tom asked.

"No."

A prolonged sigh leaked from Cindy's lungs.

"You'll be asked to make a formal identification in the presence of these detectives, myself, and the pathologist."

"What if we're not sure?" Tom asked.

Cindy moaned, the prospect of not being able to recognize her own child almost too much to bear.

"Then we'll ask you to supply us with Julia's dental records, or her hairbrush. . . ."

"Can we go in now?" Cindy interrupted, knowing that if they waited any longer, if she had to listen to any more malignant words like decomposition and discoloration, or even to formerly benign words like dental records and hairbrush, she would go mad.

Mark Evert's hand hesitated on the doorknob. "You're sure you're ready?"

Cindy marveled at the question. How could anyone ever be ready for something like this? "I'm ready," she said, feeling Tom's fingers digging into her own as the door opened, and they stepped into the morgue.

It was like a huge operating room. Cindy's eyes bounced from the cream-colored tiles on the walls to the darker tiles at her feet. In the center of the room, and running its entire width was a big, stainless steel refrigerator at least ten feet high, containing three rows of compartments. There must be room for a hundred bodies in there, Cindy thought with a shudder, wondering how the attendants removed those bodies from the lockers without straining their backs, becoming only slowly aware of the narrow table directly in front of her, of the white vinyl body bag stretched out across its smooth surface.

"This is Dr. Jong, the pathologist," Mark Evert said of the disconcertingly young-looking man doing his best to look invisible, the doctor responding with an almost imperceptible nod of his head.

He's here to cut her up, Cindy realized, a sudden, loud buzzing filling her ears, as if a thousand bees were trapped there.

"Remember," Mark Evert was saying, "you have to be one hundred percent sure."

Cindy turned to Tom. "Do you remember when Julia was a little girl, and she was showing off on that new bicycle you bought her, and she fell off and broke both her arms?"

"I remember," Tom said, clutching tightly to her hands.

"And I rushed her to the hospital, and of course, we had to wait about four hours till somebody saw us, and she kept saying, 'Why doesn't God like me, Mommy? Why doesn't He like me?' And I told her, 'Don't be silly. Of course God likes you. He loves you.' But she was adamant. 'No, He doesn't love me, or He wouldn't have broken my arms.' And we laughed about that later. Do you remember how we laughed about that later?"

"I remember," Tom said again.

"And then the poor thing couldn't feed herself or go to the bathroom with both her arms in casts."

"It didn't take her long to get the knack."

"And she was embarrassed to go to school."

"The teachers probably thought she was an abused child."

"And then you got that rock 'n' roll band you represented—who were they again?"

"Rush."

"Yeah, Rush. I remember. Such nice guys. They all signed her casts. Then she couldn't wait to get to school to show everybody. And when it came time to take the casts off, she cried and carried on."

"We had to keep those damn, smelly things for years."

"I remember that just after the doctor removed them, Julia fainted, and the doctor, who was standing on the other side of the room, came flying back and caught her before she fell off the table. She might have cracked her head open on the floor. And there I was, standing right beside her, and I didn't realize what was happening."

"Cindy," Tom said softly, "don't do this."

"If I'd watched her more closely, she would never have fallen off her bicycle."

"Kids fall off their bicycles every day."

"If I'd paid closer attention. . . ."

"Mrs. Carver," the morgue attendant said gently. "Do you think you're ready now?"

"Do you think she had any idea how much I love her?" Cindy asked her former husband, tears filling her eyes and spilling down her cheeks.

"She knows," Tom said.

"I yelled at her. The morning of her audition. I yelled at her about the dog, I yelled at her for banging on the bathroom door, I insisted she come to the bridal fitting that afternoon when I knew she didn't want to come."

"This didn't happen because you yelled at her."

"What if she was kidnapped on her way to the fitting? What if whoever did this to her saw her as she was getting on the subway and followed her?"

"Cindy. . . ."

"I should have been paying more attention."

"You're a great mother, Cindy," Tom told her.

"She must have been so scared."

"Mrs. Carver," Detective Bartolli ventured, then stopped.

Cindy confronted the young-looking pathologist. "How long does it take to strangle someone?"

"Cindy. . . ."

"Please, Dr. Jong. Tell me how long it takes to strangle someone?"

"Approximately two minutes," the doctor answered.

"Two minutes," Cindy repeated. "Such a long time." The buzzing in her ears grew louder.

"We'll get through this," she thought she heard Tom say.

Words jumped out at her only to retreat.

"Are . . . ready . . . Mrs. . . ?"

Cindy noticed the police shield on the front of the body bag as a man's hand reached for the zipper, the sound of the zipper cutting through the buzzing in her ears, like a chainsaw through a chunk of wood, one sound magnifying the other, until Cindy felt her head about to burst.

Hands parted the zipper. A head emerged, as if from the womb. Cindy saw the straight blond hair plastered against the ghostly white skin, tried not to absorb the unsightly blotches of purple, blue, and red that stained the colorless cheeks like paint on canvas.

Oh God, she thought, recognizing the once-lovely face.

And then the room filled with the sound of angry bees, and Cindy fell unconscious to the floor.

TWENTY-FOUR

"Are you all right?" Tom was asking.

Cindy opened her eyes, lifted her head from the soft beige-and-ivory-print silk of the sofa, stared at the man looming over her. "I don't know."

"Maybe this will help." He pushed a tall glass of something cold into her hands.

"What is it?"

"Vodka and cranberry juice."

Cindy pushed herself into a sitting position, took a long sip. "It's good."

Tom sank down beside her. He stretched his long legs across the wood-and-glass coffee table in front of him, laid his head back against one of the pillows. "That was quite the ordeal." He leaned sideways toward her, clicked his glass against hers. "To better days." He promptly downed half his glass in a single gulp.

"Better days," Cindy agreed, taking another sip of her drink, the presence of the vodka both flattening and emphasizing the tartness of the cranberries. She looked around the large, expensively appointed room, with its muted furniture and bright needlepoint rugs, its bold splashes of modern art against pale ecru walls, its south wall of floor-to-ceiling windows providing a magnificent view of Lake Ontario. "This is some place you've got here."

"You've seen it before, haven't you?"

"First time," she reminded him. "It's beautiful. I didn't realize the Cookie had such good taste."

"The Cookie?" Tom looked genuinely perplexed.

Cindy turned her head to hide an unexpected blush. "Sorry. Fiona."

A slow smile crept across Tom's handsome face. "You call my wife 'the Cookie'?"

"Term of endearment." Cindy took another sip of her drink. "What am I doing here?"

"You fainted. Remember?"

"Yes. I seem to be doing that a lot lately. But then I woke up."

"And said you couldn't face going home, that your mother and sister were driving you nuts."

"They mean well."

"Yes," he said cryptically. "I remember."

"So you brought me to your condominium," Cindy stated, choosing not to explore his last remark, marveling at everything that had transpired in the last hour. "Where's the . . . Fiona?" she asked, listening for the click of the woman's high-heeled shoes on the marble floors.

"Muskoka."

"She's at the cottage?"

"We decided it was probably a good idea for her to stay up there this week, what with everything that's going on, and Heather being here."

Cindy glanced toward the long hall that ran the length of the huge apartment. "Is Heather at school?"

"I think she said she has classes till six."

Cindy checked her watch. It was barely four.

Tom brought his feet to the floor, leaned forward, rested his elbows on his knees. "She's planning to go back home this weekend."

Cindy nodded gratefully. "And Julia?" she asked, speaking the name that had gone unvoiced since that awful moment in the morgue when the attendant had unzipped the white vinyl bag.

It's not her, she heard Tom whisper. *It's not Julia.*

"We wait," he said now. "What else can we do?"

Cindy jumped to her feet, her drink sloshing around in her glass, spilling onto her hand. "I feel so guilty," she said, wiping the back of her hand on her jeans.

"Guilty? Why on earth would you feel guilty?"

"Because when I saw that poor girl's face and realized it wasn't Julia, I was so relieved, so grateful, so happy."

"Of course you'd feel that way."

"I think it's Sally Hanson," Cindy said.

"Who?"

"The girl who disappeared the week after Julia. Her poor parents...."

"At least they'll know." Tom swallowed the last of his drink, then deposited his glass on the coffee table with an authority that was missing from his voice.

Cindy nodded. Would it be better to know? she wondered.

"At least there wasn't any blood," Tom said, his eyes returning to the morgue, still clearly haunted by what he'd seen.

"As we were leaving, I heard the dispatcher talking to Detective Gill about some couple who were killed in a car accident this morning," Cindy said, remembering. "He said the car exploded, and the people were badly burned. He called them 'crispy critters.'" Cindy stared at her former husband in disbelief. "Did he really say that or did I just imagine it?"

Tom shook his head. "I heard the same thing."

"I can't believe they talk that way."

"I guess you'd have to develop a pretty thick skin in order to survive in that kind of environment."

"Still . . ." Cindy shuddered. *"Crispy critters?"*

"Think they're anything like Krispy Kremes?" Tom asked.

A bubble of laughter suddenly burst inside Cindy's throat, then tumbled into the air, like a child tossed from a toboggan. Immediately, Tom's laughter somersaulted after hers, the disparate sounds becoming hopelessly enmeshed, impossible to separate one from the other. "I can't believe we're laughing." Cindy said, laughing harder.

"I'll have an order of Crispy Critters, please," Tom said.

"Hold the mayo," Cindy embellished.

"Oh, that's hurts," Tom said, doubling over from the waist, holding his sides.

"What's wrong with us?"

"We could use another drink." Tom took Cindy's almost empty glass from her outstretched hand, retrieved his own glass from the coffee table, and marched out of the room.

Cindy followed after him, as if afraid to be left alone, even for an instant. She ran her hand along the dark oak finish of the long dining room table as she walked purposefully toward the kitchen, stopping to stare at the impressive wine cabinet built into the wall between the two rooms, each bottle of wine neatly labeled behind the thick layer of glass, the bottles secured in metal berths, stacked one on top of the other. Like bodies in a morgue, Cindy thought, fresh giggles gathering in her throat. "That's quite a collection," she said, coming into the gleaming marble-and-tile kitchen, watching as Tom refilled their glasses. "How many bodies are there?"

"What?"

"Bottles," she corrected. "I meant to say bottles."

Tom smiled. "There's room for four hundred."

"You always wanted a wine cellar."

"I always wanted a wine cellar," he agreed.

It was Cindy's turn to smile. "So, what shall we toast this time?"

"How about no more visits to the morgue?" Tom offered.

"Sounds good to me." Cindy took a long swallow. This time the vodka overwhelmed the subtle hint of cranberries. She noticed that a pleasant tingle was beginning to settle around the back of her neck. Any minute, her head would separate from the rest of her body and float into the air, like a helium-filled balloon. "So, how many bodies *do* you think that thing at the morgue holds?"

Tom laughed, once again finishing half his drink in a single swallow. "You asked that question on the drive home."

"I did? What was the answer?"

"Detective Bartolli said ninety. Apparently, it's at three quarters of its capacity right now, and most bodies are in and out within forty-eight hours."

"And they use a forklift to take the bodies from the top row. I remember now."

"You were very concerned about their backs."

Cindy laughed, shook her head, grabbed the side of the island in the middle of the room to steady herself.

"You all right?"

"Feeling better every minute." Cindy took another swallow. "So, are you going to show me around this dump?"

"My pleasure." Tom made a sweeping gesture with his hands. "This is the kitchen."

"We can skip the kitchen."

"Still don't like to cook?"

"Hate it."

"Which is a real shame, because if memory serves me correctly, you were a very good cook."

"Really? How would you know? You were never home. What's down this way?" she asked before he could protest. She let go of the island, skipped from the kitchen, turned left at the hall.

"This is the library," Tom said of the wood-paneled room they came to first. Except for the southern expanse of window overlooking the waterfront, the room was essentially wallpapered with hardcover books.

"Very impressive."

"The view helps."

"And I didn't even realize the Cookie could read."

"Fiona is a very prolific reader," Tom said curtly, although there was laughter in his eyes.

"A woman of many talents."

"Yes, indeed." Tom led Cindy into the next room, its east wall completely taken up by an enormous flat-screen TV. "This is the media room."

"Still like leather, I see." Cindy gave the dark red leather sofa a seductive squeeze. "Where are the bedrooms?"

"Down this way." Tom led her back down the hall, past the marble powder room to the right of the marble entrance. "You're sure you're okay?"

"I'm fine." Cindy followed after him. Like a puppy at his heels, she thought, recognizing she was way beyond fine and teetering into plastered. It didn't take much, she thought. A dead body, a couple of vodkas—pretty soon she was sailing.

"This is the guest room."

Cindy peeked inside the green-and-white bedroom, saw a pair of Heather's jeans draped over a small, flowered-print chair, several of her blouses strewn across the white bedspread covering the queen-size bed. "It's lovely."

"It has its own bathroom, of course."

"Just like the comfort room." Cindy giggled. "Amazing how they think of everything, isn't it?"

"Amazing," Tom agreed.

"You think Granger, McAllister designed it?"

"Who's Granger, McAllister?"

"Our neighbors, the Sellicks. *My* neighbors," she corrected, leaning against a wall to keep from lying down on the floor. "He's an architect with Granger, McAllister."

"You think he designed the morgue?" Tom asked, one word sliding into the next as he directed her toward the master bedroom suite.

"No." Cindy giggled. "You're so silly."

"You're so drunk."

"I certainly hope so." Cindy kicked off her shoes, burying her toes in the plush white carpeting. "Wow," she said, her eyes sweeping across the enormous room, taking in the full-length sofa and chairs that were grouped in front of the southern wall of windows, the ornate credenza that sat against the wall opposite the bed, the bed itself a king-size extravaganza complete with tall pillars swathed in yards of cream-colored satin. "Looks like something out of the *Arabian Nights*. Spend much time in it?" she asked pointedly.

"Cindy, Cindy," Tom said, coming up behind her, his hands falling heavily on her shoulders, his slender hips pressing into her backside. "What am I going to do with you?"

Cindy felt his breath on the back of her neck, recognized the once-familiar tingle creeping between her legs. "What's in here?" she asked, extricating herself from his grasp and diving toward a small area off the main bedroom. "Wow. Do you actually use all this equipment?"

Tom moved easily between the treadmill, the StairMaster, and the stationary bicycle. There was also a large, red, exercise ball in one corner, and an impressive selection of free weights stacked against one wall. A medium-sized TV sat on a high shelf across from the treadmill. "I work out most days for about an hour. What about you?"

"I do yoga," Cindy told him, recalling her one visit to the Yoga Studio.

"Really? I wouldn't have pegged you for the yoga type."

"Why is that?"

"I wouldn't have thought you had the patience." He laughed. "I can just see you lying there, thinking, Can we please speed this up a bit?" He shook his head. "What do I know? Anyway, it obviously agrees with you."

"You told me before that I look like crap."

"I did? When?"

"In your office."

"Ah, yes. But that was before our little trip to the morgue."

"You're saying I look great in comparison to that girl on the table?"

"I'm saying you look great. Period."

"So you lied before, when you said I looked like crap."

"I lied."

"You're a liar?" she pressed giddily.

"I'm a lawyer," he agreed, and they both laughed.

"And the bathroom?" Cindy asked as he leaned toward her. "This way?" She ducked out of his reach, tripped past the two walk-in closets toward the en suite master bathroom.

It was a big room, its walls the same beige marble as the floor, with a double Jacuzzi, a large open shower stall, his-and-hers counters and sinks, and enough mirrors to satisfy even the most dedicated narcissist.

"Oh, jeez," Cindy said, seeing her reflection bounce from one mirror to the next: the old T-shirt, the sloppy jeans, the stringy hair, the zombie-like eyes. "I do look like crap."

"You look beautiful," Tom said, leaving his glass on the counter and coming up behind her.

"Lawyer," Cindy said, falling back against his chest, his arms wrapping around hers, and the side of his cheek pressing against her own as he removed the glass from her hand and placed it on the other counter. Was he really going to kiss her? she wondered, as he slowly spun her around. Was she really going to let him?

(Flashback: Cindy stands in front of her bathroom mirror, removing the makeup she painstakingly applied only an hour earlier, replaying Tom's phone call in her mind. "Sorry, babe. I can't make the movie. We've got something of an emergency going on here, and I'm going to be tied up for at least a few more hours. Give the sitter an extra couple of bucks, and see if you can line her up for next week.")

He tasted of vodka and cranberries, Cindy thought now, luxuriating in the softness of his lips, feeling his tongue slide gently across hers. Not too much, not too little. Just the right amount. Just like old times, she thought, recalling her mother's words.

What about Neil? she thought, seeing his reflection in the mirror behind Tom's head.

You're the most courageous woman I know, she heard him say.

"It was always so good with you," Tom was whispering, his hands tugging at her T-shirt, expert fingers disappearing beneath it, unhooking her bra. "God, real breasts. I'd almost forgotten how good they feel."

(Flashback: Cindy lying in bed, her pillow moist with her tears, as Tom crawls in beside her, reaches under her nightgown, cups her breasts in his hands. "Sorry I'm so late," he says, kissing her neck. She smells the wine on his breath, as his fingers reach between her legs. "Client wouldn't stop talking. I thought dinner would never end." He buries his face in the side of her neck. Cindy inhales another woman's perfume as he enters her from behind.)

"Come here," Tom said now, guiding her between the treadmill and the stationary bicycle toward the bedroom, pulling her T-shirt over her head as he pushed the layers of satin aside, her bra falling from her shoulders, disappearing into the white carpet, like a child's mitten into snow. "You always had such beautiful breasts," he marveled, pushing her back on the bed, and unbuttoning his shirt.

What am I doing? Cindy wondered, again thinking of Neil.

Three years of being a nun and suddenly I'm the town slut? I don't feel so great, she thought as Tom's tongue found her nipples, and his fingers struggled with the button of her jeans.

(Flashback: Cindy in bed, chilled and nauseous, sipping herbal tea and fighting the urge to throw up, when she hears the front door open and the sound of a woman's laugh. She crawls out of bed and staggers to the top of the stairs.

"Can I get you a drink?" she hears Tom ask from the kitchen.

"Hello? Tom?" she calls, watching as Tom emerges at the bottom of the steps, clearly surprised to see her.

"What are you doing home? Isn't this your day to help out at Heather's school?"

"I wasn't feeling well. I had to cancel. What's going on?"

"Forgot my briefcase," Tom says breezily. "Look who I ran into coming down the street," he adds, almost as an afterthought.

A woman's head pops into view. Cindy recognizes her as the mother of one of Heather's friends.)

What on earth was she doing? Cindy wondered now, shaking her head in an effort to clear it, the motion making her dizzy and nauseous.

"We had some pretty good times together," Tom was saying, clearly oblivious to her discomfort.

As always, Cindy thought. "When you weren't cheating on me," she said flatly.

A nervous chuckle. "You took all that much too seriously. You know it meant nothing to me."

Was that supposed to make her feel better? "It meant something to me."

Silence. His hand froze on her bare skin. "You're killing the mood here, babe."

"You'd really make love to me in this apartment? In this bed?"

"Jesus," Tom said, sitting up and lifting his hands into the air, as if there were a gun pointing at his head. "You can't just relax and let things happen, can you? Damn it, Cindy. You haven't changed at all."

"Damn it, Tom. Neither have you." Cindy pushed herself off the bed, rezipped her jeans, her eyes searching through the white carpet for her bra. Probably not a good idea to move so fast, she decided, falling to her knees and locating the bra with her fingers, already back on her feet when she heard the voice from the doorway.

"Dad? What are you doing home so early?"

It was too late to do anything but turn around.

"Oh, wow!" Heather's eyes opened wide with disbelief, moving from her bare-chested father to her half-crouching, half-naked mother.

"It's not what you think," Tom said lamely, fiddling with the buttons of his shirt.

"Nothing happened," Cindy said, pulling her bra into position, securing the clasp at the back. First her mother and sister walk in on her and Neil; now her daughter finds her with Tom. That's what I get for not having sex in three years, Cindy thought.

"Sure. Okay. Wow."

"It was a momentary lapse in judgment," Cindy explained.

"I thought you had classes till six."

"Does this mean you're getting back together?"

"Absolutely not," Tom said forcefully.

"God, no," Cindy echoed.

"Okay, well, wow. Okay," Heather said, backing out of the room. "I think I should probably get going."

"Sweetie . . ." Cindy called.

"I'm fine. Don't worry about me. I'll phone you later." The front door closed after her.

Tom looked at Cindy. "I hope you're proud of yourself," he said.

TWENTY-FIVE

WEDNESDAY, September 11, Cindy stayed in bed watching TV as the country relived the agony of the previous year's terrorist attacks on the World Trade Center.

Like everyone else she knew, Cindy could recall the exact time and the place she'd been when she'd learned the devastating news. It was during the film festival, and she and Meg had just emerged from the Uptown after a screening of the British film, *Last Orders,* starring Michael Caine and Bob Hoskins. It was around 11 A.M. and they were heading up Yonge Street to meet Trish and grab a sandwich before their next movie. "Where is everyone?" Cindy asked, wondering at the lack of a lineup for the next movie.

"Something's happening at the corner," Meg said.

When they reached the intersection of Yonge and Bloor, they joined a crowd of several hundred people standing in stunned silence, watching the gigantic TV screen on top of the low-rise building on the southeast corner, as the two hijacked planes flew repeatedly, and from a multitude of sickening angles, into the giant twin towers. She and Meg had watched in openmouthed horror as the buildings collapsed, peeling downward from top to bottom, like the skin of a banana, the resultant debris spilling over onto the streets of New York, covering everything in its path in a sickening gray dust.

At the time, Cindy thought nothing could be worse.

Leigh walked into the bedroom. "You've got to talk to Mom," she was saying, dimpled knees peeking out from under light khaki shorts, her white sleeveless blouse in sharp contrast to her deeply tanned arms. "She canceled the fitting with Marcel. What are you watching?" She reached toward the bed and pressed the OFF button on the remote.

"What are you doing?" Cindy grabbed the remote, flipped the TV back on.

Leigh wrestled the unit from Cindy's hands, switched the TV off. "You shouldn't be watching this."

"What do you mean, I shouldn't be watching it? What are you talking about?"

"It'll only upset you."

"Give me that," Cindy told her younger sister, whose response was to hide the remote behind her back. Cindy jumped off the bed, tried reaching around her sister. "Leigh, I'm warning you. Give it back."

"No."

"Leigh . . ."

"I won't."

"Oh, for Pete's sake." Cindy marched back to the television and triumphantly pressed the manual ON switch.

Her sister was right behind her, pressing it off.

"What the hell do you think you're doing?"

"I'm protecting you."

"Protecting me? From what?"

"From yourself."

"From myself," Cindy repeated, incredulously.

"Your judgment isn't the best lately."

"My judgment isn't the best." Cindy shook her head. "What are you talking about?"

"I'm talking about the fact that first you slept with your accountant, then you went to bed with your ex-husband. . . ."

Cindy rolled her eyes. "Neil is not my accountant, and I didn't go to bed with Tom."

"Only because Heather walked in on you."

"It was over by the time she walked in."

"What was over? You said nothing happened."

"Nothing *did* happen."

"But it almost did. Which is my point exactly."

Cindy sank down on the bed. "This conversation makes no sense whatsoever."

"You need to get dressed," Leigh said.

Cindy glanced down at her yellow cotton nightshirt. "I'm fine."

"It's almost noon, and you're still in your pajamas."

Cindy gave her sister a look that said, So?

Leigh marched into Cindy's closet.

"Where are you going? What are you doing?"

Leigh returned seconds later carrying a pair of black capri pants and a green-and-white-striped jersey. She threw them on the bed, along with some freshly washed underwear. "Here. Wear this."

"I don't want to wear that."

"I'm not leaving this room till you get dressed."

"Well, then you might as well make yourself comfortable because I'm not wearing that."

"For Pete's sake, Cindy. You're worse than my kids."

"For Pete's sake, Leigh. You're worse than our mother."

"Cindy. . . ."

"Leigh. . . ."

Stalemate, Cindy thought.

"So, what's it going to be?" Leigh asked, the remote seemingly attached to the palm of her right hand, both hands on her hips.

Cindy shook her head. "Okay. Okay. You win."

"You'll get dressed?"

"I'll need some help with this." Cindy pulled at the front of her nightgown.

Leigh approached warily. "What kind of help?"

In the next second, Cindy lunged at her sister, knocking her to the floor as she grabbed for the remote.

"What are you doing?" Leigh gasped as Cindy collapsed on top of her. "What's wrong with you?"

"Give me that thing."

"No!"

"Give it to me."

"Mom!"

"Give me the goddamn remote."

"Mom!"

"Coming," their mother called from downstairs. "Is something wrong?"

"You're such a baby," Cindy told her sister, scratching at her arm.

"You're such a brat."

Norma Appleton ran into the room, took one look at her daughters rolling around on the floor, and threw her hands up into the air. "What on earth is going on in here?"

"She scratched my arm."

"She took my remote."

"Stop this. The two of you. Right now."

The girls stopped struggling, sat on the floor glaring at one another.

"It's my remote," Cindy said petulantly.

"Give her back her remote," their mother instructed.

Leigh tossed the unit to the floor. Cindy promptly scooped it up.

"Look what she did to my arm." Leigh extended her forearm, displaying a thin red scratch running above her elbow.

"Apologize to your sister," Norma Appleton said.

Cindy shook her head, looked the other way.

"Apologize to your sister," her mother repeated.

"Sorry," Cindy mumbled under her breath.

"What did you say?" Leigh asked. "I didn't hear you."

"Mother," Cindy warned.

"Don't press your luck," their mother said, helping her younger daughter to her feet.

"Oh, sure. Take her side."

"I'm not taking sides."

"Don't press your luck? What would you call that?" Leigh practically shook with indignation.

"Oh, darling, your 'Hi, Helens.' " Norma Appleton pointed with her chin toward the underside of Leigh's arms. "Maybe a different blouse. . . ."

Cindy started laughing.

"You're both nuttier than fruitcakes. You know that?" Leigh said.

Cindy scrambled to her feet, laughed harder.

"What's so funny?"

"You are. You're being ridiculous."

"*I'm* being ridiculous? *I'm* being ridiculous?"

"*You're* being ridiculous."

"Girls, please."

"Am I the one who's refusing to get dressed? Am I the one whose daughter walked in on her half-naked with her former husband?"

"Heather was not half-naked," Cindy said.

"Sure. Make jokes. Correct my grammar. It's easier than facing the truth."

"The truth being?"

"Girls . . ." their mother warned.

"The truth being that you're behaving irresponsibly."

"What!"

"You're always flying out of this house without telling anyone where you're going or what time you'll be back."

"It's my house. I'm an adult. I didn't realize I had to report to anyone."

"It's not a matter of reporting. It's a matter of consideration."

"What if I don't know where I'm going or when I'll be back?"

"That's exactly what I'm saying. You go off half-cocked."

"You're starting to sound like Tom, you know that?"

"Well, maybe he's right."

"Sorry if I'm not behaving completely rationally these days."

"Since when has it ever been any different?" Leigh scoffed. "Cindy does exactly what Cindy wants to do, just as she always has. Where do you think Julia gets it from?"

"Whoa," Cindy warned.

"If Cindy wants to get married when she's eighteen and her parents are dead-set against it, no problem," Leigh continued, undeterred. "She'll just elope to Niagara Falls. Doesn't matter if her parents go crazy with worry for two days, wondering where the hell she is. Doesn't matter that they miss their younger daughter's performance in *Our Town*. So what if she's the lead and she's been rehearsing for months? Hell, it's only a school play. There'll be plenty of other opportunities. Isn't that what you said, Mom?"

"Sweetheart," their mother demurred, "where is all this coming from?"

"*Our Town*?" Cindy marveled. "You've got to be kidding."

"Why? Because it was important to *me?*"

"Leigh, darling, please. . . ."

"Please what, Mother? Please don't make a fuss? Please don't be upset because you still can't find any time for me?"

"If this is about the fitting I had to cancel this afternoon. . . ."

"You didn't *have* to cancel the fitting, Mother. You *chose* to cancel the fitting."

"It just seemed like there were other things that were more important. . . ."

"More important than your granddaughter's wedding?"

"I didn't say that."

"Why is Cindy's daughter any more important than mine?"

"In case you hadn't noticed," Cindy interrupted, "*my* daughter is missing." She burst into a flood of angry, confused tears.

"Cindy," her mother said, rushing to her side.

"Leave her alone, will you. Stop babying her."

"What's the matter with you?" Norma Appleton demanded of her younger daughter. "Why are you acting this way?"

"Because I am sick and tired of being ignored."

"Who's ignoring you?"

"I all but abandon my family to come over here, I cook for you, I clean up after you. . . ."

"Nobody asked you to do any of that."

"I've been doing it all your life," Leigh snapped. "After you got married, who was there for you? Who made sure things got patched up between you and Mom and Dad? Who was there after that wonderful husband of yours walked out? Who sat beside you and listened to that damn message he left on the answering machine, over and over again? Who rushed over after Julia decided she wanted to live with her father? Who sat up all night with you while you cried your heart out?"

"*You!*" Cindy shouted, punching her fists into the air, like a boxer flailing at an invincible opponent. "*You. You. You.* Always the first one at the scene of an accident. Always available in times of crisis. Tell me, when else do you ever come around?"

Silence.

"When else do you ever let me in?"

The two sisters stared at one another. The doorbell rang.

"Shit," Cindy said.

"Shit," echoed Leigh.

"Shit," said their mother.

Nobody moved.

The doorbell rang again.

"I'll get it." Norma Appleton said finally, walking slowly toward the hall. "Can I leave you two alone?" she asked, turning back.

The doorbell rang a third time.

"Coming." Norma Appleton hurried down the stairs. "I'm coming. Hold your horses."

"Are you expecting anyone?" Leigh asked.

Cindy shook her head, listening for the sound of voices. "I know it's stupid," she said, "but every time it rings, I think it might be Julia."

"Me too," Leigh said.

In the next instant, Cindy was in her sister's arms, crying on her shoulder.

"Oh, Cindy," Leigh whispered, crying too. "I'm so sorry. You know I didn't mean any of those things I said."

"No. You're right. I've treated you very badly."

"No, you haven't."

"I haven't thanked you for any of the things you've done."

"I don't need thanks."

"Yes, you do," Cindy told her. "You need to be thanked. You deserve to be valued."

Leigh smiled sadly, hugged her sister tighter to her chest. "It probably wasn't the best time to bring up *Our Town.*"

"I'm sure you were terrific."

"I love you."

"I love you too." Cindy brushed an errant curl away from her sister's face. "Did I tell you how much I like your hair this color?"

"Really? 'Cause I was thinking of maybe adding a couple of darker streaks."

"That would be nice too."

"Cindy," her mother called from the front hall. "Come look at what just arrived for you."

"What is it?"

"Looks like a plant of some kind." Norma Appleton was already tearing at the cellophane by the time Cindy and Leigh reached the bottom of the stairs.

Cindy unpinned the small white envelope from the side of the wrapping as her mother extricated a lovely arrangement of African violets.

Thinking of you, the card read. *Martin Crawley.*

Cindy laughed, tucked the card into the pocket of her night-shirt, felt it warm against her breast.

"Who's it from?"

Cindy smiled. "My accountant," she said.

"He seems like a very nice man," Leigh acknowledged, lifting the plant from her mother's hands and carrying it into the kitchen. "So, I was thinking of making my famous lemon chicken that Julia loves so much, maybe freezing it," she called back, "so that she can have some when she comes home. What do you think?"

"I think she'd like that very much," Cindy said, following her sister into the kitchen.

"Good. Then that's what I'll do."

"Leigh?"

"Hmm?"

Cindy paused, took a deep breath. "Thank you," she said.

TWENTY-SIX

WHAT did you say to get them to leave?" Neil was asking.

"I said 'please,'" Cindy answered. "Something I haven't been saying nearly enough these days." It was almost midnight and she and Neil were sitting naked in her bed, having finished making love for the third time since his arrival some two hours earlier. Elvis lay on the floor beside them, as if he'd sensed their need for privacy. Or maybe he'd just gotten tired of the constant motion, of having to adjust his position to accommodate their fevered acrobatics. "Actually, I think they were quite happy for the break. My brother-in-law's been pretty patient, but I'm sure he's glad to have his wife back, even if it's only for a day or two. And my mother's been here since . . ." Cindy stopped, reluctant to say Julia's name out loud, to bring the continuing agony of her daughter's disappearance into bed with them, when being in bed with Neil was the only respite she'd had since Julia went missing.

But it was already too late. Her pain, which had gradually morphed from constant, daggerlike thrusts to her chest and abdomen into a steadier, duller, though no less constant, ache that infused every fiber in her body—a chronic illness as opposed to a

LOST 285

surprise attack—had already wormed its way under the sheets to insinuate itself between them.

"What say we watch some TV." Cindy flipped on the television set, began restlessly surfing through the channels.

"What's that?" Neil asked as Cindy's fingers froze on the remote. The screen filled with the distorted image of Edvard Munch's masterpiece, *The Scream,* now reborn as a hideous mask, hiding the face of a merciless killer as he stalked a group of nubile teenagers.

"*Scream,*" Cindy said with authority, shaking her head at the irony that such a breathtaking work of art had achieved its greatest fame via a series of teenage slasher movies, then shaking her head again with the realization that she'd seen the entire *Scream* franchise.

No, I won't see Scream 3 *with you,* Julia had protested when the film was first released. *It's supposed to be terrible. I can't believe you're going. How can you like that garbage?*

Before Julia went missing, Cindy had an easy answer, similar to the one she'd given Neil on their first date. She enjoyed such vicarious torment, she'd told Julia, precisely because it *was* vicarious. She could relish the thrill of danger without experiencing its real threat. The danger was entirely illusory. She was perfectly safe.

Except no one was safe, she understood now. It was the notion of safety, not the threat of danger, that was the real illusion.

The monsters were very real.

Cindy flipped to another channel, then another and another. "Stop me if you see anything interesting."

Neil gently removed the remote control unit from her hand, turned the TV off. "It's late. Why don't we just get some sleep?"

"Did you ever cheat on your wife?" Cindy asked suddenly, carefully monitoring Neil's reaction.

"No," he said. "Not my style."

"Tom cheated on me all the time."

"Tom's an ass."

"Yes, he is, isn't he?" Cindy smiled, although this time the smile was genuine and not the stiff, automatic reflex that normally accompanied each reference to her ex-husband.

The divorce was seven years ago, she heard Julia say. *Get over it.*

Amazing, Cindy thought, her smile widening. I *am* over it.

"You hungry?" she asked Neil, suddenly energized. "Thirsty?"

"Just sleepy."

Cindy felt her body tense. *To sleep,* she thought uneasily. *Perchance to dream.* "Quick," she said. "Name all the seven dwarfs."

"What?"

"From *Snow White.* You know Sleepy, Bashful, Grumpy, Doc, Happy. . . ."

"Cindy, what's wrong?"

"Wrong? Why do you think something's wrong?"

"Because it's midnight and we're talking about *Snow White and the Seven Dwarfs.* What is it? Don't you want me to stay?"

"No, of course I want you to stay."

"You're sure? Because if you're not comfortable. . . ."

"It's not that." Cindy reached for her robe and climbed out of bed, crossing to the window and opening the shutters, staring past the backyard toward the roofs of the large homes along Clarendon, wondering absently what secrets were hidden beneath those roofs.

"What is it?" Neil asked, coming up behind her, surrounding her with his arms.

"It's just that I'm a bit of a restless sleeper these days."

"That's understandable."

"I'm not so sure how understanding you'll be when my screaming wakes you up a couple of hours from now."

"You've been having nightmares?"

"I don't know what you'd call them. They're so stupid." Cindy told Neil of waking up in a sweat night after night, convinced she was dying because she'd forgotten to take some nonexistent pills. "My mother says it's hormonal. My sister says it's a natural by-product of my anxiety. Either way, it's making me crazy."

"I think I might be able to help you," Neil offered.

"Really? How?"

"Come here." Neil led her back to bed and sat her down, then disappeared into the en suite bathroom.

Seconds later Cindy heard him rummaging around in her medicine cabinet, heard the sound of water running from the taps.

"I don't want any sleeping pills," she said as he reentered the room, a glass of water in his right hand.

"You need to sleep, Cindy."

"Not everything can be cured by taking a pill."

"Try these." Neil perched on the side of the bed and opened the fist of his free hand.

Cindy stared into his empty palm. "What's this—the emperor's new pills?"

"Take as many as you need."

Cindy smiled, stared into the deep blue of his eyes. "You really think this is going to work?"

"Can't hurt. Go on. Doctor's orders."

Cindy's fingers hesitated over the invisible pills. She took one, raised it to her mouth, then dropped it onto the tip of her tongue, and swallowed it down with some water. Then she reached over, took another one.

"Why don't you have one more, for good luck."

"For good luck," Cindy agreed, swallowing the third invisible pill and returning the glass of water to Neil's waiting hand. "Now what?"

Neil deposited the empty glass on the night table beside the bed, then climbed into bed beside Cindy, sliding down under the covers and taking her in his arms. "Good night, Cindy," he said, kissing her softly. "Sleep well."

* * *

WHEN CINDY WOKE up at seven-thirty the next morning, Neil was already in the shower. "Well, what do you know? The damn pills actually worked." She laughed out loud, was considering joining Neil in the shower when the phone rang.

"Cindy, it's Ryan Sellick," the voice boomed across the phone wires. "I know it's early, and I'm probably the last person in the world you want to be hearing from under the circumstances, but . . ."

Neil emerged from the bathroom, towel-drying his hair.

"Is something wrong?" Cindy asked, the expression on Neil's face asking the same thing. "My neighbor," she whispered, her hand over the mouthpiece.

"Believe me, I wouldn't be calling you if I weren't absolutely desperate."

"What is it, Ryan?"

Neil crossed the room, kissed Cindy's forehead, began gathering up his clothes.

"It's just that you've always been so kind to Faith, and I don't know who else to turn to."

"Is Faith all right?"

"She's had a really rough couple of days. She was up most of the night, and she just fell asleep about fifteen minutes ago. Unfortunately, I have to be in Hamilton all day."

"You want me to look in on her?"

"I was wondering if you could take care of Kyle until Faith wakes up. I know it's a hell of a thing for me to be asking. Especially when you think I might have. . . ." He paused. "It's just that I'm being picked up in less than half an hour, and. . . ."

"Okay," Cindy told him, watching Neil get dressed.

"Okay?"

"I'll be over in fifteen minutes," Cindy said.

"Thank you. Cindy. . . ."

"What?"

Silence. Then, "Please believe I had nothing to do with Julia's disappearance."

"I'll be over soon." Cindy hung up the phone.

"You're sure that's a good idea?" Neil asked.

Cindy shrugged. She wasn't sure of anything anymore. "Maybe immersing myself in someone else's problems for a few hours will take my mind off my own."

"You're amazing," Neil said.

"I had a good night's sleep."

Neil kissed her gently on the lips. His hair smelled of green apple shampoo. "I better go home, get changed for work."

"Thank Max for me for letting his father stay out all night," Cindy said as she was walking him to the front door minutes later.

"I'll call you later."

Cindy watched Neil drive off, then hurried upstairs to get dressed, realizing she was feeling better—more positive—than she had in days. Was it because she'd actually slept through the night for the first time in weeks? Because she was having sex for the first time in years? Because she thought she might be falling in love? "How can I even be thinking about falling in love at a time like this?" she asked the silent house, discarding her terry-cloth robe and standing naked in the upstairs hall, knowing that she was completely alone, that her mother wasn't here to warn her of the dangers of catching a draft, her sister wasn't waiting to point out that she too could have a flat stomach if she had the time Cindy had to work out, that Heather wasn't gasping in embarrassment and dismay at what the future held in store, that Julia wasn't here to tell her to *please* put something on. . . .

That Julia wasn't here.

"I'm all alone," Cindy said as the dog rushed over to lick at her toes. "Well, maybe not *all* alone," she amended, surprisingly grateful for the animal's presence. She knelt to stroke his side, watched him roll over to offer his belly. "Thank you for being here," she told him, obliging him with a few heartfelt scratches. Elvis groaned his pleasure, stretched himself out to his full length, pawed at the air for more.

Don't stop, he seemed to be saying. *Don't stop.*

Don't stop, she heard herself cry out in joyous abandon as Neil buried his head between her thighs.

"I'm doing it again," she said out loud. How can I be happy? How can I be hopeful for the future when the present is so unsettled?

And yet hope was exactly what she was experiencing. Was it some kind of premonition? Cindy wondered as she showered and dressed. Was her intuition telling her that things were about to change, that all was not lost, that there was indeed reason to be optimistic?

Maybe at this very instant, Julia was being rescued, Cindy projected, racing down the stairs to the kitchen. Maybe any minute now, the police would be turning up at her front door with the good news. "And I won't be here," she said, deciding to call Detective Bartolli, tell him where she'd be. Just in case. She left the Sellicks' phone number with the officer who answered the phone, then shut Elvis in the kitchen, and quickly exited the house.

She arrived at the Sellicks' door at the same time a black Caprice was pulling into the driveway.

"Would you tell Ryan his lift is here?" an attractive young woman called, leaning out the window of the driver's seat.

Cindy smiled at the woman, whose long coral-colored ringlets hung past the shoulders of her low-cut, floral-print blouse, acknowledging the young woman's request with a nod of her head as she rang the bell.

"Cindy, thank God," Ryan said as he opened the door.

"Your lift is here." Cindy motioned toward the driveway, stepped into the hall.

Ryan signaled with his index finger to the young woman, then closed the door. "The baby's asleep," he said, straightening his dark blue tie, speaking quickly. "Faith's been expressing her milk, so there are a few bottles in the fridge. All you have to do is heat one up for a minute in the microwave. . . ."

"Ryan," Cindy interrupted gently. "It's okay. I know what to do."

"Of course you do." His eyes swept across the floor, like a broom. "Damn it. Where'd I put my briefcase?"

"Is that it?" Cindy pointed to a black leather briefcase propped against the wall next to the kitchen.

"That's it." He took two giant steps toward it, scooped it into his hands, held it tight against his gray suit, his eyes shooting from the kitchen to the living room. "I'm sorry the place is such a mess."

"I'll try to straighten up a little."

"Oh no, please. You don't have to do that."

"It's fine. Gives me something to do."

Outside, a car horn honked.

"I've got to go."

"Go."

"I look okay?"

"You look great."

"Very important potential client or I'd send somebody else."

"Knock 'em dead."

"You're a godsend, Cindy. I don't know how to thank you."

You can find my little girl, she thought. "Your ride's waiting," she said.

Ryan opened the door. "I've left my cell phone number on the kitchen counter, in case there are any problems."

"There won't be."

"I'll call you as soon as I get two minutes."

"Try not to worry."

Ryan ran down the front steps to the car, then stopped, his hand on the door handle. "Has there been any news?" he called back, an obvious afterthought.

Cindy shook her head. "Drive carefully," she advised the impatient young woman behind the wheel of the car.

"I'll phone you later."

Cindy waved as the woman backed her car onto the street and turned west toward Poplar Plains, not envying them the traffic they faced. Hamilton was almost close enough to be considered a suburb, but rush hour traffic would add at least twenty minutes to the normally hour-long drive. And that was providing there were no accidents along the way.

(Typical Altercation: "It was an accident, for God's sake," Julia, age thirteen and already towering over her mother, stares unapologetically at the broken Lalique vase her careless hand has swept off the mantel above the fireplace.

"I know it was an accident," Cindy says evenly. "I just said you should be more careful."

"It's just a damn vase. I don't know what you're getting so bent out of shape about."

"It was a birthday gift from Meg. And please watch your language."

"What'd I say? Damn? You call that language?"

"Julia. . . ."

"I hear you say much worse."

"That doesn't mean. . . ."

"It means you're a hyprocrite."

"Julia. . . ."

"Mother. . . ."

Stalemate.)

Cindy closed the front door, leaned her head against it, trying not to hear the echo of Julia's recriminations clawing at her through the years. I have to stop doing this, she thought. I have to stop projecting Julia into every scenario, stop putting her inflection into every casual utterance.

How do I do that? she asked, pushing herself away from the door. How do I stop thinking about my daughter? How do I get used to living without her?

She walked into the living room, the hope she'd felt only moments earlier rapidly dissipating as she surveyed the chaos. Pillows from the living room sofa lay scattered on the hardwood floor. There were used coffee cups everywhere. Something sticky grabbed at the soles of her shoes. A plate of leftover pieces of Kentucky Fried Chicken sat largely untouched on the water-stained coffee table in the middle of the room. Cindy carried the plate into the kitchen, swept the food into the garbage disposal under the sink, the sink full of dirty dishes. "What a mess." She stacked the dishes in the dishwasher, then rinsed out by hand the half dozen wine glasses on the counter.

Was Faith drinking? Or was it Ryan?

Does your daughter drink? Detective Gill had asked.

No, Cindy said.

Occasionally, Tom corrected.

"Stop it," Cindy said out loud. Not everything is about Julia.

Julia's reflection winked at her from the large window overlooking the backyard. "Of course it is," she said, as upstairs, a baby started to cry.

TWENTY-SEVEN

CINDY hurried up the stairs to the nursery, glancing toward the closed doors of the master bedroom as she tiptoed past, hoping the baby's cries wouldn't disturb Faith. "It's okay. It's okay," she cooed at the screaming infant, his face scrunched into a tight, wrinkled ball, like a roll of bright pink yarn. She reached into the crib and drew the baby gingerly to her chest, kissing his soft, sweet-smelling forehead as she rocked him gently back and forth. "It's okay, baby. Don't cry. Don't cry."

Amazingly, the infant stopped howling almost immediately.

That was easy, Cindy thought, standing by the side of the crib, continuing her rhythmic rocking. Too easy, she realized, as seconds later, the baby stiffened in her arms, his hands and feet shooting from his body like the limbs of a leaping frog. A fresh round of screams pierced the air. "My goodness," Cindy muttered, tapping the door to the nursery closed with her foot. Had Julia ever screamed this loudly? "Do you need changing? Is that the problem?"

Cindy looked around the nursery, noticing for the first time what a lovely room it was. Pale blue walls, bleached wood crib and hand-painted dresser, a high shelf filled with soft, colorful, stuffed animals that ran along three of the walls, a Bentwood rocking chair by the small side window, its curtains the same delicate blue-and-white gingham as the crib sheets. A mobile of dancing elephants hung from the overhead light fixture; another mobile, this one of pastel-colored butterflies, dangled over the crib. "Everything you could ask for," Cindy told the crying infant, lying him across the changing table against one wall and reaching for the giant box of disposable diapers at her feet. "We'll get you all cleaned up and then you'll be happy. You'll see." She unsnapped the baby's clean white sleeper and removed his diaper with a sure and steady hand. "Just like riding a bicycle," she told the baby, whose response was to scream even louder. "Not too impressed, I see." And not wet either, she realized, replacing the dry diaper with another, then leaning forward to secure the tabs just as a sudden arch of urine sprayed into the air, narrowly missing her eye. Cindy pulled back, startled. "Oh, my," she said with her mother's voice. "Well, I only had girls. They didn't do things like that." She wiped off the top of the changing table and replaced the now-wet diaper with another clean one, then gently maneuvered the baby's wriggling feet back into the legs of his sleeper, before carrying him out of the room. "Ssh," she cautioned, hurrying past the master bedroom and down the stairs. "We don't want to wake Mommy. Mommy needs her sleep." Mommy needs a psychiatrist, Cindy thought, proceeding past the messy living room into the now-tidy kitchen. Or, at the very least, a housekeeper. She reached into the fridge, located one of the baby's bottles, and popped it into the microwave, the baby screaming steadily in her ear. "It's okay, sweetheart. We'll have you all fixed up in no time."

Or not, Cindy thought when the infant refused to take the bottle. "Come on, sweetheart. You can do it. Mmmm. Warm milk. Yummy delicious. Try some."

Cindy carried the baby into the living room, and sank down

on the pillowless green velvet sofa, cradling Kyle the way she remembered cradling Julia. She'd nursed Julia for almost a year,
she remembered fondly, as Kyle's lips bounced across her white
T-shirt, searching for her breast. "Oh, sweetheart, I'm so sorry. I
don't have any milk. But I have this yummy bottle." She slid the
rubber nipple into his mouth, even as Kyle tried turning his head
away in protest. "Come on, sweetheart. Give it a chance."

Kyle's lips suddenly locked around the rubber nipple, his crying shuddering to a halt as he devoted all his energy to draining
the liquid from the bottle.

"That's a good boy. Yes, that's it. Now you've got it."

Julia used to suckle with that same ferocious determination,
Cindy found herself thinking, recalling the hard tug at her breast
each time Julia would settle in against her to be fed. She kissed the
top of Kyle's down-covered head, tried remembering the same
scene with Heather. But Cindy had few memories of nursing
Heather, and those few she did have revolved more around Julia,
who'd sit screaming at Cindy's feet, her arms wrapped tightly
around her mother's knees, every time Cindy tried breast-feeding
her younger child. Ultimately, everyone involved was a nervous
wreck, and Cindy switched Heather over to a bottle when she was
barely two months old.

"Well, well. Look at you go." Cindy watched the milk rapidly
disappear from the bottle. When the bottle was empty, Cindy
lifted Kyle over her shoulder and gently patted his back until she
heard him burp. "What a guy," Cindy murmured, rocking him
back and forth in her arms until he drifted off to sleep.

She'd always loved this part. The baby part. She knew a lot of
women didn't, that they had trouble relating to their children
until their children started relating to them. Maybe Faith was one
of those women. Maybe once Kyle started responding to her, she'd
stop viewing his outbursts as evidence of her own failure. Maybe as
the year progressed, and Kyle started sitting up, trying to stand, to

walk, to talk, she'd realize what a miracle she and her husband had created together, the tremendous gift they'd been given, and she'd be happy.

Except it wasn't as easy as that, and Cindy knew it. Postpartum depression, if indeed that's what Faith was suffering from, couldn't be cured with simple platitudes or even common sense. Another case of hormones running amok, Cindy thought, wondering if Ryan had taken her earlier advice, talked to Faith's doctor about prescribing stronger medication.

I certainly can't keep running over here every time there's a problem, she thought, carrying Kyle up the stairs to the nursery.

Why not? she wondered. What else do I have to do?

Cindy felt an unexpected tear wend its way down her cheek, then drop onto the top of Kyle's head. He stirred, his little fist shooting instinctively into the air, as if preparing to defend himself. Cindy pressed him tighter to her breast, hunkered down in the chair, began rocking back and forth.

Within minutes, she was fast asleep.

(Dream: Cindy is walking down the empty corridor of Forest Hill Collegiate, where she attended high school, trying to locate the principal's office. *It's over there,* Ryan tells her, appearing out of nowhere to pass her in the hall. Suddenly Cindy is standing in front of the long reception desk in the middle of the main office. *I'm looking for Julia Carver,* Cindy tells Irena, who is too busy ironing a pair of men's slacks to look up. *Room 113,* Irena says curtly. Cindy races down the hall, past a drinking fountain that is shooting water blindly into the air, then bursts through the door to Room 113, her eyes sweeping across the rows of curious student faces. *Where's Julia?* she demands of the dwarflike man at the head of the class. Michael Kinsolving lowers the script he is holding to his sides and walks menacingly toward her. *Who's Julia?* he asks.)

Cindy woke with a start, causing the infant in her arms to stiffen and cry out. "It's okay," she reassured him softly, coming fully awake, grateful when the baby's body drifted back into sleep. She took a deep breath, carefully adjusted Kyle's position, and checked her watch. Eleven o'clock! She'd been asleep almost two hours. She checked the time again to make sure, then pushed herself out of the rocking chair, her legs wobbly, her shoulders and arms stiff. "Those pills of Neil's were really something."

Slowly, with meticulous care, Cindy deposited Kyle on his back in the crib, then crept from the room, closing the door after her. She proceeded down the hall to the master bedroom, each step a deliberate exaggeration, then cocked her ear against the closed door, wondering if Faith was still asleep. After several seconds, she pushed open the door, and stepped inside.

The room was dark and stuffy, an etherlike pall filtering through the air, like a miasmal mist. Cindy inched her way across the clothes-strewn broadloom toward the huge cast-iron bed that sat against the far wall. Faith lay on her back in the middle of the bed, one arm tossed carelessly above her head, one foot peeking out from underneath a pile of heavy blankets, her uncombed hair matted against her forehead, her mouth open, a series of snores emanating from between parched lips. Cindy smoothed the damp hair away from Faith's face, then replaced her foot beneath the covers. How many times had she done the same thing for Julia? How many times had she tucked in errant toes and smoothed away stray hairs?

Don't do that, Julia would protest, slapping at her mother's hand, even in her sleep.

Cindy was halfway down the stairs when she heard the steady sound of barking and realized it was coming from next door. Elvis! She'd forgotten all about him. Had he been barking the whole time she'd been away?

"I should run home and let him out," Cindy said to an imaginary panel of judges. "It'll just take two minutes." Except it wouldn't. You just didn't let Elvis out. You escorted him around the block and waited while he sniffed each blade of grass until he found just the right one on which to do his business, and then you went through the whole ritual again. And again. And again. There was no such thing as two minutes with Elvis. Twenty minutes was closer to the truth. And she couldn't leave Kyle alone for twenty minutes, even with his mother sleeping in the next room. Faith was practically comatose. She couldn't just take off. Who knew what might happen? How many times had she read articles about children dying in fires while their caregivers were out of the house? *I only left him alone for two minutes!*

"Okay, so what do I do?" Cindy asked the empty hall.

Shouldn't have been so quick to get rid of me, she heard her mother say.

Please, her sister added. *You think this is a problem? You should spend a day at my house.*

The baby started crying.

"Well, that settles that." Cindy scribbled a note for Faith telling her she was taking Kyle for a walk, then left it on the floor outside her bedroom door. "We'll change you later," she told the baby, carrying him down the stairs and grabbing the house key hanging from a nail near the front door.

She located the large English-style carriage hidden along the side of the house, and laid Kyle inside it, the baby's fierce screams bracketing Elvis's angry barks. Leaving the carriage in her drive-way, she bounded up the outside steps and unlocked her front door. Elvis shot out at her, as if from a cannon, almost knocking her over. "How did you get out of the kitchen?" Cindy asked in amazement, watching as Elvis ran down the front steps, and peed against the wheel of the carriage. "Great. Oh, that's great. Okay, wait. Let me get your leash." Cindy opened the hall closet, her hand whipping across the floor in search of the dog's leash. "Where is it? Damn it, where are you?" Where had she put the silly thing? "Okay, stay there," she directed the dog, whose response was to bark loudly four times, then run toward the sidewalk.

"Where's the leash?" Cindy yelled at the empty house, racing into the kitchen, checking the countertops, trying not to look too closely at the floor.

She finally located the leash in one of the drawers she reserved for old birthday cards and unsolicited stationary that had been sent by various charities trying to pressure her into making a donation. "Elvis," Cindy called out, carrying the leash outside, seeing the dog disappear around the corner. "Come back here." Cindy pushed the carriage to the sidewalk, then stopped dead, her heartbeat freezing in her chest.

The baby was gone.

She knew it even before she looked down.

She'd left him alone for no more than sixty seconds, and in those sixty seconds some lunatic had jumped out from behind a nearby maple tree and absconded with her neighbor's child. Already the abductor was in his car, speeding toward parts unknown. She'd lost another child. The Sellicks would never see their baby again.

"No," Cindy pleaded, fearfully lowering her eyes to the carriage, her knees buckling as she saw Kyle's huge blue eyes staring up at her, his tongue poking out between his lips, a cascading bouquet of tiny bubbles balanced on its tip.

He was there. He was safe.

Cindy crumpled to the sidewalk, as if her legs were made of paper, her heart all but exploding in her chest. "You're going to give yourself a heart attack if you keep this up," she whispered into the sweaty palm of her hand. And suddenly Elvis was at her side, licking her face and poking his head toward his leash, his tail pounding eagerly against the side of the carriage.

What are you doing goofing off down here? he seemed to be asking.

Cindy attached the leash to the dog's collar, then pulled herself to her feet. Kyle lay on his back, kicking his legs into the air and gurgling happily. "Thank you, God," Cindy whispered, pushing the pram toward Poplar Plains, then continuing south toward Edmund. So much construction going on, she thought absently, noting the new fence going up around a sprawling Tudor-style home on the corner of Clarendon and a concrete porch being erected in front of a modern town house just across the street. Large trucks were everywhere. Workers in hard hats and tight jeans toted heavy rocks and tall ladders, nodding as she walked by. How long had they been in the neighborhood? Long enough to notice Julia?

Nobody struts a street quite like Julia, Ryan had remarked.

On Edmund Street, Cindy turned left, her eyes flitting warily between the large duplexes on the north side of the street and the single-family homes and large apartment buildings on the south. Was Julia somewhere inside one of these structures?

Cindy had always considered the area around Avenue Road and St. Clair to be so safe.

Was it?

Hadn't Julia stepped onto these very streets—soon after eleven o'clock in the morning, almost the same time as now—and disappeared without a trace?

Cindy shivered, feeling cold despite the unseasonable heat, and picked up her pace, all but colliding with a frizzy-haired woman juggling an empty stroller while trying to maintain a grip on her squirming toddler's hand. That's right, Cindy urged the woman silently. Hold on tight. It's not as safe as you think.

It's not safe anywhere.

Elvis balked when they rounded the corner back onto Balmoral, obviously sensing his brief walk was about to end. "Sorry, boy," Cindy told him, dragging him up the outside steps of her home and pushing him through the front door. Clearly there was no point in trying to lock him in the kitchen. "I'll take you for a really long walk when Ryan gets home. I promise. Please don't pee on the floor."

The baby started crying almost the second they were back inside the Sellick house. Cindy carried him into the kitchen and retrieved another bottle of Faith's breast milk from the fridge, then popped it into the microwave oven. She fed the baby, took him back upstairs, retrieved the untouched note she'd left for Faith, and changed Kyle's diaper, careful this time to stand well out of the line of fire. After swaddling him tightly in a soft blue cotton receiving blanket, she laid him on his back in the crib and stood over him, gently rubbing his tummy until he fell asleep.

Her own stomach started rumbling, and she realized she'd forgotten to have breakfast. How many times in the last several weeks had she forgotten to eat, despite the constant prodding of her mother and sister? Her face was starting to look thinner, more drawn. Her bra was feeling a little roomy. *Women gain weight from the bottom up and lose it from the top down,* Julia had once remarked.

And Julia would know. Julia knew about such things.

Cindy checked on Faith to see if she was awake and interested in lunch, but she was still fast asleep, her bare toes once again protruding outside their covers. Cindy closed the door, found herself staring down the narrow upstairs hallway toward the bedroom at the front of the house. What was in that room? she wondered. Why was the door closed?

What if Julia is inside? she suddenly thought, marching down the hall and reaching for the doorknob, knowing she was being ridiculous, but unable to keep such thoughts out of her head. What if the Sellicks were a couple of deranged perverts who'd kidnapped Julia and were deriving sadistic satisfaction from having both mother and daughter under the same roof at the same time?

(Image: Julia, bound and gagged, struggling against her restraints, unable to give voice to her desperate cries, while her mother, oblivious to her daughter's presence, changes diapers in the next room.)

Was it possible?

She'd read that murderers often attended their victim's funerals, prolonging their sick pleasure by luxuriating in the family's suffering.

Was it possible such monsters lived right next door?

The door fell open and Cindy stepped over the threshold, both relieved and disappointed by the thoroughly ordinary room that greeted her eyes, its furnishings utilitarian and undistinguished. Obviously Ryan's home office, Cindy realized, noting the cluttered desk, the stacks of books, the architectural drawings spread across the large drafting table in front of the window. Black-and-white photographs of local buildings adorned the walls. Cindy's eyes swooped into each corner of the room, seeing no trace of her daughter anywhere. Had she really expected to find anything?

The phone rang, poking her in the back like an accusing finger.

Cindy gasped, grabbed for the phone on the desk before it could ring a second time. "Hello?"

"Cindy, it's Ryan," the voice said evenly. "I'm so sorry, but this is the first chance I've had to call you all morning. How's it going?"

"Everything's fine." Cindy noticed a closet in the far corner of the room. What did they keep in there? "Faith and the baby are both asleep."

"That's good. Look, we're almost finished here. Shouldn't take too much longer, and then we'll head home. Think you can hold out another couple of hours?"

Cindy checked her watch. A few more hours and it would be almost two o'clock. Her eyes returned to the closet door. "No problem."

"I can't tell you how much I appreciate this."

"I'll see you soon." Cindy hung up the phone, walked to the closet, pulled open the door.

(Image: Julia, her mouth covered by duct tape, her hands bound behind her back, her feet tied at the ankles, sits naked and shivering in a corner of the closet.)

The closet was filled with winter clothes, each item freshly cleaned and hanging inside a long plastic bag. Cindy examined each article of clothing—a man's heavy brown coat, a woman's purple fleece jacket, men's wool suits in brown, gray, and navy, a woman's black dress, a long teal skirt. She rifled through the built-in shelf full of sweaters, extricating a strong-smelling bar of soap from inside the layers of soft wool. By the time she realized someone was watching her, it was too late. Cindy spun around, the bar of soap flying from her hand and landing at Faith Sellick's feet.

Faith looked from Cindy to the closet, then back to Cindy, her eyes as cold as steel. "What the hell are you doing?" she asked.

TWENTY-EIGHT

F AITH. I didn't hear you."

"What are you doing here? Where's Ryan?" Faith shifted from one foot to the other, her toes disappearing into the soft pile of the beige broadloom. She was wearing a pair of red tartan flannel pajamas that were too big for her body and too warm for the weather, although she didn't seem to notice either. Several hairs drooped lazily into her eyes and she made no effort to push them aside.

"He had to go to Hamilton. You were sleeping. He didn't want to wake you."

"So he asked you to come over and baby-sit his incompetent wife."

"No, of course not. He just wanted you to catch up on your sleep."

"What time was this?"

"Around eight. Apparently he had an important meeting. . . ."

"They're always important." Faith looked toward the window. "What time is it now?"

Cindy glanced at her watch. "Almost noon."

"So I've been unconscious all morning," Faith noted dully.

"Obviously you were exhausted."

"Kyle . . . ?"

"Sleeping like a baby," Cindy said, hoping to elicit a smile. Failing. "I've fed him twice, taken him for a walk around the block. . . ."

"You've been very busy."

Cindy cleared her throat, coughed into her hand. "Are you hungry? I could make us some lunch."

"You can tell me what you were doing snooping around in my closet."

"I'm really sorry about that," Cindy said, stalling, trying desperately to come up with a believable excuse. "It's just that I was feeling a little cold, and I thought you might have a sweater I could throw on."

Faith's shoulders relaxed as she rushed to embrace the lie. "It *is* cold in this house. I keep telling Ryan that, but he insists the temperature's just right. If it were up to me, I'd do away with air-conditioning altogether." She pointed to a long yellow sweater hanging from a thick wooden hanger toward the back of the closet. "Try that one."

Cindy slipped the luxurious cashmere sweater from its hanger. "That's better," she said, the warm wool lying like a sunburn across her back.

"Color looks good on you."

"Thank you."

"You should keep it."

"What?"

"It looks better on you than it does on me. You might as well have it."

"Oh no. I couldn't do that."

"Why not?"

"Because it's yours."

Faith shrugged. "Ryan's in Hamilton, you said?"

"Actually, he just called, said he should be home in a few hours."

"Is Marcy with him?"

"Marcy?"

"Orange hair, big boobs, lots of teeth."

"Sounds like the woman who picked him up."

Faith nodded knowingly. "Marcy Granger. The senior partner's daughter and Ryan's close associate." She verbally underlined the word "close." "I'm pretty sure they're having an affair." She bent down and scooped up the bar of soap. "You think soap really keeps moths away?"

"I don't know. I've never tried it."

"Your husband used to cheat on you all the time, right?" Faith asked.

Cindy tried not to look too shocked by the question. Had she heard Faith correctly?

"Sorry. I guess it's none of my business."

"Who told you my husband cheated on me?"

"You did."

"I did?"

It was Faith's turn to look flustered. "Last week. When I had tea over at your place."

Cindy fought to remember the conversation over tea. She vaguely recalled talk of children, of Faith's concerns for the future, her calm recitation of family suicides, her concern that Ryan no longer loved her. She remembered clarifying that the Cookie was Tom's wife, but she had no memory of having mentioned anything about Tom's assorted infidelities.

"I'm hungry," Faith announced. "Did you say something about lunch?"

Cindy took the soap from Faith's hands, returned it to the middle of the pile of sweaters, and closed the closet door, her mind racing. If she hadn't said anything to Faith about Tom's affairs, who had?

Julia?

Questions began racing around Cindy's brain, like a dog chas-
ing its tail. Was it possible Julia had told Faith about Tom's indiscre-
tions, even though the two women barely knew one another? Or
was it more likely that Julia had confided the information to Ryan
during a romantic encounter? Had Ryan then carelessly passed the
juicy tidbit along to his wife?

"I think there's some leftover tuna in the fridge," Faith was
saying, already halfway down the hall. She stopped in front of the
nursery door. "I guess I should check on Kyle," she said with obvious reluctance, making no attempt to go inside.

"Why don't we just let him sleep?" Cindy led Faith down the
stairs, hoping for more time alone with her. There was no telling
what she might say.

Relief washed across Faith's face. "Did he give you a hard
time?" she asked, making herself comfortable at the kitchen table
while Cindy rifled through her fridge, looking for the tuna.

"No. He was great. Although he *did* almost pee in my eye."

"I think he does that on purpose."

Cindy was about to laugh when it occurred to her that Faith
was actually serious. There was a strange flatness to her voice that
belied any attempt at humor. Disconcerted, Cindy did a final sur-
vey of the contents of the fridge, ultimately abandoning the search
for tuna, and emerging with a handful of eggs she hoped were rea-
sonably fresh. "How about I make us an omelet?"

"With cheese?"

"Do you have any?"

"I love cheese," Faith said, as if this were answer enough.

"One cheese omelete coming up." Cindy located a large chunk
of old Cheddar at the very back of the fridge, as well as several loose
sticks of butter and a container of milk that had never been opened
and was one day short of its expiration date. The salt and pepper
were in plain sight on the counter, but she had to search through
several cupboards for a medium-sized bowl and a frypan. "I think

that's everything," she told Faith, who said nothing. Nor did she say anything as Cindy cracked open the eggs, mixed them with the milk, and stirred them in the frypan. Only when Cindy was adding the Cheddar did Faith show any interest in what she was doing.

"I love cheese," she said again.

They ate in silence, Faith cutting her omelet into neat little bits, then slowly chewing and swallowing each piece. Cindy watched her as she ate, wishing she could pick the young woman up by her heels and shake her, as if she were a branch on one of the outside maple trees. How many loose acorns would fall out? Cindy wondered, thinking, Does she know something? Something she's not telling me?

Something about Julia?

"Is there anything new with the investigation?" Faith asked suddenly, as if reading Cindy's mind. She laid her fork down, pushed her plate into the middle of the table, sat back in her chair, her knife in her right hand.

"No," Cindy said. "Nothing new."

"It must be horrible for you."

"It is."

"So many horrible things in this world." Faith lifted the knife toward her face, checked her reflection in the narrow sliver of stainless steel. "I look like shit," she said.

"No, you don't."

"Do you ever wish you could just crawl into bed and never wake up?"

"Faith . . ." Cindy began, not sure what to say next.

"I'm tired." Faith pushed her chair away from the table, struggled to her feet. "I think I should lie down for a while." Without another word, she turned and walked purposefully from the room. It was only when Cindy heard her opening the door to the nursery that she realized Faith still had the knife.

* * *

CINDY RACED UP the stairs, the omelet sitting heavy in her stomach, like a large stone, impeding the flow of oxygen to her lungs. Why hadn't she been paying closer attention? What if she was already too late?

Too late for what?

"Faith!" Cindy ran down the hall, Faith's sweater slipping from her shoulders and sliding off her back. "Faith, wait!"

A baby's screams filled the air, followed by the sound of Faith's tortured cries. Together they shook the floor beneath Cindy's feet, like a powerful earthquake.

"No!" Cindy threw herself into the nursery, stopping dead in her tracks at the horrifying sight that greeted her eyes.

Faith Sellick was standing over her son's crib, one hand pulling at her hair, her face a twisted mask of grief and fury, the other hand on her baby's chest, his tiny body convulsing with outrage.

"Faith, no! What have you done?" Cindy pushed Faith out of the way with such force that Faith lost her footing and fell back against the rocking chair before collapsing to the floor. Cindy scooped the baby from the crib, her eyes frantically searching his white sleeper for blood. But there was no blood on the baby's sleeper. Just as there was no blood on the sheets. No blood anywhere, Cindy realized with audible relief, seeing the knife lying innocently at the foot of the crib. "What happened in here?" she demanded over Kyle's continuing howls. "What did you do to him? Tell me!"

"I didn't do anything," Faith cried helplessly. "I was just looking at him, and he opened his eyes and started screaming."

"Did you poke him with the knife?"

"What knife?" Faith asked, her confusion palpable.

"You didn't touch him?"

Faith shook her head, covering her ears with her hands, trying to block out the baby's cries. "He hates me," she whimpered. "He hates the sight of me."

"He doesn't hate you." Cindy returned the screaming baby to his crib, lowered herself to the floor beside Faith.

"Listen to him."

"Babies cry, Faith. It's what they do."

"I can't stand it when he cries."

"I know." Cindy took Faith in her arms, rocked her back and forth, as earlier she had rocked the woman's infant son. "I know."

"Sometimes when he cries, it feels like my head is going to explode."

"I know," Cindy said again. What else could she say? It was the truth. She *did* know. There was nothing worse, nothing more heartbreaking, than the sound of your child's unhappiness. "You need to see a doctor," she told Faith gently. "I'll talk to my friends. Find out the name of a good psychiatrist."

"You think I'm crazy?"

"No. I just think you need more help than I can give you."

Faith shook her head. "You think I'm crazy," she said.

RYAN WALKED IN the house at just after four o'clock, his arms full of blood-orange roses. "For you," he told Cindy, laying them across her arms. "Along with my heartfelt apologies for being so late."

"Your meeting went on longer than you thought," Cindy stated rather than asked. This was familiar territory after all. Tom had long ago given her a tour of its terrain.

"I'm really so sorry. When I phoned you, I honestly thought we had everything all worked out."

Cindy did her best at a sympathetic smile.

"We resolved everything eventually," he said, as if seeking to reassure her.

"You got the commission?"

"Just in time for the start of rush hour traffic. It was brutal."

"You must be exhausted."

"I'm more than a little drained, to tell you the truth. I could use a drink. How about you?"

Cindy thought she already detected a faint odor of booze on Ryan's breath. "I really should be getting home, get these flowers in water."

"One little drink. To celebrate my success." Ryan disappeared into the dining room, returned minutes later with a bottle of red wine and two glasses. "Red okay with you?"

"Fine."

He uncorked the bottle as Cindy lowered the roses to the coffee table. "To you," he said, clicking his glass against hers. "With my undying gratitude."

"To Julia's safe return." Cindy lifted the glass to her mouth, took a long sip, the taste of blackberries lingering on her tongue.

Ryan winced. "How are you holding up?"

"Just barely."

"I wish there was something I could do."

"Me too."

"Honestly, Cindy, I told the police everything I know." Ryan took another sip of his wine, glanced toward the ceiling. "It's so quiet."

"Everyone's asleep."

"Amazing. You obviously have the magic touch."

"Your wife thinks you're having an affair," Cindy said matter-of-factly.

"What?"

"Your wife . . ."

"My wife's imagination is working overtime these days," Ryan said testily, cutting Cindy off before she could say it again.

"Women are usually right about this sort of thing." Cindy watched the color drain from Ryan's face as effortlessly as he drained the wine from his glass.

"My wife is depressed . . ."

"That doesn't mean she's delusional."

"You know as well as I do how strange she's been acting lately."

Cindy had to admit he was right. "What does her doctor say?"

Ryan shook his head. "I've been meaning to call him. It's just that I've been so damn busy."

"Your wife needs help, Ryan."

"Agreed," Ryan said briskly, finishing the wine in his glass, looking sorry he'd ever suggested she stay for a drink. "I'll call him first thing in the morning."

As if on cue, the telephone rang.

Cindy carried her glass to the kitchen and left it in the sink, wondering how long it would be before someone got around to washing it. "I should get going," she said, waving good-bye as Ryan picked up the phone.

"Don't forget your flowers," he whispered, hand over the mouthpiece.

"Oh, right." Cindy returned to the living room, scooped the two dozen roses off the coffee table, pricking her finger on an unseen thorn. She brought her injured finger to her mouth, sucked at the blood, thought it sweeter than the wine.

"Just a minute," she heard Ryan say. Then, walking toward her, extending the portable phone in his hand, "It's for you."

"For me?" Cindy suddenly remembered she'd left the Sellicks' phone number with the police in case they needed to reach her. Had something happened? Had her earlier premonition been correct? Had they found Julia? Cindy lifted the phone to her ear as Ryan moved a discreet distance away. "Hello?"

"Mrs. Carver, it's Detective Bartolli."

"Has something happened?"

"Are you all right?"

"Yes. Of course. Have you found Julia?"

"No." A pause. Then, "Is Ryan Sellick in the room with you?"

Cindy felt her pulse quicken. She stole a glance at Ryan, who was standing at the window, pretending to be engrossed in the late afternoon sky. "Yes."

"Okay, I want you to listen to me, and not do anything stupid. Do you understand?"

"Yes, but . . ."

"No buts. I want you to make whatever excuses are necessary and get out of that house as quickly as possible. We're on our way."

"What are you talking about?"

"Just do what I tell you."

"I don't understand."

"We did a check on those crank calls you've been receiving. Several of them came from the Sellick house."

"What?"

"You heard me."

"What does it mean?"

"We don't know what it means, but we intend to find out. Now get the hell out of that house, and let us handle it."

Cindy clicked off the phone as Ryan turned around.

"Problems?" he asked.

"I have to go."

"Was that the police?"

Don't say anything, Cindy cautioned herself. Don't do any-thing stupid. Just listen to Detective Bartolli, and get the hell out. Let the police handle things.

"Cindy?"

Cindy dropped the roses to the floor. "What have you done with my daughter?" she demanded, hurling the portable phone at Ryan's head. "What have you done with Julia?"

TWENTY-NINE

THE phone whizzed by Ryan's head like a bullet, missing the side of his skull by mere centimeters, and slamming into the piano, taking a crescent-shaped nick out of its ebony side. It crashed to the floor, then lay on its back, its underside exposed and vulnerable, like a dead turtle.

"Cindy—Jesus!—what the hell are you doing?" Ryan swayed from one foot to the other, as if not sure whether to bolt for the door or wrestle her to the ground.

Cindy made the decision for him, throwing herself at his chest and grabbing hold of his dark blue tie, weaving it between her fingers, and pulling it up and out, like a noose. "Where is she? What have you done with her?"

Ryan tried wriggling out of her grasp, but Cindy's grip on his tie was unyielding. His complexion went from soft pink to angry red, as his right hand reached for his throat, and his left tried in vain to ward off the blows of her open palm.

A sudden jolt of pain shot through Cindy's arm, like an electric shock, as Ryan succeeded in grabbing her wrist and twisting it back. Cindy responded with a sharp kick to his shin.

"Cindy, what the hell . . . ?"

"Where's Julia? Where is she?"

"I don't know."

Cindy hauled back and slapped Ryan, hard, across the face.

"Shit!" he yelled, his cheek whitening with the imprint of her hand. The slap seemed to knock him into action, for suddenly he was all masculine strength and rage, his arms extending and corralling and subduing. In seconds, he overpowered Cindy's intemperate flailings, reducing them to an ineffectual montage of arms and legs, hands and feet, fingers and toes.

Cindy cried out as she felt the point of his shoe crack against the back of her knees, then watched helplessly as her body was propelled into the air, before falling—ass over teakettle, as her mother might say—to the floor. Her elbow smacked against the top of the piano stool, and she swore, the word *fuck* flying from her mouth in a sudden rush of air, as Ryan fell on top of her, pinning her arms to the floor above her head. Roses scattered in all directions as Cindy tried to sit up, to push him away, to roll out from under him, but she couldn't move. "Shit! Fuck!" she sputtered, sounding increasingly weak, her words having lost their power to shield and protect. After several more minutes of aimless showboating, she gave up, stopped struggling, lay still.

"Okay, now," Ryan began, his voice that of the conqueror, despite his shortness of breath.

Cindy stared up at the man lying on top of her, gravity pulling on his handsome face, distorting his delicate features, like a silk sweater that's been left too long on a hanger. Ryan was bruised and sweaty, and his dark hair fell across his forehead like loosely shredded bits of carbon paper. Anger intensified the black of his eyes; confusion softened it. But something else was present in those eyes, Cindy recognized. Mingled with the anger and confusion was an unmistakable glint of excitement. Ryan Sellick was enjoying himself.

"Tell me what the hell is going on," he said.

In response, Cindy expelled a wad of saliva from her mouth, aiming it directly at Ryan's face. Unfortunately, the gesture proved more symbolic than successful, with only a tiny fraction of the spittle reaching its intended target, and the rest raining back across her lips.

"Are you crazy?" Ryan was shouting now. "Have you completely lost your mind?"

"Let go of me."

Ryan tightened his grip on her wrists. "Not until you promise to calm down."

"You're only making things worse for yourself."

"What are you talking about?"

"The police will be here any minute."

Ryan suddenly let go of her arms, sank back on his hips. "The police?"

"They know all about your affair with Julia," Cindy improvised.

Ryan fell away from her then, leaning back against the stubby front leg of the piano, the color draining from his face in uneven bursts, leaving jagged splotches of red on his cheeks, like too much makeup haphazardly applied. "That's ridiculous," he said, but his words lacked the moral outrage necessary to sustain them, and they burst upon contact with the air, like soap bubbles.

Cindy scooted along the floor on her rear end until she felt the sofa at her back. She was too tired to stand up, too spent to launch another attack. "Just tell me where Julia is," she said softly, when what she really wanted to say was, Just tell me Julia's alive.

"I don't *know* where she is."

"The police think you do."

"The police are wrong."

"Just like they're wrong about the crank calls I've been getting?"

"What crank calls?"

"The ones telling me my daughter is a tramp, that she got what she deserved."

"I don't understand."

"The calls coming from this house."

"What!"

"Are the police wrong about that too, Ryan?"

A shadow fell across Ryan's face. Like in the movies, Cindy thought, when the screen slowly fades to black. His eyes registered disbelief, acceptance, and alarm almost simultaneously, and he shook his head, muttering, "No, it's impossible. It can't be."

"What can't be?" Cindy asked, distracted by the sound of footsteps on the stairs. She turned, saw Faith standing in the doorway. She was wearing the same red tartan pajamas she'd been wearing all day, and the smell of sour milk emanated from her body like an unpleasant perfume.

"What's going on in here?" Faith asked, her eyes flitting between Cindy and her husband.

Cindy remained on the floor as Ryan struggled to his feet, limped toward his wife.

"What happened to your face?" Faith touched her husband's cheek. "What's going on?" she asked again, her voice flat and faraway, as if she were talking in her sleep.

"Faith," Ryan began, then stopped, smoothed the hair away from his wife's forehead with a solicitous hand.

"The police are on their way over," Cindy informed her.

"The police? Why?"

"They think we know something about Julia," her husband explained.

"But you already talked to them."

"Apparently some calls were made from this house . . ."

"What are you talking about?"

"The police have a tap on my phone," Cindy said, her voice cold, her sympathy spent. "Apparently it's not unusual in cases like this for the victim's family to receive crank calls," she continued, bracing herself for Faith's heated denials.

Instead she heard, "You think Julia's the victim here?"

"What?" asked Cindy, rising quickly to her feet.

"What?" echoed Ryan, his hands dropping to his sides.

"Trust me," Faith continued, tugging at the bottom of her pajama top, pulling it up and away from her leaking breasts. "Julia's no sweet, innocent little victim."

"Faith," Ryan began warily. "I don't think you should say anything else."

"Yes, you'd like that, wouldn't you? You'd like me to be the good little girl, the quiet little mouse, the perfect little wifey who stays home and cooks and cleans and looks after your demon seed, all the while smiling and looking happy, never saying a word about the fact that her husband is busy screwing everything that moves."

"Faith, please. . . ."

"What? You think I don't know? You think I don't know about Brooke, about Ellen, about Marcy?" She paused briefly. "About Julia?"

"What about Julia?" Cindy asked quietly, almost reluctant to interrupt, to interfere with the violent flow of words.

Faith abruptly shifted her focus from Ryan to Cindy. "Well, I hate to be the bearer of bad tidings, knowing how special you think your precious Julia is, but your little girl was just one of the crowd. Wasn't she, Ryan? Pick a number—the line forms to the right."

"Faith," her husband warned. "Enough."

"Enough? Are you kidding? What's ever been enough for you?"

"Look. You're upset. You're exhausted. You don't know what you're saying."

"I'm saying you're a lying, cheating piece of shit who sleeps with his clients' wives, his partner's daughter, and his neighbor's

pride and joy. Except there's not a whole lot to be proud of, is
there, Cindy? Trust me on this: Julia's no innocent little victim.
She wasn't lured into the backseat of a stranger's car by a piece of
candy. She was sleeping with a married man, and in my book, she
deserves whatever happened to her."

"Faith," Cindy urged, trying desperately to maintain control,
"if you know where Julia is . . ."

"Have you checked the Yellow Pages under 'Whores'?"

Ryan's hand suddenly sliced through the air, came down hard
across his wife's cheek. "Shut up, Faith! Just shut up!"

Faith staggered back, grabbed the side of her face. "I will not
shut up," she screamed. "I am not a silent partner in this relationship, and I will not be quiet any longer."

"If you have any idea, any idea at all, what happened to
Julia . . ." Cindy pleaded.

Faith squinted at Cindy as if she were staring directly into the
sun. "You think I had something to do with your daughter's disappearance?"

"Did you?"

Faith emitted a low, guttural sound, halfway between a scoff
and a snarl, then sank to the living room sofa. Above their heads, a
baby began to cry. "Well, what do you know? Another quarter
heard from. What took you so long?" she hollered at the ceiling.

"Did you have anything to do with Julia's disappearance?"
Cindy pressed, aware that Ryan was staring at his wife with equal
intensity.

Faith caught the question in her husband's eyes and made another sound, this one more moan than defiance. "You think I actually did something to your golden girl?" she asked, ignoring
Cindy, directing the question at Ryan. "Tell me, when was I supposed to have done this? In between breast-feeding and changing
diapers? Between putting your son down to sleep and trying to get
some sleep myself? How about between blow-jobs?"

"Faith, for God's sake. . . ."

"I didn't touch your precious Julia," Faith told Cindy. "I have absolutely no idea where she is or what happened to her." She lowered her head into her hands, spoke through slightly parted fingers. "Yes, I made those calls. Don't ask me why. You've always been so nice to me. My friend. My *only* friend." She lifted her legs off the floor and curled into a fetal position on the couch, her arms wrapping around her head, as if seeking to protect herself from further blows. "Oh God, would somebody please get that damn baby to stop screaming."

"How long were you involved with my daughter?" Cindy asked Ryan, her voice low, her eyes locked on his wife.

"Cindy. . . ."

"Please don't insult me by continuing to deny it." She turned slowly in his direction.

Ryan nodded. "Two months. Maybe a bit more."

"Why did you lie?"

"What else was I supposed to do? Tell me, Cindy. What was I supposed to do?"

"You were supposed to tell the truth."

"And what good would that have done? What good does knowing about my relationship with Julia do anyone? Is it going to help find her?"

"I don't know. Is it?"

"Honestly, Cindy. If I thought for one minute that telling the police about my affair with Julia would have helped find her, I would have done it. I was just trying to protect her."

"Protect her? The only person you've been trying to protect in this whole mess is yourself."

"I don't know where Julia is," Ryan said again. "Yes, I lied about my involvement with her, and yes, I'm a no-good piece of shit who cheats on his wife. But do you have any idea what it's like being married to someone who's constantly depressed, who acts as if she's the only woman in the world who ever gave birth, who looks at her own son as if he's some infectious disease? So yes, I tend to respond favorably when a beautiful woman looks at me with adoration instead of contempt. But that only means I'm human. It doesn't mean I had anything to do with Julia's disappearance. Please, Cindy, you have to believe me. I would never hurt Julia."

"Do you love my daughter?" Cindy asked, hearing the police car pull into the driveway, the sound of car doors slamming.

Ryan looked away, said nothing.

Of all times not to lie, Cindy thought. "You really are a jerk," she told him, listening as heavy footsteps bounded up the outside steps, and impatient hands pounded on the front door.

IT WAS ALMOST nine o'clock that night when the police finally phoned Cindy to say they'd concluded their questioning of the Sellicks, first at their home, then at the police station, and ultimately decided to release them.

"What do you mean, you released them?"

"We have nothing to hold them on," Detective Gill explained.

"What do you mean, you have nothing?" How many times did she start sentences these days with the phrase, What do you mean? "Ryan Sellick admitted he lied about his affair with Julia. His wife admitted calling my house."

"Yes, and we questioned them for more than four hours. That's *all* they admitted."

"Four hours? My daughter's been missing for two weeks!"

"Mrs. Carver," Detective Gill interrupted gently. "Of course we will continue to investigate all angles here, but Ryan Sellick's alibi checks out, and it's highly unlikely that Faith Sellick could have been involved in Julia's disappearance. Think of it logically. It means she would have had to follow Julia to her audition, wait for her, ambush her. . . ."

"She wouldn't have had to ambush her," Cindy protested, knowing she was grasping at straws. "All she'd have to do was pretend to be in the area shopping, and then casually offer Julia a lift. . . ."

"And the baby?"

"Maybe she left him at home. Maybe he was in the backseat. Maybe she used him to lure Julia into the car." Like offering a child a piece of candy, Cindy thought, recalling Faith's own words. There was a second's silence. Cindy could almost feel Detective Gill shrug. "Are you going to get a search warrant?"

"That won't be necessary."

"What do you mean, it won't be necessary? Why not?"

"The Sellicks have already given us their permission to search their cars and premises."

"They have? What does that mean?"

"It means we're unlikely to find anything."

"And that's what you think?" Why was she asking him that? It was obviously what he thought.

"I think we have to wait and see if forsensics can come up with any real evidence linking the Sellicks to your daughter."

"And if they can't? Can't you arrest them anyway?"

"We need evidence to arrest people, Mrs. Carver," Detective Gill reminded her patiently. "We could charge Mrs. Sellick with making those crank calls, but I'm not sure there's any point to that, given her delicate emotional state."

Cindy took a deep breath, swallowed the scream that was building in her throat. Elvis, lying on the kitchen floor, rolled to his feet and ambled over to where she was sitting, then laid his chin in her lap. Cindy found herself smiling in spite of her distress, and patted the top of his head appreciatively. "What about Sean Banack?"

"His alibis have pretty much checked out."

"Pretty much?"

"It seems unlikely he was involved in Julia's disappearance."

"What about Michael Kinsolving? Duncan Rossi? Any of Julia's friends?"

"So far, nothing."

"So you're no farther ahead than you were two weeks ago. In fact, if anything, you're farther behind." Hadn't she read somewhere that the longer a case dragged on, the colder its trail became? "What exactly are you people doing to find my daughter, Detective?"

"Our job, Mrs. Carver," the detective said simply. "And you're not making things any easier for us by barging into people's homes and interfering with our investigation."

"I didn't barge into the Sellicks' house. I was asked to come over."

"You know what I mean."

"So I'm just supposed to sit back and do nothing?"

"That's exactly what you're supposed to do."

"I don't think I can do that."

"You have no choice here, Mrs. Carver."

Cindy clenched her fists in her lap, swallowed another scream. Elvis immediately poked his wet nose into the palm of her hand, demanding to be stroked. Cindy absently obliged, replaying Detective Gill's words in her mind—*You have no choice here*—and wondering how many major events in her life had been decided without her approval. There was no such thing as choice, she was thinking. It was an illusion, a comforting yet basically specious concept that human beings had developed in order to fool themselves into believing they had some control over their lives.

Control—another illusion.

"Mrs. Carver," Detective Gill was saying. "Did you understand what I just said?"

"I understand, Detective Gill. I'm not an idiot."

"Then please stop acting like one," he said, a sudden sharpness cutting through his soft Jamaican lilt. "You could end up sabotaging this whole investigation," he continued, softening. "Or worse. You could get hurt. And what good would that do anyone?"

"You're right." Cindy looked around the kitchen, thinking that if she didn't get off this phone, get out of this house, she would go insane. "I'm sorry, Detective. It won't happen again."

"We'll keep in touch."

"Thank you." Cindy hung up the phone and jumped to her feet, Elvis leaping to attention beside her. "We have to get out of here," Cindy told the dog, who promptly dragged his leash to the front door, understanding her intent, if not her words.

Seconds later, the two were running down the street toward Avenue Road.

THEY RAN DOWN the steep slope between Edmund and Cottingham. Even after nine o'clock at night, Avenue Road was still busy. Three lanes of traffic moved steadily in each direction, and pedestrians ambled along both sides of the street—joggers, people walking their dogs, couples out for an evening stroll. Such a nice night after all. Still warm. Summer hanging on, more stubborn than usual.

A few more months and this hill would be as treacherous as a mountain of ice. Cindy remembered winters when this stretch of road became almost unnavigable, when cars on the ascent stalled and faltered, their wheels spinning aimlessly before succumbing to the pull of gravity and sliding back down the hill, colliding with other automobiles powerless to get out of the way, causing traffic tie-ups all the way to Queen's Park.

Cindy passed an elderly couple strolling hand in hand, the wife using the handrail that ran along the side of the street to help her manage the incline, then scooted past a jogger in bright orange shorts and the latest in running shoes. What was she doing? she asked herself. She wasn't a jogger, let alone a long-distance runner, yet here she was running much too fast down a steep hill, wearing jeans that were way too tight and sandals that offered no support at all, a rambunctious and unpredictable terrier at her feet. She'd be stiff as a board in the morning, she thought, and laughed out loud, the sound scraping at the darkness, like a pick through ice. Oh well. At least that would keep her from barging into people's homes and offices, from interfering with the police investigation. Hah, she thought, and laughed again.

At the bottom of the hill, she turned right, running along Cottingham, glancing at the semidetached brownstones that lined both sides of the wide street, wondering what mayhem was being unleashed behind thin venetian blinds and antique lace curtains. She slowed her pace as she drew near two young women who were talking beside a low, white picket fence. Both were blond. Neither was Julia.

"What's your favorite film so far?" one was asking the other.

"It's between *The Magdelene Sisters* and *L'Homme du Train*. They were awesome."

"Am I wrong, but is the quality of films better this year?"

Cindy resumed her former pace, passing the two young women, then turning left, then left again, and running briskly down Rathnelly, a quirky little avenue whose even quirkier inhabitants had once declared their street a republic. She turned left again, Elvis beside her, somehow knowing not to stop, to keep running, to keep turning left, then right, then left again, then right, watching one familiar street blur into another. Cindy kept on going, hoping to disappear, to lose herself in the welcoming darkness.

She ran beside the railway tracks along Dupont, past the tiny Tarragon Theater on Bridgeman, where she'd once had a subscription, past majestic old Casa Loma, where Meg had held her wedding reception, then across the bridge at Spadina, back up to St. Clair, and finally back down Poplar Plains to Balmoral.

She reached the corner in time to see Ryan and Faith Sellick pulling into their driveway, climbing out of their car, and carrying their infant son up the front steps, before disappearing inside their home.

Home, she thought, coming to an abrupt halt.

All her running, and where had it gotten her? Back where she started.

She couldn't get lost if she tried.

AT JUST AFTER two o'clock in the morning, Cindy's phone rang.

"Is this Cindy Carver?" a voice asked, jolting her awake.

"Who is this?"

"It's Officer Medavoy from Fifty-third Division. We have your daughter, Mrs. Carver," the officer began.

He was still speaking as Cindy threw down the phone and raced for the door.

THIRTY

T H E Fifty-third Division of the Metropolitan Police Department is a vine-covered, redbrick building with a dramatic glass atrium over its entranceway, located on the southwest corner of Eglinton and Duplex, across from the Eglinton subway station. Cindy pulled her car into the narrow lot at the rear of the building, parking it between two black-and-white police cars, and running along Duplex to the front of the three-story structure. Her legs were cramping as she reached the glass double doors, and she stopped to rub behind one knee, taking several deep breaths in an effort to calm herself down.

They'd found Julia. She was alive.

"I'm Cindy Carver," she announced as she burst through the front door and threw herself at the long counter that cut across the middle of the large, high-ceilinged room. "Where's my daughter?"

A dark-haired woman with a wide forehead and a long, pinched nose was sitting at one of four desks behind the counter. She immediately jumped to her feet, glancing anxiously over one shoulder, before returning wary eyes to Cindy. "I'm sorry?" she began, absently smoothing the creases of her police uniform.

"My daughter, Julia Carver. Someone called me. . . . Officer Medavak. . . ."

"Medavoy," the policewoman corrected.

"Where is he?"

"I'll see if I can find him."

Cindy nodded, her eyes quickly scanning the bulletin board to her left, crowded with pictures of missing children, as the policewoman shuffled slowly toward a door at the back of the room. Cindy had to bite down on her tongue to keep from yelling, Move!

The officer suddenly stopped, turned back to Cindy. "I'm sorry. Your name again?"

"Cindy Carver." What's the matter with her? Cindy thought. Doesn't she know who I am? Doesn't she read the papers? Hasn't she seen Julia's photograph plastered across the front pages for weeks now? Although there'd been no pictures of her for several days, not since the police arrested Sally Hanson's boyfriend for her murder and eliminated the likelihood of a serial killer on the loose. Was it possible Julia had already been forgotten? That Tom had been right—out of sight, out of mind?

"Tom," she thought, saying his name out loud. Was he here? Had anyone thought to phone him?

Certainly she hadn't, she realized guiltily, although she hadn't been thinking too clearly when the police officer called. It had been all she could do to remember to put on some clothes before tearing out the door. She looked down at her black V-neck sweatshirt, hoped it was clean, that she didn't smell. She couldn't remember the last time she'd done any laundry. Not since her sister left, she thought, thinking she should call Leigh, tell her the good news. And her mother. She should phone her. And Tom. Somebody should phone Tom.

She reached for the cell phone in her purse, felt her fist close around it, then released it, brought her hand back to her side. She wanted some time alone with Julia first, time before Tom arrived.

It was horribly selfish of her, Cindy knew, but she also knew that once Tom swept onto the scene, she might as well disappear. There was no question where Julia's first allegiance lay. Cindy wanted— needed—at least a few minutes alone with her daughter before Tom effortlessly assumed control. She needed those precious minutes alone with Julia to touch her, hold her, tell her how much she loved her. Time to stake her claim.

Unless it was already too late.

Unless Tom was already here. Unless they'd called him first— of course they'd called him first— and he'd arrived before her. A five-minute drive, for heaven's sake, especially at two in the morning with only a few cars on the road, and it had taken her almost three times that long to get here. Imagine taking the wrong turn, heading west on Chaplin when she knew to go east, getting stuck behind some joker doing five miles an hour. Where was the idiot going anyway? Why wasn't he home in bed? What was he doing out at two in the morning, this middle-aged man with thinning hair and watery eyes, who scowled when she passed him on the inside lane? And then forgetting what side street was quickest, getting lost *now,* now when her daughter had finally been found.

Tom had undoubtedly proceeded with appropriate calm, had announced himself with the proper politeness to the officer behind the desk, who, of course, had been totally charmed, and who'd immediately ushered him into the backroom without unnecessary prompting. He'd probably asked for a few minutes alone with his daughter, and that's what was taking so long now.

Or maybe he'd already taken Julia home with him, and that was why it was taking forever to find Officer Madavak or Medicare or whatever his name was. Why wasn't he here? And where were Detectives Bartolli and Gill? Why hadn't they been the ones to phone her with the good news?

Unless the news wasn't good, Cindy realized, her stomach

suddenly doing flip-flops, her already sore knees buckling. Unless there was something they weren't telling her.

The front door opened and Cindy spun toward the sound. A uniformed policeman—surprisingly short, beefy, standard-issue bull neck, crossed the room, smiled, and said hello.

"Officer Medavoy?" Cindy asked hopefully.

"No, sorry. Are you looking for him?"

"I'm Cindy Carver. Officer Medavoy called my house to say you have my daughter." Had he? Cindy wondered. Or had it been just another crank call? Why hadn't she thought of that possibility before? Maybe there was no Officer Medavoy.

"Let me see if I can find him for you," the policeman was saying, his voice cheerily noncommital, his demeanor friendly and nonjudgmental, as if she looked like a normal human being, and not like some escapee from the Clarke Institute, as if her skin wasn't ghostly white and her eyes weren't swollen with worry and fatigue, as if her hair wasn't sticking out in a variety of weird angles, as if she didn't smell fetid and stale, her breath heavy with sleep, as if talking to half-crazed mothers at two o'clock in the morning was something he did every day.

And maybe he did, Cindy thought, understanding there was a whole other world that operated between the hours of midnight and 7 A.M., an inverse world where people lived and worked and carried on relatively normal lives. Except what was normal? Cindy wondered, watching the officer disappear into the station's inner sanctum.

Almost immediately, the policewoman reentered the main room from another door. "Officer Medavoy will be with you in a moment," she told Cindy, before returning to her desk and pretending to busy herself with paperwork.

"Can I go in? Can I see my daughter?" It was taking all of Cindy's self-control to keep from leaping over the counter.

"Officer Medavoy would like to talk to you first."

"Why? Is something wrong? Is my daughter all right?"

"She's been throwing up."

"Throwing up?"

"They're getting her cleaned up now."

"I can do that. Please—just let me see her."

"I'm sorry. You'll have to wait for Officer Medavoy," the policewoman cautioned as the other officer reappeared.

"Officer Medavoy will be right with you," he said, stooping to search for something behind the counter.

Cindy watched in growing amazement as the two officers went about their business. What's the matter with everybody? she wondered again. Why are they so calm, so blasé, so indifferent? Why won't they let me see my baby?

Something isn't right here, she decided. Why such a lack of concern, especially if Julia was sick and throwing up? Didn't they realize who she was? Where were Detectives Bartolli and Gill? Why weren't they here?

"Are Detectives Bartolli and Gill here?" Cindy asked, louder than she'd intended.

The two officers exchanged glances, although neither head turned. "I don't believe so," the woman officer responded. "No."

"Why not? Why hasn't anybody called them? What's going on here?"

Both officers approached cautiously. "Mrs. Carver, are you all right?"

"No, of course I'm not all right. I want to see my daughter."

"You have to calm down."

"Calm down? You expect me to calm down? What's the matter with you people?" Had she dreamed the phone call after all? Was this whole episode nothing but a cruel hoax?

Another door opened at the back of the room, and a tall, heavyset man stepped inside. He was about forty, with brown hair, a square jaw, and a nose that had been broken several times. "Mrs. Carver?"

"Where's my daughter?"

"I'm Officer Medavoy," the man answered, coming around the counter, extending his hand.

Cindy shook his hand because it was obviously expected. What she really wanted to do was swat it aside and push the imposing figure out of her way. Why all the formalities? Why couldn't they just take her to Julia? Why the need to talk to her first? What grim reality were they preparing her for? "Please, Officer Medavoy. I need to see my daughter."

He nodded. "You understand she's not in the best of shape."

"No, I don't understand. I don't understand anything. Where did you find her? *When* did you find her?"

"We picked her up about an hour ago in an underground parking garage off Queen Street."

"An underground parking garage?"

"She'd been in a fight with some other girls. They smacked her around a bit."

"A fight?"

"Apparently over some guy."

"I don't understand."

"Well, she was pretty drunk."

"Drunk?"

"She's been throwing up for the last ten minutes," Officer Medavoy said matter-of-factly, leading Cindy around the counter toward one of the backrooms. "Maybe you should go easy on her. At least until morning." He opened the door.

"Julia!" Cindy cried, rushing toward the young girl who sat, battered and wan, on a gray plastic chair in front of a dull brown desk.

Tear-soaked blue eyes stared back at Cindy. "Sorry, Mom," Heather replied, her voice breaking as she wiped a thin line of spittle away from her bruised chin. "It's only me. Sorry," she said again.

"Heather! My God—Heather!" Cindy didn't know whether to laugh or cry, so she did both. Heather, not Julia. She hadn't even considered the possibilty it might be Heather. "Oh, my poor baby," she said, falling to her knees in front of her younger child. "What happened? What did they do to you?" Her fingers fluttered nervously in front of Heather's trembling chin.

Heather turned her head away, revealing a large scratch on her left cheek. "It's nothing. I'm okay."

"The police said you were in a fight with some girls. . . ."

"It was so stupid. I was at this club. There were these girls—I thought we were getting along great. They offered me a lift home. We got to the garage, and next thing I knew they were all over me, saying I was flirting with one of their boyfriends. It was so ridiculous. He wasn't even cute."

"Did you arrest the girls?" Cindy asked the officer.

"They took off before we arrived. Your daughter claims she can't identify anyone."

"Heather. . . ."

"It was dark. It's no big deal."

"Of course it's a big deal. Look at you."

"I'm okay, Mom. It's not important. Please, can we just go home?"

Cindy looked to Officer Medavoy for help, but he only shrugged. "Maybe you should take her home, let her sleep on it. Her memory might improve after a good night's sleep."

Cindy put her arms around her daughter, helped her to her feet. "Are you okay to walk?"

"I'm fine," Heather insisted, clinging to Cindy's side as mother and daughter staggered out into the night.

THEY DROVE HOME in silence. Several times Cindy turned toward her younger child and tried to speak, but the words froze on her tongue, like pieces of dry ice.

(Flashback: Heather, at eight months, her cherubic little face aglow as she sits on her bedroom carpet watching her big sister dance around the room; Heather, at thirteen months, a proud smile filling her cheeks as she sits on the potty, happily chanting, "Pee pee, pee pee"; Heather, three years old, listening intently as Cindy reads her a bedtime story, the second and fourth fingers of her right hand stuffed inside her mouth, her index finger rubbing a disintegrating pink blanket against the tip of her upturned nose; Heather, at six, dressed as an angel for Halloween; Heather, age twelve, tears filling her eyes as she watches her mother watch Julia drive away in her father's car.)

"Can I get you anything?" Cindy asked as they walked through the front door, Elvis jumping all over them. "Some hot chocolate? Tea?"

"It's three o'clock in the morning," Heather reminded her mother, as she bent down to let Elvis lick the scratches on her cheek.

"Maybe you shouldn't let him do that," Cindy cautioned.

Heather straightened her back, headed for the stairs, stopped. "Is Leigh still sleeping in my room?"

"She went home for a few days," Cindy told her. "Grandma too."

Heather looked relieved. "Then I think I'll take a bath, if that's all right."

"Do you want me to get it started?"

"I can do it." Heather was already half out of her clothes by the time she reached the top of the stairs.

"Why don't you use my tub?" Cindy offered.

Normally Heather jumped at the chance to use Cindy's bathtub, with its extra leg room and high-powered Jacuzzi. Tonight she just said, "Okay."

"Maybe tomorrow you should see the doctor," Cindy said over the sound of running water. "Make sure nothing's broken."

"Nothing's broken, Mom."

Cindy watched her daughter shed the last of her clothing, then climb into the still-filling tub. "Don't make it too hot."

"I won't."

"You want some privacy?"

Heather shook her head. "You can stay."

Cindy lowered the lid on the toilet seat, sat down, gazed at her daughter's wondrously slim body through her reflection in the mirror, a million questions free-floating around in her brain: What were you doing at that club alone? What were you drinking? How *much* were you drinking? *Why* were you drinking? Instead she asked, "Still feeling sick?"

"No. I'm okay now."

"You're sure?"

"I don't usually get drunk, you know."

"I know."

"I don't usually drink at all."

"That's good."

"Are you going to tell Dad?"

"I don't know."

"Have you seen him since . . . ?" Heather's voice evaporated along with the steam rising from the tub.

"No."

Heather turned off the taps, then pressed the button on the side of the tub to start the Jacuzzi. Instantly, water began flooding into the tub from several strategically placed openings.

"What about your blind date? Have you seen him again?"

Cindy pictured Neil's handsome face, tried not to picture it between her legs. "He was here last night."

"Yeah?"

"Does that upset you?"

"Why would it upset me?"

"Because I know that children of divorce are always kind of hoping their parents will get back together one day."

"I'm not a child, Mom."

"I know that."

"I just want you to be happy," Heather said.

"Isn't that supposed to be my line?"

"You can use it too."

Cindy smiled. "Have you heard from Duncan?"

"We had a long talk. You were right. We're too young to be so settled. We should be out sleeping around. Like you said."

Dear God, Cindy thought. Of all times to start listening to me. "How about sleeping with me tonight?"

It was Heather's turn to smile. "About you and Neil . . ."

"What about him?"

"Just that I have a good feeling about the two of you." Heather closed her eyes, didn't open them again until the automatic timer turned the Jacuzzi off.

ELVIS WAS ALREADY asleep on Cindy's bed when Cindy guided Heather between the covers. Grudgingly, the dog moved over to accommodate them, eyeing them warily, as if remembering the acrobatics of the other night. Cindy threw her arm across her daughter's hip, and hugged her close, Heather's round little bottom snug against the inverse curve of her mother. They lay together in silence for several minutes, like spoons in a drawer, one breathing out as the other breathed in, two parts of the same whole. My baby, Cindy thought. My beautiful, beautiful little girl. "I love you," she whispered.

And suddenly Heather was sitting up and sobbing in her arms, her slender body convulsing in unexpected anguish. "Oh, Mom, I'm so sorry. Please forgive me. I'm so sorry."

"What are you talking about? Sweetheart, there's nothing to forgive."

"I've been such a brat."

"No, you haven't."

"I wasn't thinking clearly when I gave the police your phone number. I didn't realize you'd assume it was Julia they had in custody. Of course you'd assume it was Julia. What else would you think? And that awful look on your face when you saw it was only me, how disappointed you were. . . ."

"No, sweetheart, no. You just caught me off-guard."

"I said such awful things to her that day, Mom. I told her I never wanted to talk to her again, that the sight of her made me sick."

Cindy thought of her recent altercation with Leigh. "We all say things in anger that we regret. Julia knows you didn't really mean them."

"Does she? I told her I was sorry she'd ever come home, that I wanted her to get out and never come back. Mom," Heather wailed, "I told her I wished she was dead."

Cindy slowly pushed Heather away from her side, held her at arm's length, stared deep into her eyes. "Heather, listen to me. This is very important. No matter what happens, no matter where Julia is or what's keeping her from us, it has nothing to do with you. Do you understand? You do not have that kind of power. You are not to blame. Do you hear me? You are not to blame."

Once again, Cindy folded her daughter into her arms, rocking her gently until eventually, Heather drifted into a restless sleep. Through a steady stream of tears, Cindy watched the minutes tick away on the digital clock radio on the nightstand beside the bed. Occasionally Heather muttered something in her sleep, and Cindy strained to make out the words.

"I'm not to blame," she was saying. "I'm not to blame."

THIRTY-ONE

A<small>T</small> exactly seven o'clock the next morning, Cindy got out of bed, sliding up and out from between her daughter and the dog, and tiptoeing into the bathroom, where she showered, brushed her teeth and hair, put on a little makeup, then headed for the closet, where she dressed in a pair of coffee-colored chinos and a crisp white blouse. It had been a long time since she looked crisp, she knew, and it was important that she start keeping up appearances. For Heather's sake, as well as her own, she decided. She had *two* daughters after all. Not just one.

Heather was still sound asleep when Cindy returned to the bedroom. Elvis had shifted his position, and was now curled up on Cindy's pillow. He lifted his head as Cindy approached, as if to question what she was doing up after so few hours sleep, then lowered it again as she walked out of the room.

Cindy also questioned what she was doing up so early, but the truth was that she'd never really fallen asleep, and she was getting stiff just lying there in bed. It was better to be up and moving, to try behaving like a functioning adult, to make a pretense at normalcy. When Heather woke up, she would find her mother dressed and presentable, fixing her pancakes, and eager to hear her plans for the upcoming weekend.

But for now, she would let her daughter sleep.

Cindy walked down the stairs and into the kitchen, prepared a pot of coffee, then sank down at the kitchen table and stared out the sliding glass door. Outside was another perfect day. Leaning back in her chair, Cindy studied the early-morning sky. A large pink cloud, backlit with just a hint of yellow, hung heavy over the Sellicks' backyard, its lilac underbelly exposed and friendly, like a puppy sleeping on its back. Several wisps had broken free and were drifting to her right. The drifts were purple and in the shape of a woman's mouth, imprinted on the air like a blot of lipstick on a tissue. Cindy watched the stray fragments gradually fade, then get lost in the deepening blue of day.

Everything disappears, she was thinking. Clouds, people, entire civilizations. Human beings were as fragile, as fleeting, as cool wisps of air.

She stretched her legs out in front of her, hearing her joints groan, like hinges needing to be oiled. Yesterday's impromptu run had been a foolish venture, especially since she hadn't worked out in weeks. This is how the body slips into middle age, she thought, patting the slight rounding of her belly as she pushed off her chair, feeling her thigh muscles cramp as she headed for the front door. She needed to start exercising again, she decided, thinking she'd ask Leigh to join her at the gym one afternoon.

The *Globe* and the *Star* lay at her feet when she opened the door, and Cindy scanned the headlines, noting that the unflattering picture of the Prime Minister was the same on both front pages. "Well, what do you know?" she asked him, bending down to scoop up the papers. "It's Friday the thirteenth." Cradling both papers in her arms, she backed into the house, about to close the door when she heard another door opening beside her.

Cindy froze as Faith Sellick emerged from her house and hurried down her front steps, clutching Kyle tightly to her chest, and disappearing around the side of the house. Like Cindy, Faith was neatly dressed for the first time in weeks, the slovenly tartan pajamas replaced by a calf-length, blue cotton dress, her hair pulled into a neat ponytail that pointed, like an arrow, down the center of her back. Seconds later, Faith reentered her line of vision, pushing Kyle's carriage toward the street, the baby crying loudly inside it.

Where would they be headed this early in the morning? Cindy wondered, straining to see where Faith was going, then abruptly pulling her head back inside her door, like a startled turtle returning to its shell, when Faith suddenly spun around, as if aware of Cindy's watchful eye.

Cindy waited half a second, then peeked back outside, her eyes following Faith's swift departure. Ryan's car was still in the driveway, and Cindy wondered if he knew where his wife was going, if he was even aware she was gone. She thought of phoning him, alerting him to his wife's absence, then thought better of it, knowing she was the last person in the world he would appreciate hearing from under the circumstances.

Whatever had possessed Julia to get involved with a married man? She could have her pick of any man she wanted. Why choose this one?

Cindy knew the answer even before she'd finished asking herself the question. Julia had been attracted to Ryan Sellick because he was a younger version of the man she loved best in the world. Deliberately or subconsciously, Julia had picked a man just like dear old dad.

"And so it goes," Cindy muttered, watching Faith push the carriage into the middle of the road from between two parked cars. Where is she going in such a hurry? Cindy asked herself, dropping the newspapers to the floor and stepping onto her front landing, watching Faith turn left onto Avenue Road, heading north.

Almost without thinking, Cindy grabbed her purse from the hall closet and chased after her, careful to stay in the shadows, to keep a comfortable distance between them. Faith was moving quickly, and Cindy's legs were stiff and hurting from last night's ill-conceived marathon. They rebelled each time Cindy tried to widen her stride, pick up her pace. She almost lost Faith at the corner of Avenue Road and St. Clair when Faith caught the traffic light and she didn't, but she spotted her again several blocks later in front of Granite Place, two large apartment complexes that sat well back from the main street.

Faith stopped at the corner of St. Clair and Yonge, despite the green light that indicated she had the right of way. Once more she spun around, as if suspicious she was being followed, and Cindy had to duck into the doorway of Black's One-Hour Photo to keep from being spotted. Her breath was labored and audible. A thin trickle of perspiration ran down the open V of her blouse, and she flicked it away with her finger before it could reach inside her bra. Seven-thirty in the morning and already the outside temperature was creeping toward eighty degrees. Already she was hot and sweaty, the humidity twisting her hair into tight little curls that crept around her head like vines. So much for keeping up appearances, she thought, hearing wary footsteps approach. Cindy took a deep breath, braced herself for yet another unpleasant confrontation with her neighbor.

But the woman who hurried by cast only a furtive glance in her direction, careful to keep a wide berth between them, as if afraid Cindy was one of those crazy ladies who wandered the streets, asking for money and talking to themselves. And maybe she's right, Cindy thought. Maybe I *am* crazy. How else to explain what she was doing, trailing after her neighbor, like some middle-aged Nancy Drew, only a day after the police had ordered her to back off. What was the matter with her? Why couldn't she just mind her own business? So much for acting like a functioning adult.

"Go home," Cindy told herself. "Go home now."

But even as she was saying the words, she was running across the already busy intersection at Yonge and St. Clair, trying to locate Faith. "Where is she?" Cindy muttered underneath her breath, her eyes shooting back and forth across the four corners, seeing no trace of her neighbor. Maybe she went into McDonald's, Cindy thought, glancing toward the tiny takeout restaurant that was squeezed between the Bank of Nova Scotia and the St. Clair subway station.

It was then Cindy saw the baby carriage. It was standing outside the subway's glass doors, blocking the entranceway, until a man in a hurry shoved it rudely to one side. "Kyle?" Cindy called, rushing toward the carriage. But the carriage was empty. The baby was gone.

Why would Faith abandon an expensive carriage in the middle of the street? Had she spotted Cindy, decided it was faster and easier to proceed without it? And where was she taking Kyle so early in the morning? Did she have a plan, or had she impulsively opted for an early-morning subway ride, much as Cindy had opted for a late-night run?

"Did a woman with a baby just go through here?" she asked the bored-looking attendant who sat in a large glass booth inside the subway entrance. "It couldn't have been more than a few minutes ago," Cindy continued when the attendant failed to respond.

"Wasn't paying attention," the man answered finally. Then, "You're holding up the line."

Cindy tried to push through the turnstile, but it refused to move.

"You need a token," the attendant reminded her.

"I don't have a token."

"Then it's two dollars and twenty-five cents."

Cindy fished in her purse for the correct change, as several disgruntled commuters wove past her impatiently, while those forced to wait in line behind her groaned as one. "Sorry," she said, the apology floating toward the ceiling, like steam from a kettle, as she offered the money to the attendant, who rolled his eyes and pointed at the proper container.

Cindy ran down the stairs on the other side of the turnstile, trying to guess if Faith had headed north or south. She opted for south, running down a second set of stairs to the subway platform, her eyes panning the yellow tiles that lined the walls for any sign of Faith and her baby. Had she missed them? Had the southbound train already come and gone?

It was then she heard a baby's loud wail and saw Faith standing at the other end of the platform on the opposite side of the station. She was rocking Kyle in her arms and smiling calmly. She looks okay, Cindy thought, and waved, a broad gesture that caught Faith's attention. Faith smiled, as if seeing Cindy in the subway at this hour of the morning was not unexpected, then turned her attention back to the baby squirming in her arms.

Something's not right, Cindy thought, walking briskly back toward the stairs, pushing against the crowd surging in the other direction, vaulting up one set of stairs and down the other. Seconds later, she reached the north platform, the tunnel stretched out before her, like a long, dark pipe.

"Careful," a man cautioned as she ran beside the wide yellow stripe that ran along the edge of the platform. "Shouldn't get so close to the edge."

Cindy heeded his advice, moving closer to the wall and proceeding quickly to the far end of the platform.

"No need to run," she heard someone say. "A train just left." Was he talking to her?

"Damn, I'm going to be late," another man replied. "How long till the next one?"

"Couple of minutes."

Cindy continued walking toward the far end of the platform,

watching Faith's smile broaden as she approached, as if she were genuinely pleased to see her.

"Cindy. What are you doing here?"

"I was just about to ask you the same thing."

"Kyle has a doctor's appointment."

"So early?"

"It was the only time she could fit me in."

"Is the baby all right?"

"He has this rash."

"Rash?" Cindy hadn't noticed any rash yesterday.

"I called Dr. Pitfield as soon as I saw it. She said to bring Kyle in first thing this morning, and she'd have a look at him."

"Isn't Dr. Pitfield's office on Wellesley?" Cindy had recommended Dr. Pitfield to Faith when Faith first found out she was pregnant. Dr. Pitfield had been both Julia's and Heather's pediatrician.

"She moved."

"Really? She was on Wellesley forever. Where is she now?"

"Lawrence."

"Well, that's great. We can go together."

"You're going to Lawrence?"

"Yoga class," Cindy said quickly, wondering why Dr. Pitfield had suddenly uprooted her practice after more than thirty years in the same location. And why wouldn't Ryan have driven his wife to the doctor's instead of letting her struggle with public transportation? Why was Faith being so nice to her after what had happened yesterday? "Was that Kyle's carriage I saw in front of the station?"

Faith shrugged. "Never liked the stupid thing," she said. Then, "You look nice." As if this was the most natural of follow-ups.

"Thank you. You too. New dress?"

Faith glanced briefly down, as if she couldn't remember what she was wearing. "No. It's old."

"It's very pretty. The color looks great on you."

"You think so?"

"I do."

Faith smiled. "Another beautiful day," she said.

"Yes, it is."

"They get kind of boring, after a while. All that sunshine."

"I guess we could use some rain."

"That would be nice. I like the rain, don't you?"

"Sometimes," Cindy agreed. "There's nothing like a good thunderstorm." Were they actually talking about the weather?

"Lightning scares me," Faith confided.

"Me too."

"Have you ever seen a tornado?"

"A tornado? No, not a real one, anyway. I saw that movie though, *Twister,* I think it was called."

"I saw that," Faith said, nodding. "It wasn't very good."

"No. The story was pretty lame."

"The special effects were great though."

"Yes, they were. What's your favorite movie?" Cindy asked.

Faith raised her eyes, pursed her lips, as if giving the question serious consideration. "I don't think I have one."

"Really? What about *Titanic?* Did you see that? Or *The God-father?"*

"I saw that on television. On Bravo, I think. They were show-ing it over and over again. You couldn't miss it."

"Did you see the sequel? People say Part Two was even better than Part One, which is really rare in a sequel, although Part Three was lousy."

"I didn't see Part Three."

"You're lucky."

The baby renewed his squirming. Faith began rocking him ab-sently, looking over her shoulder for the train.

"My favorite movie is *Invasion of the Body Snatchers,*" Cindy contin-ued, a growing unease spreading through her joints, although she wasn't sure why. "The original, with Kevin McCarthy and Dana Wynter, not the remake."

"I don't know that one."

"I have a tape of it at home. I could show it to you."

"I don't know. It sounds kind of scary."

"I guess it is, a little. I could watch it with you, if you'd like."

Faith shook her head, began rocking back and forth on her heels. "I don't think so. Thanks anyway."

"Have you ever been to the film festival? I go every year with a couple of friends. Lots and lots of fabulous films. Maybe next year, you'd like to go with us."

Faith smiled, said nothing. The baby in her arms began whimpering. "Ssh," Faith told him, as several sharp cries pierced the air. "Come on, Kyle. Be a good boy. Please don't cry."

"Would you like me to hold him for a few minutes? He must be getting pretty heavy."

Faith shook her head, took a few steps back. "He's okay."

"He sounds hungry."

"No. I just fed him."

"Maybe he needs changing."

"He's fine." Faith began turning around in small circles, each spin bringing her a little bit closer to the edge of the platform.

"Be careful," Cindy warned. "You're getting too close to the edge."

Faith smiled, said nothing.

In the distance, Cindy heard the rumble of an approaching train. "I have an idea," she said. "Why don't we go somewhere and have breakfast?"

"I'm not hungry."

"Coffee, then. There's a million places we could go for coffee."

"I don't want coffee."

"Faith, you're not thinking about doing anything foolish, are you?"

"Foolish?"

"You know what I'm talking about." Cindy felt the rush of air from a southbound train as it pulled into the station on the opposite track, knew she didn't have much time before a northbound train came barreling along.

"I think you should go now," Faith said.

"I'm not leaving here without you."

Faith looked confused. "Why are you doing this?"

"Because you're my friend. Because I'm worried about you."

"There's nothing to worry about. Everything's all right now."

"It is?"

"Yes. I've worked everything out."

"Worked what out?"

"What I have to do."

"You have to move away from the edge of the platform," Cindy told her evenly. "Please, Faith. I know that whatever you think you have to do, you wouldn't want to hurt Kyle."

"I'd never do anything to hurt Kyle."

"Then move away from the edge of the platform."

"I'm not the one who'd hurt him," Faith said. "It's you."

"Me?"

Faith glanced past Cindy to the other people standing idly by. "All of you."

Cindy's eyes also scanned the waiting crowd, trying to transmit her concern. But no one was watching them. "Nobody here would do anything to hurt Kyle," she said loudly, trying to attract someone's attention.

"The world isn't a very nice place, Cindy. You know that better than anyone."

"Yes, I do," Cindy said, wondering whether she should scream for help, afraid such action might only make things worse. "I do know that. But I also know that no matter how grim things may seem, they always get better."

"You really believe that?"

"I have to believe it."

"And if things don't get better? What then?"

Cindy's eyes filled with tears. "Then we have to go on."

"Really? Why?"

Cindy pictured Heather asleep in her bed. "Because there are other people who need us, who would be devastated if we did something so final, so irreversible." She heard a low roar, and realized with horror that it was the sound of an approaching train. "Please, Faith. Listen to me. Things will get better. Honestly, they will."

"You promise?" Faith whispered, her eyes aching to believe.

"I do. I promise," Cindy repeated, crossing her fingers for both of them, balancing on the balls of her feet, preparing to throw herself at the other woman, to wrestle her to the ground, if need be.

And then Faith took a long, deep breath, and smiled, her shoulders relaxing. "Okay," she said simply, allowing Cindy to wrap her in her arms.

Thank God, Cindy said silently, clinging tightly to the other woman, slowly leading Faith away from the edge of the platform toward the stairs.

"Oh," Faith said, stopping suddenly.

"What is it?"

"Could you hold Kyle a minute?" Faith pushed the crying infant into Cindy's arms before Cindy realized what was happening. Then she wriggled away from Cindy's grasp, ran toward the end of the platform, and threw herself in front of the oncoming train.

THIRTY-TWO

(INSTANT Replay: Cindy hears a noise, like distant thunder, and realizes it is the sound of an approaching train. She pleads with her neighbor. "Please, Faith. Don't do anything foolish. Things will get better. Honestly, they will."

"You promise?" Faith asks imploringly.

"I promise."

Faith takes a long, deep breath, her shoulders relaxing. "Okay," she says, collapsing into Cindy's arms.

"Thank God." Cindy clings tightly to the other woman, begins maneuvering her through the crowd toward the exit. They are almost at the stairs.

"Oh," Faith says, stopping abruptly, as if she's forgotten something.

"What is it?"

"Could you hold Kyle a minute?")

Cindy sat on one of the sofas in her living room, staring at the far wall, trying to keep her gaze from drifting to the window, to keep the awful events of the morning from reflecting across the dark panes of glass. But all it took was one flicker of the midnight moon peeking through the clouds, and suddenly she was back on the northbound platform of the St. Clair subway station at the beginning of the early-morning rush hour, her arms gripping the shoulders of her seemingly acquiescent neighbor, and one second they were walking peacefully toward the exit, the crisis miraculously averted, and the next second, Faith was pushing her baby into Cindy's arms, then bolting from her side and throwing herself in front of the speeding train. Cindy heard the awful thud of flesh against metal, the sickening squeal of brakes, the horrified screams of onlookers.

And then chaos.

(Chaos: People running in all directions. Passengers locked inside the subway cars, banging on the doors to be let out. The smell of vomit. The ashen-faced conductor, his forehead pressed against the glass of a side window, yelling into his radio transmitter. Sirens wailing somewhere above their heads. Paramedics and police arriving. The police demanding information. Someone pointing at Cindy, sitting on the dirty floor, her back against the dull yellow tiles, her feet stretched out in front of her, like a lifeless rag doll, cradling the now-sleeping baby in her arms and staring blankly into space.

"Can you tell us what happened?" a policeman asks, kneeling down in front of Cindy, forcing his massive shoulders into her line of vision. "You knew this woman?"

Cindy stares at the young man, whose face refuses to register beyond the deep brown of his eyes. "She's my neighbor," an unfamiliar voice responds from what seems like a great distance away.

"Can you tell us her name?"

"Faith Sellick. Faith," Cindy repeats, the irony of the name imploding against her lungs, the strange voice floating to the ceiling, like a moth to light. "Is she dead?"

Silence.

Silly question, Cindy thinks, as the officer's eyes close in confirmation.

"Is there someone we can notify?"

"Her husband." The voice supplies the officer with the necessary information. Cindy watches him jot it down in his notepad. How many times has she seen that lately? Too many times. Way too many. "This is Kyle," the voice continues. "Faith's baby."

"We'll need you to tell us exactly what happened here." The officer signals to a colleague for help. "Can you do that?"

The two uniformed officers take hold of Cindy's elbows, help her up, although the ground feels less than steady beneath her feet, as if she is standing on a moving sidewalk. Cindy clings tightly to Kyle, resisting attempts to take him from her.

"Are you going to be all right?" the policeman with the brown eyes asks, although his words are garbled, as if someone is playing them at the wrong speed.

Cindy nods, walking slowly between the two officers as they guide her toward the exit.

"We'll need your name," the police officer is saying as Cindy's attention is diverted by a sudden movement on the subway track.

"Cindy," the unfamiliar voice answers, and for an instant Cindy wishes this person would stop talking, let her answer for herself. "Cindy Carver."

"Cindy Carver?" the second officer repeats, stopping in almost the exact spot as Faith stopped only moments before. "The mother of that missing girl?"

And then Cindy sees the paramedics carefully lifting Faith's hopelessly twisted body onto a stretcher, and notices a torn fragment of Faith's blue cotton dress lying across the tracks. She turns back, sees bits of human flesh dripping from the blood-soaked front window of the train.

"Are you Julia Carver's mother?" the first officer is asking, staring at Cindy with his puppy dog brown eyes.

A persistent buzz fills Cindy's ears, almost blocking out his words. *Are . . . Julia Carver's mother? Are you . . . Carver's mother? Are you Julia . . . 's mother?*

And then the unfamilar voice once again assumes control. "Excuse me," it says calmly as Cindy hands Kyle to the policeman with the puppy dog eyes, in much the same way Faith earlier handed him over to her. "I think I'm going to faint." And then Cindy feels her knees bend, her hips sway, her eyes roll back in her head, everything happening in slow motion, as her body begins folding in on itself, like a collapsible chair. I'm getting rather good at this, she thinks as she falls toward the hard tile.

"She saved that baby, you know," someone says, as strange arms reach out to block her fall. "She should get a medal. She's a hero."

I'm a hero, Cindy thinks, and might have laughed but for the darkness that envelopes her.)

"So, according to the eleven o'clock news, I'm a hero," Cindy said now, watching Neil walk toward her with a freshly brewed cup of tea. He was wearing khaki pants and a beige shirt, and Cindy thought he was the most welcome sight she'd ever seen. On either side of her sat her mother and sister. Leigh stood up as Neil approached, moved to the other sofa, scooted in beside Heather, Meg, and Trish.

"Not feeling very heroic?" Neil sat down beside her, stroked the back of Cindy's neck as she gingerly sipped her tea, Elvis keeping close watch on everyone from the floor.

Cindy smiled at the handsome man who'd rushed to her side when she'd regained consciousness and phoned him from the subway station. "I feel like such a fraud."

"How are you a fraud?" Meg asked.

"Because I didn't do anything."

"You saved a baby's life," Trish reminded her.

"*Faith* saved him, not me."

Joy Fielding

"It's only because of you that they're not both dead," Cindy's mother said.

Cindy shook her head. "This whole thing is my fault."

"How can it possibly be your fault?"

"Because I'm the one who drove her over the edge," Cindy said, the words she'd been trying to swallow all day spilling from her mouth in a sudden rush. "Literally. I did everything but push her over the side of that platform myself."

"Cindy . . ."

"I'm the one who rubbed her nose in her husband's affair with Julia. I'm the one who called the police, who had her hauled off to the station for questioning when she was so tired she could barely stand up. I knew how fragile she was, I *knew*, but that didn't stop me from flinging all sorts of ridiculous accusations in her face, even after the police warned me to back off, even after they ordered me to stop interfering with their investigation. And now look what's happened. . . ."

"Cindy . . ." her mother said.

"Please don't tell me it's not my fault."

"Do you really think you have that kind of power?" Heather asked, using the same words her mother had used the night before.

Cindy smiled sadly, holding open her arms as her daughter slid into them.

"Thanks for being here," she said, kissing the top of Heather's head. "All of you."

"Where else would we be?" everyone answered, almost in unison.

Heather had been waiting for her when Neil brought her home from the subway. Her mother and sister, who'd been at the dressmaker's, rushed over as soon as they heard the news, as had Meg and Trish several hours ago. Only Tom hadn't bothered to call. Probably halfway to Muskoka when the reports were first broadcast.

Normally, subway suicides went unreported in the media, lest it encourage others to take similar action. But Cindy's presence at the scene had changed everything. The fact that Julia Carver's mother had been instrumental in saving another woman's child from certain death had been the lead story on every newscast on every radio and television station in the city, and the fact that the victim was Cindy's next-door neighbor had only added to the intrigue. Reporters had been calling or knocking on her door since early this afternoon, theorizing about a possible connection between Julia's disappearance and her neighbor's attempted suicide. The story was sure to make tomorrow's headlines, Cindy understood, sighing audibly, especially once the press got wind of Ryan's affair with her daughter, as surely they would.

"Are you okay?" Neil asked.

"I should have realized what was happening sooner."

"Then she might have jumped sooner, taken Kyle with her."

Cindy looked toward the front door. "Is the house still surrounded?"

"I thought I saw someone from CITY-TV lurking in the bushes about an hour ago, but I think he finally gave up and went home."

"What about you?" Cindy asked reluctantly. "Shouldn't you be heading home? It's almost midnight. Your son . . ."

"I can stay a little longer."

The phone rang. Everyone looked toward the sound. No one made a move to get up.

"You want me to answer that?" Meg asked.

Cindy shook her head. "Let voice-mail take it."

After four rings, the phone went silent. Two minutes later, it rang again. And again, two minutes after that.

"Persistent little devil," Trish said.

"Maybe it's important," Leigh added.

"It isn't." How many crank calls had she received already today? Between the reporters and the kooks, her phone had been ringing almost constantly, although it had tapered off in the last several hours. At one point, things had gotten so disruptive—the phone ringing, cameramen banging their equipment against the windows, the dog barking each time someone came to the door— Cindy had briefly considered grabbing Neil and taking refuge in a hotel. But she knew her mother and sister would insist on coming along, as would Heather, Meg, and Trish, and the thought of all of them crowded into a small hotel room had been enough to put the kibosh on that idea.

Cindy pushed herself off the sofa and shuffled into the kitchen, where she checked her voice-mail for messages. "Nothing," she informed their eager faces upon her return. "Whoever it was didn't leave a message."

"Next time it rings, I'll answer it," her mother said.

"Why don't you go upstairs to bed?" Neil suggested.

"I don't think I could sleep. Every time I close my eyes, I see . . ." Even when I don't close them, she thought, as once again, Faith materialized to hurl herself in front of an oncoming train. Cindy heard the helpless squeal of brakes, the gut-wrenching thud of cold steel against warm flesh, saw the torn sliver of baby-blue cotton clinging to the coal-black of the subway tracks, Faith's blood splattered across the front window of the car, like mud, burning its way into the glass, like acid rain, branding itself into her soul.

"I may have a few of those pills left," Neil whispered underneath his breath.

"Really? What kind of pills are those?" Leigh asked. "Because I haven't had a good night's sleep in months."

"Have you heard anything from Detective Bartolli?" Trish asked.

Cindy grimaced, remembering how angry Detectives Bartolli and Gill had been upon hearing the news of Faith's suicide and Cindy's presence at the scene, how Detective Bartolli had gone so far as to threaten to arrest her if there were any further incidents. "Listen, you guys, you don't have to stay. Really."

"Do you want us to leave?" Meg asked.

"No," Cindy admitted. "I want you to stay forever."

"Okay," they all said, and Cindy smiled.

They sat together for another hour, exchanging idle chatter, hugs, and sighs, until Norma Appleton announced she could no longer keep her eyes open, and she and Leigh went upstairs to bed, as did Heather ten minutes after that. Meg and Trish reluctantly said goodbye several minutes later, both promising to call the next day.

"Your turn," Cindy told Neil, standing by the open front door.

"You're sure?"

"Only if you promise to come back tomorrow."

"How's breakfast? I'll bring bagels."

"If memory serves, my family loves your bagels."

Neil smiled. "Maybe I'll bring Max. He likes bagels too."

"I'd like that."

Neil leaned over, kissed Cindy tenderly on the lips. "See you in the morning."

Cindy watched him drive off before retreating back inside the house. She was about to close the door when she stopped, stepped back onto the landing, her eyes staring through the darkness toward several cars parked at the far end of the street. How long had they been there? And were they empty or was someone sitting inside them? Cindy squinted, trying to differentiate between flesh and shadow. More reporters? she wondered. The police?

Probably no one.

Cindy locked the door and headed upstairs for bed, trying to shake the uncomfortable feeling she was being watched.

THIRTY-THREE

SHE was almost asleep when she heard something outside her bedroom window. Cindy sat up in bed, careful not to disturb Heather, who was curled up beside her, Elvis at their feet. She waited, the silence of the night swirling around her head like a potent perfume. And then she heard it again, a tap on the glass, quick and sharp. And then another.

Cindy's first thought was that it was a bird, pecking on the glass to be let in. But birds didn't fly at night, she knew, climbing out of bed and going to the window, peeking through the shutters. Almost immediately, something slapped against the windowpane, and Cindy gasped, pulled away from the glass, her heart pounding wildly, convinced someone had fired a bullet at her head. But the glass hadn't shattered. It hadn't even cracked. Cindy inched back toward the window as once again, something ricocheted off the glass. A pebble, she realized.

Someone was throwing stones at her window.

Cindy reached for her robe and raced down the stairs to the kitchen, flipping on the light over the back patio.

A man, dressed entirely in black, was standing in the middle of her backyard. Cindy stifled a scream as he turned his head toward the light, the scream freezing in her throat when she recognized the familiar look of consternation on his handsome face.

"Tom?!" Cindy unlocked the sliding glass door, watched her ex-husband toss a fistful of pebbles to the ground, then bound up the stairs. Immediately, the Cookie, also entirely in black, stepped out of the darkness to follow after him. "What on earth are you doing here? What are you *doing?*"

"Trying to get your attention, damn it. Why didn't you answer your goddamn phone?"

"What?"

They stepped into the kitchen, the Cookie closing the door as Tom flipped off the patio light, the full moon falling into the space between them, like an errant spotlight. "What was going on here tonight? A party?"

"You were watching the house?"

"I need to talk to you. I couldn't do it when everyone was here."

"I don't understand. Has something happened?" A feeling of dread trickled into Cindy's veins, like a transfusion of tainted blood. She felt her body grow cold, as if a hand had reached out to her from beyond the grave. "Does this have something to do with Julia?"

Tom pushed his fingers roughly through his hair. "Okay, listen. I recognize this is going to be a shock, but it's very important that you stay calm. I understand it's already been one hell of a day for you, but I need your assurances you aren't going to freak out."

"I think you'd better tell me what's going on."

"I came here to prepare you."

"Prepare me for what?"

Tom said nothing for several long seconds, then he reached back to the sliding glass door and pulled it open. "Okay," he said to the surrounding darkness. "You can come in now."

The night air stirred as a shape began forming inside it, gradually separating from it. Cindy held her breath as the shape assumed human form, began its slow ascent up the patio steps, its face hidden by the hood of a black sweatshirt.

And then there she was, standing in the doorway, the hood falling from her head to reveal the straight blond hair beneath, looking as impossibly beautiful as she had the last time Cindy saw her over two weeks ago.

Julia.

"JULIA!" Cindy threw herself at the apparition, casting an invisible net over its head, and trapping it in her arms before it could fly away, as if she'd stumbled across a rare butterfly. She knew her mind was playing tricks, that the awful events of the day combined with her fatigue had disrupted the normal patterns of her brain, so that not only was she seeing lost young women jumping from her side, she was seeing other lost young women miraculously appearing to take their place. "Julia," she uttered, staring at the vision in the black velour jumpsuit, touching her face, her shoulders, her hair. "Julia," she said again, as if the repetition of the name would be enough to give the ghost weight, provide it with the substance needed to sustain it. "Julia," Cindy cried, bracing herself for her daughter's sudden absence.

And then the mirage that was Julia was folding herself inside Cindy's arms. And Cindy was hugging her and kissing her, and her skinny frame felt solid and real, and her soft, smooth skin smelled of Angel perfume. Cindy tasted her daughter on her tongue, like tiny bubbles of champagne. "Are you really here?" Cindy cried, squeezing Julia's broad shoulders, her toned arms, her slender hips. "Are you really here?"

"I'm really here," the apparition said, sounding just like Julia.

"It *is* you. You're here. You're real."

Julia laughed. "I'm real. I'm here."

And now Cindy was sobbing, her whole body shaking as she pulled her daughter to her chest, as if trying to solder them both together, all the while smothering the side of Julia's face with kisses, as if she couldn't get enough of her, as if she intended to devour her.

Julia was back. She was in her mother's arms. She was alive and well. And she looked wonderful. She looked rested and beautiful, more beautiful than ever. No bruises stained her flawless complexion; no nameless terrors clouded her eyes. "You're here," Cindy kept repeating. "You're all right."

"I'm here. I'm all right."

Despite the assurances, Cindy refused to relinquish her daughter's hands. If she did, the dream would surely end. She'd wake up. It would be over. Her daughter would be gone. "You're not hurt?"

"I'm fine," Julia said again.

"You're fine," Cindy repeated, unable to staunch the flood of tears streaming down her cheeks. Her daughter was alive and well and back home where she belonged. She wasn't a ghost. She was really here. And no harm had befallen her. How was that possible? "I don't understand. Where have you been?"

Julia looked from her mother to her father, who nodded his silent encouragement. "You have to promise you won't be angry."

"Angry?" What was Julia talking about? "Why would I be angry?"

"Promise me you'll at least try to understand."

"Understand what? What's going on? Tom," Cindy implored, her eyes veering reluctantly from her daughter to her ex-husband. "Tom, what is she talking about? Where did you find her?"

"Don't you get it yet?" he asked, looking at Cindy with a mixture of pity and scorn.

"Get what?"

A second's hesitation before Julia's simple response. "I was never lost."

The words ripped through Cindy as if fired from a gun. She

staggered back, dropped her daughter's hand. "What are you talking about? Where have you been?"

There was a long pause, a second exchange of glances between father and daughter before Julia answered. "At the cottage."

"What?"

"She insisted on coming back as soon as we heard the news about Faith Sellick," the Cookie interjected quickly.

"Is Ryan okay?" Julia asked. "The news reports barely mentioned him."

"You've been in Muskoka all this time?" Cindy's head was spinning. Her daughter was back. She wasn't injured. She hadn't been kidnapped, or raped and murdered, then buried in a shallow grave. She was alive and well. Wasn't that all that mattered? What difference did it make where she'd been, that it appeared she'd been relaxing in the country while her mother was going crazy in the city, that instead of being concerned about her sister, her grandmother, her aunt, she was asking after Ryan, that even more astounding, she seemed oblivious to the hell she'd put her family through these awful last two weeks?

Cindy turned toward Tom, another horrifying thought slowly crystallizing. "Did you know about this? Did you know where Julia was all along?"

"You promised you wouldn't get angry," Julia reminded her.

"Maybe you should sit down," Tom said.

Without protest, Cindy lowered herself into a kitchen chair, braced herself for whatever staggering revelations might follow.

"This doesn't leave this room," Tom warned, closing, then locking, the sliding glass door.

Julia took a deep breath, blew it out slowly, as if she were savoring a forbidden cigarette. "As you know, two weeks ago, I had an audition with Michael Kinsolving for a part in his next movie. Dad said you saw the tape."

"Yes," Cindy acknowledged quietly. "You were wonderful."

Julia smiled proudly. "Thank you."

"Unfortunately, wonderful auditions aren't enough these days," Tom continued, assuming control. "There are too many beautiful, talented actresses out there, and Julia needed something that would give her an edge over the competition, something that would get her the attention she deserves." He paused dramatically. "And what better way to get noticed than to disappear?"

The room went in and out of focus as Cindy shook her head in disbelief. Surely she'd misunderstood. Surely she'd misinterpreted what her daughter and ex-husband were trying to tell her. "You're saying this was a publicity stunt?"

"I just wanted a chance, Mom. Michael was auditioning so many girls. He hasn't had a hit in a while, and Dad said the studio was pressuring him to give the part to a name Hollywood actress. We knew we had to do something to level the playing field."

"So you concocted this scheme . . ."

"To make Julia as recognizable as any of the famous actresses in town for the festival," Tom continued, unable to disguise his enthusiasm. "Cindy, I'm an entertainment lawyer. I know how this business works. I knew we had to do something pretty drastic to get the results we needed. And it worked. Hell, Julia's practically a household name. *Entertainment Tonight* did two whole minutes on Michael's possible involvement in her disappearance the other night. Do you have any idea what that kind of exposure is worth? Michael would be a fool not to give her the part now, and trust me, Michael Kinsolving is nobody's fool. He knows a good story. So does the studio. And they also know everybody likes a happy ending."

"Good story?" Cindy repeated incredulously. "Happy ending?"

"Okay, Cindy. It's obvious you're upset. But can you at least try to keep an open mind?"

"Why didn't you tell me?" Cindy looked at her daughter through wide, disbelieving eyes. Could her daughter really be so unfeeling, so monstrously self-absorbed? "Do you have any idea what I've been going through? What we've *all* been going through? Why didn't you tell me?"

"We thought about it," Julia began.

"You *thought* about it?"

"We couldn't tell you," Tom said curtly. "We knew that, at the very least, you'd feel compelled to tell your mother and Heather. And then Heather would tell Duncan, and your mother would tell Leigh, and then where would we be? Don't you see? It wouldn't have worked if you didn't honestly believe that Julia was missing. Your daughter's the actress in the family, Cindy. Not you. The police would have seen through you in a heartbeat."

"Besides," the Cookie added matter-of-factly, "we knew you'd never agree to it."

Cindy felt suddenly sick to her stomach. "That afternoon at the morgue . . ."

"Not my idea, believe me." Tom waved his hands in front of his face, as if to rid himself of the memory. "I wouldn't want to go through that again."

"And what happened afterward in your apartment . . ."

"What happened in our apartment?" the Cookie asked.

"All the people the police questioned—Sean, Duncan, Ryan—people whose lives have been turned upside down as a result of this little charade. And Faith. My God, poor Faith!" Again, Cindy saw the hapless young woman hurl herself in front of the speeding train, heard the sickening thud of metal against flesh.

"Faith didn't kill herself because of me," Julia protested.

"She was suffering from postpartum depression." Cindy struggled to stay calm, to keep her voice down. "Do you think it helped her to be hauled into the police station for questioning? To find out you'd been sleeping with her husband?"

"And exactly whose fault was it she found that out?" Tom asked, narrowing his eyes accusingly.

"I'm really very sorry about what happened to Faith," Julia said. "But she was Loony Tunes to begin with. You can't blame me for what she did. We had no way of knowing she'd pull something like this."

"You had no way of knowing that *she'd pull something like this?*" Cindy repeated incredulously.

"Kindly lower your voice," Tom instructed.

"Kindly go fuck yourself," Cindy shot back.

"I told you it was a mistake coming here," the Cookie said, throwing her hands into the air in defeat.

"You didn't consider that there might be consequences to your actions?" Cindy asked her daughter. "It never occurred to you that not everything works out exactly as planned? That sometimes the things we set in motion have a way of spiraling out of control?"

"I just want to be famous," Julia said evenly, as if this made everything understandable, as if it made everything all right.

"So the end justifies the means?" Cindy stared at her daughter, the young woman whom only moments before she would have given her life just to hold in her arms. Julia was her father's daughter, she realized in that instant. She always had been.

(Flashback: Julia, four years old, Shirley Temple curls tamed into two long braids, holding tightly to her father's hand as they walk down the street; Julia, age eight, proudly sitting on the shiny red bicycle her father bought her for her birthday; Julia, at thirteen, wearing a fancy brown-and-blue-striped taffeta dress, posing beside her father, so handsome in his tuxedo, before they leave for the annual Havergal father-daughter dinner-dance; Julia the following year, packing her clothes into the new Louis Vuitton suitcase her father bought her, then carrying it outside to his waiting BMW, leaving her childhood—and her mother—behind.)

"So what happens now?" Cindy asked, her energy sapped. "What exactly are you planning on telling people? That Julia was a victim of amnesia?"

"It's simple," Tom said. "We tell them that Julia was feeling down because she thought she'd blown her audition, so she wandered the countryside for a couple of weeks, trying to clear her head, didn't even look at a paper until today. . . ."

"The police will never buy it."

"Are you kidding?" Tom reminded her. "It was their idea."

"And I'm just supposed to go along with this charade?"

"Do you have any other choice?"

Did she?

"I could tell them the truth."

"You could, yes," Tom agreed. "But then, in all likelihood, Julia will be arrested, a promising career will be nipped in the bud, and I'll be disbarred. Is that what you really want?" Tom paused, allowed his words the necessary time to sink in before continuing. "Look, Cindy. Right now you're hurt and you're angry, and that's completely understandable. You've been through hell these last few weeks. Nobody knows that better than I do. But I urge you to think this through, and consider our daughter's best interests."

"Our daughter's best interests," Cindy repeated numbly.

"Please, Mom. I'm so close to getting everything I've ever wanted."

"You can't really want to see your daughter go to jail," the Cookie said.

"I thought all you ever wanted was for Julia to come home," Tom reminded Cindy.

"I thought so too," she said.

There was a noise in the hallway and Elvis suddenly galloped into the room.

"Elvis!" Julia fell to her knees, hugged her dog to her chest. "How are you, boy?"

Heather appeared in the kitchen doorway. "I heard voices," she said, falling silent when she saw her sister.

"What's going on?" Norma Appleton called from the top of the stairs.

"Julia's home," Heather shouted back at her.

"Julia?! Leigh, wake up! Julia's home."

In the next instant, Cindy's mother and sister came flying into the room, crying happily, and gathered Julia inside their arms, smothering her face with kisses.

Moments later, the women sat huddled together at the kitchen table, their bewildered faces heavy with anger, relief, and pain, as they tried to recover from the shock of the early-morning revelations.

"I'm really sorry," Julia told them, standing next to her father on the other side of the room. "I honestly didn't think everybody would be so upset."

"You didn't think we'd be upset?" Her grandmother's head shook from side to side in disbelief.

"You didn't think, period," Leigh said bitterly.

"How could you do this to Mom?" Heather asked.

"I said I was sorry," Julia said testily.

"Okay," the Cookie chirped into the silence that followed. "I think we've said everything that needs to be said. There's nothing to be gained from going over the whole thing ad nauseum."

"I'll call the newspapers first thing in the morning," Tom said. "Tell them Julia's come home." He squeezed Julia's hand. "That she's ready for her close-up."

Julia smiled, her free hand automatically reaching up to smooth the side of her hair.

Cindy stared at her older daughter. Still just a child really, despite her twenty-one years. Maybe there was still hope. Maybe time would bring some measure of maturity. Or maybe not. Maybe Julia would always be a bit of a monster. Maybe her single-minded self-absorption was the very quality that would make her a star, her obvious contempt for the feelings of others resulting in her being adored by millions.

Her father's daughter all right.

But her daughter too.

Cindy walked to the phone and punched in the number for the Fifty-third Division. "I'd like to speak to the officer in charge, please."

"What do you think you're doing?" Tom demanded.

"If you tell the police the truth, I'll deny it," Julia said quickly. "I'll say you were in on the whole thing from the beginning."

"This is ridiculous," the Cookie snapped. "You're just doing this to get back at Tom and I."

"Tom and *me,*" Heather said from her seat at the kitchen table.

"What?"

"Object of the preposition," Heather said.

"I don't believe this! Tom, do something."

"Mom, please," Julia pleaded. "I just want to come home."

The words tugged at Cindy's heart.

"Officer Medavoy," a familiar voice announced in Cindy's ear.

"Officer Medavoy, it's Cindy Carver. We met the other night. My daughter Heather . . ."

"Yes, of course. How is she?"

"She's wonderful. Wonderful," Cindy repeated, her eyes absorbing the miracle that was her younger child. All these years she'd overlooked Heather's quiet light because she'd been so blinded by the raging fire that was Julia. All those years Cindy had given short shrift to one daughter because she was so busy mourning the loss of the other. And now Julia was back, and she was saying exactly what Cindy had been waiting a lifetime to hear: *Please, Mom. I just want to come home.*

And it was too late.

"It's my other daughter I'm calling about. Julia."

A collective intake of breath.

"She's home," Cindy told the officer. She closed her eyes, shook her head, a cry escaping her mouth as she tried to continue. Could she really tell the police the truth, knowing that her daughter might go to jail, her dreams of stardom over? Hadn't the last two weeks seen enough misery and shattered dreams to last a lifetime? "She waltzed in about an hour ago," Cindy announced, "totally unaware of everything that's been happening."

"Thank God," she heard the Cookie whisper, as Julia burst into a flood of grateful tears against her father's chest.

Cindy continued reading from the invisible script her ex-husband and daughter had prepared, surprised by how convincing she managed to sound. Tom was right. When all was said and done, what other choice did she have? "Thank you," she told the officer before hanging up the phone and facing the others. "He said he'll let Detectives Bartolli and Gill know what's happened, that they'll probably contact us first thing in the morning."

"Thank you so much, Mom," Julia whispered.

"You did the right thing," Tom said.

Cindy glanced toward the kitchen table, expecting to see at least a hint of recrimination in her mother's eyes, a scowl of disapproval on her sister's lips, a look of disappointment on Heather's face. But all three women were nodding their tearful support. There were no judgments here, Cindy realized. Only love.

Tom kissed Julia's forehead. "Try to get some sleep, sweetie. You want to look good for the reporters in the morning." He touched the Cookie's elbow, began leading her toward the hall.

"Wait," Cindy called out. What was she doing now?

"Cindy, we're all beat. Can't this wait until tomorrow?"

"Julia can't stay here." The words were out of Cindy's mouth almost before she realized they were in her head.

"What?" Tom stopped abruptly.

"What?" Julia echoed.

"You can't stay here," Cindy said again, the words sounding no less strange for having repeated them.

"I don't understand."

Cindy took a deep breath, releasing the air slowly from her lungs, feeling her heart about to burst. "I love you, darling. I always will. You know that. And I'm so sorry." She glanced from Julia to Tom, then back again. "It's just that I can't spend any more time living with someone I don't really like."

Julia's eyes filled with unexpected tears. She quickly lowered her head, her hair falling across her face as it had during her audition for Michael Kinsolving.

(Fantasy: Julia raises her head, tears falling the length of her cheeks. "I'm so sorry," she says. "Please forgive me. I never meant to hurt you. I love you more than anything in the world. I promise I'll change. I promise things will be so different from now on.")

Julia remained in that posture for several seconds, then a toss of her hair, a shrug of her shoulders, brought her head back up. When her eyes next met her mother's, the tears were gone. "Whatever. I'll stay at Dad's."

The Cookie's eyes widened in alarm.

Could she really do this? Cindy wondered. Could she really send her daughter away? Was she prepared to lose her again, possibly forever? Cindy felt her body shudder, as if finally absorbing the fact that Julia had been lost to her a long time ago.

Julia stood in the middle of the kitchen, not moving, as if giving her mother a few extra seconds to change her mind. "Okay, then. If that's the way you want it. Come on, Elvis. We're going back to Dad's."

"Oh no," the Cookie wailed. "I will not have that mangy mutt peeing on my good carpets again."

"Come on, Elvis," Julia repeated, as if the Cookie hadn't spoken.

Elvis slowly raised himself up from his position underneath
the kitchen table and lumbered over to the middle of the room to
where Cindy was standing. Then he barked loudly three times, and
stretched himself across the top of Cindy's feet.

"Fine." Julia rolled her eyes in exasperation. "Stay here, if that's
what you want."

"Thank God," the Cookie muttered.

"Shut up," Julia snapped.

"You shut up."

"Ladies, please," Tom implored, ushering the two young women
toward the front door without so much as a backward glance.

Cindy followed, her eyes trailing after them as they walked
down the street. She saw Julia climb into her father's car, watched
that car pull away from the curb, then turn the corner onto
Avenue Road.

And then she was gone.

(Flashback: Julia, age fourteen, her ponytail waving behind
her, carries her suitcase into her father's waiting BMW, leaving her
childhood—and her mother—behind.)

"Are you all right?" Heather asked, coming up behind her.

Cindy nodded. "I'm okay," she said, realizing that she was.

Maybe nothing would ever completely heal the wound in her
heart, maybe there would always be a part of her that wanted to
run down the street after her older daughter and beg her to come
home. But it was too late for that. Julia wasn't fourteen anymore.
She was all grown up now. An adult, with a mind and a will of her
own. And, thank God, she was healthy and strong and safe. Hell,
she was indestructible.

They were the ones who'd been battered and bruised and
beaten these last few weeks, Cindy realized. For fourteen days
they'd been treading water and holding their breath, struggling to
keep their heads above the cruel current. Their lives had been
turned upside down and inside out. And now, suddenly, it was

over. Just like that. Two weeks of slow torture resolved in mere seconds.

And yet those seconds would resonate with all of them for the rest of their lives.

"How are you guys?"

"Tired," said her mother.

"Exhausted," said Leigh.

"We should get to bed."

"What do you think will happen tomorrow?" her mother asked.

"I don't know."

"Neil's coming over with bagels," Heather reminded them.

Cindy smiled at the three women. "I love you," she said simply.

"We love you too," they said in unison.

Elvis lifted himself off Cindy's feet and stared at her expectantly.

"Don't worry," Cindy told the dog. "We love you too."

(Final images: Cindy drapes one arm across her daughter's shoulder as the other arm stretches to accommodate both her mother and sister; the dog's tail snaps hopefully against her leg as she guides everyone toward the stairs.)